THE **KENNETH ANDERSON** OMNIBUS

THE KENNETH ANDERSON OMNIBUS

VOL I

RUPA

Published by
Rupa Publications India Pvt. Ltd 2000
7/16, Ansari Road, Daryaganj
New Delhi 110002

Sales centres:
Allahabad Bengaluru Chennai
Hyderabad Jaipur Kathmandu
Kolkata Mumbai

Edition Copyright ©Rupa Publications 2000

This is a work of fiction. Names, characters, places and incidents
are either the product of the author's imagination or are used fictitiously
and any resemblance to any actual person, living or dead, events or
locales is entirely coincidental.

All rights reserved.
No part of this publication may be reproduced, transmitted,
or stored in a retrieval system, in any form or by any means,
electronic, mechanical, photocopying, recording or otherwise,
without the prior permission of the publisher.

ISBN: 978-81-716-7455-8

Twenty-fourth impression 2022

30 29 28 27 26 25 24

Printed in India

This book is sold subject to the condition that it shall not, by way
of trade or otherwise, be lent, resold, hired out, or otherwise circulated,
without the publisher's prior consent, in any form of binding
or cover other than that in which it is published.

Contents

Tales from Indian Jungles   1
Introduction   3
Ghooming at Dawn   5
The Bellundur Ogre   17
The Aristocrat of Amligola   62
The Assassin of Diguvametta   87
Tales of the Supernatural   118
The Strange Case of The Gerhetti Leopard   158
The Lakkavalli Man-eater   185
What the Thunderstorm Brought   206

Man-eaters and Jungle Killers   231
Introduction   233
The Marauder of Kempekarai   236
Alam Bux and the Big Black Bear   273
The Mamandur Man-eater   288
The Crossed-Tuskar of Gerhetti   308
The Sangam Panther   330
The Ramapuram Tiger   352
The Great Panther of Mudiyanoor   371
The Mauler of Rajnagara   386

Tales from Indian Jungles

Introduction

THE MAN SITS WITH HIS BACK TO A TREE AND THE LIGHT FROM THE campfire waxes and wanes, throwing him into sharp relief along with the tree-trunk against which he rests, to fade the next instant into obscurity and gloom. Leaning against the tree beside him is a .405 Winchester rifle of ancient vintage.

Someone throws a fresh log on the flames and myriad sparks soar upwards, lighting the heavy boughs of the great tree that overshadows the camp. For an instant the man's countenance, too, is lit brightly and we see that he has a beard and moustache, and that firmly held in the corner of the mouth is an old briar that has long gone out. A battered 'Gurkha' hat, its brim curled up at the left side, slopes rakishly to the right upon his head.

The man is speaking. He appears to be telling a tale and it is clear that he is so intent upon it, so absorbed, that he has forgotten his pipe and all else around him.

The flames die down, then flare up again, their momentary gleam revealing the absent look in the man's eyes, as he lives again the incidents he describes. The past has become so real that he is oblivious of his audience, squatting around him on the ground beside the fire, listening to his words.

The sparks fly upwards to merge, fade and disappear in a thick spiral of smoke that curls yet higher until it is lost in the gloom of the heavy foliage of trees that encircle the camp and accentuate the jungle night.

Except for the crackle of the flames and the drone of the man's voice, the forest is lost in silence, and a heavy, oppressive, uncanny quiet that we feel cannot last much longer. And we are right. The roar of a tiger breaks suddenly through the blackness, to be answered by the scream of an excited elephant. 'Aungh-ha! Ooongh! Aungh-ooongh!' comes that awful sound as the tiger stalks boldly down the jungle aisles, while the distant trumpeting of the elephant 'Tri-aa-a-ank! Tri-aa-a-ank!' announces that the challenge has been met.

But the man seems not to hear these sounds, so engrossed has he become in the story he is telling. He appears to be of the jungle himself, and we get the impression that he belongs there. This is home for him and here is the place he would want to die; the jungle is his brithplace, his haven and his resting place when the end comes.

Let us give heed, then, to what he tells. Stories of the denizens of the forest; tales of incidents, macabre and ghostly sketches of himself. The man seems happy as we listen and he warms to his theme.

For he loves to speak about the jungle and its people, and who should know that better than I.

For I am that man!

One

Ghooming at Dawn

THE POOJAREE AWAKENS US WITH HIS PERSISTENT SOFT CALLS OF *'Dorai, Dorai; yeancheko, knarl munni agadho!;'* meaning, 'Master, master; wake up, it's four o'clock!'

    He whispers the words into our ears, first mine and then yours; for to touch either of us with his hands would be considered disrespectful. Have not the poojarees, for as long as man can remember, been regarded as outcasts, whose very proximity to any ordinary person—let alone their touch—is abhorrent in the extreme?

    We sit up abruptly, for in the jungle a tardy awakening may spell the difference between life and death, to view the glowing embers of the fire whose light barely extends to the trunks of the giant trees of the forest that hem us in on three sides. On the fourth we see a whole stretch of water, lit by the stars, which is the Cauvery river, and we hear the dull rumble as the flood swirls past us, appearing out of the darkness of the jungle night and vanishing just as swiftly.

We are camped in the open upon the river bank, a few yards from the fringe of the forest and only a short distance from the water's edge. The poojaree has remained awake all night, to stoke the fire that protected us while we slept from an unwelcome visit by some wandering elephant that might have come for a drink, or perhaps an unusually daring crocodile. The sands of the river bank on which we have been sleeping have been a deterrent to our smaller but equally unpleasant foes such as snakes and scorpions, who do not like crawling on such a surface.

We throw off our light coverings, for it is comparatively warm. The heat from the embers has helped to protect us from the dew. I place a small kettle of water on the fire to brew some tea, that ever-refreshing drink that is always welcomed by persons who sojourn in wild places, and while the water boils accompany you the few paces to the water's edge for a quick wash of teeth, face and hands.

By the time we return, the kettle is boiling, and soon we sit with a steaming mug in hand, while cold buttered *chapatties* and some ripe bananas—called plantains in India—a complete breakfast, unfit for kings perhaps, but of which there is no equal for good health.

This brief meal is soon over, and now we attend to the rifles that we are going to carry on this early-morning 'ghoom' of the foothills that start less than a quarter-mile away and rise steadily and culminate in a peak called Ponachimalai, over 5,000 feet high and about six miles distant as the crow flies.

My silent, but trusted friend and companion over many years and through many adventures, a somewhat battered .405 Winchester of which everybody makes fun, needs little or no attention. Like me, it is an old-timer that seems to look after itself. In any case, it appears very inferior to that 10-shot U.S. 3006 Springfield rifle of yours, which you rightly treat with such care.

It is still dark when we leave camp. Our poojaree companion is eager to accompany us, but as we are embarking upon a prowl during which I would like to try to show you a few interesting things, I decide to leave him behind on the pretext of looking after the few possessions we have brought. A hunter, pure and simple, Byra, our poojaree friend, would greatly disapprove of my pointing out to you some grand old sambar stag instead of shooting it; while if I draw your attention to the mother-love of a spotted doe, offering herself as a target in an attempt to shield her fawn, he would be positively annoyed with me for not pulling the trigger and bagging both mother and fawn.

The air becomes chill within a hundred yards, and seems to grow even colder as we start to climb the sloping ground to the summit of the first foothill.

It is still dark and we progress slowly. Stumbling over stones and brushing through the undergrowth will certainly betray our movements and turn the first phase of our little walk into a failure. For it is the season when the *jumlum*-tree casts its purple fruit so prolifically over the ground, and this astringent delicacy is an article of diet absolutely irresistible to sloth bears, who will cover miles in a night to visit such a tree. Only yesterday I noticed a grove of these *jumlums* close to the riverside and barely two furlongs from camps, with the tracks and droppings of many sloth bears that have been visiting them each night to feed upon the fallen purple fruit.

The hillock we are now ascending is adjacent to the grove and will form the direct line of retreat for the sloth bears that will be still gorging there. As is their custom, they will begin to make for rising ground as soon as the false dawn breaks. That time is close upon us now, and a momentary lightening of the sky heralds this curious phenomenon.

But within a few minutes a pall of darkness once again envelopes the land, till a wider spreading glow in the eastern sky, perhaps twenty minutes later, announces the true dawn and the beginning of another day.

This false dawn deceives not only the hunter new to the forests, but the inmates of the jungle as well. Junglecocks begin to crow, peafowl awaken to voice their brassy calls, carnivores on the prowl turn back to the lairs, and the hyenas and jackals that have been sneaking after them in the hope of a meal from what is left of their kills, turn back to their burrows in the ground and under the rock, where they shelter during the day.

The grumpy and greedy sloth bears that have been concentrating their energies on gormandizing the fallen *jumlums* will also be deceived by the false dawn. Reluctantly they will abandon the few fruits they have been unable to force down their throats and will make for the haven of the hillsides where they will be left in peace, there to spend the hot hours of noontide sound asleep in some cave or grassy hollow in the ground, or perhaps beneath the shade of a gnarled old tree.

But we ourselves are not misled and hasten to take up our positions before the short-lived glow lapses into pre-dawn darkness. We should be in hiding if we are to hear the sloth bears' approach and perhaps glimpse one of them in the light of the true dawn when it breaks. It would never do to be surprised in the murk of that short-lived twenty-minute interval.

The sloth bear shares with its relatives of all lands the evil reputation of being irascible, excitable, resentful and aggressive should one stumble upon him unexpectedly. Scores of jungle dwellers in India carry horrible scars because they happened to encounter a sloth bear coming round a corner or floundered upon one sound asleep. Many have lost eyes and noses under their raking talons.

This rock, which we have come upon, will suit our purpose admirably. It is about four feet high by perhaps six long. Both of us can crouch behind it and await the coming of a bear. It is, of course, just a chance that may or may not come off, for after all the bears have the whole jungle to roam in and there must be many other *paths* and byways by which they could climb the hillock without passing in this particular direction.

We chance our luck and wait in silence for a few minutes, hearing only our own breathing. Then the faint thud of a stone, somewhere at the base of the hillock, raises our hopes. Only an animal, generally clumsy in its habits or in search of the grubs that hide under such stones, would have betrayed its presence by making such a noise. Decidedly not a deer, for it would be afraid; and certainly no tiger or panther would advertise its passing. The other possibility might be an elephant. This we will know in a few moments.

Now we can hear the sound of laboured breathing, as if some old man is climbing the hillock with great difficulty. This removes any doubt that a sloth bear is indeed approaching sniffing at holes under the rocks and at the roots of bushes in search of grubs and other succulent morsels.

The eastern sky is beginning to brighten with the approach of the real dawn, but it is still dark behind the rock where we crouch, when the bear reaches us. You are to my right, and the bear is to the right of you, maybe ten feet away. I press your arm tightly and you understand my unspoken signal to remain motionless. It might not see us, for it is notoriously short-sighted. It is also very deaf. It might attack should we betray our presence, and we do not want to shoot it, for normally a bear does us no harm.

The snorting and the grumbling, the huffing and snuffing pass. All we can glimpse is a black blur against the bushes; then the bear has disappeared as it ascends the hill and the sounds of its progress grow fainter.

The dawn breaks apace and the sky to the east across the river displays a pattern of ever-changing colour, starting from dark grey and deep purple and trailing off into violet, green, blue, orange and vermillion, till at length the sun's rim rises above the jagged heights of distant mountain peaks. Its diffused rays are not yet bright enough to keep us from staring with unshielded eyes at that glorious fiery ball.

In salute, birds large and small, far and near, burst into song. The twittering of a hundred *bulbuls*, the call of the black-and-red crow-pheasant, the cry of a brain-fever bird rising to crescendo, fall upon our ears from the hillside, while from the heavy cover by the river we hear the challenge of junglecocks, 'Wheew! Kuck-kya-kya-k'huckm,' and the metallic notes of a far off peacock 'Miaoo! Miaoo!'. We can imagine it with the glorious plumes of its tail spread like a large fan, strutting and dancing before a bevy of admiring hens.

Crack-a-a-ack! We hear the sound but once, rather faint but quite unmistakable. Something heavy is coming up the hill, perhaps another sloth bear, but I think not. Bears are continuously noisy, while this animal, except for that initial accidental sound, is otherwise, silent.

We crouch quietly behind the rock with just the tops of our heads and eyes showing. To remain absolutely still is the first secret of successful concealment in the jungle. Even if an animal sees you, it will not be able to make you out provided you remain absolutely motionless. The second factor, of course, is the direction in which the wind is blowing. The sense of smell rather than of sight is far more developed in most wild creatures, particularly members of the deer family. Provided the wind is not blowing directly from you to the quarry, and provided you remain absolutely still, you have a good chance of ambushing practically any animal successfully.

We put this to the test a moment later when the bushes before us part with a faint rustle to reveal the head and shoulders of an enormous sambar stag. His giant antlers are spread in perfect symmetry, and he is near enough for us to see their gnarled thickness, equal to your forearm, at the base.

The stag is closer to us than the sloth bear was a moment earlier, and directly in front, yet he does not see us. He hesitates cautiously before advancing into the clear space on the other side of the rock behind which we are hiding. Then he steps forth and we see his massive body in all its grandeur.

He is an old animal, as revealed by his dark brown colour, the shagginess of the mane around his neck, and the long coarse hair on his flanks, which is not quite thick enough to cover completely the skin on his sides. These factors and the massiveness of his antlers indicate the stag's advanced age.

Now I will show you how inquisitive a sambar can be. Plucking a thick stem of grass at my side, I allow the plumed end to protrude above the rock, while holding the stem between finger and thumb. Then I begin to twirl it around and the effect on the stag is instantaneous. Soundless and slight as is this movement, it registers on those ever-watchful eyes. He stops abruptly, his two large ears flicking forwards and backwards, and then forwards again. Impatiently he raises his right leg bent at the knee-point, and stamps it hard upon the ground. His hoof makes a metallic click against a stone.

The stag repeats this action while staring harder than ever at the stem of grass which I continue to revolve. All his suspicions are aroused now as his instinct warns him that something strange is going on. He has seen stems of grass many a time swaying in the breeze. But never has he seen one twirling round and round!

We can read the stag's thoughts behind those staring eyes. Instinct alerts him and urges him to flee. But curiosity impels him to find out more about the stem of grass that twirls around in such a peculiar fashion. The sambar takes a step forward, hesitates for a full minute, and then comes forward again. Every muscle in his frame is taut, attuned to flee at a moment's notice; but he just cannot overcome his inquisitive urge.

This natural inquisitiveness among the deer and antelope families is the reason why thousands of them are slaughtered each year by experienced poachers, who do just what I am doing at the moment, or adopt some other trick to entice them to their doom. The stag is so close now that he could be transfixed by a spear-throw; and he is coming even closer! Clearly this foolish animal must be taught a salutary lesson and I decide to give him the fright of his life.

Springing up from behind the rock, I yell 'Wroff! Wrooff! Wrooff!' at the top of my voice. To say that the stag is taken aback by this sudden apparition of a human with a tiger's voice describes the situation mildly. He rears up on hind legs, slips on a stone, falls to his knees, struggles erect and lets out a strident cry of danger.

'Oo-onk!' he screams.

Then he lays his antlers back along his sides so as not to get them caught in the branches of trees, and crashes down the hillside. So precipitate is his flight that we can follow his movements by the rattle of displaced stones till he reaches the shelter of the heavy forest beside the river. There the stag evidently halts to see if he is being pursued, and resumes his warning to all the jungle that danger and death lurk upon the hillside.

'Oo-onk! Dha-ank!' he bellows, again and again.

The general excitement is taken up by the watchman of the band of langur monkeys that have been feeding contentedly in the *jumlum*-grove. We can just glimpse him from where we hide, standing erect on two legs on a tree-top as he strives hard to catch sight of the danger that the sambar has announced. Try as he may, he cannot see us. Obviously he is puzzled and wants to identify the nature of the foe. Then the big male langur decides he must do his duty to his band and the other wild creatures at large by joining in the alarm and passing on the warning.

'Harr!' he screams gutturally; and then a moment later, 'Harr! Harr-harr!' in quick succession. The forest is disturbed in right earnest now, and from the far side of the river a jungle-sheep, about to quench his thirst, takes fright, scampers away and voices his dog-like bark as he goes, 'Kharr! Kharr! Kharr!'

A herd of spotted deer, grazing somewhere on the other side of the hillock on whose slopes we are hiding, hears the commotion and passes on the warning. 'Aiow! Aiow! Aiow!' call the hinds to each other in quick succession. In the distance an elephant trumpets shrilly.

The excitement dies down at length and we decide to resume our early-morning prowl, for there is nothing to be gained by continuing to hide. The sambar has made too great a commotion for anything further to come our way.

Do you see that shrub with the tapering leaves resembling the tea-plant that thrives only in higher altitudes? Many such bushes grow all around. It is known as the 'vellari' plant. The leaves, in a compress or poultice form are very useful in relieving rheumatic pains and swellings of any sort. The five-pointed leaves of this large tree, green above and silver-white below, produce excellent effects when applied to raw wounds or a contusion; the silver-white side is placed in contact with the troubled area. That little plant that grows on the hard ground, barely a foot high, with the silver-grey, almost spiked leaves, is said to be a remedy for poisonous snakebites, and that other tiny plant with white, daisy-like flower and the serrated leaves, is renowned for stopping bleeding where the juice from the leaves is squeezed into a wound. It also lowers high blood pressure in a patient as rapidly as can any medicine prescribed by a doctor.

Truly the jungle is filled with all manner of herbs and plants whose leaves, stems, seeds, flowers and even roots are remedies for most of the maladies from which the human race suffers. They grow in the forests and also in civilized areas, even along the railway track.

You must often have noticed the myriads of pink and white flowers peeing out from among the green leaves of the common Indian periwinkle shrub that thrives practically everywhere, particularly on railway embankments. Forty leaves of this plant, brewed like tea and drunk in a large cupful of water or milk every day, stimulates the pancreas by helping the secretion of insulin, thus controlling diabetes. But there are other roots and leaves that are even more effective in treating this malady, one of them a little creeper common in every jungle. It is known as the 'sugar killer' because, after chewing only one leaf, sugar loses its sweetness and tastes like sand in the mouth, this effect lasting for about three hours.

But we are digressing and in the meanwhile have arrived at the top of the hillock and begun our descent on the other side. We must move cautiously now, for in places the going is steep, and should one of us dislodge a stone or make some noise, the family of spotted deer that has now stopped calling and that we hope to see soon, will surely take alarm. Luckily the breeze is blowing up the hill, so they will not scent us.

We reach the base of the hillock and tread our way around bushes of thorn and lantana on tiptoe till we arrive at a grassy glade. There, feeding placidly, is a herd of at least forty of the deer we had hoped to find. Fortunately, none of the hinds on sentinel duty have observed our approach and we stop just in time behind a crop of young redwood trees.

The sight before us is magnificent. The stags are in the centre of the group, antlers spread and tapering, as they toss their proud heads and sniff the air before stooping to graze again. Around them on all sides are the does and fawns, the former ever alert, with ears cocked forwards and twitching to catch the faintest sound. Now and then a head and neck dips quickly to earth to grab a mouthful of grass or leaves, but is raised again quickly, ever observant, always vigilant.

The fawns have no such responsibilities and death will strike many of them down cruelly and suddenly, before the survivors learn that the great secret of continued existence in the jungle is to be 'ever watchful at every moment; for death lurks everywhere.'

They gambol and play among themselves, one chasing the other round and round. A few of the very young members nuzzle up against their mothers, slyly dipping their tiny heads under udders hanging temptingly close, to sneak a drink of milk. The mothers in turn stop their feeding now and again to lick their little offspring affectionately, but never for a moment do they halt their close scrutiny of the surrounding jungle for a possible foe. Their eyes seem to stare in every direction, with ears strained forwards to catch the slightest sound, and nostrils dilated to detect the faintest scent of danger.

On a tree directly above the grazing deer is a small family of langurs. Two of these jump to earth and playfully chase a spotted fawn. Then one leaps back to a low branch where, hanging by its legs, it grabs the fawn by the tail and half lifts if off the ground. The fawn enjoys the game but its mother does not seem to approve.

A scene apparently of utter peace, beauty and tranquillity. But out of the corners of our eyes we notice the faintest of movements beneath a large bush, well away to our left. We look harder at the bush, but the movement has now ceased.

A hind with her young fawn, grazing close to that bush, has seen it too. She raises her head abruptly to stare hard, both ears cocked forwards and muzzle aquiver. The she raises her right foot to stamp the ground and voice the first syllable of her warning cry, 'Aiow!'

But it is already too late. An elongated form, golden and spotted in the rays of the early morning sun, springs from under that bush and in two bounds reaches the little fawn. In the next second it is dead, while the panther glowers and growls over the small quivering body.

Then we witness a scene that is as touching as it is magnificent. The fawn's mother, forgetful of her own safety, rushes forward to defend it. The panther leaves the little carcass and springs upon the hind, seizing her throat and bearing her to the ground. Her hoofs drum out their death-agony on the green grass, already stained a deep red by the blood that flows from her torn throat.

I watch you as you raise your 10-shot Springfield to cover the still growling panther, in order to exact what you feel is just retribution for the murder that has just been done. But I stretch out a hand to hold the muzzle and deflect your aim.

'Don't shoot, John! It's the law of the jungle. The panther has killed for food, not wantonly.'

The panther hears my voice, then sees us. In the next instant it has vanished. But it will come back.

Two

The Bellundur Ogre

BELLUNDUR IS A HAMLET SITUATED ON THE SHOULDER OF A HILL AND about three miles from the village of Tagarthy, in the district of Shimoga, in Mysore state.

For centuries this part of Mysore has been the home of tigers, which had become so numerous as to have almost eliminated, simply by devouring them, their lesser cousins, the more subtle but far less powerful panthers that also, not long ago, roamed in large numbers through the area. These lesser cats, as a matter of fact, had created havoc in their time. Far bolder and more clever, and more difficult to circumvent, they could hide themselves better, being smaller than tigers; they haunted the precincts of villages which they raided systematically each night after sundown, carrying away fowls, dogs, goats, sheep and calves with equal disdain and impartiality.

Humans they seldom harmed unless they were wounded, but on those rare occasions when they were guilty of this crime, to exact retribution against them was difficult because of the cover afforded by the dense jungles of the area, well watered as they were by heavy monsoon rains.

When my story opens, however, tigers were the ruling factor, while in Bellundur lived a necromancer who was reputed for his ability to provide charms and talismans of all sorts for all purposes. These last were said to be particularly efficacious in procuring a loved one, or contrarily, in ridding yourself of one whom you did not love quite so well. They were also rumoured to be very effective in securing a job that had been applied for or the success of petition.

Among his other abilities, this magician was far famed as possessing the power, by charms and incantations, to 'tie up' the jungle, so that any hunter operating in that area would meet with total failure. The game would either not appear before his rifle; or if they did, the rifle would not go off; or if it did go off, the bullet would not strike the quarry even at a few yards' range. I had met this character some years ago, and have written about him in one of my earlier stories.* Like most members of his calling, he enjoyed a little flattery. Otherwise, I had found him quite friendly and had found nothing wrong in his weakness. After all, we all like to be flattered.

But the 'Ogre of Bellundur,' about which I am going to tell you, began its career in more or less the usual way, as a very ordinary and inoffensive tiger. Nothing was heard of it in its younger days. Evidently it had confined its attentions to killing and eating spotted deer, sambar and pig, which swarmed everywhere in those times. Then the government began encouraging programmes of cattle-rearing, and as rich pasturage abounded, herds of cattle were introduced which

---

* See *Nine Man-eaters and One Rogue*.

multiplied into many thousands within a short period, to the detriment of the wild deer and pig that previously had grazed undisturbed.

'The Ogre,' as it came to be known later, now made its presence felt by varying its taste for wild game with a liking for prime beef, and this inclination grew rapidly to the exclusion of any other kind of meat. It killed and it ate, and it ate and it killed, till it had accounted for many herds of cattle and the villagers at last began to feel that something should be done.

The Indian villager is a man of unbounded patience, an attribute easier to understand if one observes his complete apathy, his capacity for resignation and for accepting whatever misfortune it may be the will of God to bestow upon him. So, when I tell you that at last the villagers had had enough of this tiger and were determined to put a stop to its depredations you will realize that the Ogre had really gone too far. They decided to set a trap, catch it and then kill it.

A deep rectangular hole was dug in the centre of a game trail; the mouth was carefully concealed by thin interlaced bamboos covered with leaves and twigs, and the bait, in the form of the least valuable calf in the village, was tied to a stake at the farther end of the rectangular pit. A direct approach to the bait from any other direction except across the rectangular pit was made impracticable for the tiger by a vast mass of thorns packed tightly around it on both sides and beyond, leaving only the one approach open.

Everything went according to plan and on the third night the tiger fell into the pit.

The following morning all the inhabitants of Bellundur village turned out, including the necromancer, to gloat over their erstwhile enemy and throw firebrands at it, before putting it to death by the simple but rather slow process of spearing it from above. Evidently nobody had a gun, and the question

THE KENNETH ANDERSON OMNIBUS

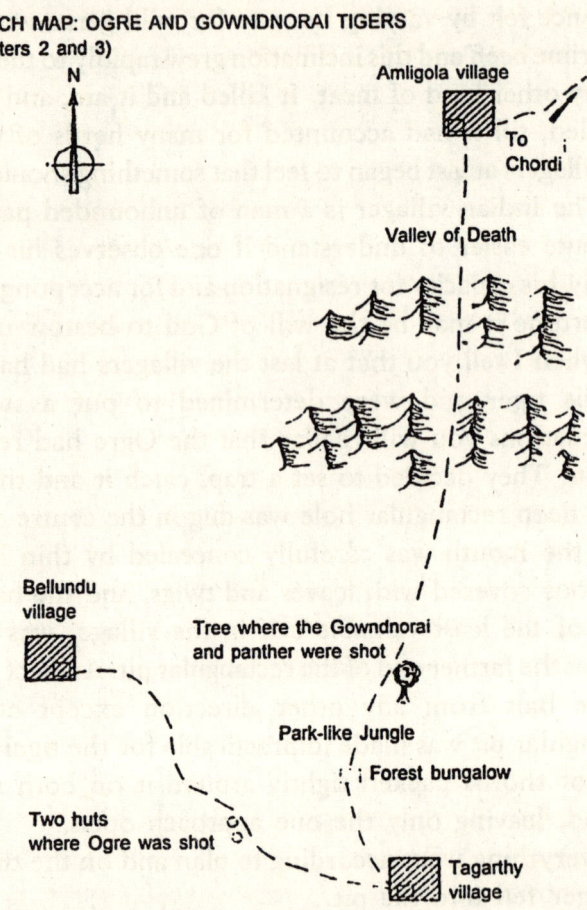

SKETCH MAP: OGRE AND GOWNDNORAI TIGERS
(Chapters 2 and 3)

of cruelty, of course, did not occur to anybody. For was not this animal the tiger which had killed and devoured so many of their cattle?

Not only did the inhabitants of Bellundur have no guns, but they did not appear to be very rich in spears either. I discovered afterwards that just two people had spears, or articles that might pass as such. One was a short affair, less than four feet long and entirely blunt at the end. The description fitted more a crowbar than a spear. The second was a true spear and belonged to the local temple. It was reputed to have been used in a war two and a half centuries ago, but was now as blunt as the aforementioned crowbar, having been employed many times for digging yams out of the earth. In any case, the shafts of both weapons were too short to reach the tiger from the surface of the pit, but this mattered little, as each of their owners was confident that, with a single throw of his particular weapon, he could transfix and kill the imprisoned beast.

Much argument is said to have arisen as to who should cast his weapon first. Finally, but I do not know on what grounds, the owner of the crowbar won the dispute. Taking careful aim, he hurled his weapon; no sooner had it left his hand than its blunt point was deflected and the side of the weapon rather than its blunt point, struck the flank of the tiger with a dull thud.

As might have been expected, the tiger did not take lightly to this form of treatment. It roared its defiance and glared up at its tormentors. There was widespread tittering amongst the assembled crowd as the second spear-man, after glancing contemptuously at the crestfallen owner of the crowbar, prepared to make his cast. The 250-year-old spear flew downwards to its target, the blunt point embedding itself fairly in the tiger's hindquarters.

Now Bellundur was totally unarmed! And the Ogre lost its temper. With a burst of unexpected energy, it sprang upwards to the rim of the pit, groping with the talons of its forefeet. They reached it, held and embedded themselves in the soft soil. The hind feet, kicking the air madly, found purchase against the sides of the pit and levered the beast upwards. And the next moment the tiger was free, leaping out of the mouth of the pit like a demon from hell, and far more dangerous.

Just one of the crowd stood in its *path* to freedom; all the rest had fled. The tiger leaped over the man before it, kicking backwards with all four feet extended, and the claws of one of those dreadful feet met the back of the man's skull before he, in turn, could gather his wits to run. It was only a glancing blow, comparatively light considering the force that the tiger had put into it, for if the paw had struck the head fully the skull would have been smashed like an eggshell. As it was, the tips of the claws caught in the skin at the back of the man's neck, and the weight of the tiger, as it leaped over the man's head, did the rest.

Then the tiger had gone. The man fell where he had been standing but he was quite alive. The whole of his scalp, removed neatly from the bone, now hung over his face, the long hair streaming down before him instead of behind. It took three days for this man to die, for to the very last moment he lived in the hope that his scalp could be put back. He was the Ogre's first victim although admittedly unintentionally so.

Naturally, with the healing of his wound, the tiger grew cunning. Other baits were tied out for it with various forms of traps, but they were studiously ignored. All its killings of cattle thereafter were done in broad daylight, generally in the afternoons while the herds were placidly resting after having grazed all morning and their attendants were huddled asleep in the shade of the bushes. Those who were awake or had been awakened by the short cry of the stricken victim, at first attempted to drive the Ogre off by shouting and throwing stones. But the Ogre soon put a stop to such tactics by leaping upon one of the graziers and mauling him severely. Strangely enough this man made a complete recovery, though the lesson that had been given was salutary enough. Thereafter, at sight or sound of the tiger all herdsmen fled, leaving their charges to its mercy.

The situation at Bellundur went from bad to worse. Cattle owners could no longer trust their animals to the forest for grazing, but endeavoured to feed them at home, and this of course cost a lot of money. Correspondingly, the tiger's hunger grew as the supply of Bellundur beef was cut down, so it extended the range of its operations to include Tagarthy and some of the smaller neighbouring hamlets. Its fame for daring as a cattle-lifter began to spread far and wide.

That was how a gentleman, whom we shall call Mr Johnson, came to hear about the tiger.

Johnson was an officer in railway service who had lately been transferred to the area from some other part of India where tigers did not exit. This made him very keen to attempt to bag the beast that was the talk of the neighbourhood, and as he had a rifle he made his way to Bellundur, which was only about seven miles from the railway track, on the few days' leave during which he hoped to succeed. And this is where old Buddiah, the necromancer, comes into my story.

Hearing that a white man had arrived and was making inquiries about the tiger, Buddiah donned his ceremonial saffron robe, plaited the long roll of filthy false hair that he kept for such occasions in a coil around the crown of his head, smeared ashes liberally across his forehead, which he further decorated with vermilion marks of a religious significance, hung his chain of large amber wooden beads around his neck, and holding his gnarled walking-stick, blackened by being soaked in oil, in his hand, presented himself before Johnson, offering his services, claiming that they were absolutely indispensable if the white man wished to succeed in shooting the tiger.

Now the situation was really very simple. To anyone of moderate experience, it was obvious that old Buddiah was endeavouring to earn a few rupees but more than that he was taking the opportunity to impress his fellow villagers with his greatness as a magician. He wanted them to feel that even a white man had to come to him for help. If Johnson had used a little psychology and common sense, he would have recognized these things and given the old man a boost with a few rupees to humour him. Instead, Johnson lost his temper, told the magician to get out of his presence, and when Buddiah began to remonstrate indignantly, made matters worse by threatening to break his neck!

So, the necromancer stalked away in fury: his prestige with the villagers, which he had been endeavouring to enhance, had been severely lessened by the white man's words. He felt his companions would laugh at him secretly, although he was still confident that they feared him too much to do so openly.

The villagers, on the other hand, felt abashed. Although none of them had any liking for Buddiah who had exploited them systematically since childhood, he was, nevertheless, their own magician. One of themselves. To be spoken to in such a fashion by the white man, and to be threatened with a beating, reflected scant respect for their magician and incidentally for themselves and the village as a whole. Thus by his hasty words, Johnson had made enemies all around instead of friends. The villagers left him where he stood and refused to have anything more do with him. Nor would anyone sell or hire him a bait to tie out for the tiger.

Being of a determined nature, Johnson made up his mind to succeed in spite of the local noncooperation. He made his way back to Tagarthy where, by exercising the tact he should have displayed at Bellundur, he was able to buy two ancient bulls. Engaging herdsmen, he had these two animals driven back to the outskirts of Bellundur, where he tied each up in a *nullah* said to be frequented by the tiger, or so he was told by the herdsmen he had engaged; but as these men were from Tagarthy and not from Bellundur, they did not know very much about the tiger's movements.

The following morning Johnson and his herdsmen visited the baits. One had disappeared. It certainly had not been taken by the tiger, for there were no pug-marks to be seen in the sandy bed of the *nullah,* which bore a number of human footprints instead. Had these been made by his own men the previous day, or by others? The other bait had not been touched.

Johnson rightly came to the conclusion that the villagers of Bellundur had stolen his first bait. He stalked into the village with a loaded rifle, demanded the return of the bull, and then threatened to inform the police. To all of which the villagers assumed an air of injured innocence. They maintained that the human footprints he had seen in the sandy ravine were those of his own men when they had tied the bait and asked him to prove otherwise. To Johnson's dire threats to shoot the thieves, the yokels turned a deaf ear and smiled.

Fearing the second bait would also disappear, Johnson ordered his two men to construct a *machan* over it, in which he sat that same afternoon, perhaps more to protect his bait from being robbed than in the serious hope of bagging the tiger. But the unexpected happened. I am told the tiger turned up while it was still daylight. Johnson fired, succeeding only in wounding the animal, which got away.

Throughout the next week, Johnson, with commendable determination, scoured the jungles in search of the tiger. No one came forward to assist him; even his two henchmen refused to accompany him on the plea that it was too dangerous. Unaided, the white man lost his way on one occasion and was compelled to spend the night in the forest. In the end, bitterly disappointed, Johnson had to return to duty without bagging his tiger.

Everything was quiet for some time after that. The Ogre did not show up and the villagers of Bellundur had to admit that, in spite of their best efforts at noncooperation, the *sahib* had rid them of the pest that had been exacting such a heavy toll of their cattle. Buddiah, the magician, was more aggrieved than ever. He saw his pride and reputation at a still lower ebb, for he had announced boastfully that the *sahib* would not or could not shoot the tiger; he had done so nevertheless and had rid Bellundur of the hated cattle-lifter.

So the cattle were driven out to the jungles once again each day for grazing. That is, until the inevitable happened!

Early one afternoon a herd rushed pell-mell back to the village minus one of its members—and minus the nineteen-year-old youth who had gone out with the animals that morning to graze them. Nobody worried about the matter till nightfall. Then the relatives of the boy grew a little anxious about him, while the owner of the missing cow grew far more anxious about his valuable animal. A search the next morning revealed the cow lying dead: her neck had been neatly broken by a large tiger whose pug-marks were clearly to be seen in the field where she had been struck down. A hundred yards away, hidden under a bush, was the body of the missing youth.

There was, however, this difference between the two carcases: the cow had not been eaten, while rather more than half of the youth's body had been devoured by the tiger. The familiar pattern had appeared once more: an innocent tiger had been turned into a man-eater through being wounded and left to fend for itself.

Tragedy succeeded tragedy after that and the pattern of events was repeated. The people of Bellundur locked themselves in their huts at sundown while the cattle were kept starving in their pens. Old Buddiah's prestige was at its lowest ebb.

Lack of human prey drove the tiger into extending his operations towards Tagarthy and more distant villages, and that was when the beast began to be referred to as 'The Ogre,' a name that was whispered with bated breath behind locked doors and only during daylight hours. Otherwise it would surely hear and bring dreadful vengeance upon the man who dared refer to the creature as a tiger.

After darkness the Ogre was about! It roamed everywhere and a man was not safe even in a locked room. The Ogre, or one of its spies, an evil spirit of the air in the form of a bat or an owl, or one of the many devils that lived in the jungle, might hear what was being said and carry words to the dreaded man-eater.

Then the man who had spoken against it was indeed undone! It would be only a matter of time before the Ogre exacted a terrible revenge. His fate was sealed and there was no means of escape. That was the universal opinion.

At this stage my old friend, Doctor Stanley, the medical officer of Tagarthy village, wrote a long letter to me and related this story, inviting me to join him in an attempt to end the Ogre's career. This doctor, who owned only a .12 bore shotgun and no rifle, had shot many tigers himself in his younger days, parelleling Dick Bird, the Postmaster of

Santaveri, whom I have mentioned in another story. Now that he had grown older, he felt that his rather antiquated gun, although still a trusty weapon, might not be quite up to the mark for a man-eater.

I met him three days later in the front room of his dispensary-cum-hospital, after motoring to Tagarthy in my Studebaker. The first thing he insisted upon was a tremendous meal, with gallons of tea, after which, over clouds of pipe-smoke, we discussed 'old times' for about three hours. Generally long-suffering by nature, at times I become impatient; finally I reminded the good doctor that there was a job of work to be done. Obviously the first step was to visit Bellundur and pick up the trail from there.

The Studebaker had a hard time to reach this village. The track, which was always bad, had become really terrible after the last rains. The doctor, who sat next to me, said we should have walked. Having reached Bellundur at last, I set about undoing, as far as possible, some of the mischief that had been done by the tactless Johnson. I called upon Buddiah, who was sulking in his hut, asked him to don his ceremonial robes and make *pooja* for me and repeat all the mantras he knew, to enable me to succeed in shooting the man-eater, presenting him with ten rupees to cover incidental expenses.

He brightened up at once. In no time at all he stalked out into the marketplace, all dressed up for the occasion, where the first thing he did was to demand another five rupees from me to cover the cost of a black fowl and a bottle of the local spirit called '*arrack*.' The fowl was to be killed, cooked and eaten by him, presumably to placate the spirits of the jungle, and the *arrack* was to be drunk, also by Buddiah, presumably for the same purpose. The old man declared that only thereafter would he be in a proper condition to utter the mantras that would lead to the downfall of the man-eater. Dr Stanley and I, knowing what state that would be, pretended hearty agreement.

I handed over the money and resigned myself to a further delay of another hour at least, which would be the shortest possible time for the cock to be half-cooked while Buddiah had conditioned himself with *arrack* for saying his mantras. But the old man, and the villagers of Bellundur especially, had to be humoured if the damage done by Johnson was to be repaired.

The doctor and I chatted while the unfortunate black cock was procured, slaughtered before our eyes, parboiled into a curry and then devoured by the greedy old necromancer. With scarcely an interval he proceeded to empty the bottle of *arrack* by the simple process of applying the neck to his mouth and pouring the contents down his throat. Why he did not choke in the process amazed me.

This done, the magician staggered to his feet. He was dead drunk and could hardly stand erect. With bloodshot eyes and an inane smile, he produced what looked like a bracelet of twisted and dried jungle vines from a filthy cloth-bag that he brought out from somewhere on his person. Asking for my rifle, he proceeded to pass this bracelet over the end of the muzzle and down the length of the barrel three or four times. He was so drunk that he missed his aim once or twice, but I was able to rectify the error unostentatiously by quickly guiding the end of the barrel so as to allow it to be encircled by the bracelet.

That was the end of the mantra. The tiger's doom was sealed! It would fall to my rifle! The spirits of the jungle, in the person of old Buddiah, had eaten and drunk well. The crowd of villagers, who had been watching every detail while they stood around us in a circle, breathed this assurance loudly. In any case the mantra, together with their assurances, ended just in time, for the next moment old Buddiah fell to earth as if pole-axed.

The important thing was that good feeling had been restored. Buddiah's prestige was up again, as was that of the villagers and of Bellundur village itself. Dr Stanley and I were smiled upon as 'good fellows,' while the activities of the Ogre were momentarily eclipsed. Just then it was no more than an ordinary tiger, waiting to be shot.

It was now dark, and the trip back to Tagarthy in the Studebaker was a nightmare. We made it, however, without any broken axles or springs, but resolved that henceforth we would walk there and back rather than risk a breakdown, which would be inevitable if we tempted fate too much.

Stanley procured two baits at Tagarthy, which we duly tied out the next day at suitable points near the track to Bellundur, for you will remember that I told you that the tiger was by this time, operating throughout the area. After lunch we walked the seven miles to that village, and we were able there, without any difficulty, to procure another three animals as additional baits. Obviously the little show we had organized with Buddiah the previous evening had had its good effects. These baits were tied out at points which the villagers informed us were often visited by the Ogre.

Time was against us, however, and we were in too much of a hurry to be able to set up a *machan* above any one of the five baits we had laid that day. This is against my usual practice of constructing a *machan* first and tying the bait in full view of it afterwards, which has two advantages. Firstly a 'kill,' if it occurs, is in proper view of the *machan* and does not have to be shifted. Secondly, no noise is made in building the *machan*, which would be inevitable if the 'kill' occurs first. Such sounds may arouse the suspicion of the tiger if it is lying up or otherwise lurking within hearing.

It was again pitch-dark when we walked back to Tagarthy, keeping a sharp lookout with our torches against a surprise attack by the man-eater, but the only animal we encountered was a pangolin foraging amongst the dead leaves, out much earlier than usual for these creatures.

None of the five baits we had tied out was touched that night, but late in the morning of the third day, a man came running to the doctor's dispensary to announce that his cousin had been taken by the tiger. The victim and his wife, together with our informant and his wife, lived in two huts constructed side by side and only a short mile away along the track to Bellundur. The sun was at meridian when this cousin, who was returning from a visit to Tagarthy for provisions, came into full view of the other three members of the little community, gathered before their huts and were chatting together. They had been about to call out to him when he had screamed loudly and then vanished into thin air.

Our informant stated he had then grabbed his axe and set out to see what was the matter, accompanied by his cousin's wife, wringing her hands and lamenting aloud. The thought of the man-eater had never occurred to them. Rather they suspected that an evil spirit from the forest had done away with their companion.

Reaching the spot where the man had disappeared, they were terrified to find the pug-marks of a tiger in the soft sand of the trail. Prevented by fear from going farther, they were about to turn back when the wails of the woman, which had now increased in volume, annoyed the man-eater who had just begun to taste his victim not far away. The tiger growled fiercely, whereupon both the man and the victim's wife fled. Stopping long enough to enable the two women to lock themselves into one of the huts, the man had come running to Tagarthy by a round-about route to inform the doctor and me of what had happened. The Ogre would be there still, he affirmed, feasting upon his cousin, if only we had the courage to come at once and shoot it.

Grabbing rifle, torch and warm coat, I set out at a jog trot with our informant, Stanley bringing with him the .12 bore gun and another torch. I was younger in those days than I am now, and the doctor younger still, so that we reached the two huts in fairly good shape, if a bit breathless. Minutes later, with the man in the middle, Stanley to the left of him and me to the right, we approached the place where the tragedy had taken place, determined to flush the man-eater on its kill.

The tiger sensed we were coming long before we knew where it was, for we heard no sounds of eating or the breaking of bones. As likely as not it had seen our arrival at the two huts, which were, as I have said, in full view of the spot where the Ogre had seized its victim.

When we were quite close, the man-eater began to growl, and its protests grew to hideous volume. Clearly, it was bent upon driving us away. If we beat a retreat now, while the going was good, all would be well. But if we continued to advance, it would either rush at us, or its courage might fail at the last moment, it would then run away.

We hesitated only a second before Stanley and I nodded to each other. With my left arm I thrust back the man who had called us, motioning to him with my hand to go away. Then we advanced, shoulder to shoulder. We could not see the tiger yet. Roar followed upon roar, and the bushes in front of us shook violently. We stopped, gun and rifle to respective shoulders, awaiting the onslaught that was inevitable.

It never came! At the last moment the man-eater shirked the encounter! It was accustomed to chasing and killing men. Never before had human beings deliberately followed and approached it. With a final shattering roar, the tiger sprang away from the spot and I was just able to catch a fleeting glimpse of a reddish-brown form hurtling into a bush; then it disappeared. I could have fired. Why I did not do so I just cannot say, but I was to regret my mistake.

The tiger must have been really hungry, for we discovered it had made the most of its opportunity by devouring over half its victim, leaving only the head, arms, legs and a few ribs uneaten. Stanley and I did not speak to each other. We were both experienced enough to know that the human voice carries a long way. Instead, I looked about to see if there were any possible places to conceal myself and await the man-eater's return should it decide to come back to finish what scraps were left.

But the Ogre put an end to my reflections by its next action, as unexpected as it was sudden. It might have been hunger or natural ill nature, or maybe the fact that as it fled it saw only two humans and not a crowd, had dared to follow. Anyway, this extraordinary animal stopped in its tracks, turned about and started to come for us, roaring louder as it approached. The ground literally shook with the intensity of the sound, while its ever-increasing volume indicated that the tiger was getting dangerously close. You must bear in mind that all this time we could not see the beast for it was hidden by the bushes. What we could see was the bushes shaking violently as it came closer and closer.

What was happening just goes to indicate the axiom I have so often repeated in my earlier stories. There are no fixed rules in the jungle and no two animals are alike. Like us they are individuals; they react differently under different circumstances and the unexpected often occurs.

Standing shoulder to shoulder once more, the doctor and I turned to face the man-eater, which was making things easy for us and solving the problem by attacking. In another minute the tiger would have to show itself and then all would be over.

But the minute never came! For the Ogre was wily beyond expectation. At the last moment it changed its mind once more and began to circle us and the remains of its meal without showing itself, still snarling and roaring for all it was worth. The animal's tactics were now clear. Again its courage failed when it had been about to press home its attack. Now its intention was to drive us away with the noise it was making.

Then I had an idea. Its success depended on just how observant the tiger had been, how persistent was its memory, and how alert its instinct. It had seen the two of us approaching. That much was evident. Now if one of us went away and the other hid in the grass somewhere near the remains of the victim, would the tiger be aware of the fact? Would it think the coast was clear and return to its meal? Would it be tempted to follow and attack the one who was retreating? Would it see through the trick we were trying to play by stalking whichever one of us had remained behind and leaping upon that one from the rear?

There were too many imponderables in the situation and I confess I did not like them at all. Moreover, the doctor was armed only with a shotgun. If I suggested that he should go back and leave me behind, it was possible the tiger might decide to stalk him, when Stanley would be at a decided disadvantage. Alternatively, if I left the doctor behind and walked away myself and the man-eater decided to attack him instead of me, the same disadvantage would be there. As a last resource, I could offer the doctor my rifle and take his gun.

Frankly, I did not relish that last solution. I was accustomed to my .405 in emergencies. No doubt Stanley had the same feelings for his shotgun. If we exchanged weapons we would both be unfamiliar with the firearm each of us was handling, and a shotgun, moreover, was hardly suitable for a meeting with a man-eater.

Evidently these very thoughts were passing through Stanley's mind and he solved the problem for me by whispering to me to hide while he would go away. Without speaking, I thrust my rifle towards him and reached for his shotgun, but Stanley turned it way from me, motioning impatiently towards the bushes for me to hide.

The tiger was creeping about now, circling our position and continuing to snarl and roar alternately. A single bush, not more than four feet high, grew about thirty feet or so away, its base hidden by the usual carpet of grass and greenery. There was no other large tree or rock that offered shelter. I tiptoed to the bush and took up my position behind it, crouching on the ground with my weapon ready. We waited till the tiger had reached a point that was opposite the direction in which the doctor would have to go to regain the track leading towards the two huts. Then I motioned to him to get away quickly.

With the purpose of letting the man-eater know that he was departing and that the coast would be clear to return to the meal, Stanley coughed slightly and began to talk to himself as he began to back slowly towards the track. I watched him looking intently in the direction where the man-eater was still demonstrating, his .12 bore gun ready for instant action should the animal charge.

But Stanley had made a mistake by talking. Instead of returning to its kill now that the coast was clear, as the doctor had hoped, this most unusual animal did the unexpected thing once again. Circling the scant clearing in which the remains of its victim reposed, and incidentally myself, the tiger began to follow the departing doctor. Worse still, it stopped roaring and snarling. Clearly, the man-eater now meant business. Whatever the Ogre was doing at that moment, or intended to do at the next, was to be done in silence. Stanley, already handicapped with only a shotgun, was going to be still further handicapped by not knowing from which direction the man-eater would attack him.

This thought worried me. It was hard to sit idly behind a bush while my friend's life might at that moment be in great danger. Without weighing the consequences I decided to creep after the tiger. No greater folly could have been committed than by my action at that moment, and I will tell you why.

Try to imagine the doctor stepping backward, a foot at a time with his shotgun loaded in both barrels ready for instant use pointed towards where he thinks the tiger is, creeping upon him unseen and in silence. He does not know that I have left my shelter in the bush and am following him and the tiger. Then put yourself in the tiger's place, your composure now regained after any exhibition of bad temper. You move softly and silently, bent upon putting an end to this interfering human being who has dared to follow you. At the same time, you are aware that you are close enough for a final spring, but instinct warns you that to do so will court disaster. And you do not know that a second human being is following you. Behind them both am I, creeping forward with equally great caution, my Winchester cocked and ready for use at the first glimpse of the tiger. But I cannot see it, nor Stanley. All I can hear is the faint rustle of a bush here and there before me, as either Stanley or the tiger brushes against it despite their caution. Finally, do not forget that the distance between the doctor and myself cannot be more than forty or fifty yards now, with the tiger somewhere in between.

If only that tiger had had a little reasoning power, what fun it could have had that day! All it had to do was to conceal itself and then mimic the sound of a charging tiger by roaring 'Wroof! Wroof! Wroof!' Stanley and I would have opened fire. One or the other would have shot his companion. Perhaps with a spot of luck—or bad luck—we might have shot each other. I would have made more tender eating in those days than now! So would the doctor, even if he smelled faintly of iodoform! And what headlines for the newspapers! *Shikaries* after man-eater shoot each other! Man-eater eats both!'

So intent was I on following the tiger that all this did not dawn upon me at the time. The man-eater, unaware of being followed, kept steadfastly after Stanley; while the doctor, naturally worried by the silence that had succeeded the tiger's threatening roars, except for a faint and furtive rustling now and again as the tiger came after him, was wondering if he would reach the track to the huts before the attack came.

Then things happened! The doctor! The doctor reached the track. The tiger broke the silence with a shattering roar! Seeing nothing but hearing everything, I did not know right away whether the man-eater was launching its attack upon the doctor or myself. The doctor fired, and slugs from his gun spattered through the undergrowth uncomfortably close to me. The tiger, frightened by the sound, lost its nerve, turned, and dashed past me at full gallop. I saw the tiger coming, threw the rifle to my shoulder, and pressed the trigger at almost point-black range.

Stanley told me a few minutes later that my bullet whizzed past his head within inches. The only thing that kept it from parting his hair, he affirmed, was that he was bald! Inadvertently the Ogre had almost succeeded in accomplishing what it had been unable to do by the power of reasoning. The doctor and I had narrowly escaped shooting each other.

We still had hopes, however. We both had considerable hunting experience. Both had been ready to fire when we had actually pressed our triggers. Both had fired at point-blank range. The tiger must be lying mortally wounded close by, perhaps it was even dead. One of us must have wounded it at least. In the excitement, we overlooked the fact that I had heard the slugs from Stanley's gun, while he had heard my bullet.

So we searched far and wide, but not a speck of blood did we come across. Of dead or wounded tiger there was neither sight nor sound! Then it dawned upon us. Hard though it was to admit, the truth stuck out a mile. We had both missed, although the Ogre had met us almost face to face. Stanley looked woebegone. I do not know what I looked like; but I know what I felt like!

We made our way in silence back to the huts, where to the man and the two women still hiding there we confided all that had happened. We were half a furlong from Tagarthy before my mind, numbed with disappointment, started to function again.

Normally a tiger, after being fired upon, avoids the place where that had happened for a long time. This tiger, it should be remembered, had been fired upon not once, but twice! Therefore, by all the rules, it should leave the neighbourhood and not appear there again. But was there just a small chance to the contrary? The Ogre had already shown itself to be of a most unusual disposition on two occasions. It fled and then turned and crept back again. And it had deliberately followed Stanley when the way was clear to return to its kill. Would it once again display its singular nature by returning to a place where, at least instinct must tell it, it had suffered two narrow escapes? The chances were 99 per cent against. That left a one per cent chance that the tiger might return!

I halted in my tracks as the thought came to me. The doctor stopped also, wondering what was the matter. I told him. Stanley frowned and puckered his forehead in thought. Then he shook his head. But he was too much of a hunter himself not to realize the chance was one that could not, must not, be missed. So we retraced our steps to the huts.

The man and the two women, now all locked together in one of the huts for mutual safety, were surprised at our early return. When we told them why we had come, they were really pleased. But they were honest enough to say they did not think we had any chance of success. It was the man's opinion that the tiger would be many miles away by now.

Stanley and I retraced our steps to the place where the remains of the man-eater's victim lay strewn about, exercising extreme caution while negotiating the patch of jungle through which the doctor, the tiger and I had played our strange game of hide-and-seek. There was neither sight nor sound of our quarry.

A strange mixture of relief and disappointment filled us, relief that the Ogre had not launched another attack and disappointment at the feeling that it might never return.

My earlier survey of the possibilities of concealment, although made in such a hurry, had about summed up the chances accurately. Apart from the four-foot-high bush where I had stood while the doctor retreated there was no other place in which to conceal myself. Hiding behind that bush in daylight for a man-eater, as I had done already, was one thing; but remaining there after darkness was quite another. The tiger, with its ability to see at night, would spot me immediately as it approached what was left of its victim from any angle other than directly opposite the bush behind which I would be hiding, while for me to see it would be impossible. Further, should it indeed return in spite of being shot at twice only a few hours earlier, the man-eater would undoubtedly make an extremely cautious approach and I would not be able to hear it. Lastly, there was no possibility of erecting any sort of shelter behind that scanty bush that would not immediately betray my presence.

What could I do? I was reluctant to forgo that tiny possibility of the man-eater's return. To commit suicide, and that too in a most painful manner in the jaws of the tiger, I was still more reluctant.

There seemed no solution as we thought about the matter without speaking, till suddenly the doctor had a brainwave. Would it not be possible, with the help of the man and the two women in the near-by huts, to dig a narrow hole just where the human remains were scattered? He would hide in the hole which would be wide and deep enough to conceal him, wait until the tiger returned, and shoot it at point-black range.

Several obstacles to the execution of this plan presented themselves. Firstly, the tiger might discover the hole and shy away; worse still, the tiger might decide to investigate it. Secondly, admitting that the man-in-the-hole was hidden from the tiger, the tiger was equally hidden from the man-in-the-hole, who would necessarily have to stand erect to be able to shoot the beast, during which process the latter would surely spot him when he appeared, as it would seem, out of the very ground. When that happened, the tiger would be frightened, yes; but it would also be decidedly annoyed. What transpired after that would depend upon which of the aforementioned reflexes gained the upper hand.

Well, there was no use thinking further about it. The chance, and the risk would have to be taken or the whole plan dropped. Time was passing and it was now after 3 p.m. We would have to work fast. We hurried back to the huts, where the inmates gladly volunteered to help us, but stated they had no implements of any sort to dig with. The doctor, who in his capacity of village medico wielded much influence, solved this by returning to Tagarthy at the double, from whence he came back in an incredibly short time with six helpers, two with pickaxes, two with crowbars, and two with large baskets in which to remove all traces of the earth we dug out. With the three earlier helpers and ourselves, the eleven of us set to work, with the result that astonishingly soon the hole had been dug and all traces of loose earth removed and thrown far away.

I knew that as the father of the plan, Stanley had prepared the hole to sit in it himself. I also knew that no amount of persuasion would dissuade him. If I tried to tell him that his shotgun was not an effective weapon against so dangerous a quarry, he would reply that it was just the right thing at such close range. Nor would I be able to gainsay the truth of his assertions as, in reality, at point-blank range a .12 bore gun has its merits. So I resigned myself to inactivity for once by spending the night at Tagarthy.

Our helpers were just gathering their tools together, prior to departing with me, when Dame Fortune once again took a hand in this strange adventure. Two men burst upon us, having run all the way from Tagarthy in search of the doctor. One was the village *patel*, quite a young man for such a responsible post; the other was his servant. The *patel* annouced that his wife, who was heavily pregnant, had slipped and fallen while carrying her pot of water from the well. She had aborted and was bleeding profusely. The doctor must come at once.

While he was still speaking, the young man summed up the position and realized that Stanley was preparing to sit up for the tiger. So to make his summons more forceful, he started lamenting aloud that the doctor, as his best friend, must come to his aid at once to save his wife's life, while in the same breath he denounced the woman as a stubborn wench. How often had he told her not to carry weights, particularly the water pot from the well. Was he not the village *patel*? Did he not have servants enough for this task? Yet in her wilfulness she would never listen to him. Now this was the result. And never mind the tiger; was his wife's life not far more important?

Stanley looked at me, chagrin written large upon his face. Then he gripped my arm tightly, affectionately.

'Good luck, Andy,' he muttered, 'and be careful, please. Would you like to use my gun?'

'Thanks, doc,' I replied, 'you know how it is. Old Winny will do the trick.'

In another minute Stanley and the other members of the group, which had grown to twelve, were lost to sight. I was alone with the remains of the dead man.

Dusk was fast approaching and there was not a moment to be lost as I slipped into the hole we had prepared, to squat at the bottom and look upwards at a circle of sky above my head. By canting my Winchester, loaded and cocked, at an angle with the butt against my right thigh and the foresight-guard leaning against the wall of the hold opposite me, we had made sure, by means of measuring Stanley's .12 bore gun in just a position, that the end of the muzzle would not be visible above ground level.

In the excitement and hurry of forming and executing what I now began to realize was a rather insane plan, we had overlooked the fact that it would be terribly hot inside the hole. The earth around had been exposed to the sun's rays all day, no air could enter, and with my body in close proximity to the sides of the cavity, air could not circulate anywhere. I soon began to perspire profusely.

Fortunately in those days there were no wild elephants around Tagarthy or, for that matter, in any of the districts to the northwest of Mysore state. Those were the times when tigers roamed in hundreds, but things have now changed and carnivora are scarce, but 'jumbo' in his wild state has extended his wanderings into those jungles and herds of elephants have now made their home there, where once there were none.

I remember that it was almost deathly silent inside the hole and I could scarcely hear the roosting calls of peafowl, junglecocks and other birds as they settled down for the night. To hope to hear the man-eater's arrival by any faint sound that it might make was out of the question. I would only be able to hear it if it roared or snarled nearby, and the Ogre was hardly likely to do that—or so at least I thought till I recollected that the tiger had in fact done just that only a few hours earlier. How I hoped it would repeat its performance rather than decide upon a silent approach!

It was almost dark when the circle of sky above my head was crossed by an elongated black form that passed silently by. A nightjar, with wings outstretched, had flown low over the spot, evidently to investigate the possibility of devouring the insects that were already assembling to feed upon the exposed flesh that hung in shreds from the human bones and devoured portions of the carcase of the tiger's unfortunate victim. I could hear the bluebottles as they buzzed across the opening above my head to settle on the mess, while the stench of decaying flesh, increased by the sun's rays in which it had been baking all day, seemed to cling to the ground and flow into the hole as an invisible, nauseating liquid.

Would the tiger come? Would it start eating right away? Or would it know that something unusual was afoot? It might have been watching us from the cover of some distant bush. It might even know, at that very moment, that one of its hated foes, a man, had gone into hiding somewhere in the ground. Now would be an excellent opportunity for the tiger to unearth and devour that enemy. The thought was not a very bracing one!

Where there had been an oval of sky above, two stars now twinkled down upon me and I knew that night had fallen. They seemed so serene and peaceful up there, oblivious to my predicament down in the hole. My thoughts focused upon them and I wondered at what other tragedies, taking place at that moment in other remote corners of the earth, they also twinkled upon so impartially.

The next moment the two stars seemed to become endowed with a baleful significance. They turned into two cruel eyes that glowered down upon me in hostile anticipation. Of what?

I forced myself to cast off this depressing idea and to think of something else. It is amazing what strange and often irrelevant thoughts come to one when in danger, as I was then. Perhaps this is nature's way of providing protection from panic. I wondered if Stanley would be able to save the life of the *patel's* wife.

That was when I first heard the sound: faint but distinctly heavy breathing.

It must be the tiger! It had located me and was creeping upon its stomach to get close enough to pull me out of my hiding place. Involuntarily, my hand reached towards the rifle. The touch of metal and wood, warm like everything else in that wretched pit, was very comforting to my nerves.

The sound ceased for a while. Then I heard a sudden, loud hiss, followed by silence again. Could this be a passing panther?

I have already mentioned that panthers were scarce in this area as the tigers had driven them out simply by devouring them. Nevertheless, there were one or two to be found here and there, and it was possible that an odd member had happened to be passing and had stumbled upon the exposed kill, creeping forward to snatch a mouthful. The heavy breathing and the hissing sound could certainly have been made by a panther, bent upon stealing from the tiger's kill.

I did not hear anything more for quite a long time. Then came a dull, scraping sound, as of something gliding over the ground above my head. Could a large snake be the cause? A hamadryad? There were quite a number of them to be found in these forests, where the vegetation and jungles were of the 'wet' variety, unlike the forests farther south.

Silence followed, while I strained my ears to pick up the faintest of sounds, and my eyes stared upwards at the faint light of the hole above me till they ached. The two stars still twinkled down upon me, but whether in disdain or mockery I did not know. I saw that they had shifted farther towards the edge of the circle above me and would soon disappear from view, indicating that time had passed since I had first observed them. I would miss their company and then would really be alone. Would their place be taken by other stars, I wondered?

This thought was still in my mind when at last the heavy silence was broken. There was a loud crack and the man-eater began to gnaw the bone it had just broken.

The noise made by a feeding tiger indicates its mood. Generally it is one of great contentment, and the sounds of mastication, gnawing, chewing and the tearing and rending of flesh follow one another as the feast progresses. Should there be a second tiger present, or the killer be a tigress with cubs, there is a lot of growling and wrangling, accompanied by threatening snarls when the other tiger, or a cub, approaches too closely. For despite the ties of mother love, which are considerable—and instances have been known where a tigress has sacrificed her life for her cubs—when it comes to eating, instinct seems to tell a feasting tigress that food is something not to be shared too soon, and to urge her to eat her fill before allowing her companion, mate or even her cubs to approach and eat what may be left.

The tiger above me began to growl. I knew then that it could not be alone. Perhaps there were cubs, perhaps another tiger, accompanying the man-eater. The situation was decidedly complicated and more than what I had bargained for. None of us had considered this possibility earlier in the evening, when this sitting-in-the-hole idea had occurred to Stanley.

I thought hard what to do next. Obviously, in order to take a shot at the tiger, I would have to locate it first by peeping over the edge of the hole and then by drawing the rifle right out of the hole and placing it on the ground outside so as to take aim. All this would entail considerable movement; I might even make a sound of some sort; the rifle might knock against the ground. The feeding animal would hear me and attack before I could free my weapon. There might be a slight hope of escaping the tiger's attention should he, or she, happen luckily to be facing the other way.

But there was a second tiger present. Even cubs could give the game away if they saw my head and shoulders, followed by my rifle, emerging from the ground. It was certainly straining imagination and luck too far to hope that all the animals above me would have their backs to me and be looking in the wrong direction. And if there should be two tigers above me, which of them was the man-eater? A silly question, that: obviously the one that was eating. But had both developed the man-eating habit, or only one? I must not kill the wrong tiger. Therefore, I must shoot both to take no chances.

The alternative course of action was to sit in silence in the hole, allow the animals to finish their meal and afterwards go about their business, then call it a day. But I had come here to shoot the man-eater; not to hide from it. I thought of the man it had killed and was now eating. What would Stanley and the villagers say of me when they came in the morning to find the ground covered with tiger pug-marks, the scraps of the man otherwise completely devoured, and me hiding in the hole?

Well, here goes, I said to myself, and a millimetre at a time, if such slow movement can in truth be possible, I began to position my feet so as to support me. Then slowly, very, very slowly, I started to raise myself, to bring my head to ground level. This in itself, took a long time, for I had to avoid making the slightest sound, and my thighs and legs were cramped from squatting so long on my haunches. The tiger continued feeding, growling and snarling now and again to keep the other tiger, or perhaps the cubs, away.

At last I was on my knees and toes and I stretched my two hands downwards to help support my weight on my outstretched fingers. Then very slowly, I began to raise myself.

Time had passed, and the strain on my hands and legs began to tell. But I must not hurry. Even now, as my ears came closer to the surface above, the tiger's growls grew stronger. I began to be frightened.

My hands were beginning to tremble with the sustained strain of supporting my weight, when I sensed that the top of my head must have reached about ground level. I could not delay longer, for the tiger or tigers would be able to see me should they be looking in my direction, whilst I would not be able to see them. I therefore quickly raised my head, until my eyes were level with the earth.

A terrifying sight confronted me. Luckily, through sitting in the darkness of the hole for so long, my eyes had grown accustomed to the gloom, so that I could see, only a few feet away, and lying broadside on, the enormous form of a tiger extended on its belly, chewing some part of the victim which it was holding between its front paws. Worse still, there was another form, also at full stretch, slightly farther away from me and a few feet from the feasting tiger, but facing it, and watching anxiously as the latter swallowed mouthful after mouthful. This second tiger, facing the first, was also facing me, and could not fail to see the top of my head popping out of the earth.

It let a snarl of surprise and scrambled to its feet. I ducked into my hole like a jack-in-the-box, grabbed my rifle, and looked upwards, expecting to find one or both tigers attacking the opening. I was wondering whether to sit tight, or to raise myself and the rifle quickly to ground level and risk a shot, but I remembered there were two tigers, not one outside. So I funked it and decided to sit tight.

All this occupied only a few seconds, but in that time the feasting tiger had not been idle. Hearing its companion snarl, and seeing it spring to its feet, this animal, not knowing that the sight of me was the cause of the excitement, concluded that its companion had decided to fight for a share of the kill. There was a second loud roar, followed by a fearful din, as the feaster, who was obviously the man-eater, attacked the tiger that had spotted me.

Now is my chance, I said to myself, for their attention was so distracted that they would not notice me.

I quickly raised myself. First the rifle, then head and shoulders, reached ground level. For a moment I could see nothing and do nothing because of the dust that was raised by the fighting animals. But neither tiger was anyway in sight, nor was there any growling or snarling to be heard.

I could not understand it. Perhaps the second tiger had fled with the first in pursuit. But if that was so, I should have heard some sounds at least, snarls and growls as one animal chased the other away. Perhaps they saw the rifle, or even the top of my head emerging from the hole, and fled at such an unexpected apparition. Then, too, there should have been growling and snarling; at least some sounds of departure.

As it was, the jungle was silent. I could not fathom it; it was eerie. The thought then occured to me that, if the man-eater had chased its companion away, it would undoubtedly return to finish what was left of the kill. So I ducked back into the hole to await its return and the renewed sounds of eating.

I waited in vain. Maybe half an hour had passed when I heard a loud, sustained human scream. It shattered the silence, rose to a crescendo, and then faded into choking sobs and was still. Then I heard other yells and shouts, and could make out a deeper voice and a more shrill one. These were the voices of the man and one of the two women from the two huts not far away. They were screaming for help.

That was when I grasped what had happened. The second woman had been taken by the man-eater! In chasing its companion away from the feast, or perhaps in its headlong flight after seeing my rifle and myself appear out of the ground, the man-eater must have passed the two huts where the man and his wife, and the widow of the late victim, were sheltering. But how did the Ogre get its second victim? Perhaps it was in such a towering rage that it just dragged her out of the hut in which she was sleeping. This tiger certainly was not hungry enough to justify such an action as it had been feasting all this while.

I wondered what to do. Should I remain where I was, or hasten to the huts? In either event, there was not much that I could do. There was little chance that the man-eater would return to the bones of its first victim when it had a fresh one at its disposal. And I would not be able to follow it up with the second kill, because of the darkness. That could be done only after daybreak.

I decided to remain where I was. It was just possible that the second tiger—the one that had been chased away—might return to the scant remains lying above me. If it did so, I would shoot; even if it were not the Ogre itself, this second tiger would undoubtedly become a man-eater in time. I remembered how, a short while ago, it lay anxiously waiting for a chance to eat the human remains, though held at bay by the feasting man-eater.

I spent a sleepless night after that, uncomfortably hot and stung by tiny ants and other insects that had decided to share my shelter. Nothing came, and no sound disturbed the silence till about four o'clock. Then a hyena discovered the bones above me and a great commotion began. The hyena smelt the tigers and knew it was about to commit the unpardonable crime of robbery. It also knew that to be caught by the owner or owners would mean death. It was undecided, therefore, between satisfying its hunger and its fear of being killed, and in this state of indecision made a great noise, letting the whole jungle know that it was faced with a tremendous dilemma. I could hear the creature running rapidly round and round, uttering weird sounds of every conceivable dilemma. 'Chee-ah! Chee-ay! Chee-ay!' it chattered, then growled like faraway thunder. 'Goodoo-Goodoo-Grooo!' Then it decided to be mournful about the whole business: 'Mee-ay! Mee-ay! Mee-ay!' it pleaded piteously, like a cat begging for food.

But the problem remained unsolved: the tiger did not show itself, but might come at any moment, and that would be the hyena's last if it lingered. All this amused me and served to distract my thoughts from the fearful tragedy that must have been enacted so close to me while I was powerless to intervene.

The opening above me grew a little brighter with the coming of the false dawn before the hyena, who had remained noisily persistent all this time, finally summoned up enough courage to start eating. I heard the crunch of a few bones for a short while, then fear must have returned to its craven heart, for I heard the pattering sound of its departure. I could picture the poor beast slinking quickly away, a human bone between its jaws, for gnawing later in the safety of its shelter among the rocks, or in a hole in the ground, far from this place of danger and lurking death.

I awaited the advent of the true dawn before raising the Winchester and myself very cautiously above ground level. The coast was clear and I dragged my cramped legs out of that awful hole, stamped about for a few minutes to restore the circulation, and set off for the huts to see what had happened. There I came upon a dreadful sight.

The terrified man and his wife, still hiding in a corner of one of the huts, told me a very harrowing tale. Along with the widow of the man-eater's victim, they had decided to sleep in one of the huts, the one they felt was the more secure of the two. The man had taken good care to sleep in the centre of the floor, equidistant from all the walls while his wife had slept to the left of him. The second woman had been forced to sleep somewhere by herself. So she had laid down a little distance away. Naturally she must have felt a little nervous, but as modesty forbade her to lie down to the right of the man, she had been compelled to sleep as far away as possible from the couple. So she lay down near the wall of the hut and opposite their feet.

The hut was comparatively small. It was roughly a square, about twelve feet by twelve. Allowing six feet for the man and his wife who were sleeping in the centre of the hut, and another three feet in order to be clear of their legs, the second woman was, therefore, lying at the most not more that a yard from the wall. The foot of the walls of such huts, in the damper parts of India, are kept a few inches from the ground so that termites cannot climb them overnight and destroy a large part of the structure by daylight. This practice leaves a slight opening around all four sides at ground level.

The man-eater who had passed very close to the hut, either in pursuit of its companion or in flight from me, was probably in great rage. It must have caught a glimpse of the sleeping woman, or sensed her presence, through this small opening, and had decided to drag her out. It had inserted one of its paws under the opening, grabbed the woman and had begun to pull her out.

Her screams and wails, which I had heard, had awakened her two companions, who in turn had started to yell and call for help. Meanwhile the man-eater had succeeded in dragging the woman's head and neck outside the hut, and had killed her by tearing out her gullet. But the rest of her body was stuck inside, for in dying, the woman clung to two of the bamboos supporting the wall of the hut. These had broken, and the end of one of them, piercing her saree and jacket, had gone right into the flesh of her side, thus wedging her body against the bamboo wall.

The pandemonium caused by her wails, and the shouts of her companions, seemed to have acted as a deterrent; the tiger changed its mind and abandoned the victim. The carcase of the woman as it lay before me was a dreadful sight. The tiger's claws had pierced the chest and torn one breast to ribbons. Then the Ogre had bitten right through her gullet and had wrenched out her windpipe, leaving the bones of her neck and the skin behind to keep her head from being totally severed. She lay in a pool of her own blood most of which had soaked into the dry earth, except for some that coagulated here and there.

The two survivors, man and wife, crouched wide-eyed and paralysed with fear in a far corner of the hut, expecting the man-eater to return at any moment. In fact, they were so terrified as to be oblivious of the fact that it was already daylight outside. Hearing my approaching footsteps, and thinking they heard the tiger returning they started to gibber in fear.

I called aloud to reassure them. The man and the woman then hurled themselves at the door of the hut, opened it, and rushed outside, to fall on the ground trembling and crying in terror and relief at the same time. They were quite hysterical and took a long while to calm down enough to tell their story.

I had entered the hut and was reviewing the dreadful sight inside when Stanley and some of the men who had helped us the previous evening arrived upon the scene. Stanley had been awake all night but had not heard any report from my rifle, the sound of which would have carried to Tagarthy village. He therefore concluded that the tiger had not returned—or that I had been killed—and was hurrying to find out what had happened.

I fear my first question took the good doctor aback: 'How is the *Patel's* wife?'

He looked rather pained at my irrelevance, then muttered, 'She's safe. But what has happened?' I told the story. Our plans were soon laid.

We bundled the two survivors and their belongings out of the hut, an action that did not require much persuasion, and advised them to return, with the rest of our party, to the village. Stanley would hide in the other hut, while I would conceal myself in the one with the corpse of the slain woman. Ordinarily, the man-eater might be expected to return to its kill, but as there was a second tiger which was potentially a man-eater, if not already one, the doctor would be available to deal with it.

We laid our plans carefully. To begin with, neither of us would fire in the direction where the other was hiding. Secondly, should Stanley see one of the tigers, or both of them first, he was to hold his fire till the actual man-eater approached the carcase of its victim in order to give me the chance of a shot at the real culprit. As soon as I had fired, the doctor was to shoot the second tiger if it was still within sight. These precautions were necessary to avoid a mistake at the last moment for should the doctor fire first, he might shoot the wrong tiger and the man-eater would escape. We had to account for the Ogre primarily, although for reasons I have already given the second tiger had to be shot too. But the man-eater must die first and we could not risk its escape.

As I was tired after a sleepless night, while Stanley was less so, even though he had spent a good part of the night attending to the *patel's* wife, it was agreed that I should go back to Tagarthy for a meal and some sleep, returning by three o'clock, bringing the doctor's lunch and some food for both of us to eat later on besides drinking water, tea and the torch that Stanley fitted to the barrels of his shotgun. It was wise that one of us should remain on guard, just in case either of the tigers took the unusual step of returning to the kill by day.

Another idea then occurred to me. I told Stanley and he agreed to it. We took a gunny sack from one of the huts and walked down to the remains of the earlier kill. My plan was to remove all that was left of it, so that should either of the tigers, or both of them, think of revisiting the old spot, they would find nothing. That would urge them to come to the huts, where we would be in hiding.

A slight hitch arose when we asked our men to do this job. Being of high caste, they recoiled with horror and flatly refused. There was nothing but for Stanley and myself to do the job ourselves. Stanley did not mind, for he was a doctor, but it was an unpleasant undertaking for me. What little remained of the meat was two days old and stank abominably. Further, bluebottles had laid their eggs in the remains, and in the hot sun maggots had already hatched in myriads. The flesh was covered with a seething mass of them.

We gathered all the bits and pieces and put them into the sack. Since none of our followers would touch it, I had the unhappy task of conveying this nasty burden on my shoulder all the way to the village. It was surprising how heavy those bits and pieces turned out to be, although they represented so very little of their owner.

I smelled dreadfully and was in a bath of perspiration; some sticky fluid had oozed through the sacking from the putrefying flesh and bones within. It was on my hands, shoulders and neck when I dumped my grisly burden at the entrance to the local police *chowki*. The constable on sentry gazed at me goggle-eyed. For once in his life he was too taken aback to ask for a statement. I remembered about the statement well enough, but did not care to remind him. Why should I? There was going to be a hell of a row in any case, when the sub-inspector and other busybodies from headquarters arrived at Tagarthy. Whey had we removed the remains from the scene of the tragedy? How were the police to know the man had been killed by a tiger? He might have been murdered? Perhaps he had committed suicide? Time enough to answer these questions later. What I wanted was a bath, tea and plenty of it, a hot meal and some sleep.

I hastened to the little quarters occupied by the doctor, which he had invited me to share with him, and yelled to his servant-boy to prepare a gallon of tea. Then I divested myself of my stinking clothes and washed my shirt. Next I had a bath, and what a bath!

Emerging at least two pounds lighter in weight, I set about the tea and had consumed maybe two quarts when the doctor's servant seriously suggested I leave some room for lunch. But there was no lunch left when I stood up from the table. I observed the servant had conceived a new respect for me as a glutton of great capacity.

I told the boy to put the doctor's lunch aside and to make dinner for both of us, saying that I would take the three meals with me to the two huts at three o'clock. In sadness, the youngster shook his head and replied aggrievedly that there was no lunch left. I had eaten it all. So I gave him money to make some lunch; also the two dinners. And I told him to awaken me at 2.30 sharp.

When he awakened me it was nearly three o'clock, but as the meals were ready and packed, together with two flasks of tea and two canteens of water, I had only to pick up the doctor's torch and place it in a large bag with the food and flasks, sling the canteens and my rifle over my shoulders, and set out for the huts.

Walking fast, I soon arrived to find a very hungry doctor who had no news of the tigers. He swallowed his lunch while we reviewed our plans in whispers and drank some water. The flasks of tea we decided to keep for the night.

At four o'clock we separated; I went to the neighbouring hut where the woman's body lay, taking my rifle, torch, dinner and a flask of tea with half a canteen of water, leaving Stanley in the other hut with his share of the tea, water and food. Taking up my position at the farther end, as far away as possible from the spot where the corpse was lying half in and half out of the little structure, I made myself comfortable in preparation for the long vigil of fourteen hours till dawn.

I have cultivated the habit of sitting cross-legged for hours on end, practically motionless and without sound, a habit essential if ever you have to sit up for game. The slightest movement, or the faintest sound, will betray your presence to any wild creature, animal or bird. If your quarry is an animal possessed of a keen sense of smell, the direction in which the prevailing breeze happens to be blowing has also to be taken into account, and the stronger the breeze, the farther your scent is carried. For this reason, poachers of deer in India seldom go out on a windy night. Falling rain prevents scent being carried far, but equally so all animals, except tigers, take shelter from the elements, and if the rain is really bad, even tigers and elephants restrict their movements.

Now, as tigers have only a very poor sense of smell, that factor did not trouble me. What I had to be careful about was that the man-eater should not discover my presence by sight or sound. After the adventure of the previous night, and the scare it had received, we could expect both tigers to be very cautious. It is remarkable how instinct enables a man-eater to differentiate between a possible victim, helpless and defenceless, and a would-be hunter capable of taking its life.

Having been sheltered from the sun, the corpse was not smelling yet, and it was otherwise pleasant inside the hut, offering a great relief from the conditions of the previous night, in the hot and tight-fitting hole. Everything about me was quiet, for, in fear of the man-eater, the herdsmen of Tagarthy and the neighbouring villages for miles around had abandoned their usual habit of driving their herds out to the jungles to graze.

The afternoon passed in silence except for the buzzing of flies that had discovered the dead body and were busy laying their eggs in the raw flesh. The darkness of evening was accentuated within the hut and it soon became difficult to see, although I could perceive the lingering daylight outside, visible right around me through the few inches of space between the base of the walls of the hut and the floor.

Because of the scarcity of panthers and the larger species of wild cats, jungle fowl, which are the normal prey of these animals, swarmed in this area and their calls, together with those of spur-fowl and peafowl, told me the sun was about to set. Silently, I munched the food I had brought with me for dinner, and drank some tea.

In due course the cries of the birds died away, to be replaced by the calls of a nearby herd of spotted deer and the belling of a more distant sambar stag. This told me the sun had set, although by now it was already quite dark inside the hut where I was sitting.

Soon the nightjars began their teasing cries and a night-heron wailed in the little stream at the bottom of the valley. Then I knew that night had fallen indeed, and I could now see nothing in the interior of that hut. If the man-eater came and started to remove the cadaver of the woman, I would be compelled to use my torch.

This raised a problem. When I used the torch, its beam would necessarily strike against the inside of the wall of the hut and be reflected back into my eyes. I would not be able to see beyond, or to look through the gap between the wall and the floor. In other words, the man-eater would not be visible to me. The thought began to trouble me and I decided to change my position. I would lie prone on the floor, as close as possible to that part of the woman's body which remained inside. This would give me a great advantage. By keeping my rifle extended on the ground before me, all I would need to do, when the tiger came, would be to point the barrel in the animal's direction and press the trigger. The man-eater could not avoid making some noise when it began to pull the woman's carcase out of the hut, for, as you will remember, in the struggle of the previous night the end of one of the bamboos of the hut-wall had become embedded in her flesh. The tiger would have to tear the body free from this obstruction.

Gathering the flask of tea and my weapon, I crept quietly across the floor till I reached the woman's body, and then lay down beside it, the rifle on the ground before me with the butt under my armpit and the end of the barrel only a few inches from the opening. Accidentally my shoulder touched something that was cold and hard and very stiff. It was the corpse's leg and I drew a few inches away.

Three hours passed with no sign of any tiger. It was well after ten o'clock. Tigers generally return to their kills around eight; panthers very much earlier, and I was beginning to think our quarries had decided to keep clear of the huts when the leg which had touched my shoulder three hours ago touched it again.

What was far worse, that cold stiff leg was now moving very distincly. It was not only rubbing against my shoulder now, but moving gently forwards.

Not a sound could I hear. But the leg moved again! The hair at the back of my neck stood on end. Panic seized me. I was on the verge of scrambling to my hands and knees and getting as far away as possible from that awful, mangled human thing that had come to life. Then reason returned. I could feel myself trembling and the perspiration was pouring down my face as I discovered the solution. The leg and its owner had not come back to life, nor did it move of its own volition. The man-eater was moving it!

I could see nothing. There was no sense in sticking the barrel of my rifle forward and firing blindly; that would only scare the tiger away, to continue its depredations elsewhere. At the most I might wound it. I had first to make certain what I was firing at.

Then it was that I heard a faint scratching sound, coming from somewhere very close to me and a little to my right. I could still see nothing. I was tempted to switch on my torch, but remembered in time that to do so might result in dazzling myself. Yet it was imperative that I should find out where the scratching sound came from and what was causing it.

I did an extremely stupid thing. Not being able to see, I thought I might be able to feel what was going on, and with this in mind, I stretched my right arm very slowly forwards in the direction of the scratching.

I did not have far to reach. My questing fingertips contacted something hairy, something sinewy, and the next instant all hell was let loose. The man-eater, perhaps remembering its difficulty of the night before to free the body of its victim, or maybe in an endeavour to secure a better grip on the corpse, had extended its paw into the gap below the wall and was groping for a hold on something solid. That movement of its paw was the cause of the scratching sound I had heard a moment before. When my fingertips touched its skin, not having heard of ghosts, the tiger knew there was something alive inside the hut.

An ordinary tiger would have bolted. But the Ogre who was no ordinary tiger and had always done the unexpected, lost its temper. It let out a terrific roar, then grasped the wall of the hut in its jaws and began to tear it apart.

My task after that was easy. A great hole appeared before me and the beam of my torch revealed a horrifying tiger with the matting of the wall still stuffed in its mouth. With only a few inches to find its target, the bullet of my .405 entered high into the throat; then I rolled over and over with my rifle to get out of range of what I knew would follow. I was near the far end of the hut when the Ogre hurled itself through the gap. But I had time to put two more shots straight into its head. With the dying animal threshing about the floor, I rushed to the door of the hut, flung it open and leaped out, only to be confronted by yet another terrifying spectacle.

Another tiger was there, about twenty feet away and to one end of the farther hut! But it was lying on the ground, stretched on its side and still twitching. Stanley had killed the second tiger, almost at point-blank range, with lethal balls fired simultaneously from both barrels of his shotgun. Because of the noise made by my own rifle, and because of my own excitement, I had entirely failed to hear Stanley's shots.

The doctor related afterwards that he heard the man-eater's roar, followed by the report of my first shot. Then the sounds of the hut-wall being demolished. Disregarding our agreement, he had dashed out to my aid, to be confronted by the sight of the second tiger, standing broadside on to him a few yards away, watching its mate and obviously undecided what to do. He had fired both barrels of his shotgun, loaded with lethal balls, into the animal's heart, killing it instantly.

As we suspected, the man-eater turned out to be a tigress, the other animal her mate.

There was much tom-tomming and rejoicing at Tagarthy until dawn, and when the news reached Bellundur next day old Buddiah strutted about, filled with pride. Was he not the greatest of all magicians? Had not his mantras brought about the doom of the man-eater and also of her mate? Buddiah was happy indeed. With his fame as a necromancer soaring once again, he could look forward to many feasts of cock curry and many more bottles of that fire *arrack* for which the villagers of Bellundur were famed. He was dead drunk by midday, when I called to thank him.

Three

The Aristocrat of Amligola

THE TITLE OF THIS STORY WILL LEAD YOU TO EXPECT THAT THE creature I am going to tell you about had nobility and fearfulness, and that he came from a place named Amligola, but you might not guess that the story really concerns a very large tiger that had other characteristics which I am sure you will agree were far from noble. Very few of you will have heard of Amligola, for it is situated in the remoter jungles of the district of Shimoga in Mysore state, and was only a hamlet at the time of my story.

People called him 'Gowndnorai' in the Kanarese tongue, being a term approximately equivalent to 'aristocrat,' and he earned his title by his unexpected behaviour at the time he first appeared in the thick forests surrounding the hamlet. It was rumoured that he came from the jungles of Tagarthy, a place renowned for tigers and only eight miles away; while others said he had strayed from the Karadibetta Tiger

Sanctuary, which he had deserted in disgust because his kindred in the sanctuary were numerous and the quest for food had become more competitive.

The 'Gowndnorai,' apparently, did not like this sort of thing. It was bad enough to have to hobnob with the proletariat of the tiger species, but when it came to having one's quarry snatched from under one's nose, as frequently happened, by younger and fleeter tigers, or the whole hunt thwarted and the prey driven away by a fledgeling tigress, he felt it was time to shift to more select jungles, where there were fewer of its species and more game for him to hunt.

There is a small hillock in the forest about two miles from Amligola which borders the track leading from this village to Tagarthy, and it came about that around five o'clock one evening, woodcutters returning home along this *path* were surprised to see a tiger sprawled on a rocky promontory of the hillock, basking in the rays of the sun that had still an hour to go before it would sink behind the tops of the towering teak trees to the west.

They quickened their footsteps. Everyone knew that these dense jungles were the homes of tigers, although such animals rarely showed themselves in broad daylight. The tiger they were now watching although fortunately from an appreciable distance, was an enormous brute and, to judge by his attitude of lazy indifference, seemed to care little about their presence. They were talking loudly and he could see and hear them, but he continued to lie on the warm rock as he turned his huge head in their direction with the mildest curiosity.

Thus the woodcutters judged it better to get home while the going was good and before darkness overtook them. Against such a monster they would have no chance whatever, once the sun sank and the brief jungle twilight merged into gloom.

Quite often thereafter, the graziers, woodcutters and forest guards saw this tiger of an evening, at about the same time, sunning himself on the same promontory and looking at them quite unconcernedly, as they moved through the jungle or followed the footpath that wound around the base of the hill on its way to Amligola.

None of them remembered having seen a tiger do this sort of thing before. Panthers had been seen quite often, on the same rock, on other rocks, sunning themselves of an evening; but never a tiger. The larger carnivores are too cunning and too shy to expose themselves in this way to an easy shot from a rifle.

Nobody fired at the basking tiger, for the very good reason that nobody in Amligola at that time possessed a rifle, while the range was too great for the ordinary muzzle-loading gun, a couple of which, unlicensed of course, were owned by local villagers.

For the first few months this seemingly inoffensive tiger had been content to confine his attentions to the spotted deer and other wild fauna of the forest. Then, as rarely happened in this area that was so close to the Western Ghats and received a heavy rainfall, the southwest monsoon failed one year and the jungle became dry. The grass withered, the fields lay fallow, and the wild creatures that fed on the grass and the grain were compelled to move away to regions where a little water was still to be found and some grass for their bellies. The herds of cattle that had hitherto fed along with the deer and had not been molested by the tiger so far now found themselves alone.

Nevertheless, this tiger was choosy about his meals. He left the herds and wandered into the village postmaster-cum-schoolteacher's field, where he started by killing the owner's large white bull that used to draw his cart all the nineteen miles to Sagar town once a week, on shandy (market) day. Not only did the tiger slay the huge bull with one slap of his paw and a twist of its neck, but he slung the quarry across his back and walked off with it in broad daylight, neatly leaping the six-foot-wide *nullah* that divided the field from the forest.

The field was at the back of the postmaster's house, and the owner was in the backyard, washing his clothes at his little well, and saw the whole thing happen. He shouted at the top of his voice, hoping to frighten the tiger into releasing its prey, although this would have done no good anyway because the white bull was already dead. But, far from being alarmed, the tiger was not even perturbed. He walked majestically at the same pace towards the *nullah*, the dead bull across his back, jumped the obstruction, and disappeared into the forest beyond.

The tiger killed again, and quite often after that, but strange to relate, on each occasion his prey was a lone, large bull or a fat, sleek cow. Never did he attack the herds, as other tigers and panthers had done before him, to choose and kill the first animal within reach.

This tiger spent a long time in reconnoitring and selecting his victim, and it always had to be the biggest animal he could find, proportionate to his own colossal size, revealed by the immense pug-marks he left on the fields and in the wind-blown sands of the pathways leading into the forest.

At that time I happened to visit Tagarthy, a favourite haunt of mine, where I came to hear about the Gowndnorai and his colossal size. As this animal was killing normal prey I had no intention of interfering with him, but repeated stories of his extraordinary size made me curious to catch a glimpse of him if I could.

So I set out on foot one dark night along the jungle track that led through dense forest to Amligola, the rifle across my back in case of emergency, a three-cell spotlight torch in my hand and a set of spare cells in my pocket.

I remember that night well. On the way, the beam reflected the green light of the eyes of spotted deer and sambar, bobbing up and down as they tried to avoid the torch-beam; the single, red eye of wild boar that refused to face the light but rushed away; the wide-set blue light from the eyes of a bull-bison that stared morosely as I passed; the red-white light of a panther's eyes as they sank behind a small shrub and then peeped at me from over the top; and the pinkish-blue eyes of a sloth-bear as it sat on its haunches to watch me as I padded past in my rubber shoes, not ten feet away.

I had entered the fields bordering Amligola when I met the Gowndnorai and immediately recognized him, although I had never set eyes upon him before. Two great blobs of light blazed white-red like brilliant stars suspended just above the tops of the grasses that were swaying gently to the night breezes as they blew down from the small hillock. It might have been a hundred yards away.

This tiger was, indeed, of colossal proportions.

The Gowndnorai gazed back at me unflinchingly as I stopped to watch him with the beam of my torch directed at him steadily. We returned stare for stare, and thus we remained for what might have been the better part of ten minutes. Then the tiger did a strange thing. With a low grunt, and eyes still blazing into the bright rays that confronted him, the Gowndnorai started to walk towards me.

No ordinary tiger would have done that; it would have bounded away. No wounded tiger, or even potential man-eater, would have done so either; it would have charged towards me, roaring in furious attack, or have melted away into the jungle, refusing a direct encounter.

The Gowndnorai did neither. He advanced upon me slowly, inexorably, determinedly, a guttural grunt issuing from his slightly opened mouth as he came, no signs of anger or of fear upon his striped visage.

One fact soon became evident. This strange animal, whatever his reason, was obviously quite determined to come right up to the torch and find out what it was all about.

I must confess his attitude rather unnerved me. I had no wish to shoot the beast, for he had done no harm to the human race. But what he might do when he came right up to my torch and found a man behind it was anybody's guess.

The tiger was now less than fifty yards away and still approaching, pace by pace, when these thoughts rushed through my mind and the reason for its strange behaviour dawned upon me. There were just four days until Christmas and this was the middle of the mating season. Without doubt the tiger was a male, and a tigress was sitting on her haunches somewhere near by, regarding the scene with admiration, as to her adoring eyes the Gowndorai displayed his prowess and contempt for danger.

Tigers can be very dangerous if encountered in the mating-season in company with their newly-found spouses. Their desire to flaunt themselves and their natural aversion to any intruder who disturbs their lovemaking, together with a fear that some harm might come to their mates, combine to turn them into creatures of destruction that will wipe out the intruder, man or beast.

Then came the disquieting thought that the tigress might even be creeping up behind me in the darkness, in support of her mate. I did not want to remove my torchbeam from the Gowndnorai's eyes, in case such action might precipitate a charge; at the same time the possibility of the close presence of the tigress behind me left no alternative.

Taking a chance, I whipped around, allowing the torch-beam to flash through the jungle in a quick semicircle to my right, and then behind. Sure enough, that was exactly where the tigress was. She was seated on her haunches, like a great big cat, directly behind me, awaiting the oncoming of her mate.

The reason for the tiger's strange behaviour was evident enough after that. He had been approaching the tigress when I had happened to move between them, and the mating urge had been too strong to deflect him from his purpose. I had no illusions about what he would do when he found me standing between him and his girlfriend. It was time to get the hell out of there!

This I proceeded to do forthwith, and with dispatch, by stepping sideways as rapidly and as silently as possible, while still keeping the torch-beam directed upon the tiger. The Gowndnorai halted abruptly and his grunt turned into a loud growl. What was worse, I could hear the tigress growling behind me. It seemed that a concerted attack was imminent.

With my left arm I unslung the loaded rifle, slipped the butt into my shoulder, and pressed the button of the other torch that was clamped to the barrel of the weapon, using my thumb for the purpose. The two beams shone together for a moment as I prepared to slip the three-cell torch into my trouser-pocket prior to placing my right forefinger upon the trigger.

Perhaps it was the two torches, shining together, that averted disaster. Maybe the Gowndnorai did not like the sight, and the potential danger revealed by the presence of a second light appearing so suddenly where a moment before, there had been only one. With a series of snarls he bounced obliquely forward in the general direction of his mate, and understanding the situation, I followed his movements with both torches still alight. As soon as he had reached her, the two animals turned to face me. Now two pairs of white-red eyes glared back at me resentfully.

Then I began to pace backwards in order to escape. Easier said than done, indeed. Have you ever tried to walk backwards, in pitch darkness along a twisting footpath, through heavy grass and jungle, with a rifle balanced awkwardly against your shoulder in your left hand, your thumb pressing against a torch switch, and another torch held in your right hand which is also helping to keep the rifle in place, while a pair of mating and naturally resentful tigers confront you?

I succeeded in the manoeuvre for a short distance and then, as the two tigers had shown no inclination to follow me, I whisked around in order to hurry along the footpath for a few seconds and afterwards whisked back again to see what the tigers were doing. They were in the same positions, obviously glad that I was departing.

Soon I reached Amligola and the hut of the headman, who was my friend, where I related my adventure. Ramiah, the headman, was a widower and invited me to spend the rest of the night with him. Perhaps in daylight I could study the tigers under better conditions, he suggested.

Along with numerous mugs of milk, and some rather stale *vadais* (small pungent cakes) that he offered me, Ramiah and I began to chat, but it was not long before loud roaring and growling from the forest told us that the tigers had begun their mating in right earnest. The din continued for quite a while. Then there was a period of silence, after which the noises started all over again. This sort of thing continued till we fell asleep.

Next morning I was in no hurry to investigate, for I knew that both would be resting after their strenuous mating-sessions and my appearance too early might precipitate a showdown. Besides, I was feeling inordinately sleepy after the rather restless night I had spent in Ramiah's hut.

It was nearly ten in the morning when I awoke and, after another bout with Ramiah's now tough *vadais*, followed by at least three cups of coffee which (rather than the tea that I would have much preferred) is the normal beverage of the Kanarese villager, I prepared to investigate the scene of the previous night's noisy mating. Ramiah excused himself from accompanying me on the plea of urgent field work, so I set out alone.

The spot whence the noises had come, when at last I located it, may be a little over a furlong away, revealed the energy that the two tigers had put into their lovemaking. Although fairly hard at this time of the year, the earth was scored and dug up in clods, the smaller shrubs having been ripped from the soil, roots and all, by the antics of the gambolling beasts.

From this place the ground dropped into a densely vegetated ravine, where scratchings upon the bark of a tree, along with freshly-shed dung which—unlike the panther—a tiger leaves exposed rather than covered with earth, indicate the way the lovers had entered the ravine. Curiosity prompted me to follow, although I knew that what I was doing was rash; so with rifle at the ready and eyes that endeavoured to see through and behind every bush, I advanced in silence, taking care my rubber-soled shoes did not tread upon any dry leaf or twig.

No sooner was I in the shadow of the large trees that grew in this hollow than the sweetish stench of death was borne to my nostrils and I knew I was approaching an animal that had been killed. A few yards farther, and I found it. The partial remains of a huge wild sow that had been slain by the Gowndnorai and upon which the two tigers had feasted hungrily, for tigers love pork. Although a sow, the pig had put up a fight, as could be seen by her hoof-marks in the ground.

I did not examine the sow very carefully, for you may be sure I was watching all around me against being surprised by one or the other of the terrifying lovers, and it was while I was doing this that I caught a glimpse of something white that showed through the leaves of a jungle-plum bush, perhaps thirty yards away. I approached this object, and it turned out to be the pelvis bone of a sambar doe also half-eaten by the tigers during their spree the night before. There was no means of knowing which of the two animals—the sow or the sambar—had been killed first, but it was clear that the latter had been slain some distance away and then brought to the spot by the Gowndnorai for the benefit of his mate, for no wild animal would have come anywhere near a spot where a kill had already been made.

The presence of the three crows, flying down from a branch to the earth and up again, betrayed a third kill slightly farther away. The fact that the crows were flying to the ground indicated that neither of the tigers was near. This kill turned out to be a spotted stag which the Gowndnorai had also brought to the ravine after killing it elsewhere. Little of the stag had been devoured, for by this time the tigers were too stuffed with food to do more than sample the meat.

But I had not finished yet with finding kills. In fact, I tripped over the carcase of another sambar doe that lay most halfway between the carcase of the spotted deer and the sow. There was little left of this sambar, most of it having been devoured by the tigers. I was almost certain now that this sambar, and not the sow, as I had thought, had been the first of the four victims. The sow had followed next, her hoof-marks on the ground showing she had fought before she had been killed. She ought not to have come near the dead sambar. Perhaps one of the tigers had chased her there. The other sambar and the spotted stag had been carried to the spot later, for nowhere had I seen any traces of dragmarks upon the ground, which made clear that the tiger had carried his victims, one at a time, across his back. If I needed further proof of his size, here it was indeed.

There is a strange satisfaction in reasoning out the facts of apparent jungle mystery, and I felt this as I reached my conclusion. The ravine was, in fact, a veritable charnel-house; the stench of death hung heavy in the air, and suddenly I grew afraid.

Something warned me that I was being watched. I took a quick pace to the rear to bring my back against a tree and so shield myself against attack from behind. Then I began to scan every bush and tree-trunk in the immediate vicinity.

Not a breath of air stirred in the forest that grew hotter with the passing hours, as the sun climbed higher into a cloudless sky, although I could not see it at that moment because of the trees. Not a whisper of sound broke the stillness; even the two cicadas that had been calling from trees higher up the banks of the ravine were now silent. The crows had seen me and watched the scene with mute expectation, heads cocked slightly to one side, beaks partly open and panting with the heat. It was as if the jungle lay in breathless suspense, awaiting the next act in the drama that was about to be played at any instant.

Out of the corner of my eye I saw a tuft of grass, frail and feathery, suddenly sway for an instant and then become still. It had no business to sway on that breathless forenoon, unless something had pressed against the stem near to the ground.

The something must be one of the tigers!

Most tigers—even a man-eater—will hesitate to attack if it feels that a man has discovered its presence. It prefers to have the element of surprise on its side. I knew this from my own experience, so I opened my eyes as wide as possible and stared hard at the spot where the grass had just moved. This would tell the tiger I had discovered where it was hiding.

For a moment I could see nothing. Then two black protuberances, tipped white behind, seemed to rise slowly from beyond the grass, and I knew that I was looking at a tiger's ears. An instant later, the animal raised its head a fraction higher and I was gazing into the baleful eyes, of one of the tigers. I knew it was the female. Her head was too small to belong to a male of her mate's size. That left the tiger to be contended with. He was probably in hiding at the moment, I knew not where, gathering courage for a sudden onslaught, if for no other reason than to prove to the tigress, who was watching closely, what a great brave creature he was.

Nothing happened while the tigress continued to peep at me over the top of the grass, and after a while I began to hope that she was alone. Maybe her mate had gone to look for a fifth victim!

It must have been ten minutes later when the tigress began to make a peculiar sort of noise. I might say she was mewing, but it was too guttural and hoarse a sound for that word to convey. She was summoning her mate. As she had not attacked me all this while, it was clear that the tigress, by herself, lacked the courage. What would happen when the tiger arrived would be quite another thing.

I decided that discretion was the better part of valour and I slipped behind the tree-trunk that I had stood against all this while. Then I started to back away.

The next moment a loud roar from the top of the ravine behind me told me I was too late. The Gowndnorai had arrived. Something in his mate's mewing calls seemed to warn him that all was not well. I could hear him crashing through the dead leaves and undergrowth now, coming directly towards me at the gallop.

I am far from being a good climber, but sheer funk lent me agility and I dragged myself up the tree with commendable speed, the rifle hanging on my shoulder. The first fork was hardly eight feet from the ground. I reached it and tried to climb higher, when the rifle slipped awkwardly from my shoulder down to the crook of my arm. I hitched it up again, and just as fast it slipped down once more.

The Gowndnorai arrived at the base of my tree and my movements made him look upwards and see me. I decided I must face him and bring the rifle from the crook of my arm to my shoulder. I expected him to make a bound at me at once, but strangely enough he did nothing of the kind. He crouched on the ground instead, looked up, and snarled and snarled and snarled.

Rather foolishly, as I think of it now, I changed my mind and decided to try to climb higher, but in any case I could not go very far. I managed another seven feet perhaps when I found I had gone as high as the thinning branches would permit. At this juncture, the tigress, confident of the protection offered by her mate, emerged and advanced towards him in gambolling leaps till the two of them were together barely fifteen feet below.

I hoped that neither of the tigers would try to follow me, as the bough to which I was precariosly clinging was too frail to support any additional weight, while by my own foolishness in ascending higher I had put myself in a nasty plight. I was obliged to cling to the branch with both my hands and knees, and this prevented any possibility of using my rifle, which I could not unsling, since I would fall from the tree if let go my hold. Moreover, the strain on the muscles of my hands and legs was tremendous, and I could not possibly maintain the position for long.

It occurred to me that I might try to shoo the tigers away by shouting aloud. The ruse would probably succeed; but again it might not. The sound of my voice might irritate the animals, particularly the tiger, who till now had behaved like a gentleman.

The two tigers settled the matter after a few minutes, as if by mutual consent, when they calmly walked away side by side. Allowing another five minutes to pass, I descended cautiously, but there was no sign of either animal even after I climbed the bank of the *nullah* and started walking to the village. I really owe the Gowndnorai and his mate a debt for sparing my life.

Shortly afterwards I was trudging back to Tagarthy, thinking I had heard—and seen—the last of the tiger. But as I was soon to discover, that thought was entirely wrong.

Hardly had I been a month in Bangalore when the headman of Amligola, with whom I had spent the night listening to the Gowndnorai and his mate, wrote me a postcard which he had tramped all the way to Tagarthy to post, informing me that the big tiger was growing overbold and begging me to come and shoot him. It was only a matter of time, he said, before the Gowndnorai would turn man-eater.

I oppose hunting tigers that have not molested man, and I was not going to accept the headman's fear of something that had not yet happened; the Gowndnorai might never become a man-eater and I had certainly no justification for shooting an animal that had spared my life on two occasions.

It happened that I had a few days to spare and could think of no more pleasant occupation than trying to see my benefactor, the huge tiger, once again. But things had changed by the time I reached Amligola, although it was only a matter of a few days since Ramiah had written. The big tiger had grown bolder indeed, killing more of the villagers' choice cattle. Ramiah had already lost his best bull, and now the Gowndnorai saw it fit to slay his second best.

This was too much for the already exhausted patience of the headman. Disdaining to wait for my arrival, Ramiah journeyed to the town of Kumsi, about twenty miles away, borrowed his cousin's .12 bore shotgun, and sat up to ambush the tiger when he next visited the outskirts of Amligola in search of prize cattle. Having succeeded so many times before, the Gowndnorai walked into the trap all unsuspectingly, to receive a charge of slugs full in his face from Ramiah's borrowed weapon. The tiger then dashed away roaring terribly as he went. So great was his anger, caused by the wound, that he entirely demolished a bamboo platform erected by the villagers on a field from which to drive away the birds that fed upon their grain, and which stood in the tiger's *path* as he rushed back to the forest.

All that day and night, and throughout the two nights that followed, Ramiah and his companions were forced to listen to the pain-racked roars of the wounded tiger as he voiced his woe and anger to the jungle at large, while they cowered within their huts.

Unaware of what had happened, as nobody told me anything at Tagarthy, I arrived late in the evening of the fifth day at Amligola, having walked through the jungle in blissful ignorance for eight miles without hearing or seeing a thing. We did not hear the tiger that night, but the morning of the sixth day brought the first result of Ramiah's ill-timed shot.

It was just after nine o'clock and I was about to set out on my return journey to Tagarthy, when a man staggered into Amligola and fell exhausted in the one lane that formed the main village street. He said that he and another man had started out from the village of Chordi, which was some miles away, just before dawn, and had been travelling to Amligola when, about two miles from their destination, they had seen a tiger following. Accustomed to tigers and not knowing that the Gowndnorai had been wounded, they were not unduly perturbed, but decided to keep a sharp lookout behind them as they walked.

For the next two or three hundred yards they saw nothing. Then they glimpsed the tiger, and this time he was not more than thirty yards behind them. Sensing that the animal was bent upon mischief, the two men had broken into a run, whereupon the tiger roared and charged them.

The man who had staggered into Amligola had escaped merely because he happened to be the faster runner. He told how the tiger had quickly caught up with his companion, who was racing just a yard or so behind. His friend's dying scream had compelled him to look back over his shoulder and the lucky woodcutter affirmed that the sight he had seen would remain in his memory for ever. The tiger's countenance had been dreadful to behold. It was badly mangled and a mass of blood. He did not think the animal had any eyes left: its ferocity vented upon the victim it had just seized, was truly awful. Not daring to look back any longer, the man had raced to Amligola for all he was worth, to reach its shelter utterly exhausted.

The wounded Gowndnorai had killed its first victim. To judge by what we had heard, Ramiah's slugs had blinded the unfortunate beast.

Without delay, I hurried to the place where the attack had been launched, Ramiah and the surviving woodcutter reluctantly accompanying me. The tiger must have been ravenously hungry; he had eaten the most of his victim on the spot. Then he must have heard us coming, for he had carried away what remained as he dashed into the undergrowth, perhaps only a matter of minutes before our arrival. We knew the tiger had eaten well, for his victim's head, hands and feet lay scattered about, a sure sign of a hearty meal.

The trail was fresh, but the undergrowth was extremely lush. Ramiah and the woodcutter were Kanarese and not of the stuff of jungle-men and trackers. They flatly refused to come any farther. So I followed by way of the broken weeds and the bent branches of his victim. It was difficult to watch ahead and both sides against a surprise attack while moving fast at the same time.

The Gowndnorai, for all his size, did not stop to fight it out. Probably his recent wound, and the pain he was suffering, made him reluctant to risk an encounter with another armed man. It is uncanny how a wild animal is able to sense the presence of a human being who may spell danger and distinguish him from one who is helpless, unarmed, or bears no hostile thoughts.

The trail led through the belt of thick forest into lighter scrub, where it was more difficult to proceed, and then down a steep decline where the tiger had finally jumped into a narrow ravine, more a watercourse than anything else. Here I had to go down on hands and knees and within a few yards it became too dense to go farther. In any event, pursuit was fruitless as I could never hope to overtake my quarry under such conditions.

Disappointed as I was, two facts were now established beyond any doubt. Firstly, the Gowndnorai had not been totally blinded by Ramiah's pellets. Therefore he remained a very real danger to the human race and would continue to be so till he completely recovered from his wounds and went back again to killing cattle and wild game. That was extremely unlikely to happen, however, as once a tiger has tasted human flesh and comes to realize how easy it is to kill a man, it rarely abandons the habit. In other words, here was a man-eater at the beginning of his dreadful career. Secondly, despite his enormous size, this tiger did not have a fighting heart, so he was likely to prove more cowardly, cunning, elusive and much more difficult to bring to book than most ordinary tigers, normally more daring and so liable to expose themselves.

How correct both my surmises were was revealed in a comparatively short time. My visit to Amligola could not be prolonged as I had to return to work to the aircraft plant in which I was employed at that time. So leaving instructions with Ramiah to keep me closely informed of events as they occurred, I returned to Bangalore the following morning.

It did not take long for Ramiah to write again. He related that the Gowndnorai had turned into a dangerous and elusive brute. No longer did he sun himself on the slopes of the small hillock, in full view of every passer-by. Now there was no sight of him, no sound to be heard. Only his huge, saucer-sized pugmarks betrayed his passing, and with each such visit some traveller, who had set out on a journey, failed to reach his destination.

Ramiah said that the tiger had taken to haunting the most lonely section of the footpath leading from Amligola to Tagarthy, from where he would snatch the last of a group of travellers. Apparently this had happened on three occasions, and now people shunned this track. They preferred to walk twenty-five miles by a circular route to Tagarthy.

Having covered the short cut many times myself, I knew exactly the spot to which Ramiah referred. It was a dip through a valley running between two low hills, where the vegetation consisted of tall bamboos and fairly heavy evergreen scrub that provided ideal cover in which a tiger could spring an ambush upon a group of passers-by.

I left for Tagarthy the next day, parked the car at the rest house of the forest department that stood in a beautifully wooded setting a mile away, and set out to cover the eight-mile footpath to Amligola, which would lead through what had become the valley of death, in which the Gowndnorai launched his attacks. It was exactly two in the afternoon when I started, and it was a cloudy, cool day. The conditions for a tiger to be early afoot were ideal.

I would have to progress slowly and carefully and timed my arrival at Amligola at about six o'clock or at most half an hour later, just as it was getting too dark to see. To stay out after that would force the use of my torch, and realizing I was dealing with a very shy and crafty animal, I felt he was less likely to show himself then, and would probably prefer to launch his ambush at a time when he thought the traveller was unprepared.

For the first mile or so, the pathway traverses beautiful park-like country, and here peacocks, which had just begun to grow their new plumage after dropping their tail-feathers subsequent to the mating season, grubbed under the bushes and flapped heavily skywards as I appeared around a corner.

Gradually the vegetation grew more dense, the trees higher and the undergrowth thicker. After the second mile, I could only see the track ahead and snatch a quick glance around at it behind me. To my left and right a wall of impenetrable green hid everything more than a yard away from sight.

The dangerous valley about which I have spoken, where the Gowndnorai had thrice launched his ambushes, still lay three miles ahead, beginning at about the fifth mile along the track I had come, with another three miles to my destination, Amligola.

The closer I approached this valley, the more dense became the vegetation. Actually, this sort of jungle is not favoured by tigers as a rule, who prefer the park-like country I had already come through. Bison, elephant, sambar and barking deer are at home here, the felines choosing the more open jungles where their main prey, such as spotted deer, wild pig, and of course village cattle, graze on the plentiful grass that grows there. It was another indication of the Gowndnorai's craftiness that had induced him to change from the habit of his species to haunt a place affording him the maximum cover for his ambushes.

At last I tipped down the foot of the hill, the base of which marks the start of the valley of death. It is three-quarters of a mile, or perhaps seven furlongs, to the point where the *path* starts climbing the next hill, and dense bamboos with lush undergrowth press heavily upon the narrow trail on both sides.

I halted for a moment to pick up a handful of sand, which I raised to shoulder level and then allowed to trickle slowly from my fingertips. There was little breeze, but what there was carried the sand earthwards slightly to my left. The wind was therefore blowing from right to left, and the tiger, if he attacked, would almost certainly do so from the left-hand side of the track and not from the right. My deduction was based upon a fundamental law of the jungle.

Felines prey upon deer and such creatures as have a keen sense of smell. To do so upwind would render their stalk abortive, for the currents of air would betray their presence and their quarry would escape. Carnivores have therefore learned by instinct always to approach downwind, that is against the wind, so that their own scent will not give them away before they can attack.

Unlike deer, the human being has practically no sense of smell so far as self-preservation is concerned, and the average person would not be able to scent a tiger or a panther, even in hiding a yard away, whatever the direction of the wind. But the feline does not know this and so applies the same rules to stalking a man as it would to stalking any other jungle creature. For this reason, I was almost sure that the Gowndnorai, if he came for me, would attack from the left;

and being the coward that he was, ten chances to one from behind me.

Having established all this by reasoning, I began to walk silently forwards along the track, alert for anything that might happen.

The first quarter-mile or so was fraught with apprehension. Every little while I glanced backwards to see if I was being followed. Once, as I looked back, I was in time to see a bush I had just passed sway violently, then come to rest.

I swung around. I knew that I could not see beneath the bush; it was far too thick. But I could watch the top of it. A tiger cannot spring out of the middle of a bush, it has to creep forwards to break clear of its branches before he makes its leap, and when it creeps the tops of the bushes will shake. If you keep watching the tops of the branches you will be able to see them move, then you will know it is coming.

Sure enough the top of one of the branches very near the edge of the pathway shook slightly as something brushed against its base. This is it, I said to myself, and raised the .405 to my shoulder.

A moment later the branch vibrated more noticeably and out walked a wild boar into full view. Seeing me suddenly, it swerved head-on, the bristles on its neck rising like spines, head bent low with tusks aimed at me, small red eyes looking upward angrily.

I felt like laughing, but sighed with relief. The fact of the boar appearing from my left indicated that the tiger was not in the immediate vicinity.

Noticing that I stood motionless and made no move towards him, the boar decided that I must be harmless after all, although something to be regarded with grave suspicion. With head still bent at an angle to keep me in view and charge if necessary, the pig crossed the track to plunge into the thickets on the right with a loud brushing of the leaves. The next instant it was gone.

This time I really sighed. I went on again, relief making me a trifle less cautious perhaps, and was soon within reach of the end of the valley. I saw nothing in front of me; I looked back, but nothing was there. I looked in front again, when something urged me to turn around.

And there was the Gowndnorai, or rather his head, emerging from a wall of green to my left that I had just passed. Not a sound had he made. My rifle came to my shoulder and I squinted down the barrel.

But the tiger was no longer there to aim at. Instinct and his inherent cowardliness warned him that here was no defenceless passer-by. He vanished as silently as he came.

Confidence made me bold and I stepped forward to catch a glimpse of him, if possible. A low growl, and then the rustle of leaves several yards away in the undergrowth, told me that the big tiger would not stay to fight. He was running away.

I arrived at Amligola shortly before dark to recount my adventure to an astonished Ramiah.

I did not know quite what to do the next day. Ramiah said it was useless to tie out cattle as bait, for the Gowndnorai would not look at them. In any case, there were very few cattle in Amligola, and none of their owners would sell for this purpose. I would have to wait to walk back to Tagarthy the following morning if I wanted to buy a bait.

That afternoon the Gowndnorai broke his own rule. Perhaps he was over-hungry. Maybe he thought the valley was too dangerous for him to haunt for a while, with me in it. So he killed a man in the park-like jungle I have told you about, a mile or so from the Tagarthy forest rest house where I had left my car. The victim's three companions came hurriedly through the valley to bring me the news. They knew it was safe enough to traverse while the tiger was engaged in eating this kill. It was nearly three in the afternoon when they arrived and I had seven miles to cover to reach the site of the incident. We found what was left of the man a little after four-thirty.

The Gowndnorai had attacked his victim in the expected fashion from behind a bush, out of the centre of which grew a wild-cashew tree, killed him and carried him back to the same bush, behind which he had set to work and eaten more than half the body. The three men who had been walking in front of the victim had practically run the rest of the way to Amligola.

The wild-cashew tree growing on the spot was a very lucky factor. Its many branches and large leaves made the construction of a *machan* a quick and easy matter. Although I made a bet with myself that the Gowndnorai would never show up, because he was far too cunning for one thing, while the noise the men made in building the *machan*, in spite of all their efforts to work silently, must have been heard by him where he lay, probably not very far away, there was always the slimmest chance that he might appear. By six o'clock I was in the *machan*, quite a snug affair considering the short time in which it had been made, and the three men hurried back the mile to Tagarthy which they had covered that morning in the company of the unfortunate man now lying mangled behind the bush.

This was the Indian spring and it soon began to grow dark. Within another hour the remains of the corpse on the ground beneath me was hidden from sight. There was no moonlight and I was relying upon the torch, clamped to the barrel of my rifle, to light the scene if the tiger returned.

All was silent for nearly an hour except for the calls of a few night-birds and the flapping of the large fruit bats around the tree. I glanced at the luminous dial of my watch. It was eight o'clock, the time when tigers generally return to their kills!

Almost punctually to the hour, a group of spotted deer began to call in alarm from the park-like jungle to the east. Their cries were dying away when an animal moved in the bush directly below me. The Gowndnorai had come. In another moment he could start to eat and then would be my chance.

This was precisely the moment when I heard a tiger growl, but it was at least a hundred yards or more away; certainly not below me. So the Gowndnorai had a companion!

This fact raised complications. Was this the man-eater after all? I remembered his cowardliness. Maybe another tiger was the true man-eater. Or perhaps both had the habit!

My thoughts were interrupted when the animal below me snarled; then dashed off at top speed. After that I heard neither of the tigers and thought they both had gone when, a few minutes before nine o'clock, a twig snapped and this was followed by the crunching of bones. One of the tigers had returned. So I slowly raised the rifle to my shoulder in preparation for a shot.

An instant later pandemonium broke out. A series of shattering roars came from the darkness a short distance behind me, a coughing snarl issued from directly below, and this was followed by the sound of a large body frantically clawing its way up the trunk of the tree upon which I was sitting. At about the same instant a second body crashed against the tree, which shook under the impact, and started tearing at the trunk.

The tree swayed as if struck by a hurricane and I felt I would be hurled out of the *machan*. Roars, growls and snarls from below my very feet threw me into panic. Hastily pointing the rifle-barrel downwards, I pressed the torch-button. The light cut through the night and fell upon a panther, only two feet below. But it was gazing downwards.

I moved the barrel slightly, and now, I looked into the blazing eyes of the Gowndnorai, who would never have had the courage to attack the tree on which I was hiding had not the panther, stealing from the kill, thought fit to take refuge in it. Neither animal knew the tree was already occupied by me.

The first was an easy shot—between the eyes. The Gowndnorai fell backwards as his roars came to an end. So was the second. The panther looked up in startled amazement to provide another easy shot, also between the eyes. I could not afford to spare him, though I would have liked to do so. He had been eating from a human kill and might turn into a man-eater himself.

The Gowndnorai was perhaps the largest tiger I have ever shot; and surely the most cowardly.

Four

The Assassin of Diguvametta

IF YOU WERE TO TRAVEL IN A SOUTHEASTERLY DIRECTION BY METRE-gauge railway from Guntakal junction in the state of Andhra Pradesh, you would pass the large town of Nandyal and shortly afterwards enter a delightful stretch of hilly country, heavily forested and intersected by numerous streams. Over these you would rattle, halting briefly at the jungle stations of Basavapuram and Chelama, and traversing two tunnels, one short and one extremely long. Finally you would cross a verdant valley by a picturesque high viaduct, with tree-tops far below. In a few miles you would probably observe a large stone water-column at the right-hand side of the line, always overflowing, next to which stands the 'outer' signal that heralds the advent of Diguvametta railway station, where the hills and the jungle end and the cultivated plains begin again.

The 'assassin's' operations extended from this station as far as the very long tunnel in the valley crossed by the long viaduct, but it was particularly active in the vicinity of the dripping water-column and the 'outer' signal beside it.

I have always had a sneaking fondness for the forests between Chelama and Diguvametta, not because they are particularly well stocked with game or carnivora, but for the utter peace and solitude of the area, and the friendly disposition of the wild Chenchu tribesmen who inhabit the extensive jungles in this section of the Eastern Ghats. I have found that even the ordinary villager of Andhra Pradesh is, on the whole, much more friendly than his counterpart in Mysore state, where I live, while the folk in Madras state reveal a disposition between the two.

Also, the nature of the vegetation here is quite different from that growing farther south, and while no elephants or bison occur, this area represents the southernmost limit where the nilgai or blue-bull, a large animal of the antelope species, looking like a sambar deer, is to be found.

So to Diguvametta I travelled by train one day, passing through the long tunnel and over the long bridge, both of which always held for me a childish fascination, skirting the signal and dripping water-column, to alight at Diguvametta with my small bedroll, campkit, and rifle. A couple of urchins grabbed the bedroll and campkit, and with my rifle slung over my shoulder, we began walking up the road that ran parallel to the railway track in the direction from which the train had just come.

It was perhaps half a mile to the forest bungalow, a wonderfully cosy structure for so old a building; a plantation of teak seedlings lay to the south of it, the jungle lay east and north, while to the west was the road leading to the railway station, and after that again the railway-line, as I have just said. The signal and water-column stood a bare half-furlong away. My old friend, Aleem Khan the caretaker of the forest bungalow, welcomed me at the gate with his expansive smile, at the same time shouting to the urchins to get a move-on with my *samaans*.

The bungalow had two suites of rooms, and as usual Aleem was good enough to put me into the better one, the one that faced the road and the railway. It was better because the bathroom attached to this suite was fitted with a shower, while that on the other side had none.

Aleem was a Muslim and had only two wives, while so many of his co-religionists had four, the maximum allowed to a Mohammedan legally. He had told me once before that he felt that two were just enough. Without further ado he summoned these two women and set them to operate the hand-pump together. This contrivance drew water from a large well and fed it to a zinc water-tank situated on the roof of my bathroom. For half an hour, while I unpacked and then drank tea, hastily prepared for me by the caretaker, I could hear the clank-clank-clank of the hand-pump, and the chatter of the two wives as they argued with each other and then started to quarrel, each accusing the other of shirking her bit of the pumping. The dispute was brought to an end by the sound of water pouring off the bathroom roof. The tank had been filled to capacity!

Then came the much anticipated pleasure of a shower bath, or rather a series of shower baths, one after the other, the cool water trickling over my body in fine jets. Outside the temperature was well over 100° F as the sun shone down with the merciless intensity usual to Andhra, but inside that bathroom it was so cool, so damp, so heavenly. I smiled maliciously to think I was so callously wasting the precious liquid those two women had worked so hard to pump for me.

Refreshed, and stretched at length in an armchair on the veranda, I drew placidly on my pipe and drank mug after mug of tea. A goods train clanked past heavily, an engine at either end, the one in the front blasting clouds of black smoke from its funnel and tugging for all it was worth, while the one at the back came along unconcernedly, as if there was nothing to bother about at all.

Aleem Khan squatted on his heels on the ground at the side of my armchair, telling me some of his family troubles. His only sister had lost her husband, a forest guard who had died suddenly of tuberculosis, leaving his wife and two children unprovided for. They had immediately come to Aleem for shelter and the problem was now a major one. Aleem's first wife had three children, the second had two; and now his sister with her two children and himself made a total of four adults and seven children to be fed on his meagre salary.

Could I do something about it? Aleem confided that, in spite of her two children, his sister was still a comely lass, good to look upon, with a fine figure, amiable disposition, and all the attributes required to make a very desirable wife. In a moment of temptation, I closed my eyes and let my thoughts run wild. What fun it would be for me to announce my conversion to Mohammedanism! I could then marry Aleem's sister and take two more wives into the bargain. With the one back in Bangalore, this would make the fully permissible four.

Then the expense side of the question hit me a sharp blow, and the troubles that would follow as a consequence hit me a sharper one. I opened my eyes in horror to think of what a predicament I was in, and then smiled when I remembered it was all in the realm of speculation.

Hastily I told Aleem I would inquire in Bangalore for a suitable candidate, and then, equally hastily, changed the topic. Were there any tigers or panthers about?

A tiger had been poached just ten days ago he confided, by some government official in a jeep, using a spotlight, on the forest department's fire-line two hundred yards from the rest house. This fire-line, I must tell you, extended from west to east. It began at the road to the northwest of the bungalow and a furlong away, and went on in an easterly direction to another road two miles distant that traversed the forest and connected Diguvametta to a hamlet named Gondacheruvu, some forty miles away.

Aleem also mentioned that there was a panther about, and this animal was beginning to prove troublesome. Its pugmarks could be seen early in the morning around the rest house, and it had taken his dog three weeks earlier from the place where it had been sleeping on the back veranda. He added that his sister had not only brought her two children but her dog as well, and this the panther had attacked immediately outside the door of the outhouse that Aleem had allowed his sister to occupy. But this animal, unusually big for a village cur, had also a big heart. He had turned on the panther with such ferocity that the latter had fled precipitately with the cur in hot pursuit. Both Aleem and his sister had witnessed the scene in the bright moonlight.

Nevertheless, the caretaker said he was not happy about matters and felt the panther would summon up enough courage to return and would eventually get the dog. But what really troubled him was the presence of the seven children, two of whom were mere toddlers. Should the panther become sufficiently bold—or hungry—he might be tempted to run off with one of them.

Many people have asked me why I do not leave India and go to England, Australia or even Canada. I have tried to answer that question, but I do not think I have convinced anybody. This thought returned to me as I lay in the armchair that afternoon at Diguvametta. Where in England, Australia or Canada, where anywhere else in the world, except perhaps

Africa or South America, would I find the conditions of India? A journey by train or road of a few hours separated my home in Bangalore from the cold climate to be found on any of the several mountain ranges that lay within two hundred miles, or from the swelteringly hot weather of the plains that lay even closer; from the dense forests to the west, with their very heavy rainfall, and the extremely arid, semi-desert areas to the east; from the teeming millions of one of the cities and the utter solitude of a jungle within fifty miles of home; from the varied languages and dialects of the towns and the almost incoherent vocabularies of the forest tribes; from the safety and comfort of home and the ever-present hazards of death from a sudden sickness, snakebite or some wild animal. Where in the world would time be of so little, if any consequence, as in India? Where in the world would consequences themselves be of so little importance? It matters not how you dress, or whether you dress at all! The bare requirements of existence are all that do matter. Everything else is thrown in along with that, sometimes in good measure and sometimes scarcely at all; but really it does not make much difference either way and there is never any hurry about anything. There is a time to be born and a time to die and each event is as inevitable as the other. Moreover, death follows life and life follows death, so it really does not matter where you start and where you end, as it all works out to the same thing.

My friends cannot understand when I tell them that these things are the reasons why I love India, why I do not think I shall ever leave it.

My reverie was broken by trouble in the form of the forest range officer, who arrived on a bicycle to inform Aleem Khan that word had just been received that the district forest officer (D.F.O.) was passing through Diguvametta and would spend the next night at the rest house. Did I have written permission to occupy the bungalow?

I had to reply in the negative, and the range officer looked aghast. I had committed the unpardonable crime of trespass. I was occupying a government building without permission. He swallowed hard and then told me I would have to get out forthwith.

Here was the same difficulty that I had experienced in so many forest bungalows in so many jungles. This is why I have purchased so many parcels of land in so many areas, in order to be able to camp in peace without being troubled by authority, that ever-present bogy that has stalked the length and breadth of the country from time immemorial, that stalked it during the days of the British Raj and that dominates it even more since Independence.

I flattered the range officer and in no time he was eating out of my hand. Certainly, sir, he agreed, these senior officers coming on tour were a damned nuisance. Why (and being the gentleman that he knew I was, he could tell me in confidence), they did not work at all when they came. It was he and his subordinates who were the workers. These visits were only a pretext for collecting *batta*, the colloquial name for a travelling allowance, when they were hard up. Witness the fact that these 'tours' invariably took place during the last week of a month. Certainly, I could remain for the night in the bungalow, but I must promise faithfully to go before noon the following day or he would be in grave trouble should the D.F.O. find me occupying the bungalow without permission.

I promised, and then inquired if there was a vacant room anywhere in the village. The range officer did not think so.

At this stage in the conversation I mentioned that I had suffered similarly in so many other areas that I had begun purchasing small plots of land in nearly every jungle I visited and had at that moment over twenty camp sites of my own. He brightened at this idea. He had a friend, he said, in the revenue department, who owned many acres of land just beyond the railway station. Upon his recommendation, the ranger was sure this friend, whose name was Ranga Reddy, would be glad to present me with a small plot of land all my own, big enough to pitch a tent upon, as a gift and free of all charges.

Within the hour we were at this friend's place. There we drank coffee and were forced to consume two *dosais** each. Then Ranga Reddy took us to his land, which was a quarter of a mile beyond the railway station and to the east of the line, and invited me to select any spot I fancied, anywhere I wished and to the extent required.

The field was good agricultural land, consisting of rich black soil, and we had to go to the far corner to find a vacant bit, lying fallow and with earth that was not quite so rich as the rest of the field. After all, I required only a camping site and did not want to deprive my new friend of anything of value. A stream flowed a short distance away, while the main road bordered the plot on one side. An ideal camping-site! Ten cents of land would be ample for my requirements.

I told the owner of my choice. He answered with an expansive smile that I could certainly have the land. He would take me in his jeep the following day to the town of Giddalur, twelve miles away, where the formal registration of my ownership would have to be made.

I asked the price. Free, of course, he replied. This would never do, I answered. Besides, it would not constitute a legal purchase; he must accept some price. With hesitation, Mr Reddy said 'Five rupees,' and I said,' 'No, take fifty.'

---

* A fried flat cake made from rice flour.

He recoiled in horror. 'Take fifty rupees from a friend for such a useless plot of land!' Eventually we agreed to thirty rupees, which is less than two pounds in English currency.

The next morning we were at the registrar's office at Giddalur when it opened for business. Half an hour later I was the proud owner of my own camp site of ten cents of land at Diguvametta!

However, I have anticipated events a little by telling you about the purchase of the site. I should have related, in proper sequence of events, what happened on the night after I had returned to the rest house from a short stroll along the fire-line where the tiger had been shot so recently. This fire-line traversed a deep *nullah* that formed the bed of a running stream where the flow of water, now that the dry season prevailed, was not more than a yard wide. Implanted in the mud on both sides were the pug-marks of a medium-sized panther. This animal, like all its kind, had been loath to walk in the water, and so it had jumped across.

I wondered if it could be the animal Aleem had told me about. The tracks led towards the forest lodge and had probably been made the previous night. Then I stooped to examine them more closely and changed my mind. The dark-green layer of surface fungus that borders old watercourses and streams in some places grew to the water's edge on both banks, and it had been pressed down by the weight of the panther both on the side from which the animal had jumped and, considerably more deeply, upon the bank where it had landed. The fact that the dark green fungus was still pressed down on both sides was very significant. Why had it not returned to the upright position of the fungus elsewhere? It would have done so had the panther made its leap the previous night, as I had first thought. There could be only one conclusion: the facts clearly showed that the panther had crossed not more than an hour or two earlier.

It was now after six in the evening, so the animal must have passed this way between four and five, long before sunset. In this case it would be in the vicinity of the bungalow right now, unless it had gone on to cross the railway track in the direction of the water-tank. I turned back from my walk, wondering if I would hear it calling during the night.

I had just sat down to an early dinner of cold roast beef that I had brought from home when it happened. The time was exactly 7.45 p.m.; I remember this because I had just wound my watch, a habit I follow as I sit down to dinner. Aleem's sister's dog had made itself friendly and was sitting on its haunches by my chair, gazing soulfully at me in anticipation of receiving scraps from my plate. I gave it a piece of dried chuppatty.

Most dogs would have gulped the morsel and looked for more, but this creature, in common with all village curs, decided to take the mouthful outside and enjoy it in solitude. It ran out on to the veranda, and then I heard a low snarl, followed by a loud yelp from the dog.

My rifle was in the bedroom that led off from the central dining-room, and there was no time to get it. Realizing that the panther had struck and that if I wanted to save the dog I would have to act fast, I rushed on to the veranda where I was just in time to see in the moonlight a spotted form leap down from the raised plinth on which the veranda stood, with the dog in its jaws, still alive and struggling.

Shouting loudly to frighten the attacker, I hurled the first missile that came to hand at the slouching form, one of the hard wooden chairs with which all government buildings are furnished. The departing leopard was only fifteen feet away when the chair descended squarely upon it, but the panther did not let the poor dog go. On the contrary it began to bound away with the dog still held firmly.

I rushed back into the bedroom for my rifle, hastily loaded it, and followed in the direction taken by the panther. Bright moonlight lit the compound, and so I had not waited to attach my torch-equipment to the weapon. That would have taken time, and not a second was to be wasted if I were to try to save the dog.

It was quite a different matter, however, when I reached the jungle that flanked the bungalow's grounds. Darkness, cast by the foliage of the trees, enveloped me, relieved here and there by shafts of moonlight. I soon realized that to crash about in the underbrush and darkness would only serve to frighten the panther and make it carry the victim farther away. In any case, it was too late for me to save the dog's life. So I sat down in the shadows at the foot of a tree, annoyed with myself for not having fixed my torch to the rifle. It would have taken time to do so, but at least I would have been able to see.

The panther, realizing I had stopped chasing it, must have thought I had gone away, for within ten minutes it began to eat. Nor was it very far away, for I could hear its low growl now and then, alternating with the sound of tearing flesh and the crack of a bone. I was undecided whether to try to creep up to the beast or go back to the bungalow for my torch, and as so often happens when one is undecided, I chose to do the wrong thing.

Rising to my feet slowly, and treading cautiously in the darkness for fear of making any sound, I tiptoed towards the noises that reached me now and then, adopting the old hunter's practice of only moving while the sounds lasted, and stopping as soon as they ceased. For when an animal you are trying to stalk is eating or making a noise of any kind there is less chance of his being able to hear the sounds that you might make, however slight they may be, in your approach, but it would be much more likely to hear you if it were silent.

I came quite near the panther that night. I do not think it could have been more than five yards away when luck, that had helped me so far, decided to put a spoke in the wheel. Incidentally, it sealed the fate of three innocent people. A bear, pig or pangolin had dug a hole in the ground. In the darkness I did not see it and put my left foot right into that hole, bringing me down with a jerk. I stumbled forward, and the panther knew I was there. With a coughing snarl he was away, and I heard him bounding through the bushes.

Extricating myself, I went on till I found the body of the dog which the panther had started to feed upon. I could make out its form as a light blur against the darkness of the ground. When I returned to the rest house, Aleem and his family had come out, searching for the dog and wondering where I had gone.

I fixed my torch on to the barrel of the .405 then, and returned with the caretaker. Only a fourth of the dog had been eaten. Aleem carried the remains back to the bungalow, where he said he would bury them in the morning, while I decided to try to search for the panther.

It was easier now to wander in the jungle with the help of my torch, and I scoured the area right around the building within the radius of a furlong for over two hours. No sign of the panther did I see, while the presence of a small sounder of pigs showed that the spotted cat had moved away from this area completely. On the other side of the road and bordering the railway track close to the signal, a few spotted deer and a solitary nilgai cow grazed in peace, suddenly shattered by a shrill whistle of an engine and the heavy rumble of a goods train.

The panther had gone. There was considerable weeping on the part of the women and children when what was left of the dog was buried the next morning. A little later, as agreed, I moved out of the rest house, stopping at the ranger's quarters to borrow an old tent that he had promised to lend me.

Within two hours the tent had been pitched and a camp made on my new site. Two mud-pots, purchased in the marketplace and stored in a corner of the tent, served for drinking and washing water. Two fireplaces, built with stones and placed outside the tent, were ample for my needs, one for brewing tea and the other for cooking food. The earth was my bed; the stream not far away was my source of water, both for drinking and bathing; a small lantern was my illumination at night. What more did I need? Free to come and go as and when I liked! At least, as far as Diguvametta was concerned, I was henceforth rid of officials and government rules and regulations for evermore. Happy was I and very contented.

There was just one thing that could go wrong. If it happened to rain, the black-cotton soil would be churned into a sticky quagmire. I had not brought a campcot as I had intended to stay at the forest bungalow. So I would, literally, be in a mess.

Early that afternoon, after I had returned from Giddalur, a jeep came tearing down the road, and as it flashed past my tent I read 'Andhra forest department' in large white lettering on boards both behind and in front. The dark face of the occupant next to the driver stared at me hard. The district forest officer had arrived!

Later in the evening I called at the rest house on a courtesy visit. As much as I dislike government officials, one has to keep in touch with them in India if one wants to move about freely.

The D.F.O. was a young man, practically new to the service, and had been recruited directly to the department after passing through college, followed by training and a departmental examination at one of the provincial centres. Very soon I discovered that he knew nothing whatever about the jungle fauna and that he harboured the usual vague ideas regarding the terrible ferocity of tigers and panthers.

Aleem had told him what had happened to the dog the previous night without disclosing my part in the story or, most important of all, the fact that I had been occupying the bungalow.

So the D.F.O. in his turn now related to me a highly embellished account of the incident, including how the panther had leapt upon Aleem's breast and carried away the dog that had been sleeping there, to all of which I listened with an innocent, not to say surprised, expression. Apparently it did not occur to him that people ordinarily do not sleep with great hefty dogs upon their chests.

However, the upshot was that the D.F.O. invited me to shoot the panther. He inquired where I was staying and was markedly surprised to hear I was the owner of ten tents and was camping on my own site. Very generously, he suggested I should occupy the other half of the bungalow and enjoy its comforts.

Hanging my head in shame, I reminded him that I did not have 'official permission to occupy the Government forest lodge,' and slyly added that the rules of his department were very strict on this point. Permission could only be granted by the conservator of forests or by the collector of the district.

My new friend was offended. Was not he the D.F.O.? Was his permission not good enough? To hell with the conservator and the collector! 'You come along to the bungalow right away,' he said; 'we'll have dinner together tonight.'

So I came back where I started, but now as a guest, having left rather in the fashion of a vagabond. Moreover, but this

I am sure was pure luck, I was installed once more in the western or shower-bath side of the building. And it was fortunate, indeed, that I returned to the shelter of the bungalow just in time, for that night we had a heavy downpour. Next morning, my campsite was a sea of black mud.

The D.F.O. made Aleem bring a dog from the village, at Aleem's own suggestion and much against my desire, and instructed the caretaker to chain it to a teak-sapling that grew about ten yards behind the building. He was keen that I should bag the marauder. I dislike using dogs as bait. They are far too sensitive and suffer an agony of apprehension when chained up, as they appear to realize the danger they are in.

The D.F.O. had no firearm, but sat with me on another chair inside the dining-room. By keeping the door half-open we could see every detail outside in the clear moonlight, while the panther might not be able to see us in the darkness of the dining-room.

You may be sure that I kept a sharp lookout, for I did not want the dog to be killed. The cur, on its part, realizing the danger and feeling the discomfort of the chill air, began to yelp and whine loudly. The panther, if it happened to be anywhere within half a mile or even more at this moment, would certainly hear it.

The D.F.O. began to doze shortly after 11 p.m., and retired to his bed before midnight. Soon after two o'clock in the morning, with the moon behind the trees, long shadows began to fall and hide the dog, which had resigned itself to its fate. It had stopped yelping and was curled up fast asleep, and out of my sight. Should the panther attack now, I certainly would not be able to save the mongrel from being killed. Yet I hesitated till the moon disappeared behind the jungle to the west and it became pitch-dark. Then I got up from my chair, untied the dog, who wagged its tail joyously on seeing me, brought it indoors, and went to sleep myself.

After lunch the next day the D.F.O. departed on his return journey to Nandyal, while I left by the midnight train after giving my Bangalore address to Aleem, along with a couple of stamped postal covers which I always carry about with me for just such a purpose, instructing the caretaker to write to me should any unusual event occur. I had a hunch that I had not heard the last of that panther. But I forgot all about the affair before I even reached my journey's end.

It came as a surprise when Aleem's letter reached me about four months later, stating that a railway ganger had been killed by a wild animal midway between the long bridge and the water-column with the 'outer' signal close beside it. The letter said that no tracks could be found and that the ganger's body had been partly devoured. Then it went on to explain that there was a division of opinion as to what kind of beast had perpetrated the crime. Some said the killer was a tiger; others said it was a sloth bear. A few supersititious people blamed an evil spirit, but Aleem himself thought it was the panther. Would I come and shoot the creature, whatever it might turn out to be?

I answered, saying that as the killing was an old one and might be merely the odd result of a chance meeting with an irate bear, my visit to Diguvametta would be of no use just then; but I impressed upon him to write again should anything further transpire.

The next letter came about a month later. This reported that the ganger in charge of the water-column had made a practice of returning to the railway station by sunset. Invariably he and another ganger, whose duty it was to light the oil-lamp serving the 'outer' signal at precisely six o'clock every evening would meet at the foot of the signal and return together. This had been their regular habit ever since the two had become friends.

On the evening before that on which the letter was written, however, this meeting had failed to materialize. The second ganger had lighted the lamp on the signal, came down the iron ladder and found no signs of his friend from the water-tank, who should have been waiting for him there. Thinking the fellow must have fallen asleep, he called his name loudly, 'Ram! Ram!'

No answer had come, so the second ganger, apprehending no danger, had gone in search of his companion. He came upon the body at the base of the stone structure that supported the cast-iron tank of the water-column. Not much of it had been eaten: just a little from the chest. And although it was after six o'clock, there was still light enough for him to see in the sodden earth, saturated by the overflow from the water tank, a number of pug-marks, crossing and re-crossing each other. They had been made by a panther.

The ganger took to his heels and did not stop running till he had reached the station.

'Come at once,' Aleem's letter concluded urgently. 'A man-eating panther is amongst us!'

Unfortunately, I had urgent engagements that day, so I decided to leave early next morning, travelling by car so as to avoid delay and in order to carry the tent, stores and all the other kit that I would require for living on my camp site. I did not want to risk again the nuisance of being ousted from the bungalow in the midst of my operations. Moreover, when hunting a man-eater, particularly a panther, one cannot possibly conform to government rules that limits one's stay in a travellers' bungalow or a forest rest house to not more than three days.

I had just returned that evening, completed my packing and was about to have dinner, when I heard a bicycle bell outside. Then Thangavelu, my servant, came in with a telegram and the messenger's delivery book for my signature.

Hastily I signed and tore open the cover of the telegram to get one of the most unpleasant shocks I have ever received: 'Panther killed sister's child. Come immediately. Aleem.'

Before dawn I was on my way.

If you ever go to the forest rest house at Diguvametta, at the southeastern corner of the building and within twenty yards of it, you will come across a little grave under a stone slab. Inscribed on the stone is the one word: 'Mischief.'

The story goes that many years ago, in the days of the British Raj, a visiting British forest officer, or it may have been a collector, was occupying the bungalow along with his little dog whose name was 'Mischief.' A panther had suddenly pounced upon the latter and was carrying it away when the Englishman fired, killing both the panther and his own dog with the spreading shot from his gun. In sorrow, and in memory of his pet, this officer had buried it where it had been killed and had later returned, bringing an engraved tombstone to place over the spot.

Aleem told me the story of the latest tragedy as I was getting out of my car. His sister's elder child, who was a girl, had been told the story of 'Mischief' and had formed the habit of placing a little bunch of jungle flowers early each morning on the grave. That morning, for some reason, she had forgotten to put the flowers she had gathered on the stone slab, but only remembered late in the evening when it was almost dark. Meanwhile, the little bunch of flowers had withered noticeably.

'Peearree,' which was the girl's name, had told her mother, Aleem's sister, about her omission and said she would put the flowers on the grave at once. Her mother had answered that it was growing dark and the man-eater would catch her.

Besides, the flowers were already withered; she could put fresh flowers on the grave the next morning.

Without heeding, Peearree had grabbed the dying flowers and dashed out. She must have reached her destination, for the little bunch was found there. Nobody had heard a sound; neither a scream, nor a whimper, nor a growl. The child did not come back.

Alarmed, her mother had called out to her, but receiving no answer summoned Aleem and his two wives from the adjoining room. The caretaker snatched up a stick and the four of them, carrying a couple of lanterns, went to the small grave, where they found the flowers, but of the little girl herself, no trace. A few feet away lay a scattered heap of glass beads, and the string on which they had been threaded. And, of course, a little farther on, a few drops of blood!

Aleem and the three women had hurried to the village, to return considerably later with the ranger, a couple of forest guards, and quite a number of people armed with hatchets, sticks, knives and lanterns. Nobody had a gun.

They searched the undergrowth rather haphazardly that night without result, because everyone feared the panther. Next morning, they had looked again. This time they found the killer's pug-marks, and the marks left by the child's body where it had been hauled through the thicker bushes. They even found some tattered remnants of clothing. After that, all signs of man-eater and victim had vanished.

Aleem said I should stay in the rest house and not expose myself to risk from attack by the panther while in my tent. This I resolutely refused to do till he tempted me with an idea, as brave as it was dangerous. He offered to sit on Mischief's tombstone all night as bait, if I agreed to lie prone upon the veranda with my rifle, hidden behind a pillar. He said he would call softly, as soon as he felt the panther's presence. I could then switch on my torch, play the beam around, pick up the animal's eyes or form in the light and shoot it. There was no moon at this time, the nights were totally dark.

Aleem's was a magnificently brave, but an utterly absurd and foolish plan. As if he would ever feel the man-eater's presence in time to warn me before it attacked him! He would feel nothing till it was upon him, and then it would be too late. What was worse, I would not be able to fire, for if I did so, I would possibly hit him and not the panther. Even supposing Aleem sensed the panther coming and called to me, the man-eater would never show up.

'No!' I kept repeating, 'No, no, no!' But at the same time I was thinking that Aleem's scheme had possibilities and they gave me an idea: there was nothing to prevent me from dressing in Indian clothing and sitting on Mischief's grave! My usual attire might scare the man-eater away, as panthers are inordinately cunning and clever, but Indian garb would deceive him. No other party being endangered, no charge of manslaughter could be brought against me; nor could there be any idea of suicide. Should the man-eater come, and should I not be aware of it beforehand, the question of suicide could not arise, for the very simple reason that I would not be present to answer the charge. So I told Aleem of my scheme and now it was his turn to remonstrate.

I had my way, however, as I usually do in these matters, and sunset found me seated on Mischief's tombstone with crossed legs, dressed in Aleem's dirtiest clothing, my face and hands blackened with charcoal, and a filthy rag tied round my forehead to emulate a turban. The rifle lay inconspicuously on the ground close at hand, with the torch clamped to it, covered with a light layer of leaves so that the man-eater might not notice it. You may be certain I took good care to sit with my back towards the rest house so that I could watch the jungle on three sides.

The sunset hour and the corresponding break of day are the most delightful moments to be in a forest to anybody fascinated by the jungle and the wild creatures that inhabit it, for it is at these times that one hears the songs of the birds of the day at their best. The creatures and birds of the night seem to take the cue from their brethren of the day, and their calls of welcome to the hours of darkness that lie ahead mingle with those of their roosting fellows, to fade away correspondingly at break of day.

But I had no ears for such music at this moment, enchanting as it always is to me, for my ears, mind and nerves were attuned for the coming of the killer. Now was the hour, the sunset hour, when it would be afoot. It was at precisely this moment that it had taken poor little Peearree, and there was every likelihood that it would revisit the place where it had killed her in the hope of finding another victim. Thoughts such as these came into my mind and filled me with an ever-growing sense of danger.

It was soon quite dark. The rest house behind me, although so close, was a mere shapeless blur against the blacker background of the jungle behind it. Overhead, the stars twinkled here and there in the open spaces between the tree-tops that swayed slightly to the faint breeze. A short distance away a tall clump of bamboos reached heavenwards, the tops of their giant feathery culms drooping back to earth again in all directions like a graceful but huge bouquet.

Then I heard a faint rustle a little to my left. Very soon I heard it again, coming, it seemed, from a bush a few feet away. I strained my eyes but could see nothing but the blob of deeper blackness that was the bush against the blackness of the jungle beyond. My hand grasped the loaded rifle, kept ready at my feet, and in a lightning-swift motion the butt was at my shoulder and my left thumb was pressed hard upon the switch. A bright beam cut through the darkness to reflect tiny eyes that gazed back at me, brilliant as rubies, in innocent resentment. What I thought to be the man-eater turned out to be one of those huge black scorpions, common in India and particularly in Andhra state, rustling the dry leaves in its search for grubs.

These creatures grow to a length of eight inches, vary between jet black and very dark green in colour, are covered with short, bristly hairs, have a tremendous crab-like pair of pincerclaws before them and a long segmented tail, with a needlesharp point at its end. The sting of this creature brings with it intense agony for twenty-four hours and death to such of its victims as may suffer from a weak heart.

The scorpion halted in its tracks when the light fell upon it and hissed audibly with vexation. I picked up a handful of earth and tossed it at the scorpion, which hissed again before scurrying away. Then I switched off the torch, replaced the rifle carefully on the ground at my feet and, groping for the leaves I had displaced, lightly covered it once again, cursing under my breath.

The whole incident was most unfortunate. The scorpion had made me reveal my position by shining my torch. If the panther had been anywhere near by it would have seen the light, and with the uncanny instinct of man-eaters who can sense when they are being hunted, the beast would beat a hasty retreat and now be far away.

It is said that scorpions have more than two eyes. I began to wonder if this was so and which of its eyes could have caught and reflected my torch-beam, when I heard the whistle of an engine as it rounded the bend just before reaching the outer signal. The goods train rumbled to a grinding halt and the engine-driver started to whistle again, first in short, rapid bursts and then in a prolonged blast that disturbed the whole jungle. I could hear voices too, the driver and his firemen talking to each other. They seemed to be unduly excited and were making quite a lot of noise.

I began to wonder what it could be all about when what I thought to be the solution came to me. The 'outer' signal must be 'up,' against the train entering the station, because the down passenger on its way to Nandyal was coming in from the opposite direction. This meant it was midnight and time had passed much faster than I expected.

The sound of human voices continued while I heard the distant hooting of the passenger train's engine, followed by the sound of its arrival at the station. The goods train driver now whistled and started his train, which clanked slowly along. A few minutes later, the down passenger drummed by as it picked up speed on its journey to Nandyal.

The quiet that I had expected would follow did not materialize, however, for soon I heard voices again, which grew louder as a group of men carrying a couple of lanterns turned in at the gate of the rest house and approached the building. Annoyed because all hope of shooting the man-eater was now gone, I rose from Mischief's grave and approached the veranda, where I was joined by Aleem, who had been awake and listening. The party turned out to comprise the stationmaster, the ranger, and the driver, guard and one of the firemen of the goods train.

They were all worked up and told how, upon coming out of the long tunnel, the headlight on the engine had revealed what looked like a crumpled human body lying at the side of the track. Observing this, the driver had concluded that one of the earlier trains must have knocked over some man who had attempted to cross the line, and as his train was moving slowly at the time, he decided to stop and investigate, lest the blame of having killed the man be put on him later. To his dismay, however, the driver and his firemen discovered that the man had not been run over at all. On the other hand, he had been devoured by some animal, as was evident from the fact that his gnawed bones lay scattered around.

The train guard, who had joined them by this time, suggested the body might be that of some wandering Chenchu tribesman, as it was clothed only in a *loincloth*. Having heard of the depredations of the panther, the driver and his companions decided to inform the stationmaster at Diguvametta, who could report the incident by telegram to the authorities. This they had done when the stationmaster, knowing I was at hand and had come to shoot the man-eater, resolved to inform the ranger and me first, before sending out his message.

So I had been right! The panther was, indeed, far away. Perhaps it had never been near the bungalow that night. Perhaps it had come at just about the time when the big scorpion had given me a false alarm. Maybe it had seen my torchlight, scurried away, met the Chenchu near the tunnel and killed him. But this was hardly possible, considering the distance of the tunnel from where I was sitting. As likely as not the Chenchu was a traveller who had not heard about the man-eater, or perhaps he had heard and for that reason had decided to sleep inside the tunnel, thinking it a safe place where the panther would never come.

I thanked my informers and said I would do what I could. After they had departed, as there was no point in remaining any longer by the grave, I determined to snatch a little sleep, instructing Aleem to wake me after four o'clock.

He must have remained awake, for it was a few minutes to four when he called me. We brewed tea and munched a few biscuits, after which we set out in darkness, walking in single file along the railway track. Had the man-eater been a tiger, to have done this would have been extremely dangerous, for a man-eating tiger nearly always carries away the person last in line. With a panther the risk was less: the more timid, but also more cunning, it waits for the victim who is alone and helpless before launching its attack, avoiding showing itself when more than one person is present.

Dawn was just about to break when we reached the long bridge. Here we had to wait for about ten minutes before it became bright enough to attempt a crossing as this was a tricky business, involving stepping from sleeper to sleeper between the lines. One did not dare to look too much at the valley and the tree-tops far below as we glimpsed them through the open spaces between the sleepers.

It seemed an endless distance to the other end, but we made it eventually. Not far away was the yawning black hole that was the tunnel's entrance. Just before reaching it, on our left and close to the track, lay the mangled remains of what had been a Chenchu.

Examination showed that the man-eater must have returned to its meal, either after the goods train had passed or later perhaps, after the passenger train had gone in the opposite direction, for much more of the body had been eaten than had been reported to me. The head, feet and hands were now severed from the trunk and lay scattered about, leaving just a possibility, though not a strong one, that the man-eater might return.

Our thoughts were rudely disturbed just then by the rumbling sound as of distant thunder. It issued from the mouth of the tunnel, growing momentarily louder till it became a continuous roar. The up morning passenger train to Diguvametta was approaching. Making up my mind quickly and calling to Aleem to follow, I ran a few yards from the tunnel up the track to give the driver a chance to see me, stood between the rails and began to wave frantically as the front of the engine, in billows of smoke, dashed out of the tunnel.

The train was moving fast when the driver saw me. He applied his brakes while I skipped clear of the lines, but half the train had passed before it could be brought to a halt. I explained the situation briefly to the driver and guard who came running from both ends of the train, and asked them to take Aleem along and tell the stationmaster at Diguvametta to ask the ranger to issue orders through the local police, forbidding anybody to approach the bridge or tunnel that night. I intended to await the man-eater's possible return. To Aleem I gave hasty instructions, asking him to return with food, tea and blankets for both of us. A down passenger was due to pass shortly after 2 p.m., and he could safely come by it.

While I was speaking, a large number of passengers had crowded around, wanting to know what was going on. Some of these now insisted upon going to look at the corpse, so that it was over fifteen minutes before the driver could continue his journey. I watched the train as it clanked over the long bridge and disappeared around the curve.

In an incredibly short time the vultures discovered the remains. At first one appeared as a speck in the sky high above me, soon followed by other specks. Then came the loud rustle of air through their wing-feathers as they swooped to earth to alight heavily a few feet from their prospective feast, towards which they began to waddle in ungainly fashion.

Squatting at the mouth of the tunnel, I had an abundant supply of ammunition in the gravel ballast of the line. I hurled the stones at the venturesome vultures, and from such close range I managed to score a fair number of direct hits which served to keep the unwelcome birds at bay. All this helped to pass the time and an up goods train to Duguvametta roared through the tunnel without the driver noticing me, squatting to one side of the mouth, or the scattered remains of the Chenchu, though he could not have failed to observe the abnormal number of vultures that gathered on both sides of the track.

The section is not a busy one and no other trains came through till the arrival of the down passenger shortly after two o'clock, bringing Aleem, the tea, my lunch and a blanket for each of us for the night. The driver stopped his train for Aleem to alight and then stepped down himself, with his firemen and, of course, the guard and a crowd of passengers, to view the cadaver which by now was smelling strongly.

Amidst cries of 'good luck' the train rumbled away again, followed an hour later by a goods train, after which we were left to our own devices. The vultures had by now abandoned their task as hopeless and had flown dejectedly away, leaving us to make our plans for the night.

There were two possible places in which to hide. The first was the mouth of the tunnel itself; the second, somewhere above the entrance. To determine which would be the less likely of the two hiding places to be discovered, I put myself in the man-eater's place. Instinct, and a long association with the locality would have conditioned it to the fact that huge monstrosities, rumbling and roaring and billowing smoke, every now and then issued from the hole in the earth. So it would certainly watch the hole very carefully and for a long time before daring to show itself; in the course of this close scrutiny it would very likely discover us, for I would have to keep Aleem with me. There was nowhere to send him away to, and it would be most dangerous to ask him to return home unarmed.

The conclusion we reached therefore was obvious: we would hide somewhere on the hillside, as close as possible above the mouth of the tunnel, hoping that the panther would keep to the general rule of not looking upwards for an enemy. The ground above the entrance to the tunnel sloped gradually and was mostly covered with coarse grass and weeds with a stumpy tree here and there. It was quite rocky and boulders lay scattered around in profusion, varying in size from a football to the height of a man.

Grateful for the luck afforded by this cover, it did not take us long, working together, to construct a small buttress of boulders which we placed in line a little above the entrance to the tunnel-mouth in the form of a wall high enough to conceal us when lying prone behind it. Between these boulders we allowed enough space for two loopholes, one for Aleem and the other for myself, through which to keep close watch upon the remains at the side of the track below us, and a little of the terrain around it. For a wider view, and to take a shot, I would have to look over the top of the rough stone parapet we had constructed. If I were to try poking the rifle through the aperture, I might make some sound if the barrel struck against the stone. The panther would hear this, look up and spot us. The one disadvantage of our situation was that we were lying at a downward-sloping angle, with our heels at a higher level than our heads.

We were in place by four o'clock, with the sun still blazing down upon us and the ground fire-hot beneath. We lay on our blankets, but these soon became unbearably warm, while the disadvantage of the downward slope now began to make itself felt. I suppose, because of the steady accumulation of blood in my chest and head, rather than in equal distribution over my whole body, I began to experience an uncomfortably stuffy sensation, which grew more and more apparent as sunset approached. This caused me to squirm about, and I saw that Aleem was squirming too, from which I concluded that he, like me, was feeling uncomfortable. If in the short space of only two hours I could feel so suffocated, it was quite apparent that we would be compelled to change position before very long.

It was now beginning to get dark, and we could still make out the remains of the Chenchu, when a barking deer called sharply from the hill-top at the back of us. 'Kharr!' eh cried, 'Kharr! Kharr! Kharr!'

It kept barking hoarsely, but did not move away. Therefore, whatever it had seen was evidently at a safe distance, enabling it to hold its ground while continuing to give the alarm. A peacock honked loudly and left its perch on a tree, also behind us, and flapped heavily away. I caught sight of it out of the corner of my eyes as it sailed with spread wings into the valley beneath the long railway viaduct.

There was silence after that and darkness had almost fallen when a junglehen, also from somewhere on the hill behind us, fluttered from cover with a hysterical 'Kok! Kok! Kok! Kok!' I did not relish all this activity behind me. Without doubt, some animal that represented danger to the creatures that had given their alarms, was afoot somewhere behind us. It could be any tiger or panther, but far more likely it was the man-eater itself.

Within the next few minutes it became too dark to see the Chenchu any more, although I could observe the line of ballast beside the railway track, stretching away like a faint grey ribbon from the tunnel beneath me. While I was still looking, I heard a small stone roll somewhere behind me. The sound was faint, but my ears, attuned closely to any noise in the jungle, did not fail to register it.

From straining my eyes to see the ballast below, I turned my head to the left to glance uncomfortably backwards.

Aleem, next to me was doing the same. Then the thought occurred to me: perhaps the man-eater, in walking along the track, had dislodged one of the small granite stones down there. Maybe the beast had come through the tunnel itself and shifted one of the stones at the entrance. What a lucky thing we had decided not to sit at the mouth of the tunnel!

I was just congratulating myself in this way when a thought struck me with horrifying significance: perhaps the panther was not below us at all. Maybe it had seen us from the hill top above and was crawling down upon us that very moment from behind, waiting to get close enough before launching a final attack.

All further conjecture was interrupted at that moment as the earth beneath me appeared to quake and tremble. As deep rumbling increased to a prolonged roar, and a moment later a shower of sparks and black smoke shot out of the earth before me as a light engine, travelling backwards, rushed out of the tunnel-mouth. Because this engine was moving in reverse, the driver could not use his headlight, and we had no warning of his approach. All other sounds were shut out as the black silhouette of the engine disappeared into the darkness.

That was when the panther decided to attack, and it came from behind us, not from down below. Maybe it could see only one of us and therefore failed to realize that there were actually two people present, for it came bounding along in true man-eater style, but without making a sound, unlike the normal panther that 'woofs' and coughs harshly and loudly when it attacks.

We heard only the muffled fall of its soft pads on the hard ground as it leapt towards us, a faintly-scraping, hollow, bumping sound, which puzzled us. A moment more and it would have been upon us but it then discovered that it was attacking two people where it expected only one. The panther checked itself two yards away, snarling and growling in baffled rage. Then, and only then, did we know that the man-eater had indeed arrived.

I can hardly remember what happened next. I know Aleem sprang up, yelling and I know I rolled violently over and over away from where instinct told me there was danger. But I do remember switching on my light and firing into the face of the panther at point-blank range. It sprang forward then, passing between us and over the edge of the tunnel above which we were seated, to fall with a loud thud upon the railway track below.

The driver of the midnight down passenger was amazed at the sight revealed by his headlight some time later. Two men were drinking tea. Between them lay a dead panther, and but a short distance away the mangled remains and bones of a man. I wager he will remember the sight long after he retires from service. Being a good fellow, he gave Aleem and me, along with the dead panther, a lift to Diguvametta.

Five

Tales of the Supernatural

MANY PEOPLE HAVE ASKED ME IF I HAVE HAD OCCULT EXPERIENCES during the years I have spent in the jungles, and for my views on whether such things are true or fictitious, or perhaps the product of an overwrought imagination.

I have really no idea why the occult should be associated with hunting experiences and forest lore, but somehow it is so. Other hunters, far more experienced than I am, have related some interesting happenings of this sort and we have little reason to doubt them. I have had a few curious experiences myself and have told them already, like that of the dead watchman of the Kalhatti forest bungalow.* Fortunately I was not alone at that time; my son Donald was with me. We both saw the watchman as clearly as I can see this sheet of paper; yet he had been shot dead and buried long before!

---

* See: *The Call of the Man-Eater.*

Then there was the case of Captain Neide, who removed an old lamp from an ancient temple. He almost died of fever shortly afterwards and only recovered when he returned the lamp to its resting place. Practically in the same locality lived the girl who was possessed by an evil spirit or spirits, that made her vomit stones each time she attempted to eat her evening meal. I saw this for myself and I saw her cured by a religious healer. Details of both these happenings have been related by me in an earlier book.*

I am no authority on the occult and I think it is very foolish for anyone to express an opinion on a matter he knows nothing about. So I propose only to record some of the beliefs of the people of South India. Of course, this is no answer to the questions of those who have asked me for a personal opinion. In fact, I have no answer.

Perhaps the most common belief in the south of the peninsula is in a pair of evil spirits that exist as man and wife. The female is referred to in the Tamil language as a *minnispuram* and in Malayalam as a *Yakshi*. It is universally agreed that the female is very hostile and dangerous to human beings, particularly to other women, while the males are generally quite harmless, at least according to Tamil ideas. Such a view corresponds closely to our own as regards the males and females of the human race. But the Malayalees think differently: they say both *Yakshis* (female spirits) and *Gandharwas* (male spirits) are highly dangerous to humans.

The Tamils believe that *minnispurams* (female) can adopt any shape or form, animal or human, and frequently appear as tall pillars of nebulous whiteness or blackness. Malayalees say that *Yakshis* generally show themselves in a more comely

---

* See: *Tiger Roars*.

way, as graceful bare-breasted women, clad below the waist in semi-transparent lungis, their hair long and flowing down their backs, thus concealing the hollow backs that are characteristic of these spirits. Tales are rife of how a man or youth, returning home at night, had met one of these nebulous creatures and was tempted to her side; he was then struck across the head or back, began to vomit blood and died within twenty-four hours. Others have been tempted to the edges of wells or tanks and then pushed in.

There is a story of two *Namboodries* (west coast Brahmin priests) who encountered two *Yakshis* in the form of beautiful girls. They spoke to the women and were invited to their home. The priests were tempted, and the house where the two girls lived turned out to be a very nice place indeed. Each of the *Namboodries* went into a room with one of the girls. But for some unaccountable reason one of them became nervous: instead of making love he clutched in his hand his personal talisman, a palm leaf with the sacred word *Nghrie* inscribed on it.

From the next room came the sound of giggling, which stopped suddenly and was followed by the sound of crunching bones. The girl did not touch the priest, but besought him earnestly to throw away the palm leaf and make love, emphasizing the temptation by exposing to him her naked body. But the priest, by now thoroughly suspicious, clung tenaciously to his leaf.

Suddenly the crunching sound in the next room ceased, whereupon the girl grew angry, abused the priest loudly, slapped him across the face and vanished from sight. So did the house! And he found himself alone in the darkness with the mangled body of his friend.

Belief in vampirism, but in a special form, is common. Instead of sucking blood, as do the European counterparts, the Indian vampire, which also appears only at night and sleeps in the earth all day, specializes in dogging the steps of a solitary man at night, stopping when he stops and walking when he walks. This continues to within a hundred yards of the man's destination, and then the vampire strikes! It attacks from behind, then tears its victim to pieces to devour his flesh. The only way of escape is to utter a very sacred word and turn upon the vampire with a drawn knife. The vampire will scream like a stricken animal. It must be stabbed repeatedly till it falls, when it will certainly disappear in a pool of blood. Or so it is said!

Great success in business and much prosperous trading, together with the amassing of several fortunes, can occur when a man agrees to hand over his wife to a spirit of a certain genus who confers great wealth on the family in exchange for the favour. The earthly husband must live apart from his wife and have no sexual intercourse with her, although he is allowed to speak to her and even feed with her occasionally.

The wife must live in a house apart; at nine each night the doors must be locked and the earthly wife must retire to a windowless bedroom. Soon a nebulous mist appears which takes the form of the spirit-husband. He stays with her till three in the morning, which is when all respectable spirits must depart in wraithform, just as they came, while less respectable men sneak home with their shoes in their hands!

Years ago, I knew a Jewish family that came from Rangoon. The husband dealt in hardware. He had a wife and three children. They were long-married and business was not good. Then a pact was said to have been made with a spirit-husband who came to like the wife, the woman being still of comely appearance despite her three children. It is not clear whether she sought the arrangement or the business-minded husband wanted it.

According to the rules, she shifted to a house apart, closed the doors by nine o'clock and enjoyed her spirit-husband till three in the morning. The earthly husband and the three children slept in another house all night but visited her during the day. Business improved. Everything they touched flourished and turned to gold. The family became one of the most prosperous in Rangoon and fabulously rich.

Then, one afternoon, something happened. The earthly husband and earthly wife were together. The children had gone out. The wife was still a comely woman and old habits were too strong to resist. The couple were intimate.

That night there was a great commotion in the wife's house after nine o'clock. The spirit-husband appeared, and he was highly annoyed; jealous, too. He beat her soundly and said he would never come there again. He did not, and the fortunes of the family went down and down. Business failed completely. They had to sell out, and from being one of the richest, they became one of the poorest families in Rangoon.

There have been cases, too, of spirit-wives who come at night. But whether these bring material riches, or material poverty and trouble, as their earthly counterparts generally do, is not quite clear.

Very frequently I have been asked if there is any truth in black magic, and instances in the lives of close friends of mine are many. I have already related the case of Ossie Brown, to which I was a most reluctant witness.*

About twenty years ago I was guilty of having done something that I should have avoided; but it is not clear to me now whether I offended the party concerned or whether

---

* See: *The Call of the Man-Eater.*

I fell under the person's influence. Call it a subconscious fancy on my part if you like. But for more than a fortnight, at exactly 3 a.m., I would wake up with a frightening, choking sensation, as if something or someone were grasping me by the throat. Then I would hear heavy footsteps outside the window—the measured, slow tread of someone walking in army boots. I dashed out on more than one occasion with a stick—even with a gun! Yet in the bright moonlight nothing could be seen, while the footsteps ceased. No sooner did I return inside than the footsteps started once again. They would last for about ten minutes.

Things came to a head one night. I got up almost suffocated. I heard the footsteps. I dashed out with the gun as usual and searched everywhere. There was nothing to be seen. I came back and the footsteps started again. I closed and locked the window. It was all very strange, but I determined to ignore it. Switching off the electric light, I got into bed.

The next moment something soft struck against my mosquito curtain and fell to the floor. Leaping out of bed, I turned on the light. There on the ground, was a ball of wet mud as large as my fist. Where had it come from? The window was closed. My wife and children were in the next room, sound asleep.

At this stage I determined to do something about the matter—something I would normally never think of doing.

There is a seer living in Bangalore who has achieved considerable fame as a fortune-teller, a recoverer of stolen property and necromancer. His fee for consultation is one rupee (about one shilling and four-pence), to be presented to him on a betel leaf—nothing more; nothing less. I had heard a good deal about this man, and had thought him a clever rogue.

I went to see him. He had very large black eyes and a big moustache. Other than this, there was nothing outstanding about him. I came into his room and laid down my rupee on a betel leaf, feeling myself to be the biggest fool in town at that moment.

Looking at me, he calmly said: 'You are being troubled by hearing footsteps at night. Lately, a mud ball was thrown at you. You have been bewitched by'—(and here he described person concerned) 'because you refused to give the individual what was asked.'

That's easy to explain, you will say. Thought-reading is the answer; or some form of hypnotism; or both. You may be quite right. But listen to what happened next.

'Go home,' he told me. 'Measure six paces from your window in the direction in which the sun rises. Then dig a foot into the ground. You will find something. Destroy it. You will not be troubled again.'

I went home, feeling angry. I took a shovel in my hands, feeling more angry. I measured six paces from my window towards the east, and began to dig. Not only was I angry now, but also wondered how I had become such a fool. But I found something, and I had dug just about a foot deep. I found a doll made of clay buried in the earth. A crude affair with misshapen head and arms and legs. But human hair had been stuck to the head and a nail driven through it. At the pointed end of the nail was a dried lemon skin that had been sliced almost in half. The human hair looked remarkably like my own.

I was amazed; and I burned the damned thing! I did not hear the footsteps at three next morning, or ever again!

Now, how had the seer known? It could not have been thought-reading, because I did not know about the doll myself. And he could not have prepared the stage beforehand, for how did he know I would consult him?

Years later, I related the incident to a person who dabbled in such matters. He told me the clay doll with human hair was made to represent me. The nail driven through the head signified that the mantra had been made against my mind, my powers of reason. If the curse had not been removed by the seer telling me where to find the doll, I would assuredly have become insane within a short time!

This occurrence interested me so much that I made up my mind to investigate these matters more fully. As this friend was known to be a black magician, a necromancer, I began worrying him to tell me more; in fact, to initiate me into his brotherhood. But he flatly refused!

I have a trait about which some people who do not like me complain bitterly. It is stubbornness, coupled with persistence. The more my friend refused, the more I pestered him. So, at length, he initiated me as a member of the brotherhood of the Silver Armlet!

I have my silver armlet which I wear on certain occasions, and nobody else is allowed to touch it. Nor can I tell you all the mystic rites of the society as I am under oath not to reveal them; but I can give you the outline of the initiation ceremonies.

The first entails a visit to any old cemetery—the older it is the better—on the night of the *amavasa*, which is the night before the new moon. The neophyte must go alone, after midnight, carrying either a live black cock and a knife with which to cut its throat, or if he feels squeamish about cutting the creature's throat, a couple of pounds of pig's entrails and liver instead.

He must enter the cemetery, and after a brief *pooja* by lighting camphor, etc., he should cut the cock's throat and then proceed to cut up the whole bird, feather and all, into finger-long pieces. Or, if he has brought pig's liver and entrails instead, cut that up into pieces. Next he must walk through the cemetery without looking back, throwing these pieces over his left and right shoulders one by one while using the most foul language he can think of, in whichever dialect he wishes. 'Take this, you—and eat it,' and so forth. This attracts the spirit or the disembodied entity, to him.

The neophyte then goes home and performs another ceremony which makes this spirit a servant to him.

You may have heard and read of miracles performed by holy men in India who can produce from the air articles like fruit of any kind, money, sweetmeats and even certain medicines. These things are made possible by the services of a species of small genii known as *kutty shaitan,* one of which becomes attached to the individual on a sort of fifty-fifty contract basis. They each become a servant of the other and are bound together for life. The word *kutty* in Tamil and Malayalam signifies 'small;' while the word *shaitan* in Urdu and Hindi means 'devil'—a curious combination of four languages. This spirit belongs to the category of 'elementals,' but assumes the form of a miniature negro, not more than three to four inches tall, in order to make itself visible.

After midnight on any night, but particularly on *amavasa* night, when it becomes perceptible, a curious movement can be seen by a watcher concealed in a pen with a herd of buffaloes. He notices something flicking from the back of one animal to another. It looks like a large moth, or maybe a small bat, but apparently has no wings! It dances on one back, leaps to another, sways, disappears and reappears on the back of another buffalo. But the animals do not appear to see it, or notice or feel its presence.

This is a *kutty shaitan* in its natural habitat and condition. If the watcher sees this much and is satisfied, all is still well.

But if he wants to become like the other great men who can pick up anything they want 'out of the air,' so to speak, he is playing with fire! For to do this, he has to get the *kutty shaitan* into himself. He has to make a 'deal,' a bargain, with the elemental spirit: a promise that they will serve each other for life. To make the deal is simple; but to get out of it is practically impossible.

What he has to do, to make the deal, is to approach the buffaloes and go through the motions of trying to snatch and capture the little sprite—although of course he can never do this in fact—while in his mind he concentrates on the thought that he desires the services of the *kutty shaitan*. He will receive a message, sometimes at the first attempt and sometimes after two or three failures—which is generally a telepathic message to his subconscious and thence to his conscious mind—as to what to do next. Generally the message instructs him to carve, (or even purchase) a small black doll, of wood, ivory, bone or any substance, which he must keep on a table or shelf in his house, and perform a daily *pooja* to it with lighted candles, incense, camphor and other things. This little image represents the *kutty shaitan*, and this ceremony seals the bond whereby the sprite agrees to serve him.

The man can then ask for and get anything he wants, *provided he agrees to return it within a fixed time,* say a month or two. *But he cannot get something for nothing.* The little sprite will bring him money, an apple, balm for a headache, a cooked meal, even petrol for a stalled car. *But everything has to be returned at the time promised.* Otherwise, the individual, whoever he may be, has had it!

The sprite does only one free service for its patron. It warns him of approaching danger and contrives to get him out of it. But the wages demanded by this sprite are costly.

The life-span of its patron is shortened; he can have no dealings with a woman; he is hardly allowed to sleep at night; he can never accumulate wealth, although he is permitted enough for his actual needs; he will not be on good terms with his family; he will always be a wanderer, restless, unable ever to settle down.

As a member of the brotherhood of the Silver Armlet, I can assure you that black magic is a fascinating subject to study—but a hard and ruthless taskmaster if embraced!

I have another good friend, a retired army doctor who was a colonel in the India Medical Service during World War II. He told me a story which he assures me is perfectly true. While stationed at Madras, he happened to meet two brothers, Mohammed Bey and Ali Bey, who were Egyptians. He became friendly with the former, but did not know for a long time that both brothers were necromancers who had been trained in Egypt under an adept.

When he learned this, the colonel jokingly told his friend. 'Oh, then you will be able to show me a spirit. I am longing to see one and have been trying for years, without success.'

'Not only will I show you a spirit,' replied Mohammed Bey gravely, 'but I will make him your servant for your lifetime, to help you in anything you want and to bring good fortune to you. But there is one firm condition. Never, at any time, must your employ this spirit servant to do harm to another, or for any sort of evil purpose whatever. If you do, he will turn upon you and you will surely die, and most painfully too. Do you agree?'

'You have my word,' the doctor said with a laugh. 'The proposition is very attractive and I'm extremely interested.'

Mohammed Bey then asked for a writingpad and a pencil, and when he had been given these materials was busy for a while. The colonel has very kindly lent me the sheet of paper on which the Egyptian made his drawing more than twenty years ago, and I have faithfully copied it and reproduced it on pages 129 and 130.

The mantra, or words for summoning spirits, as told by the Egyptian necromancer

Ah, Ah, Sharheel wa burrhoode wa noodaju wa askeerah if alue aywhel kadhamu ma amuro bi hi min shain hathal kagadi bi hyqi sharheel us Fur Ya rooh (three times) *Tha-al* (three times) *bill amruho* (seven times).

Begin by facing the north. Then turn to the right or east, and read the above words seven times. Then turn back again to the north. Then turn to the left or west side and read the words seven times. Then turn back to the north. Next turn right around to face in the opposite or southern direction, and read the words seven times. Then turn back again to the north, where the words should be read once more seven times. After having finished the four points of the compass, turn in the direction of the cemetery you have selected for your visit and read the words twenty-one times. Lastly, breathe in slowly, hold your breath a little and then exhale slowly three times, each time concentrating upon a good manifestation of the spirit desired by the person teaching this, or that you would like to see yourself.

This procedure is to be followed for twenty-two days, beginning in such a fashion that the twenty-third day falls on a Tuesday or a Friday. That twenty-third day is the day on which to go to the cemetery. In other words, carry out the directions for twenty-two days, ending on a Monday or a Thursday. The next day (Tuesday or Friday) is the day on which to visit the cemetery.

The following drawing may be traced on a piece of paper, folded and kept in a locket or wallet for good luck:

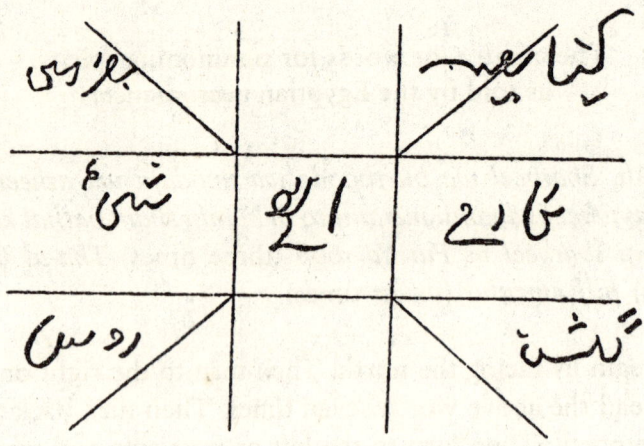

'I have written in Roman-Arabic so that you may be able to read it,' Mohammed Bey explained (Roman-Arabic is Arabic written phonetically in Roman characters). 'Next come the instructions in English. Carry these out faithfully and to the letter.'

'Order a large garland of roses to be prepared by the evening of the final day, and ninety minutes before midnight that day have a bath and dress in a clean white shirt and suit. I will call for you at 11.30 and show you what to do next. One more thing. You must fast on that last day, but you may drink a cup of milk in the morning and another in the evening. Nothing more.'

'Now let us start calculating which is the twenty-third day.'

Thereupon the Egyptian turned to a large calendar hanging on the wall, made some calculations while counting the days on the calendar with the tip of a pencil, and finally named a day and a date.

'Be ready,' he added cryptically, and the doctor agreed.

The instructions were carried out to the letter, but during the interval the colonel never met Mohammed Bey. At the end of the third week he had the feeling that his friend was deliberately avoiding him. He wondered if it was all a joke.

The final day came. The garland of roses which the colonel had ordered was ready by evening. At 10.30 p.m. he had a bath and then dressed in clean white clothes. He tells me he felt himself a fool.

At exactly 11.30 p.m., a car drew up beneath the portico of his old-fashioned residence and the Egyptian alighted. He, too, was dressed in white clothes.

'Bring the garland, doctor,' he said in a matter-of-fact voice, 'we must be there by midnight.'

Wondering where they were going, the doctor did as he was told. They reached the cemetery in fifteen minutes and, carrying the garland of roses, the doctor followed his companion through the wicket-gate. It was pitch-dark, except for a faint glow cast by the stars. Indside the cemetery the Egyptian stopped for a moment. Then he moved among the graves for some distance, as if in search of a particular one, while the doctor followed him. They found it at last. A grave with a granite slab and a rounded headstone. It was too dark to see more.

'Place the garland around the headstone, doctor,' Mohammed Bey directed, 'and stand at the foot of the grave with your arms folded across your chest. I will stand at the side. Now, whatever happens, do not be afraid. I am here; have confidence in me. We must wait for midnight.'

A few minutes later a distant clock chimed and then struck the hour of twelve. But Mohammed Bey did nothing for a few minutes more. Then he started intoning something in a language the doctor could not understand, but thought to be

Arabic. The words came in a singsong voice and the Egyptian appeared to be in a trance.

This continued for a while, and then something seemed to go wrong with the proceedings. The chanting came to an end abruptly, and was followed by angry words from the Egyptian, with an interval, and then more angry words followed. It seemed as if he was having a heated argument with some invisible person, whose voice could not be heard.

The Egyptian grew more excited. He waved his arms. He appeared to be using abusive language. Then he spat upon the grave. The next instant he fell as if pole-axed across the granite slab. His body twitched in the faint gloom, while horrible, gurgling sounds came from his throat. The doctor panicked and was on the verge of bolting, his only thought being to save himself by running for dear life.

At that moment his professional training came to his aid. He was a doctor after all. The Egyptian might be having an epileptic fit, a heart attack or a seizure of some kind. It was his medical duty to stay. Also came the paralysing thought that the Egyptain might die if left alone. When his body was found, if it was ever discovered that the doctor had been with him in the cemetery, he might be accused of murder.

So he ran forward, grasped the body of his companion that was still thrashing about and from which came dreadful gasps and groans, and attempted to raise him.

The doctor swears he encountered a force stronger than his own that was keeping the man down. A struggle followed, then the Egyptian gasped: 'Roses—the garland—give it to me.'

The doctor let go of his companion, removed the garland from the tombstone, and threw it to the prostrate man. While he still grovelled on the granite slab as if in an epileptic fit, Mohammed Bey tore the garland to shreds. And as the garland disintegrated, the black magician appeared to be gaining mastery over the situation.

Eventually he stood up, dishevelled and breathing hard. Blood trickled down his face from a gash across his forehead, where he had struck it against the granite slab.

'It's all right now, doctor,' he gasped, 'but let's get out of here. I'll tell you in the car.'

The two men hurried out to the car and began to drive back to the doctor's house. The colonel waited till his companion regained his composure. At last the Egyptian spoke.

'The spirit came all right. In fact, there were several. But they were in grotesque forms, resembling strange animals. They all volunteered to serve you. But I insisted there should be only one, and that one should adopt a human form. They refused, and were adamant that all should attach themselves to you and in their present strange forms. I would not allow it. There was an argument and suddenly the leader struck me down and they all set upon me, choking me. If you had not thrown me the garland to break the spell, I would have been killed.'

A clever piece of acting by the Egyptian, put on to deceive the doctor, you will say. The cut across his forehead against the tombstone was, of course, an unforeseen accident. Perhaps it was not blood after all, but something surreptitiously applied!

Quite possible I do agree, and a reasonable explanation. But remember, the Egyptian never asked his friend for money, or a favour at any time. Then why did he go through all this trouble?

Many Indian families, particularly on the west coast of India, believe they are guarded by what they call 'deities.' These are not evil spirits or jinns or even gods. They are thought to be superior spiritual beings. Each is distinguished from the other by the scent of a particular fragrant flower which comes from nowhere. Some bring with them the scent of jasmine; this is very common and I have smelt it myself many times in rooms and in places where flowers of any kind certainly did not exist. Superior orders are said to bring the scent of roses, or other fragrances.

Amavasa night—the night before the new moon, the darkest night of the month—is the time generally chosen for practising all kinds of black magic, and it is on such nights that many Indian families feel and hear the presence of their guardian spirits. These evidence themselves by the sound of a heavy chain being dragged or jingled, or in the case of a female spirit, by the subtle clicking of bracelets against each other. The major guardian announces his presence by making a noise as if a man were walking around the house snapping his thumb against his fingers every once in a while, or by measured, heavy footsteps.

Belief in the existence of spirits and in the occult has found its way into all religions in India. In my own opinion, all creeds, as originally preached and believed, were of pure and divine origin: Hinduism, Buddhism, Mohammedanism and Christianity all pointed the way to the Supreme Being. But priestcraft on the one hand, and superstition and occultism on the other, have become so intermingled with these doctrines that many of their followers practise a religion very different, and in certain cases quite opposed, to the doctrines of the original parent order.

The beliefs and practices of many Christian converts in India, both Roman Catholic and Protestant, are indeed a queer mixture of religion, superstition and occultism. Very properly, these people are the despair of most right-thinking priests of all faiths, although unfortunately here and there are some who encourage distorted beliefs to the point of malpractice in order to drive home that fear of hellfire by which they hold their congregations in submission.

Saint Anthony, who is regarded everywhere as a most beneficent man while alive, has come to be looked upon by many in India as an infallible means of effecting revenge upon others as well as acquiring benefits by prayer. Horrible acts of revenge and the defeat of enemies by fair means or foul, including painful illness and lingering death, are sought through him. Saint Anthony is also regarded as the main means for the recovery of lost or stolen property and for inflicting punishment, by many kinds of violence, upon the thief responsible. Some of the forms of punishment which Saint Anthony is asked to inflict upon the culprit or the enemy are of a revolting character and out of all proportion to the crimes committed. For example, in retribution for stealing a pound of rice, Saint Anthony is asked to inflict upon the thief, known or unknown, such appalling diseases as cholera and plague.

My servant is a Roman Catholic convert, but here is her procedure for recovering lost property through Saint Anthony. To find the thief, the supplicant must first take a bath. Then he must wash the statue of the saint, or (if he does not possess a statue) the glass covering the saint's photograph. To bathe the saint's likeness in milk, rather than in water, is considered more efficacious. The ceremony should be performed at sunset on a Tuesday. After this, four candles are lighted at the foot of the statue or photograph, before which an offering of flowers is made and incense burned. A small coin is tied in a cloth to the top of the frame of the photograph or placed at the foot of the statue.

A prayer is then offered to the saint to grant the favour of finding the thief, restoring the money or property, or severely punishing the offender, as the case may be. This is accompanied by a vow that, if the petition be granted, charity in some form or another will be given to thirteen beggars in the name of the saint. This charity may be in the shape of a small gift of money, or a garment, or a meal. Such prayers to the saint are offered every evening at sundown for thirteen days. It is thought certain favours of a minor kind will be granted within eight days, whereas major favours, in respect of articles of greater value, may take longer, but action by the saint will surely be evident within a month.

The recovery of lost property purchased by hard-earned money, or of stolen money, is assured by the lighting of a single candle, accompanied by incense, for thirteen consecutive evenings before the statue or picture of Saint Anthony.

In some parts of India, particularly old Hyderabad state, these supplications to Saint Anthony assume a more forceful character. The feet of the saint's statue are bound with cord, signifying that the supplicant is not prepared to release him until or unless the favour is granted. The most drastic—and amusing—instance that I have met is the procedure followed by an old Anglo-Indian living at a place called Kazipet. He was an old army man and possibly thought Saint Anthony needed a spot of disciplining now and again. For should the favour not be granted within the stipulated time, the statue of the saint was subjected to rough treatment. It was tied to a tamarind tree out in the garden and smeared with a mixture of chili-powder and other ingredients that are known to be extremely pungent. The idea was by torture to force the poor saint into granting the favour, and once that happened the old soldier brought the statue indoors again, washed it, bathed it in milk and restored it to its pedestal.

Statues and photographs of the Virgin Mary were similarly appealed to for general favours. Thursday was considered the right day for the first supplication, to be repeated for eight days in succession.

The old English method of tying up a pair of scissors, so that the two loops of the scissors rest on the fingertips of two persons and rotate at the mention of the name of the guilty party, is very widely practised in India. So is the custom of suspending a rosary over a pot of incense, so that the cross is immediately above the fire; it is then said to oscillate at the name of the guilty party.

In cemeteries in which Indian Christians are buried, it is common to see the relatives of the dead come to the grave on certain days with offerings of milk and food, presumably to sustain the departed spirit on its long journey to higher realms.

My purpose in mentioning these things is to emphasize the extent to which superstition and ancient customs have become inextricably involved with Christianity in India. Superstition and belief and fear of the unknown are rife in all walks of life in all communities and all religions. Among the upper-class Hindus it takes a higher form but is nevertheless powerful. From birth, a child's horoscope is all-important and plays a primary part in the arrangement of a marriage—the boy and girl rarely see each other before the ceremony—and the stars continue to have a major role throughout the man's life. Conspicuously marked on calendars, for every day of the month, are two lists of timings, headed respectively *rahukalam* and *guligaikalam*, meaning 'bad time' and 'good time', and no Hindu, and many who are not Hindus, will dream of leaving home at a time, or embarking on a business venture or journey at an hour which falls within the *rahukalam* or 'bad time' period. He will patiently wait till that time had passed and the *guligaikalam* or 'good time' has come. Then he will set out on his venture, very confident and assured of success.

A ring that has very magical properties in attracting the fair sex, sometimes to their great embarrassment, can be made in the following way. I took great pains to write down the formula, or whatever you care to call it. The only snag is that the mantras involved have to be acquired and learned. The secret is so valuable, presumably because the reward is so great, that so far nobody seems willing to tell me these mantras, so that I may learn and repeat them. But I am still trying to find somebody who will part with the secret.

However, you must procure a live fresh-water turtle of the dark variety of medium size. This is not very difficult. For about a rupee someone will bring one to you. They abound in fresh-water wells throughout the countryside.

Having procured the live turtle, get some dried pumpkin seeds that will germinate easily. These may be obtained readily from any seedsmen, or from any pumpkin purchased in the market, though in the latter event they should be well dried.

Next, tempt the unfortunate turtle with some food such as earthworms or a small frog. When he sticks his neck out of his shell to eat, decapitate him with a deft stroke of a sharp knife, delivering the blow just behind the back of his head and high up the neck; that is, be sure to leave a good bit of stump protruding. After all movement has ceased insert about half a dozen of the dried pumpkin seeds well into the raw stump of the neck. Then bury the turtle in an upright position in the ground, so that the neck-stump, with the seeds in it, is rather less than a couple of inches below the surface of the ground. Then water the spot sparingly every day.

The pumpkin seeds, or some of them, will sprout. Select the best and healthiest. Wait till the second shoot appears, and then carefully pluck the whole seedling, along with its roots, from the decaying neck-stump of the turtle. Clean away the mess from the roots, and cram the seedling tightly, roots and all, through the groove on the underside into the hollow of a ring, which you should have prepared in advance.

Any ring will do, but one of silver or copper is best. A hollow groove, as deep as possible, should have been cut around the ring.

After you have pushed as much as is possible of the seedling with its roots into this hollow groove, seal up the same with sealing-wax or any form of lacquer or gummy substance that will dry and harden. The ring should not be sent to a jeweller for sealing, as the heat he will apply to melt the metal to seal the ring will burn up the seedling inside.

The ring, having thus been made ready and sealed, must not be used till the next new-moon day. At midnight on the night before, that is that night of *amavasa*, a mantra has to be repeated over the ring eleven times, and it is then ready for use. Its efficacy in attracting and embarrassing females is said to last for a lifetime.

This topic will not be complete unless I tell you of an adventure that befell me near a town called Chitaldroog, in a jungle once renowned for tigers, situated to the east of the district of Shimoga in Mysore state. The village of Sampigehalli, a few miles from Chitaldroog, is surrounded by thick forest. About four miles from this village, along a track leading to another village named Budhalli, in the midst of the jungle, stands a ruined temple with a very deep well. The temple and the well are reputed to be haunted, for which reason hardly a soul will approach within a furlong of them in broad daylight, while the area is of course absolutely taboo after sunset.

Because of its isolation, a sloth bear or two invariably lived in or close to the ruins, while quite frequently a panther could shelter in the old temple close to the bears, but without having anything to do with them. Now and again a tiger decided to take up residence there for a few weeks, and when that happened the bears and the panther temporarily took themselves off to safer abodes. For either of them to dare to share the same abode with the king of the jungle might prove a costly experiment. But eventually the tiger would move on, and then the bears and the panther would come back and things return to normal.

Some time ago a villager disappeared from Sampigehalli, and a month later another disappeared from Budhalli. Nobody knew what happened to them, nor was there any sign of the remains. As villagers in India rarely leave their birthplaces voluntarily, the disappearance of these men, one after the other, left food for thought. It suggested that a tragedy of some sort had taken place.

About this time an unusually large tiger, said by the villagers to be exceptionally fierce because of the manner in which it boldly attacked their herds of cattle and never failed to make a kill, took up its abode in the locality, or even in the old temple itself. This was established by its pug-marks, to be seen early in the morning returning to the temple, superimposed upon the pug-marks it had left in the dust of the trail when it had gone forth the previous evening. The villagers felt that this tiger had devoured their two companions, one after the other, so they appealed to the authorities for help against the man-eater that they were convinced dwelt in the ruins of the old temple.

Sampigehalli was at one time a favourite haunt of mine and several of my village friends wrote to me to come to their aid. When I reached the village a fortnight later I made painstaking inquiries regarding the last movements of the two missing men, but everything seemed to be shrouded in mystery. A village girl was mixed up in the affair and it was said that both the men were her suitors. The girl was poor, whereas both the men were comparatively well-to-do, owning land in their own villages. They were married and had families, but no member of either family had the least knowledge of the large sum of money each of these individuals was reported to be carrying on his person just prior to his disappearance, nor did they know why their relative had been carrying the money about with him. All this came to light only afterwards. For India is one of the few places left in the world today where wives do not dare to question their husbands' movements or authority.

The man's word is law and women are content to confine their activities to the kitchen.

Meanwhile, there was no evidence whatever to connect the tiger with the disappearance of the two men. Casually, in the course of inquiries, I spoke about the missing men to the girl concerned and came away feeling that she knew much more about the matter than she would say. To my mind, she was much more dangerous than any man-eating tiger and far more astute; but not being a policeman, I did not feel obliged to act as an informer or a detective. I was much more interested in the tiger than in the girl's motives and movements and what had happened to her suitors.

I therefore decided to go to the old temple immediately after lunch that day, select a suitable hiding place and remain there all night in the hope of seeing the suspected man-eater. I had not made up my mind whether to shoot the creature if I did happen to see it, for something told me that it was not the culprit. In any case it was summer time, far better known in India as the 'hot weather,' and it was only a day or two until the full moon. The moonlight and the open air would be much more pleasant than spending the night in some little mudhouse, where the heat would be intense, or even in the forest department's bungalow.

After a good lunch I got together the few things I would require for the night: my rifle, ammunition, flask of tea, water-bottle, electric torch and some biscuits in a cloth bag, that would not crackle as a paper wrapper would, and set out for the old temple. In a little over an hour I reached my destination. I knew the place well enough, although I had never spent a night there. It consisted of a small central structure built of solid, irregular blocks of granite, surrounded by what had once been a fairly high stone wall. The well, which was indeed very deep, still held water and was in the courtyard to the front of the temple.

I do not know how much water was in the well, but the surface glinted down below, far beneath the level of the ground. The well itself was not more than fifteen feet in diameter, ringed at the top by a low stone parapet about a yard high. Many of the granite blocks forming the main temple, the four walls of the courtyard and the parapet of the well, had become loose and had fallen away from their original positions, while gnarled or dwarfed trees, principally the jungle fig, had been able to take root wherever the lantana shrub had not already taken possession. The scene in general was bleak and dreary, and it was clear that with time the few remaining traces of the temple and its environs would be swallowed up by the advancing jungle.

But at the moment I was not interested in the temple as a structure, historical or otherwise. What I was interested in was the hiding place of the tiger, and that did not take me long to find. The only possible place was the main temple building itself. The earth was mostly hard, but here and there were sandy patches and clearly imprinted in the soft ground, both coming and going, were the pug-marks of a large tiger, leading to and from the old ruins.

I knew that if the animal were at home at that moment it would probably be sound asleep inside. I had never been inside this structure myself, but felt safe in conjecturing that it followed the general pattern of such buildings, with a sanctuary in the form of a small separate room at the farther end of what would be the one and only prayer-room of the temple proper. This small inner room would house a Nandi or two, stone images of varying sizes of the sacred bull that is universally respected by the Hindus in India, or perhaps an image or several images of one of the many gods and goddesses.

To approach this opening would, in the circumstances, be to invite disaster. If the tiger were at home, man-eater or not, it would definitely resent such blatant violation of its privacy and would probably decide to get rid of the invader with the utmost dispatch. It was one of those occasions when brain rather than brawn was indicated, so I stood still to take stock of the situation and decide upon a plan.

And the solution lay right there before me in the broken parapet of the old well. All I had to do was to sit comfortably behind it, facing the opening leading to the main temple. If the tiger were inside, as I felt sure it was, then sooner or later it would have to come out, and this it could only do by using the entrance. I would have this entrance covered in the sights of my rifle, so that it did not matter at what angle the tiger decided to emerge. The whole thing seemed 'a piece of cake.'

The sun blazed down upon me when I took up my position behind the parapet, directly facing the temple entrance. I realized my head was above the top of the parapet, so I picked up some of the fallen stone blocks and arranged them before me, leaving a space about six inches square through which to peer. If the tiger showed up, and if I had decided to shoot him by then, I could fire through this loophole.

The only other requirement was that I should sit absolutely still. Fortunately I am well practised in that sort of thing, so that neither the heat nor the winged insects that came as if from nowhere, not even the occasional slate-black lizard with its brilliant orange and yellow back worried me when the sweat trickled down my face and the insects settled on my lips and lizards crawled over my body.

Then came the evening. The calls of roosting birds preceded the squeaking of early bats and the buzz of a passing mosquito. It was almost dark when the moon, that was not yet at the full, began to rise. Soon its glow outlined the dark shadow that was the entrance to the temple through which the tiger might, at any moment now, if he was at home, be expected to emerge. What was left of daylight faded rapidly, but moonlight took its place, so that even before I appreciated the passage of time, it was night. I shivered a little, for in those few minutes it had become distinctly chill.

That was when I heard the sound for the first time. Three distinct, sharp whistles that seemed to come from the well right in front of me. The first whistle was low, the second higher, the third shorter, sharper, louder and pitched yet higher than its two predecessors.

Who the hell could be hiding in the old well? To say the least, I was very annoyed. After all the time I had spent sitting motionless in the sweltering heat of the sun, must this so-and-so start whistling at this critical moment and frighten away the tiger that might be expected to emerge from the temple? Was it worth hiding any longer? The tiger would have heard that whistling even more clearly than I had done, and it would never show up with a human being just outside its shelter. Or would it? If it really was a man-eater it might think some victim was within striking distance.

Quite ten to fifteen minutes must have elapsed when I heard the whistling again, loud and clear, in three sharp blasts. The first low and rather long-drawn; the second louder, shorter and higher pitched; the third loudest, shortest and on a yet higher note. Then there was complete silence.

I was in the act of getting up to peer down the well and curse the intruder when a slight movement in the oblong blackness of the temple entrance caught my eye. A greyish blur seemed to pass against that blackness. It vanished, came again, and disappeared once more. A moment later, clearly outlined, sideways on the moonlight, stood the tiger!

It was obvious that it never suspected my presence for a moment, as it never even glanced in my direction. It was looking directly ahead when I first saw it, but stopped at that moment to bend its neck and lick its right foreleg. I could clearly see the movement of its head, and hear the rasping of its rough tongue over its coat each time that it licked itself. And then, for the third time, came those three loud whistles in rising crescendo.

That has done it, I thought. The tiger must surely hear them now. It would crouch, growl, spring back into the shelter of the temple, or rush away, according to its disposition or the state of its nerves. But nothing happened! The tiger continued to lick itself, unperturbed. Evidently it had not heard the whistling, and for this there could be only two explanations. Either the tiger was stone deaf, or the whistling did not register upon its hearing.

The tiger stopped licking itself and began to move forward. At the same time I heard what appeared to be the flapping of wings from the depths of the well before me. The sound was heavy, slow and distinct. It must have been made by some large and heavy bird, I decided, or a bat not much smaller than the familiar Indian flying-fox or fruit-bat.

Then for the fourth time that evening came the whistle, louder and closer than ever before. My decision whether or not to shoot the tiger was quite forgotten in this mystery.

Indeed, I did not even watch it, but stared at the top of the old well, waiting for I know not what to come out.

The heavy, slow flapping was continuous now. The large bird or bat, or whatever it was, drew nearer every instant to the top and would show itself in a moment or two. A strange fascination came over me as I stared at the opening. Once again came the three whistles, and then what seemed a large, dark shadow of indefinite shape issued from the well.

The moonlight was bright and clear and I was staring at the spot. There was no mistaking that I saw something, but it had no real form or shape: a small cloud of what seemed to be dark smoke came out of the well. It might have been six feet in diameter by about the same height.

A great lassitude seemed to come over me; a sort of strange, morbid despair. Did it matter what came out of the well? Was life worth living with all its troubles? Why not jump into the well and forget about everything?

I shook myself and stared, and as I watched the cloud hovered for a moment above the mouth of the well and in the next second was gone. The moonlight shone clearly through the spot which, a moment before, had been clouded by the indefinable shape. I had started perspiring with excitement when the tiger made its appearance, which is something I still do to this day when I see a tiger in the wild. Now I felt cold and clammy.

Meanwhile the tiger, which at least was of flesh and bone, wandered away. I knew that in all likelihood it would not return till the early hours of the morning, unless it found something to kill and eat sooner. I would therefore, in all probability, have to wait for a long time if I still wanted to shoot it when it came back. But somehow I did not want to shoot this tiger; the strange whistling, and the still stranger shadow that had emerged from the well, interested me much more. In any case, it was far better to sit there in the moonlight and the open air, than to be in the stuffy shelter I was occupying four miles away at Sampigehalli.

I forgot everything but the whistling and the shadow, and fell to conjecturing what on earth could have been the cause of what I had seen. The whistling had not resembled the call of any bird with which I was familiar. Rather, it was distinctly human in timbre. The flapping of wings I had heard could have been caused by some large bird, or the Indian flying-fox that I have already mentioned. But neither bird nor bat had emerged from the well, and I had never for a moment removed my gaze from its mouth. What had come out had been something far different and quite unexpected: a smokey shape of indefinable nature. In plain words, a small cloud. And that cloud had vanished before my eyes!

So absorbed was I in the problem that I lost all count of time and became oblivious to my surroundings till a low growl, somewhere behind me, brought me back to earth with a jolt. The tiger was standing there! It had returned from another direction and had discovered my presence. It was reputed to be a man-eater that had killed and devoured two men already.

I swung around in alarm, instinctively raising the .405 to my shoulder. About forty yards away this tiger sat on his haunches in the moonlight, staring hard at me. Then it inclined its head slightly and snarled in mild protest. As clearly as if it had spoken the words, this animal was saying, 'Can't you get the hell out of here?' That satisfied me entirely. It had had me at its mercy and could have killed me before I was even aware of its presence. This tiger was no man-eater!

I try to be grateful when a good turn is done to me and I was definitely grateful to this animal. It had spared my life and I would return the courtesy. I got to my feet, whereupon the tiger disappeared from sight.

Keeping the rifle in the crook of my arm to guard against a sudden change of mind on the beast's part, I shone the beam of my torch down the well, expecting to discover the mysterious whistler who must be hiding there. But only the water, deep down, reflected the light. There was certainly nobody in hiding, for I searched every inch of the interior. Then I turned and started to walk away from the place, thinking furiously. The tiger was nowhere to be seen.

I decided to spend the rest of that night on the veranda of the forest rest house, so I walked to the little bungalow that stood about a mile from the village and called aloud to the watchman who should have been sleeping inside. Nobody answered, although I called again and again and again. Obviously, the watchman was not on watch, but snugly asleep in some hut in the village.

This was no surprise. Those who have lived in India will know that invariably watchmen do not watch. They sleep soundly instead; perhaps even more soundly than you or I, for their minds are quite clear that night is the time when people must sleep.

So I climbed the stone leading up to the veranda which stretched around three sides of the little rectangular bungalow. The caretaker had been careless enough to leave an armchair out on one of these extensions, knowing well enough that nobody would steal such a rickety article, even if there had been a thief in so desolate a place; so into the armchair I sank to snatch a few hours' sleep.

My intention was to tell my friends as Sampigehalli the next morning that I was convinced the tiger was no man-eater, and that if they really wanted to solve the mystery of the missing men, they should suggest to the police that they question the lissom lass who was so intimately connected with both of them; particularly as to what had become of their money. Then I would head for home in the Studebaker.

But sleep eluded me for the rest of that night. Those mysterious whistles, the sound of flapping wings, the peculiar lethargy that had come over me, and above all that strange cloudy shape that had come out of the well, demanded a sane explanation. Wrestling with the problem, tired, nature finally asserted herself and I fell asleep after dawn had broken. It was late when I awoke that morning, but the caretaker of the bungalow had not yet returned.

I went to the village, where I told my friends that I had seen the tiger and that it had seen me. I explained it was no man-eater. I did not tell them about the whistling sounds I had heard nor the cloudy form I had seen, for there appeared to be no point in complicating my story unnecessarily and making myself ridiculous.

Then one of my friends inquired where I had concealed myself, and I told him that I had hidden behind the parapet of the old well. At the mention of that word, he looked at me strangely.

'Did you see anything other than the tiger?' he inquired. 'Did you hear anything?'

I did not answer for a while. Then I countered. 'Why do you ask?'

'Did you see, or hear, a huge bat? The sound of beating wings?'

The sound of beating wings! Most certainly I had heard that sound: the sound of heavy, flapping wings issuing from the depths of the well. In fact I had heard that sound several times, each time coming higher and closer to the mouth of the well, and it had ceased only after that strange smoky shape had emerged. What a fool I had been not to shine the light of my torch down the well the first time I had heard it! I might have been able to see something. Then I remembered I had been waiting for the tiger and so had not wanted to show myself.

My friend had noticed the delay in my reply. His face took on a knowing smile. So I told him everything.

He appeared horrified when I mentioned the hazy form that had emerged from the well. Evidently others had heard the whistling and the sound of flapping wings, but nobody seemed to have seen anything, because no one had waited to see.

Then my friend came up with a strange tale. According to him, a couple of hundred or more years ago—he did not exactly know when—the temple flourished and was a centre of widespread veneration, while the surrounding area was ruled by a petty chieftain who had made himself independent of the rajah whose capital was far away. In the court of this petty chieftain was an individual who played the dual role of adviser and jester, and for whom the chieftain evidently had considerable regard.

The temple itself was in charge of a number of priests—all Brahmins—governed by a high priest who was of strong character. As always happens when people of strong minds come into contact with each other, there was a clash of interests between the chieftain, his adviser the jester, and the Brahmin high priest.

Of course, all the details had been long forgotten, but it appeared that the high priest had contrived to trump up charges against his rival, the jester, who had been accused of treachery towards the ruling house. The result was that the unfortunate adviser had been publicly tried, condemned to death for treason, and forthwith thrown down the well alive, but not before he had screamed threats of vengeance against the high priest and all the temple monks.

The sequel to this story was that within a week the high priest was missing, and a couple of days later his body was found floating in the well. The jester had claimed his first victim. Thereafter, at intervals, the other priests disappeared one by one, and their corpses would show up, floating face downwards in the well just like that of their high priest. Other priests came to the temple, but each and everyone of them met the same fate.

Elaborate ceremonies were held from time to time to exorcise the spirit of the avenging jester, but to no avail, as slowly but surely priest after priest vanished and his drowned body was later found floating on the surface of the water in the well. It took perhaps a hundred years for the avenging spirit of the jester to accomplish its task, but the time came when no priest, however holy he might be, or appear to be, would risk his life by volunteering to officiate in the temple. And that was how the temple and the well came to be deserted and eventually fell into ruin.

The narrator closed his strange tale with a very significant sentence: 'Consider yourself very lucky indeed, sir, that you are alive this morning. That evil spirit could easily have thrown you down the well, as easily as it has destroyed at least a hundred priests in the past!'

Because I'm not a Brahmin priest, I retorted sarcastically, adding, 'Stuff and nonsense. Damned rot!' The words came from me violently, explosively. To say the least, I was annoyed! Did this silly fellow think he could frighten me with such old wives' tales? I fear I was very rude to my unfortunate acquaintance for the next few minutes, for I told him exactly what I thought of his story, and of him for relating it.

The poor fellow's face fell and he walked away abashed. Unabashed, I scowled after him. Then I started packing the Studebaker preparatory to returning home, which did not take me long. I wished my friends goodbye, half-heartedly and rather abruptly, noticing that the man who had told me about the temple was not among them. In the usual hospitable Indian fashion, they pressed me even at that last moment to extend my stay. In answer I pressed the self-starter, shifted the car into gear, and drove away.

I had travelled quite six miles from Sampigehalli when I stopped the Studebaker, switched off the ignition and started to think clearly. I had behaved churlishly for no valid reason. After all, the man had only told me the story as he had heard it from others. It was I who had heard the whistling, had listened to the flapping of wings and seen the strange shadow. It was up to me to believe the tale, or reject it if I could find some better explanation. The sensible thing for me to do would be to try to make further investigation into the matter by talking to more people about it. Most sensible of all would be for me to spend another night at the well to see if the phenomenon was repeated. Instead of doing either of these things, I had acted like a child and cleared off in a huff.

So I turned the car and drove back to the village, where the first thing I did was to seek out my friend and apologize. He readily forgave me saying he understood how I had felt, and was all smiles again. In fact everybody smiled at my return till I told them that this time I had not come to hunt a tiger but a ghost—the evil spirit who lived down the well at the old temple.

At these words everybody stopped smiling. Then my friend said: 'Sir, I don't want to be rude, but please go back to Bangalore at once rather than do this foolish thing. You might escape from the tiger but not from the evil one.'

That evening, having nothing to fear from the tiger, I did not go to the old temple as early as I had done the previous afternoon. It was nearly six o'clock when I settled down in the place I had earlier occupied behind the parapet of the well. I had brought my rifle along with me in case the tiger should prove to be difficult, but as there was no particular need to keep silent on this occasion, I had allowed myself a large flask of tea, bread, butter and a tin of corned mutton and even some oranges to wind up with, not to mention my battered briar pipe.

There was no sign of the tiger as I settled myself, as quickly and as comfortably as possible, in my old position, arranging the torch, flask, water-bottle and other articles to right and left of me. He might have come out of his hiding place in the holy-of-holies of the temple before my arrival, although I did not think that was likely. In this conjecture I proved to be right. The time was a few minutes after seven and it was growing very cold. The nightjars had begun to call when a stone was dislodged inside the dark opening of the sanctuary and rolled loosely down the bank outside.

I knew the tiger was standing at the opening, looking out to see if it was safe enough to emerge. It might see me now, or might already have seen me; perhaps it remembered my presence at the parapet of the well the evening before. Precisely at that moment I heard the first whistle, loud, rather low and rather long-drawn-out, followed in quick succession by a louder, far higher and shorter whistle. After that there was absolute silence.

I remembered with a sense of shock that on the evening before, the whistling had begun just before the appearance of the tiger. The same thing had happened again. The thought came to me: could it be that the thing that whistled was trying to warn the tiger of my presence?

This notion was dispelled a moment later when the tiger emerged from the dark outline of the temple's entrance, first as an indistinct shape and then as an animal of immense proportions in the early light of the newly-risen moon.

As I had observed the evening before, for some unaccountable reason these loud whistles did not register on the tiger's hearing, although they were very clear to me. The fact was uncanny and was confirmed the next moment when the three successive whistles were repeated, more insistent and louder than ever. But the tiger took no notice of them. Then I began to hear the flapping of wings again, faintly and as from a distance. The source of the sound was at first difficult to place, till it was brought home to me, with an unpleasant shock, that it came from the bottom of the deep well in front of me.

Meanwhile the tiger was standing still, clearly visible in the early moonlight. It was staring fixedly in my direction. It was evident that the tiger now remembered having seen me there the previous night. I wanted to flash my torch down the well to discover the cause of the flapping sound, but this meant taking my eyes off the tiger, something I was rather reluctant to do. The rumour that this was a man-eater came to my mind once more with renewed force. Supposing this was a fact: I would be at its mercy if it should decide to attack me while I was looking down the well.

The three whistles, coming for the third time, with the closer approach of the flapping sound, got the better of my caution. A quick glance showed the tiger was still looking in my direction when I raised myself to my knees, thrust my head and shoulders over the parapet of the well, extended my right arm with the torch grasped in my hand as far as possible down the well and pressed the button. The bright beam cut into the inky depths, then lost itself in what looked to be a cloud of thick black smoke or vapour that was heaving some distance down the well.

Forgetful of the tiger I stared down the well, transfixed with curiosity, while the cloud that appeared to be issuing from the bottom, and was dense enough to prevent my torch-beam from penetrating it, rose inexorably towards me. It would not take long to reach the surface where I was crouching.

A loud snarl brought me back to an awareness of the danger I was in from the tiger. Quickly I shone the torch in the direction where it had been standing, while I groped for my rifle with the other. But the tiger was not there! Gratefully, I realized it had seen me and bounded away, the snarl I had heard being its protest at my intrusion. In a strange way I missed the tiger, for now I did not have a material antagonist to deal with, but something intangible with which I did not know how to cope. And I can tell you the thought was most unnerving.

The flapping came again; loud, heavy and near. The torchlight, which I directed into the well, showed that the eddying billows of the smoke-cloud were now scarcely five feet from the mouth of the well and that the rays of the torch could not penetrate them. They rose rapidly upwards and soon reached the face of my torch as I held it pointing downwards. My hand began to tremble violently so that the light danced crazily.

There seemed something indescribably evil about this vapour, and it brought a reaction I had never experienced before. Unlike normal smoke this mist eddied in dense, ribbon-like trails, resembling the coils of a giant snake of interminable length that twisted and wound around and around, in and out and about itself in a seething, restless, engulfing, devouring, never-ending movement.

Soon, it had reached my head and shoulders and engulfed me as I craned myself forward to look down the well. The cloud was far more dense than it had been the previous night, rather like a pea-soup fog that could almost be felt. I am by no means a squeamish person, but for the next few moments I did not know what was happening. The feeling is hard to describe. Perhaps to say that I was taken out of myself would be nearest to the mark, although I realize that such words hardly convey any meaning.

Once again I felt unutterably tired, forlorn, depressed, altogether without hope. A deep and urgent yearning came over me to jump over the parapet and into the well, once and for all to end my misery and unhappiness. It would be such an easy, such a pleasant ending, to the tortures and troubles and trials of living. Such an easy way out! So comfortable and soothing! So Soothing! So Soothing!

And then the gas, or smoke, or whatever it was, lifted. Rather, it cleared the parapet of the well and rose above my head as a dense, heavy, whirling cloud. With its lifting my mind cleared too and I was back to earth once more, remembering in amazement my recent dismal thoughts of throwing myself into the well. The cloud rose higher and higher and thinned out as it mixed with the air. I watched it in my torchlight for a full ten minutes, by which time it must have risen to perhaps fifty feet or more, when it dispersed and I could see it no more.

I put out the torch and sat back to ponder the strange phenomenon. The words of my friend and the story he had told me came back in forceful recollection. I pondered again upon the tale of evil and vengeance, and I remembered with dismay the odd feeling of careless lassitude that had overcome me as the vapour engulfed me and passed over my head: the feeling of despair, and the comforting temptation to end all my troubles merely by jumping down the well into oblivion. I had almost, in fact, fallen a victim to the age-old curse myself. It gave me quite a jolt, I can assure you, to realize that but a few moments earlier I was dispassionately contemplating suicide.

Then there were other aspects of the occurrence that defied explanation. The three strange whistles in quick succession; the unaccountable sound of flapping wings; the fact that the tiger could not hear these sounds; and strangest of all, that the weird thing, or whatever it was that came from the well, assumed the appearance of a dark cloud.

I walked back to the forest bungalow for the second time, to seek the solace of the battered old armchair, more puzzled, more vexed in mind, more dissatisfied with myself than I had ever been before.

It was in this frame of mind that I finally drove away from Sampigehalli the next morning, after recounting my latest adventure to my village friends. All of them, without exception, had nodded and wagged their heads and repeated in varying phrases the same words, 'We told you so.' The man who had annoyed me the day before said in exultation, 'You were angry with me yesterday. Today you are indeed lucky to be alive. Fate spared you a second time from joining the others who have been drowned in that well. That was because your time had not yet come. But do not sit there for a third night, Sir. For then it might be your time and you will surely jump into the well.'

I might have argued with him and pointed out that, if indeed it was my fate to throw myself into the well on the third night, I would have been compelled to remain at Sampigehalli, whether he or I or anybody else wanted me to leave or not.

Six

The Strange Case of The Gerhetti Leopard

GERHETTI IS A TINY VILLAGE OF NOT EVEN A DOZEN HUTS, LYING A mile or so from the forest track that wandered in an almost southerly direction from Anchetty to the larger village of Pennagram in the Salem district of Madras state.

It is only seven miles from Anchetty, but to reach Gerhetti your car has to descend the winding track at an almost impossible angle, guaranteed to impose a severe strain upon the best of braking systems, bump across a couple of very rocky streambeds that hold no water for over nine months in the year, and then clamber up an equally winding and impossible gradient. In the old days of the Model T Ford, which were my young days, it would give me childish and utter delight to sit at the steering wheel of my beloved 'Lissom Lizzie', the name painted in large letters upon her rear, press hard upon the left of the three pedals that controlled her, and attain the summit in clouds of steam, billowing from a red-hot engine and a boiling radiator.

On one occasion Lissom Lizzie climbed half-way up that gradient but could not climb any more. I was bound for the forest lodges of Muttur, a dozen miles beyond Gerhetti, where I had arranged with Byra, my aboriginal poojaree friend, to help to catch a crocodile that had become stranded in the Forest department well situated upon the banks of the Chinnar river, and I had to keep that appointment. What was I to do? Praise be to Henry Ford and the wonderful adaptability of the Model T. I turned the car round, placed the hand-lever to my right in a neutral position, pressed upon the centre pedal of the three (which was the reverse pedal in the Model T) and climbed that fearful gradient backwards with ease! The car was strained and so was my neck, but we made it.

A mile or so after reaching the top of the gradient, a narrower track veers to the right, the jungle crowding in upon both sides. Another mile along this track brings one to a water hole on the right side, immediately opposite the driveway leading to the Gerhetti Forest Lodge on the left. This is a delightful little bungalow which, in those days, had but one snag. It was always locked, the reason being that the caretaker, who was also carefree and careless, and did not give a damn anyway, was away on holiday, sometimes at Anchetty but more generally at Pennagram which, although poor of soil, was rich in girls. And thereby hangs a tale.

In the old British days there was a district Forest Officer (D.F.O.) of the old school type in charge of this area. He had a double-barrelled name, was stickler for rules, and did not like me anyway. The cause of this dislike I could never fathom. Perhaps he disapproved of my wandering about the forests of which he had charge as if they were my own, and he showed his disdain, upon the few occasions I was unfortunate enough to have speak to him, by looking at me distantly, as if I were something the cat had left on the doorstep. This gentleman insisted that before occupying any of the Forest department bungalows in his area, I should apply for his permission and obtain the same in writing. As a matter of fact, this was the rule and still is. But ask anyone who has lived in India and he will agree with me that rules are made only to be broken. Everyone breaks them and enjoys the process. The stricter the rule, the more it has to be broken. At least, everyone seems to feel this way in India; and that being the case, why not I?

However, to avoid coming to grips unnecessarily with this man, I gave him on one occasion a full month's notice in advance, with my request for permission to occupy the Gerhetti Forest Lodge. As I possessed a shooting licence for the area, he could not very well refuse. Back came his written permission in due course, but along with it quite a substantial paragraph warning me not to try to break the rules and regulations in any way, not to cause a forest fire by throwing matches about, not to fail to pay the prescribed rent for the days I was in occupation and so forth.

The glad day dawned at last and I set forth in my Model T for Gerhetti. Fortunately, I had just reached the top of the ghat, when down came the rain in torrents. Model T's never worried about bad weather, and it took more than raindrops to stop a vehicle of that sturdy vintage. By the same standards they expected a passenger to care nothing too, for they were without adequate protection of the sides.

So I was soaking wet when I arrived at the front door of the Gerhetti lodge, to find it fast closed with a lock of outstanding size. And the carefree caretaker was away on his revels.

I had the written permission of the nasty D.F.O. to occupy the place. I had given him a month's notice. His office should have notified the caretaker to welcome me with open doors. Nevertheless, I was locked out. This old bounder, who was so hot upon other people keeping to the rules, had himself foundered! Besides, the rain was coming down in buckets, saturating me and my equipment.

So I staggered around the building and discovered that the bathroom door at the back was weak on its hinges. I put my shoulder to it and heaved it off its hinges. The door burst open, and that was how I got into the bungalow.

I camped at Gerhetti for the full week for which I had come, but in all that time the caretaker never showed up. Apparently his dates at Pennagram were more important. Then the time came for me to leave. The bathroom door, which had left its hinges 'by accident', could only be pulled to and closed. And there was no one present to receive the rent.

From Bangalore, I sent the rent by post to the D.F.O. and made out a strong case against his carefree caretaker. The storm, I claimed, had 'caused me, in seeking shelter, to slip and fall in the mud, whereupon in an effort to save myself my hand contacted the bathroom door. Unfortunately this mere pressure had caused the hinges, which were of ancient vintage, to give way and the door had opened'. The implication was that the security of this government building was not all it should be.

But the careless caretaker turned out to be less carefree than I had thought. He and his boss worked out as foul a plot as ever was hatched against an innocent, upright, law-abiding, Christian gentleman! The teak armchair from the bungalow and the zinc bathtub in the bathroom were missing. They had been stolen! Either I had stolen them, in which case I was liable under the rules to be prosecuted and jailed for breaking into a government building and stealing part of its furniture.

Or my irresponsible action in breaking into the building had rendered it insecure and unsafe, whereafter theft of government property had inevitably ensued, for which I was entirely responsible. I was called upon to reply within seven days, whereafter very severe action was proposed to be taken against me. Not a word was said about the caretaker's absence.

I thought fast. Had the D.F.O. been a less unpleasant individual I would have offered to pay for the missing articles. As matters stood, any such offer would be pounced upon as a clear admission of guilt. Furthermore, no thief in India would go to such a benighted spot to steal an ancient armchair and leaky bathtub, both of which would be of no value, either for his own use or for sale to any villager.

Obviously, the articles had been removed by the carefree but crafty caretaker, or by order of the D.F.O. himself, in order to 'fix' me. I could hardly believe that an English officer would do this kind of thing, however much he disliked me. So the culprit was obviously the caretaker himself. He had done this as a retaliatory act against me, when called upon to explain his absence, as reported by me. But where could the articles be? He would not have tried to sell them, because that would have left a trail. So he must have hidden them.

The obvious answer was that he had hidden them in his girlfriend's house. So off I went to Pennagram and arrived after midnight, when all were asleep. I aroused my henchaman Ranga, put the case to him and asked him where we should start searching. The question also arose as to how the caretaker could have brought the two cumbersome articles from Gerhetti to Pennagram, a distance of twelve miles. Ranga offered the answer without hesitation. In a bullock-cart, carrying felled bamboos!

From the forest around Gerhetti there was a constant flow of bamboos to Pennagaram, where the Forest department had a timber depot. As an official of the service, although a very minor one, it would be easy for this caretaker to persuade a cartman or two to convey the articles, concealed under the bamboos in a cart, to Pennagram.

More fortunately, Ranga, who had once been a cartman himself, was well acquainted with his confreres. Late though the hour was, he set out to question those that were in town and returned by 4 a.m. to give me the good news that not only had he succeeded in finding two cart-drivers, each of whom had brought one of the articles in his conveyance, but had also found out where they were hidden.

This was an ungodly hour to awaken any solitary sentry, snugly asleep in a police station, but that is exactly what we did soon after. The constable was very indignant. Moreover, claiming to be alone in charge, he declared that he could not leave his post. But when a certain exchange had been made his conscience was softened. Leaving us in charge of the station, he hastened to the police lines and shortly returned with a confederate, who had dressed himself in full uniform as befitted the occasion. This policeman accompanied Ranga and myself to the tiny house occupied, I do admit, by an exceedingly becoming lass. I was obliged to admire the taste in women of the careless but carefree caretaker. But, more important at that moment, there was the old teak armchair and the zinc bathtub, as large as life in a corner of her tiny abode.

The poor girl was arrested and the two articles removed to the police station. Later that morning the sub-inspector (S.I.) arrived, and to him I submitted two written documents. The first was a letter of complaint regarding the theft, back-dated by a few days. The second a letter of appreciation, commending and congratulating the S.I. He was delighted. I asked him, as a favour, to release the girl and capture the caretaker; but looking at me with disapproving eyes, he said he could not do that, for the girl was 'an accessory after the fact', even if she was a comely wench.

To the D.F.O. my lawyer sent a notice for defamation claiming a fabulous sum as damages, with a copy to the Chief Conservator of Forests at Madras. But time was kind to the poor fellow. He was on the verge of retirement anyhow and he disappeared overnight on furlough, from which he never returned. What gave me the greatest satisfaction, however, was the 'armchair' detection I had displayed in identifying the culprit.

You must forgive me for this digression, but my excuse is the need to let you know that even in the jungles we have our problems. India is a country that demands of its inhabitants a sharpness of wit. And this brings me to another tale.

Ticketless train-travel in India is rife. To try to combat it, the authorities institute many checks, so that in the course of even a short journey one my be required to show one's ticket to 'travelling ticket inspectors' a number of times. Now, an acquaintance of mine who emigrated from India to the U.K. was agreeably surprised to find that there were no ticket-checks on the suburban line on which he travelled to work daily. So he bought no ticket and travelled free for some months until one day he was caught.

All this, however, has nothing whatever to do with the strange leopard I meant to tell you about.

About two furlongs behind the forest lodge at Gerhetti is the small hamlet of the same name, consisting of half a dozen huts. The occupants are woodcutters, who earn a supplementary wage by working as coolies for the Forest department, repairing the road, stealing sandalwood and timber when they can, and poaching deer in the summer months when there is no water in the jungle and the animals come late at night to drink at the water hole which, I have already told you, stands a short distance in front of the lodge at the point where the 'driven-in' turns away from the main track.

The people in this hamlet had a few sheep—keeping goats in a forest area was strictly forbidden in British days, due to the destruction wrought by these animals upon seedlings—and a few fowl. There had been some cattle, but tigers and panthers had wiped them out.

The leopard in this story, being an animal of only average size, had begun its depredations by stealing a fowl here and there when they wandered from the huts to feed among the fallen leaves at the edge of the jungle. The next stage was reached when the leopard decided to go further, raiding the hut in which the fowls were kept by creeping through the wall of thorns and eating up as many as possible, killing or severely injuring the rest of the birds just for fun. It now had to turn to the sheep, there being nothing else to eat, and these it started killing one by one, whenever opportunity offered. I had been told about this leopard, but as it was reported to be quite a harmless beast—indeed, almost friendly in its habits—I had thought no more about it.

The first time I laid eyes on this animal was about 4-30 one evening. I was reclining in the armchair on the veranda of the lodge, sipping tea, when a movement at the water hole, the farther bank of which was visible from where I was sitting, caught my attention. The sun was shining brightly and the day had been a hot one. Normally, no wild animal would be afoot. The movement came again and some yellow object thrust itself out from the wall of reeds that bordered the pool. I could not make out what it was.

Perhaps a minute later, without perceptible further movement, the object turned into a panther as it emerged fully from behind the reeds. It was gazing fixedly towards the forest bungalow, knowing no doubt that if there was any danger about, it would be in this direction. I did not move in my chair. After a close scrutiny that lasted perhaps three minutes, the leopard decided all was safe. It stooped to drink, but stopped twice to look up at the bungalow to make sure that all was well.

The second time I saw this animal was when it chased a junglecock into a tree. I was returning from an early-morning prowl when the junglecock emitted its shrill alarm cry a few yards ahead and flapped heavily upwards.

'Cekh! Cekh! Cekh! Cekh!' screeched the cock, and I halted in my tracks. No doubt it had seen or heard me. But I was wrong, for an instant later a panther bounded out of the undergrowth and raced after the bird, to clamber quickly but futilely up the tree on which it had settled. The junglecock screeched again and this time flew far away, while the leopard, warned that all was not well, turned its head to look back sharply.

That was when it saw me. Releasing its hold, the panther fell back lightly to the ground, arched its back for a moment while curling its tail high above, for all the world like a friendly tabby, then turned and padded silently away, disappearing in the bushes.

The third time I saw this animal under peaceful circumstances was when I was chugging along in my Model T. I had passed the Gerhetti bungalow and the water hole, and was continuing along the track which, it will be remembered, branches off from the main route to Muttur and Pennagram.

No cars came that way in those days and bullockcarts were few. Cattle passed now and again, in the hot weather when the forest had dried up, on their way to the village of Natrapalayam and the Cauvery river, seven or eight miles away, where there was still some grazing to be had. The few people living in this area carried their loads on their heads or, when these were too heavy, on the backs of ponies or donkeys, the latter for preference because they were cheaper. The branches of the trees met above the narrow trail, for which reason the already tattered hood of the Model T had to be put down and the windshield lowered. Nevertheless, it was often needful to lie sideways on the front seat to allow a bough to scrape over the steering wheel.

Turning a sharp corner, I saw close ahead a fairly stout branch extending across the track, and lying along this bough was a panther that had evidently taken up this position in the hope of being able to ambush any animal passing beneath. It had not heard the car as I had been coursing downhill, semidepressing the left-hand pedal of Lissom Lizzie that served as gear-cum-clutch.

The panther rose on the branch when I was almost beneath it, then panicked and sprang clumsily, clearing the rear seat but landing on the back of the car, from where it took off again into the bushes, but not before the claws of its hind feet, in finding a purchase to make that second leap, tore a gaping hole in the already tattered upholstery.

There is a village along this track named Jungalpalayam. It is about half-way between Gerhetti and Natrapalayam, being two and a half miles from each. I knew it as the 'happy village', for the folks living in this hamlet, although far from civilization, medical help, schools, places of amusement and so-called cooperative centres that never seem to cooperate in anything, were always contented and laughing. It did one good to visit this little place and chat with its inhabitants. They seemed singularly free from the political consciousness that is such a dominating factor in India.

Each month, when the moon is at its full, and on two days before and two days after, the villagers would play games in the moonlight, commencing an hour or so after their evening meal, which might be at about eight o'clock, and continuing till midnight. Modesty forbade that the men and women should play together, so the women would form a circle in the centre of the village, while the men would go to the village threshing floor, a cleared space about fifty yards to one side of the hamlet. The women would mostly sing and dance, while the men played a variety of games, the most popular of which was *balchik* or *kabbaddee*, although in this particular hamlet it was known as *goddoogoddoo*, a form of the popular game of salts, played widely throughout India.

The rules of this game are simple. A straight line is drawn with charcoal on the ground, and two teams of from five to seven members each assemble on either side. Play starts when by a member from, let us say, Team A (although the villagers call the teams by such names as 'frogs', 'grasshoppers', or even less complimentary ones like 'illegitimates' or 'bastards') approaches the base line, muttering repeatedly and rapidly the word *kabbaddee* (or *goddoogoddoo*), crosses it while still muttering incessantly, audibly, and with his fingertips lightly touches a member of Team B (perhaps called the 'impotents' or 'eunuchs' or some other rude name), then springs back to the charcoal base line before any of the members of Team B can hold him down.

The point is that the man from Team A must keep on muttering *kabbaddee* (or *goddoogoddoo*) loudly and without ceasing. Should a member or more of Team B succeed in grabbing him and holding him down, so that he cannot get back to the charcoal base line, a point is lost to his team also.

After the man from Team A has scored a success or failure, as the case may be, the turn of approaching the line falls to a man from Team B, and so on. The winning side is that which first attains a predetermined number of points, usually

TALES FROM THE INDIAN JUNGLE

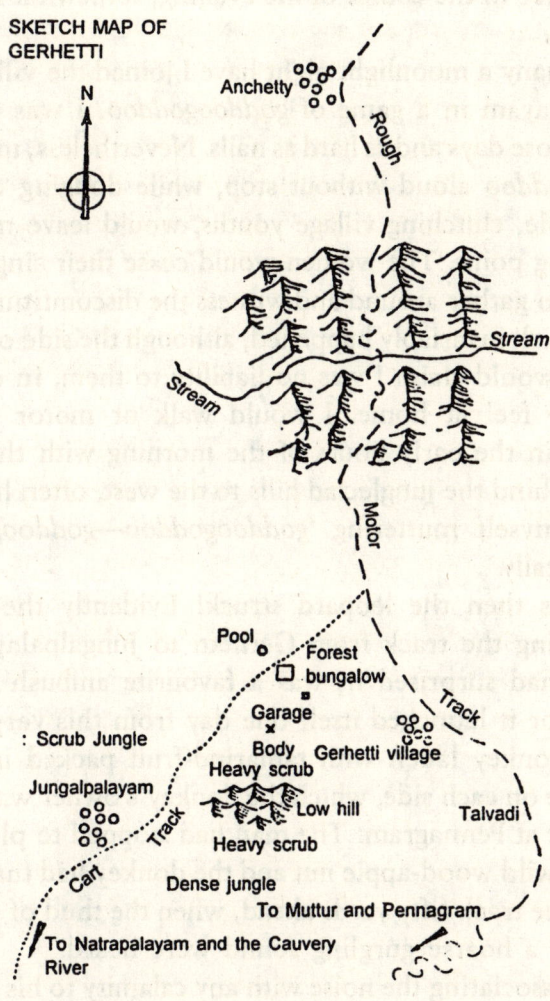

twenty-one. Sometimes a small bet is attached to the result, each member of a side ending up by winning—or losing—half a rupee in the course of the evening, somewhat less than a shilling.

On many a moonlight night have I joined the villagers of Jungalpalayam in a game of *goddoogoddoo*. I was a young man in those days and as hard as nails. Nevertheless, muttering *goddoogoddoo* aloud without stop, while dodging to avoid eager, agile, clutching village youths, would leave my lungs at bursting point. The women would cease their singing and dancing to gather around and witness the discomfiture of the *dorai*, which invariably happened, although the side on which I played would claim I was no liability to them, in order to make me feel at home. I would walk or motor back to Gerhetti in the early hours of the morning with the moon setting behind the jungleclad hills to the west, often horrified to find myself muttering '*goddoogoddoo—goddoogoddoo*' automatically.

It was then the leopard struck! Evidently the branch overhanging the track from Gerhetti to Jungalpalayam, on which I had surprised it, was a favourite ambush for this animal, for it launched itself one day from this very bough upon a donkey laden with tamarind-fruit packed into two sacks, one on each side, which the donkey's owner was taking to market at Pennagram. The man had stopped to pluck and munch a wild wood-apple nut and the donkey had turned the bend in the track fifty yards ahead, when the thud of a falling body and a hoarse gurgling sound were heard.

Not associating the noise with any calamity to his donkey, the man feared an elephant might be ahead of him. For this reason, he approached the corner slowly, while keeping a sharp lookout all round. But to his horror he saw his poor donkey dead and dragged to one side of the track, with the panther crouched against its belly, its fangs still buried in the donkey's throat, enjoying the warm blood that trickled from the severed vein.

Then the man, who ordinarily would have run away and indeed was already prepared to run from the elephant he expected to see, lost his temper and rushed at the panther whirling the stave he held in his hand. The leopard, excited by the kill it had just made, with the warmth of its victim against him and the warmer blood trickling through its jaws, was in no mood to relinquish his feast. In fact, I suppose it actually had no opportunity to do so before the angry man was upon him.

The stave thudded down across the panther's back and the panther leapt upon the man seeking for his throat, but being diverted by the long black beard this villager had grown, bit the man's chest instead. The man lost his balance, toppled backwards, and began to scream.

I happened to have come to Gerhetti at that time, but was far away at the moment, on the slopes of a hillside behind the hamlet, searching for a particular kind of beetle for my cousin who is an ardent collector. I heard those screams faintly, and thinking some man was being done to death by an elephant, ran in their direction. Most regrettably, I had left my rifle in the forest lodge. People who go catching beetles do not ordinarily carry firearms, and there was no danger to be envisaged in the area at the time from a man-eater or rogue elephant.

The screams I had heard so faintly had stopped by now, so that I was left guessing as to the point of their origin; but working on the belief that an elephant had attacked a man, I guessed that whatever had happened had taken place somewhere along the track to Jungalpalayam. So I ran in its general direction, stumbling through undergrowth and between bushes and trees till at last I reached the track.

There was nothing to be seen. Should I turn right or left? The sound had seemed so far away that I decided to turn towards Jungalpalayam and veered left, padding along as noiselessly as possible and expecting to come upon an enraged elephant at any moment.

Calling aloud but receiving no answer, I had traversed the better part of a furlong when I came upon the victim lying beside his dead donkey. The panther had left him; perhaps his screams had frightened the animal away, or may be at this, its first encounter with one of the human race, the leopard still felt some of its inherent fear of man. The man's eyes flickered open when I called to him and he managed to tell me his name was Subramaniam, that he had come from Pennagram for tamarind, and of how the panther had come to attack him. Then he lost consciousness. I lifted him over my shoulder with the intention of carrying him to the forest lodge, from whence I could take him in my car to hospital at Bangalore.

Alas, I had just reached the bungalow and laid him on the floor of the veranda, when he began to show signs of imminent death, while blood began to pour from his mouth and the terrible wounds in his chest. It was clear that his lungs had been punctured, and as I picked him up again to put him in my car he died. I will not dwell on the trouble I had in telling the authorities all that had happened, but while proceedings were still going on I returned to warn the people of Gerhetti, Jungalpalayam and Natrapalayam that the leopard might possibly turn dangerous.

Surprisingly enough, nothing happened for some months. Then the dreaded epidemic of cholera came to Pennagram and from there spread far and wide, even as far as Natrapalayam. Two or three persons died in this remote village, and because they had died of an infectious disease the villagers threw the bodies into the jungle to rot instead of burying or burning the corpses as in the normal way.

Perhaps the panther ate some of this flesh, although no one knew for certain, as no one would be bold enough to go near such a corpse. Otherwise the advent of the man-eater and the reason for the animal becoming one are shrouded in mystery.

The trouble began when a boy who had gone to the water hole at Gerhetti with his pitcher did not return. There was no reason for his absence other than supposed idleness, so his father went to look for him in the evening, carrying a stout stick to lay across the boy's back while he was still asleep. The father found his son's broken water-pot, dropped when it was full and therefore upon the return journey. He saw the boy's blood on the grass and the imprint of a panther's pugs where it had been walking down the main track before it saw the boy and pounced upon him from the wayside. A drag-mark indicated in which direction the body had been taken.

Panthers being far smaller, shorter and weaker than tiger, are unable to carry away their kills clear of the ground. They have to drag their dead victims along, for which reason they do not go far before starting to eat. Tigers, which are not only taller but immeasurably stronger, are able to lift a victim as heavy as a buffalo clear of the ground. Moreover, when a tiger intends to take its kill to some distant spot before starting to eat, it seizes its prey by the neck and, with a quick turn of its head, throws the dead body over its back, thereby supporting the weight evenly on all four legs. In this manner, tigers have been known to carry their kills for great distances, so that in the case of a man-eating tiger, their human kills, as often as not, cannot be found.

Returning to my story: the father hastened back to Gerhetti hamlet, called on its few inhabitants for help and, armed with sticks and stones, the small party followed the drag-mark. They had not far to go. What was left of the boy lay under a bush just on the other side of the water hole.

From that day nobody would move alone in the jungle. At least four men would form a party, arming themselves with wood-choppers, axes or stout staves. The news spread to Jungalpalayam, Natrapalayam, Pennagram and Anchetty. Everyone was on the lookout for the panther.

Strangely enough, the theft of an occasional fowl or sheep by a leopard still went on. Most of the people in the area had, at one time or the other, seen the harmless panther I had myself encountered upon three occasions, so nobody associated it with the animal that had struck the tamarind-merchant down and had later devoured the boy. The man-eater was thought to be some passing beast, or a leopard that had become inordinately hungry to the verge of starvation, due to sickness or wounds. A few even subscribed to the notion that the panther was mad, having eaten of the cholera corpses. For man-eaters in this region were practically unknown; there had been a couple of man-eating tigers in the past, but they had operated far away, in the region of Kempekerai. As for a man-eating panther, nobody could remember having heard of one.

A third victim followed the boy, this time a woman who was returning from the well after bathing her two-year-old child. The water in this well was very brackish and could not be used for drinking or cooking; it could be used only for washing purposes. Unaccountably the leopard did not touch the child, contenting itself with killing the mother and dragging her corpse into a *nullah* a few yards beyond the well. The wails of the infant attracted the villagers, who went to investigate.

With this tragedy, the alarm spread in right earnest far and wide. Woodcutting and all traffic in the jungle came to a dead stop, and the poachers who by night haunted the few waterholes in the forest put away their muskets and vintage muzzle-loaders until the advent of more propitious times.

My tenant at Anchetty, a young man named Narayan who cultivated the small plot of land I own there but has never bothered to pay rent, brought me the news, with a request from the *patel* of Anchetty, who was also nominally the head of the Gerhetti hamlet, to come and shoot the panther. I was tied up with urgent work at Bangalore just then and told Narayan I would come in a week, sending him back with a message to the *patel* to this effect, and an additional word of warning to the people of Gerhetti to move about only in groups and never alone. Man-eating panthers as a rule, being inherently cowardly, attack only under cover of darkness, unlike the man-eating tiger, which is braver and bolder and attacks at any time. In this respect the Gerhetti leopard was different; it had taken all its three victims in broad daylight.

On the day before I arrived at Gerhetti the panther struck for the fourth time, and the victim turned out to be the son of the bungalow-watcher, that carefree character who had tried to frame me with the armchair and bathtub. The panther took its victim in the early hours of the morning.

After the affair of the bathtub and armchair, the father had lost his job with the Forest department and had become a minor forest contractor, purchasing at public auction the right to gather fruit, various medicinal seeds and leaves, henna, honey, deers' horns that had been shed, and other lesser items. In this business the son played an active part, and at the time of his death the lad had come to Gerhetti to induce some of the poojarees living there to help him to raid the combs of the wild rock-bees that had hung their hives on the higher rock-faces of a low mountain named Periyamalai, some four miles from Gerhetti.

The lad, whose name was Nataraj, had successfully accomplished his mission and had succeeded in gathering some four or five kerosene tins of this wild honey. On an average, each of these tins held the equivalent of twenty-four bottles of honey, each of which in turn would sell for three rupees. The trip would thus earn him about three hundred rupees.

Well satisfied, he returned with the tins to Gerhetti, where he decided to spend the night, as rumours had reached the hamlet that a herd of wild elephants had recently come up from the Cauvery river and were roaming in the ravines of Talvadi, through which the road to the market at Pennagram passed. Nataraj had no intention of risking his precious honey by exposing it to wild elephants.

The forest lodge (the one from which his father had taken the furniture) was locked, but the garage was open: in fact, it had no doors! So Nataraj decided to spend the night in the garage, along with his tins of honey.

In the early hours of the morning, the people in the hamlet of Gerhetti said they heard his screams for help, but being few in number and moreover unarmed, they fastened the doorways of their huts more securely and waited for dawn. With daylight, a number of them eventually came to the garage to see what had happened. Nataraj was nowhere to be seen. Signs of a struggle were evident. There was blood on the earthen floor and one of the tins of honey had been overturned, attracting thousands of ants. There was also the impression of something heavy having been dragged across the ground and out of the open door into the jungle, which began ten yards behind.

The panther had not bothered to take him very far. His head, arms and legs, the portions that a panther, and even a man-eating tiger, is rather fastidious about and leaves for a later meal, lay scattered about in mute testimony of the panther's appetite. Rather small, as the pugs indicated the marauder to be, it had eaten a lot of meat.

I arrived at Gerhetti at ten that morning and was in time to see the remains before the police turned up from Anchetty and began their tedious and fruitless questioning. Why had I come? they asked. Had I an arms licence? A gun licence? A car licence? A driver's licence? Any question but those that concerned the panther.

I asked them to leave the remains where they were and go away as soon as possible, since this would give me a chance of sitting over what was left of Nataraj and perhaps shooting the man-eater. There was a possibility that it might return in the afternoon, and there was also the probability that it would return after dark.

The *daffedar* (head-constable or sergeant), who represented the party in the absence of his Sub-Inspector, flatly refused. He said the remains would have to stay where they were till his boss could see them for himself. And as he had to return to Anchetty, he would leave the two constables who had accompanied him to watch over these remains till the Sub-Inspector turned up, later in the evening perhaps, more probably the next morning.

At hearing the *daffedar's* words, there was unanimous disapproval of his scheme by his subordinates. One of them stated with some heat that he had not eaten his breakfast that morning, and certainly could not wait for it till next day. The other man pleaded that he was suffering from a servere cold. To this the *daffedar* rejoined that he had not heard him cough even once that day. Whereupon the constable coughed prolongedly!

Orders are orders, the *daffedar* affirmed sternly, and stalked away, to mount his bicycle and ride away to Anchetty. The two policemen stared at each other and at me, till I made them a sign in unspoken, but otherwise universally known language, that gave them the general idea; 'chins up, boys; every cloud has a silver lining'. At least this one did for them, and in a very literal sense, for with the *daffedar's* departure the two policemen were only too willing themselves to depart even if it was only as far as the nearby hamlet. Anything to get out of this dreadful place, away from those blank, staring eyes in the dead, accusing face. I was left to my own devices and the immediate problem of finding somewhere to hide and await the killer's possible return.

As so frequently happens there was no place that offered concealment. This is understandable as man-eaters—both tigers and panthers—carry or drag their kills into sheltered, dense undergrowth in order that they may enjoy their meal undisturbed. They do not leave their kills under some convenient tree from which they can be shot! There was a thick growth of lantana bushes and the panther had dragged the body of its victim between two of these bushes, where it had eaten most of it. Any attempt at constructing a hide in the vicinity would stick out like a sore thumb, and the panther would never put in an appearance. All said and done, my contemplated ambush seemed out of the question.

I thought and thought, and finally came up with an idea. It is rather difficult to describe, so I have produced a sketch which I hope may convey some notion of my scheme.

To the north of the spot where lay what was left of Nataraj was the forest lodge and the garage. To the east, not very far away, stood the hamlet and more or less open ground. To the west was light scrub, through which led the *path* from Gerhetti to Jungalpalayam. To the south was heavier scrub, flanked by a low hill. I had already walked along the *path* to the western side. No tracks of the panther coming or going showed on the sandy surface. So the man-eater had come from the hillock to the south and had returned that way.

My plan was to hide in the garage till I could hear it eating—at least I hoped I would be able to hear it. Then I would tiptoe out of the garage to the front of the bungalow, down the pathway to Jungalpalayam, and cut back from it to get between the panther and the hillock, in which direction I was sure the feline would beat its retreat.

Finally, when in a satisfactory position, I would throw some stones (previously gathered and kept ready in my pocket) as hard as possible in the direction of the garage, hoping the missile would sail over the feasting feline and fall beyond it. This would frighten it and cause it to come bounding blindly towards its only line of retreat, southwards towards the hillock, where I would be in hiding and awaiting it. Panthers have no sense of smell, so it would not be able to scent me while I tiptoed down the pathway. But they have acute hearing and it might hear me if I made the slightest sound. That was a risk I would have to take.

As an afterthought, I decided to tear up the khaki shirt I was wearing and hang strips of it on the bushes bordering the pathway, so that if the leopard did happen to break in that direction (towards the west), the sight of these strips of cloth fluttering in the breeze might turn it back again towards the south, the hillock—and me! It would not break towards the east because of the hamlet, or towards the north, as the bungalow stood there.

I do not usually tear up my shirts, particularly when wearing nothing underneath, but there was no alternative, as I was carrying no rags of any kind and the spare shirt I had brought in the car was a shade better than the one upon my back. So I removed my shirt and tore it into long narrow strips. In this way, I made some eight or ten lengths which I proceeded to tie to the lantana and other bushes bordering the pathway. They were out of sight of where the panther would be eating, but it would immediately spot them if it decided to break westwards towards the pathway, when I began throwing my stones from that direction. It would have been better if the strips had been of white or coloured material, rather than khaki, but one does not wear a white shirt when hunting.

Lastly, I went to the little hamlet to the east of the bungalow and cautioned its inhabitants, including the two constables, not to stir out for the rest of the day. I could hardly tell you my advice was unnecessary. With the killing and eating of Nataraj within a few yards of their huts, the inmates had already shut themselves up as securely as they could.

So that it should not be in the view of the panther, I pushed the Model T in which I had come to the front of the forest lodge. From there it was out of sight of the garage and any panther that might show itself from behind. And I took all the things I had in the car in the form of bedding, food, water, and the shotgun that I had brought as a spare weapon, into the garage. Here I would stay till daylight the following morning, hoping against hope that the leopard would return to what was left of its meal.

All this had taken up to half an hour to noon, and the sun blazed down mercilessly on the dry forest that throbbed to the sound of the cicadas, the cooing of the lesser speckled doves, and the calls of the black-bodied and orange-winged crow-pheasant that was diligently searching for birds' eggs, lizards and caterpillars by the edge of the jungle a few paces away.

The hours dragged by and the heat grew more intense, rising from the ground in shimmering waves. Even the crow-pheasant felt it and gave up his search, although the tireless cicadas continued to drone out their monotonous dirge.

The hours came and went while I strained my ears for the sound of crunching bones that would announce the killer's return. Not a sound did I hear other than the scream of a king vulture high in the sky. It must have spotted the remains long ago, but being those of a human being the 'king' had delayed its earthwards plunge that would be an invitation to all other vultures for miles around to foregather for a feast.

Five o'clock came, bringing a noticeable cooling of the atmosphere and a sharpening of the vulture's appetite. It delayed no longer, but plummeted to earth with the rattling rush of the wind through the tough feathers of its outstretched wings, to land with a faint thud in the vicinity of the kill. Soon other vultures would follow and nothing would be left of the panther's kill beyond cleanly-picked bones. The leopard, if it should come that night, would find nothing to eat and would wander away!

Four or five vultures joined the king at intervals, although the huge birds still hesitated to begin their meal. Nataraj's head, being left intact with its staring eyes, kept them away.

Time dragged by, and with the advent of evening the chorus of roosting birds began its tumultuous farewell to the day that is music to the ears of those who love the jungle. 'Kuck-kya-kya-khuckm!' crowed junglecocks from the foot of the hillock; 'Kee-kok! Kee-kok! Kee-kok!' challenged a partridge higher up, and 'Kee-kok-kok! Kee-kok-kok! Kee-kok-kok!' came his rival's reply from the summit of the hill. 'Wack! Wack! kuker-rawack!' growled spurfowl to each other, while far away a peacock joined the chorus 'Zank! Mia! Mia! Mia-oo-ow!'

There comes a heavy flapping of wings as the 'king' and its equally cowardly companions rose ponderously from the ground to perch on some neighbouring tree. They would wait till morning and their appetites would certainly be sharpened.

Darkness began to fall; there was a deep silence that could almost be felt. Then 'Chuck! Chuck! Chuck! Chuck-ooooo!' trilled the nightjar and 'Whooo! Whooo! Whooo!' hooted a horned owl. I fixed the two clamps that held my torch firmly to the barrel of my rifle and adjusted the beam to form a spot. Soon after that it was night. The leopard had not put in an appearance and my deeply-laid scheme appeared to be coming to naught.

I will not weary you with a description of the half-dozen hours that followed. Indeed, there is nothing to tell you, for nothing happened. The moon, that was now on the wane, had risen late, and should the panther come to its kill I would not be able to follow my plan, for the night would not be bright enough to see it when it came bounding up the hillside after being frightened by the stones I was going to throw. I would either have to let it eat, or to try creeping up on it, something that would be very difficult to accomplish and was not at all to my liking.

With these reflections I must have dozed off. Then something awoke me with a start. I could not say what it was. It was not a sound I could hear, but a feeling of deadly peril seemed to close over me. It was oppressive and heavy; it could almost be felt.

For a moment I put it down to imagination, but the sense of danger remained and became very real. It seemed to close down upon me. Without doubt something, somewhere, was threatening me.

Then I realized what it was. The man-eater was close by! That strange sixth sense that I have felt in times of extreme peril, and was to save my life so may times thereafter, was telling me as if in spoken words that the leopard was about to attack.

I closed my hands over my .405 and, without moving, I strained my eyes to look in every direction. Moonlight framed the rectangular doorway of the garage, with the rear of the forest bungalow in the centre of the scene. Then something moved ever so slightly at the bottom left-hand corner of this moonlit screen. Something black and slightly undulating. I could not quite see what it was, because it lay within the area of darkness thrown by the garage in which I was hiding and only the background of dim moonlight had drawn my attention to the faint movement near by.

The shadow moved ever so slightly and the faintest hissing sound reached my straining ears. A cobra? Or could it be the man-eater?

Luckily I had made not the least movement. Had I done so, the creature might have attacked when it realized that it had been discovered in its attempt to surprise me. But now movement—and very quick movement at that—was called for.

Springing to my feet I threw myself backwards, and was brought to an abrupt halt by the wall behind me. At the same time, I pointed the muzzle of my rifle forwards and pressed the switch of the torch. Although the beam blinded it, the man-eater launched its attack.

In describing the few moments that followed, I should write humbly and with a sense of gratitude. For it is not well to boast that 'with one shot I killed it', for any person even with a rudimentary experience of wild animals will tell you that a sambar can carry nine bullets in its body and move for miles, a bison fifteen, a wild elephant sometimes twenty-five, and a tiger or panther a great many before it falls dead. And it can tear you to pieces before it dies.

Then again the cartridge may be a dud, the cap may misfire, or the animal may turn aside just as you fire. Anything can happen. Suffice it to say that my bullet hit its mark by sheer luck and killed the leopard even while it was in midair, although to make certain I fired two more into the writhing body at my feet.

The sub-inspector arrived creditably early next morning. He was not happy to find that most of Nataraj's bones, including his head, had been taken away by the hyenas and jackals during the night.

Seven

The Lakkavalli Man-Eater

IF YOU WERE TO VISIT THE TOWNSHIP OF TARIKERE IN THE WESTERN parts of Mysore state, you would find two motorable roads open to you. On these, at a distance of not more than four or five miles from the town itself, if you had the time to stop and listen, you would hear many stories from the villagers about the depredations of tigers.

The first of these roads leads roughly southwestwards from Tarikere, passing in a curve through the village of Lingadhalli, to the south of the high horseshoe range of mountains known as the Baba Budans, crossing its lower slopes at the hamlet of Santaveri, and continuing to the town of Chikmagalur, about twenty miles away.

The second road leads northwestwards, passing the eastern and northeastern slopes of those same mountains, before curving through two hamlets, named Lakkavalli and Umblebyle, to the town of Bhadravati which itself is barely ten miles from Tarikere, by a third and more direct road.

The first and second roads in this way circumvent the southern and eastern slopes of the Baba Budan range, and the tigers that cross the hump of the mountains from the deep valley to the west and north, ringed in by these mountains, find themselves either in the vicinity of the hamlet of Santaveri on the southern road, or in the area known as the Laulbagh, west of the eastern road.

These should be kept well in mind: the hamlet of Santaveri and the area known as the Laulbagh. For it was at these places and in the area between them that the adventure with the tiger, about which you are now going to hear, took place. Santaveri, at the height of 4,500 feet above sea level, is a rocky, wild and thickly forested region, while the Laulbagh, perhaps thirty to thirty-five miles away as the crow flies, although more than a thousand feet lower and far less rocky, is correspondingly more thickly forested.

I happened to be visiting my old friend, Dick Bird, who was the postmaster at Santaveri and in private life one of the most famous tiger-hunters in the district, having shot all his tigers with a .12 bore shotgun, spurning the use of a rifle.

'Jock,' he asked me, 'have you heard about the tiger that has turned up around Kemangundi?'

I should explain that Kemangundi is about half-way between Santaveri and the Laulbagh area, and that Dick always calls me 'Jock'. For I have lived in so many places and hunted in so many forests and in so many different climates, with different fauna and flora, and have done so many different things, that I have become a sort of Jekyll and Hyde with a variety of names and nicknames. Very old friends call me 'Jock', 'Scotchie', or 'Scotch', while those met more recently address me as 'Andy', 'Kenneth', 'Ken' and 'KDS'.

At school they called me 'Snake Charmer', because of my fondness for producing these reptiles from inside my shirt and releasing them in such places as Sunday school, the school chapel, the classroom, the dining and study halls, and in cinemas and other congested spots. This was long ago, of course, and I have not been addressed as 'Snake Charmer' for some years, having dropped the habit of releasing the reptiles in public.

Most embarrassing of all, young Dudhwalla, my son's friend, insists upon calling me 'Dot'. Personally, I do not see the least resemblance or slightest connection between myself and 'any small mark with a pen or sharp point', which the dictionary gives as the meaning of 'dot'. So, because of the variety of names by which I am addressed, and being somewhat absentminded, I occasionally become confused and look around for the party addressed.

But to return to Dick's question.

'No,' I replied, 'I haven't been in the area for quite a while. I used to operate a lot in Salem district, as you know, but have had to extend my wanderings to the Nilgiris and into Andhra state. Tigers are still plentiful there.'

'Well, there are quite a few still,' Dick continued. 'But ordinary ones. You know, cattle-lifters. Snatch and grab beasts that haunt the cattle-herds. The animal I have mentioned appears to be a little different, though.'

He then went on to explain that reports from herdsmen stated a very large tiger had recently formed the habit of attacking their herds even while they were still on the roads and being driven to the grazing grounds. Before their very eyes it would seize and kill the fattest and choicest cow and carry her off, slung over its shoulders. This had happened several times and but a few miles from Santaveri itself, on the road I have told you about that led from Tarikere to Chikmagalur. The same sort of thing was reported to have taken place on another, smaller road, leading to a hillock named Kemangundi, which branched off the main Tarikere-Chikmagalur road shortly after passing through the village of Lingadhalli.

Dick went on to relate that two or three herdsmen had attempted to defend their charges by trying to frighten the tiger into relinquishing the carcase of the victim as it was carrying it away, by shouting and throwing stones.

They had soon desisted, however, when this tiger, instead of leaving the carcase and running away, had dropped the cow and charged in their direction—whereupon they had fled. Investigations later showed that the tiger had returned after chasing the herdsmen away, picked up the cow and made off with it. This tiger seemed to favour carrying its victim sluing across its shoulders rather than holding it by the neck or throat and dragging it along the ground.

We discussed this point and agreed that the indications were that either the tiger was an exceptionally bold animal—perhaps an old male—or that it intended carrying the carcase a long way before devouring it, perhaps to some distant cave, or other lair, should it happen to be a tigress with cubs. The animal was wise enough to realize that dragging its kill for a long distance would entail getting it caught in bushes and thorns; it therefore preferred to lift the carcase bodily.

'If only I would get some leave in this damned department,' Dick complained, 'I would bag it by hook or crook. But to get even two or three days' casual leave entails a hell of a fuss. A replacement for me has to be called from Tarikere or Chikmagalur, and the superintendent acts like mad. That's what comes of being a postmaster.'

My visit over, I returned to Bangalore and forgot all about the tiger. In any case, I was not interested in cattle-lifters.

Some months passed until, one morning, I happened to go to the district Magistrate's Court in Bangalore to purchase some government stamp paper, of which I was in need, when I met an Indian gentleman at the stamp vendor's booth. He was grumbling because the particular denomination of stamp paper he wanted was not available, nor were any smaller denominations that would add up to the total amount required.

I purchased the paper I needed, which was of a much higher denomination and was available.

'What name?' the vendor asked me, preparing to enter this on the back of the stamp paper, as required by rules.

'K.D.S. Anderson,' I replied slowly, spelling out the Anderson so that he could write it correctly.

The Indian gentleman with us was staring hard at me. After entering my name and receiving payment, the vendor handed me the stamp paper, and the gentleman spoke.

'Excuse me, sir,' he asked, 'but are you the Mr. Anderson who shoots tigers?'

'Well, I suppose so,' I answered with a smile. 'At least I don't know of any other Anderson who has the bad habit.' Then, as an afterthought I added, 'Perhaps you mean my son?'

'My name is Venkatasubbarao,' the man said. 'I'm the Assistant Chief Engineer working on the Lakkavalli Dam Project, near Tarikere. You see, when the vendor asked your name and you replied that it was Anderson, I pricked up my ears. I've heard of you shooting tigers all over the place. You must really come to Lakkavalli, sir. Come as my guest. I have large quarters and can put you up conveniently. You will be quite comfortable and I will make all the needful *bandobast* for you to shoot the man-eater.'

'What man-eater?' I asked in surprise.

'Haven't you heard?' he answered, evidently taken aback. 'Why, it came out in the newspaper three days ago. But come along and have a coffee with me and I'll tell you all about it.'

There is a restaurant, known as 'Tiffin Room', within a stones's throw of the Magistrate's Court, and there Venkatasubbarao and I went. Over not one, but several cups of coffee, he related the following story.

A large tiger had appeared on the road from Tarikere that led past the eastern slopes of the Baba Budan mountain range, and passed through Lakkavalli before going on in a circle to Bhadravati. It had begun by killing cattle belonging to the many herds that were taken to graze in the jungle bordering the roadside. The tiger was reputed to carry off its victims across its back, and if any of the herdsmen dared to interfere, this animal chased them off with loud growls. Invariably it would disappear in a western direction, into the jungles of the 'Laulbagh'.

Time passed. Nothing happened to any herdsmen, but the tiger continued to exact its toll. Naturally, the herdsmen grew more angry with the tiger and became correspondingly bolder. Equally naturally, the tiger grew more angry with them and grew bolder itself.

The day dawned when the anger of both sides came to a head. The tiger was moving off with a particularly fat cow across its shoulders when a herdsman, more plucky than any of his companions, rushed after it and hurled his stave. As was its custom, the tiger dropped the body of the victim and, roaring and growling horribly, charged the man, no doubt expecting him to bolt as so many others had done before.

But this man did not run away. Maybe he was braver than the others. Maybe he was stricken stiff with fear. Maybe, having cast his staff away, he thought it useless to run anyhow. Of course, not being present himself, Venkatasubbarao did not know what really happened. What he did know was that the tiger killed and ate the herdsman before walking off again with its fat victim, the cow.

Word got around and the herdsmen in the Lakkavalli area stopped interfering with the tiger. When it attacked a herd, the men in charge promptly fled, and the tiger, politely, did not bother to chase them any more. But other herdsmen, farther off, had not heard of what had transpired near Lakkavalli. They continued their old tactics of trying to drive the tiger off when it attacked their animals. The tiger, having come now to realize how helpless his human victim at Lakkavalli had proved to be, and emboldened by that experience, killed two herdsmen one after the other at Kemangundi, and one other not very far from Santaveri. These three victims it was reported to have completely devoured and, most significant feature of all, after eating them it had spurned the carcases of the cattle it had killed.

The tiger had returned to Lakkavalli after that. Once again the scene was set for tragedy. A herd of cattle was being taken out to graze by two men, a middle-aged man and his son of fifteen years. They were standing together, watching their charges, when the boy saw the head of a large tiger observing them from behind a rise in the ground. He drew his father's attention to it. Both had turned to flee, leaving their animals to the tender mercies of the tiger, when that beast, instead of attacking the cattle, had come after them.

The lad, being young and fleeter of foot, was running ahead when the father saw the tiger bound past him, overhaul the boy and pounce upon him. In heedless panic, the older man had swerved to the right and continued his headlong flight. When he reached the village he collapsed in a faint, and it was a long time before he could tell what had happened.

The villagers went to Venkatasubbarao's quarters to beg his assistance. My new friend, however, did not own a gun and so could not help them at that moment. He closely questioned the father and got from him all the details, just as he related them to me.

A runner was dispatched to Tarikere, some eleven miles away, for help. Meanwhile the herd of cattle came rushing back to the village. It was intact. Not one of them had been harmed.

The next morning a mixed posse of policemen and forest guards, nine in number and armed with lathis, arrived together with two constables with rifles and a police sub-inspector carrying a revolver. Thus a dozen men, led by the father, went to the spot where the tiger had attacked. The body of the boy was not to be seen and everybody returned.

Thereafter the problem of obtaining labour for working on the dam became insurmountable. Those who lived in huts in the village refused to go out, while many went back to Tarikere. Others—and quite a large number of them—had made a practice of cycling every morning the eleven miles from Tarikere to work at the dam, returning the same distance in the evening. These refused to undertake the journey any more. And those people who brought supplies of rice, grain, bread and vegetables from Tarikere to the technical staff working on the dam declined to travel on that dreadful road. So not only had work on the dam practically ceased, but the senior staff stationed at Lakkavalli were being starved out.

My new acquaintance had taken advantage of the inactivity to come to Bangalore on short leave, where we had met at the stamp vendor's counter. He earnestly begged me to return with him to Lakkavalli to try to rid the village of the menace that had beset it.

I had work to attend to, but yielded to my companion's pressing request and said I would come for five or six days only. I could not possibly stay longer.

Venkat, by which name I shall refer to him hereafter, was very pleased. I do not think he realized that it is practically impossible to locate a man-eater in five days. It was arranged that he should return to the hotel he was occupying, gather the bedding and the few other things he had brought with him, and be at my house by 3 p.m. the same day. We would then travel in my car to Lakkavalli.

I hastened home to gather my own equipment, which is always kept ready along with some tinned provisions, when I had another surprise. The postman brought a short letter from Dick Bird.

Dear Jock,

Hurry up and come. Be here by tomorrow. That tiger I told you about has turned man-eater and swallowed quite a few cattle-men. Yesterday, it carried off my postman while he was taking the mail bag from here to Hosoor village, three mils away. I had no time to ask for leave, so reported sick and looked for the remains of the postman to sit up over them. We searched all day and only found the poor chap's cap and slippers.

And, of course, the mail bag. (Couldn't the bloody tiger have eaten that!)

Time's up and I have to return to duty tomorrow. Now, no excuses man; I'm keeping lunch for you the day after tomorrow (that is, the day after you receive this letter), provided the tiger doesn't eat the reserve postman who carries the mail today with this letter. Poor beggar, he's in a blue funk and I can't blame him.

Your pal, Dick

Dick was surprised when he had two guests for dinner that very night. Venkat and I had made the trip in record time.

We chatted till a late hour, but this did not get us anywhere. I remembered that, beginning the following morning, I had exactly five days in which to locate the man-eater and shoot it. Dick Bird could not leave his post. Venkat, with all the willingness he evinced, knew nothing about shooting and had no weapon anyway. There was no trace of the postman's body and it was not worth searching for it, as only bones would be left.

Venkat said that he had to be back at the dam by the following noon, so we decided to motor to his place that very night. By road, it was about fifty miles away, although much nearer as the crow flies. We downed a final rum and said goodbye to Dick well after midnight. I instructed Venkat how to operate the spotlight which with the headlights of the car enabled us to search the jungle as we drove along.

We were still about fifteen miles from Tarikere, at a place named Bagavadkatte, where a stream passes under the road by a small bridge with low parapets. Dark palms thickly fringed the road both to right and left of us, with heavy undergrowth and tiger-grass growing beneath the palms. It was there that we came upon a marvellous spectacle. Standing to one side, just beyond the parapet and evidently about to cross the road was a magnificent tiger!

It turned its head towards the car as the beams from the headlights, as well as the spotlight, caught it, and the reflection from its great orbs was brilliantly white-red, like two great stars shining by the wayside. By 'white-red' I mean more of white with a tinge of red. This is how I differentiate a tiger's eyes at night from those of a panther, which are smaller, closer together, and red-white in colour—that is, more of red and less of white.

We could see the tiger's striped coat, indeed its whole form, clearly in our bright lights.

I stopped the car. Both tigers and panthers, when a bright light falls upon them, often try to take cover by sinking to the ground, although they continue to stare back at the light, thus giving themselves away. This is just what our tiger did. It sank low and then started crawling forwards on its belly, seeking to hide behind the parapet of the bridge.

Venkat was beside himself with excitement. He trembled violently and the spotlight wavered. 'Shoot! Shoot! Shoot!' he hissed, louder and louder.

The tiger heard him. It scrambled forward the few remaining feet till the parapet hid it. Then it leapt down into the stream, passed under the bridge, and we heard it growl as it disappeared to our left in the long grass and undergrowth beneath the border of date palms. I could almost see tears in Venkat's eyes as he looked at me reproachfully. His lips trembled. For a moment I thought he was going to cry.

I explained to him at some length that all tigers are not man-eaters, that we were outside the man-eater's 'limit of beat' at the moment, and that Bagavadkatte was, and had always been, a well-known spot where tigers crossed the road, or passed under the bridge, from the low range of hillocks on the one side to the low range of hillocks on the other, and that the animal we had seen was undoubtedly a perfectly harmless-to-humans, innocent beast. Moreover, it was against rules to shoot tigers on the roadside with the aid of a spotlight, and unsporting besides.

I am not at all sure to this day whether Venkat was convinced by my arguments or considered me a fool. He certainly maintained an embarrassing silence till we reached our destination, his bungalow at about 2 a.m. There he brightened up a bit.

This happened when the watchman of the place informed him that the man-eater had carried away one of the few remaining coolies working on the dam when the man was returning to the village from work shortly after 5 p.m. the previous evening. As a result the coolies had told the watchman to inform his master when he returned that they would not come to work next day. Even if my arguments at the bridge at Bagavadkatte had not excused me in Venkat's eyes for not shooting the tiger we had seen there, he now had to be convinced that the animal that had crossed the road there could not have been the man-eater.

Venkat offered me food, but I declined and said we should snatch some sleep till five o'clock in order to be ready to start our operations at 6 a.m. He thereupon conducted me to a little room with a comfortable bed, and in five minutes I was asleep.

Dawn had broken when we set forth, together with the watchman and three *coolies,* for the place where the tiger had claimed its latest prey. It appeared that these same three coolies had been with the victim when the tiger had taken him. The four men had been walking along the high bund—or wall— of the dam which was still under the process of construction. They had reached the end of it and were descending the steep slope where the sluice-gate was to be built, with the intention of climbing up the other side, when the man-eater struck. There was a piercing scream, and on looking around the fourth man was not to be seen by his mates.

A moment later they caught sight of him, held securely by the throat in the jaws of a tiger which bounded up the slope they had just come down. The beast crossed the top of the bund and disappeared from view. They delayed not a moment, but fled to report the news at the village. Next they went to the engineer's bungalow. Nobody had attempted a rescue of any kind.

We searched the cutting which was to form the sluice-gate, and there the tragedy of the evening before, in all its gruesome details, was made clear to us. The man-eater had not been lying in wait in the cuttings, as we had surmised. It had, in fact, been some distance away when it had seen the men and had deliberately followed them. The soft earth showed pug-marks where the tiger had clambered up the bund, bounded along the top, and then sprung upon the man who had been the last in line as he was descending the slope of the cutting.

The poor fellow had probably died soon after emitting his loud scream. There were no blood marks at the spot where he had been attacked, indicating the tiger had not delayed in picking up its victim and making off with him.

We found the pug-marks left by the killer as it was making off after crossing the top of the bund. Halfway down the steep slope it had skidded, and the piled-up earth showed the deep furrows left by its four feet when it had dug them into the ground to stop its slide. At this juncture it must have released his hold upon the dead man's throat, for when the tiger picked him up again, it left a trail of blood all the way down the rest of the incline and into the jungle beyond.

But for the blood trail it would have been impossible for us to follow the spoor, for the undergrowth, due to recent rain, was dense. But the vivid green of the carpet of weeds constrasted sharply with the bright red of the blood-drops which showed up clearly before us for some distance ahead.

The tiger had carried its victim westwards, and for a long distance. It had crossed the main road at a sharp curve about half a mile beyond Lakkavalli village and before the road had begun to circle back towards Umblebyle and Bhadravati. The animal was obviously making for the Laulbagh Forest Block, and I began to suspect that it must be living in some cave in this area.

A few minutes later we crossed the Forest department's 'fire-line' and were now officially inside the Laulbagh Forest

Block. Our quarry had not stopped for a moment, and it was becoming difficult to follow its trail. The blood in the body of its victim had coagulated and ceased to flow, so that the drops that had fallen were scarce and small. Our progress was consequently slow through having to search for them at long intervals, and I feared that very soon the trail would die out.

That was exactly what happened ten or fifteen minutes later. No further blood-drops could we find, nor was it possible to see the pug-marks of the man-eater. Twelve hours had elapsed since it had passed that way, and the freshening effect of the night breezes, together with the dew that had fallen, had again raised the bent stems of weeds, grass and undergrowth that had been trodden upon or brushed aside by the tiger and the body of its victim in passing. With stems and leaves standing stiffly erect, the weeds and undergrowth effectively hid from us any indication whatever as to the direction which the tiger and the victim had taken. The trail was dead.

Venkat and my other companions were bitterly disappointed. So was I. However, one piece of information had been gained from our work that morning. It was clear that the tiger lived in some cave or haunt within the Laulbagh area, as I had suspected from the beginning, and considering the distance it had already brought its victim, his hide-out could not be very far from the place where the trail had died out. I made inquiries as to the existence of a cave, but none of the villagers appeared to know about one.

As soon as we got back to the village I asked for the local forest guard. He would know the topography of the jungle within its jurisdiction. To my chagrin I was told that the guard had gone to departmental headquarters at Tarikere and would return only in the morning.

No time was to be lost, so I bundled Venkat into the car beside me and made for Tarikere without further delay. The bee that had got into my bonnet regarding the existence of a cave or other hiding place would have to be swatted before I was satisfied.

In half an hour we were at the district Forest Office, where we found not only the guard we were seeking but also his immediate superior, the forest ranger, and the divisional chief, the district officer, as well. With these people around us we related how we had followed and lost the trail of the man-eater in the Laulbagh jungle. Could they tell us if there was a cave or any other place of hiding in this block in which the tiger could have made its home?

The D.F.O. looked at the ranger, and the ranger at his guard. Then the guard looked back again, and so back and forth.

'There does not appear to be any cave in the area, Mr. Anderson,' the D.F.O announced at length.

The bee that had flown into my bonnet was dying an ignoble death. My theory was shattered! The guard, standing on one bare foot, scratched his shin with the toe of the other.

'I don't suppose the devil could be sheltering in the old Munneswara Temple, could he, *swami*?' he asked shamefacedly, addressing his immediate superior, the ranger.

'The Munneswara Temple!' ejaculated the ranger, thoughtfully; 'the Munneswara Temple!'

'The Munneswara Temple!' the D.F.O. exploded exultantly. Then, to the guard who was hanging his head in disgrace, 'You fool! Why didn't you say that before? That's it! That's where he is! The old Munneswara Temple!' The D.F.O. pranced about in the his excitement.

When emotions had died down I was informed that an ancient temple, almost in ruins, stood a short distance within the border of the Laulbagh Block. From the directions given by the guard, we must have been very near it when we had lost the trail that morning. The inner room, or sanctuary of the temple, was said to have partly caved in, but sufficient room was left for the tiger to live in, the guard thought.

Back we went to Lakkavalli, the D.F.O., the ranger and the guard following in government jeep. They said they wanted to be in at 'the kill', although they promised me they would remain in the village and not hamper me while the actual killing was taking place.

It was now past lunch-time, but with expectation at fever heat I decided to forgo the meal and set out with the forest guard on foot for the ruins of the old temple. We passed the spot where we had lost the blood trail and had gone another mile or more when there was a sudden dip in the ground. The centre of this little bowl or depression was an island of tangled undergrowth and bushes, and peeping through the varied foliage I could see the grey ruins of a small temple.

Instructing my companion to climb one of the taller trees and remain at the top, a suggestion that he did not delay a moment in executing, I picked my way on tiptoe towards the ruins, taking advantage of every intervening bush to cover my advance. The hot sun poured down on the scene and I was in no hurry.

In my excitement I discovered I had forgotten to ask the guard the direction the temple faced. This was important, if I hoped to take the man-eater by surprise. It would never do for me to be watching the rear of the temple while the tiger slipped out in front, circled around under cover of the undergrowth and attacked me from behind.

Eventually, on closer approach, I could make out the opening that led to the temple-sanctuary. It faced a little to my right and was partially blocked by debris. I was lucky. All I had to do now was creep up beside this opening, take cover, draw the man-eater out, and shoot it.

This is what I proceeded to do. Edging forwards, I reached the corner of the square that formed the outside of the temple. This struck me as being a very suitable place in which to hide and ambush my quarry. I would be safe from attack when the tiger rushed out. Naturally, it would charge straightforward and not think of looking for me to its right or left.

But there was a snag. If I hid behind one corner of the building, what was to prevent the tiger hiding behind the other corner at the back of me and pouncing upon me from the rear? It might not be in the temple at that moment, for all I knew. Perhaps it was watching me from the cover of some bush while It was searching for it.

I decided to creep up to within a couple of feet of the temple entrance and flatten myself against the wall. At least that would prevent me from being attacked from behind while I was peeping around the corner in front. This I did and was in position at last. Now it was a matter of drawing the tiger out. I had to avoid frightening it, and I should not anger it. It had to do itself out of curiosity.

So I moaned faintly, imitating the call of a tiger far away. Nothing happened! Perhaps the tiger had not heard me, although I could scarcely credit that. I moaned again, and still nothing happened. I moaned a third time, and much louder. That distant tiger had made a remarkably fast approach! Yet nothing transpired and I concluded that the tiger was not in the temple. I peeped around the corner very carefully; then I grew bolder and entered the broken opening, stooping double. A damp, mouldering smell greeted me. The dust at the entrance showed no pug-marks. Nor was there any trace of human remains. Not only was no tiger here, but no tiger had been here for months. Clearly the Munneswara Temple was not the man-eater's hiding place.

We were so disappointed that the huge lunch my friend Venkat had had prepared for himself and me was sufficient to feed the D.F.O. and the ranger also. Moreover, a little was left over, sufficient to give the forest guard a snack.

Sitting on the plinth of the veranda of Venkat's bungalow smoking, a short while later, I chafed at the delay while my friends continued to talk over events. Time meant everything to me, but nothing to them. It is the one thing in India that has never been rationed; and never will be.

In the afternoon sunlight, a Lambadi herdsman grazed his buffaloes outside. With the man-eater about, it was far too dangerous for him to take them into the forest, while the sparse grass in the compound of the engineer's quarters offered a meagre substitute. Attracted by the sight and smell of the assorted fumes from my pipe, Venkat's cigar and the cigarettes smoked by our two friends of the Forest department, this individual became sufficiently emboldened to approach us and beg for a cigarette. The D.F.O., threw him one and we forgot his existence, after seeing him move off to the rear of the bungalow where we heard him and the forest guard talking to each other.

A few minutes later the guard approached. He was excited, but also hesitated to interrupt the conversation of his exalted superiors.

'Well?' muttered the guard with great diffidence. 'I prey your honour not to get angry, but the outcaste Lambadi tells me there is an overhanging ridge of rock a mile beyond the Munneswara Temple under which there is sufficient space for a tiger to shelter. In fact, he says he saw one sunning itself on top of the rock one evening when he was returning with his buffaloes, and before the man-eater came amongst us. Of course, he ran away and his animals followed. He says he had not been there again.'

We summoned the Lambadi without delay and closely questioned him. His reply was exactly what the forest guard had just told us. The only new piece of information he offered was that he felt certain that the tiger he had seen and the maneater were one and the same animal, bearing in mind the fact that the tiger had not turned man-eater at that time. Within a few minutes I was on my way again, the forest guard accompanying me rather reluctantly this time. But the Lambadi was in better spirits.

It was half-past four when we passed the temple, and close upon five before the Lambadi pointed out to me, about two hundred yards ahead, a slight rise in the ground above which peeped a sloping rock. He told me that, although we could not see it from where we stood, owing to the intervening jungle, when I came close enough I would find that the rock made a low overhanging cave, the entrance to which was not more than two feet in height. This, he thought, had been caused by the rush of rainwater during the monsoons, for the cave was not a very deep one. On his previous visit he had been at almost the same spot on which we were now standing and had noticed the tiger lying at full length and sunning itself on the top of the rock. He had run away as fast as he could.

Once again I told my companions to climb trees and to remain there till my return, and for the second time that day I crept forward on tiptoe as cautiously as possible.

This time my advance lay through fairly thick jungle, and not through open country like that which formed the depression in which the old Munneswara Temple mouldered. I looked to right and left and behind, to guard against flank and rear attacks. There was an oppresive silence and I glanced momentarily downwards at each pace that I made. On no account must I step on a leaf that might rustle or a twig that might crackle. Now and then, despite all my precautions, some part of my body brushed against a bush and made a faint rubbing sound.

I said to myself: 'I must not do that again: the tiger will hear me.'

I was now very near the rock, but the undergrowth in front still hid the ground level opening mentioned by the Lambadi. I halted for a few minutes. Maybe I could hear the tiger if I strained my ears. I did so, but I heard absolutely nothing.

'A few steps more,' I said to myself, 'and I will be able to see.'

I looked down. No leaf, or twig, no loose stone in front. It was safe for me to take another step forwards.

I took that step, but I overlooked an insignificant little shrub to my right. That shrub had thorns, and the thorns did the trick. They rasped audibly against my trousers, held for a moment, and then let go with another rasp.

Before I could guess whether the man-eater had heard me, it had in fact done so. Instinct warned it that this was no bird, no hare or other small creature that was approaching just out of sight. It knew full well that no living thing that could fly, walk or creep would dare to come so close to its dreadful presence. Therefore this must be an enemy, and more over, an enemy that was stalking it, the tiger, no doubt to kill it in turn.

Its reflexes gave it this message and there was no delay. The tiger charged, its shattering roars of 'Wroof! Wroof! Wroof!' rending the silence.

The bushes before me parted and its head and body catapulted through them before it caught sight of me. It halted for a moment prior to making the final spring. Perhaps it never expected to find a miserable human being confronting it instead of running away. Head and paws at ground level, hindquarters and tail sticking up, the tiger looked a bit ridiculous.

I fired twice into its head. Then I leaped quickly aside, for one must never forget to spring aside after firing at a tiger at close quarters, as the odds are ninety-nine to one that it will rush straightforward, even if it must die the next instant. A dying tiger can in fact do you an awful lot of harm.

The man-eater did as I expected, and I shot it twice more behind the shoulder. As it twitched and then began to stiffen, I saw that it was quite an old animal, past the age from hunting game.

The bones of the coolie for whose body we had been searching were strewn about the entrance to the shallow cave. They had been gnawed clean. Red ants were devouring what small strands of flesh adhered to them still.

The three of us returned in darkness, unafraid this time. There was another feast at the bungalow, and it gave me indigestion. Dreams of tigers rushing out of temples troubled me till the early hours. Then came a farewell to Venkat and my friends of the Forest department.

I was at Santaveri by nine in the morning. Dick offered me lunch, but I declined. My stomach was still rumbling in uncomfortable protest as I swallowed a quick rum. By four I was home, having accomplished my mission well within time.

Eight

What the Thunderstorm Brought

DONALD, MY SON, WAS IMMENSELY PLEASED WITH HIMSELF. HE HAD just tied for the first place in a clay-pigeon shooting competition held by the Rifle Association of Mysore state.

Now clay-pigeon shooting is something we in India do not normally indulge in, at least so far as I know, perhaps because there are so many wild pigeons that we cannot be bothered with the clay variety, or whatever substance it is that goes to make a clay pigeon. More likely, because up to this time nobody had the apparatus to eject these little things, these clay pigeons into the air. Certainly, I had never seen them before. I am sure I could not hit one myself. I am essentially a rifle shot and almost useless with a gun. My attempts years ago at snipe and duck convinced me of that.

Donald, however, is a natural good shot with both gun and rifle. Like me, he had never seen a clay-pigeon-shooting gadget, and therefore certainly had had no chance to practise.

But he entered for the competition and tied for the first prize. And now he suggested that we should make a trip to the jungles to celebrate the occasion.

To the jungles? What a strange place to go to celebrate! But the truth is we both love the jungles. In them we are at home; there we find peace. So it did not take much persuasion to get me to go.

This time we decided to try our hand at photographing tigers by night rather than shooting them. Donald had borrowed a wonderful camera with a flashlight apparatus from his old friend of schoolboy days, young Dudhwala, who was young no longer, and about whom I have told a tale in an earlier book.* For a long time Don had been wanting to try his hand at the most difficult and I might also add, most highly-skilled sport of night-photography and this was his chance.

I will not tell you to which jungle we went because it is one of the very few places remaining in southern India where tigers are yet to be found. Some enthusiasts have read my books and gone to places I have named, bent upon trying their luck, and it has become a matter of necessity, from the point of view of Indian conservation, no longer to name them. For tigers, panthers and bear are becoming very scarce in southern India. The heavy shooting which resulted from the influx of foreigners into India during World War II began their decimation. The Indian poacher particularly, of the kind that uses jeeps with spotlights, continued the process. Then came the deadly insecticide of which I have already spoken, which the government still supplies almost free of charge to protect the villagers' crops against various pests, but ryots whose cattle or goats have been killed by tigers and panthers have no compunction about smearing the flesh

---

* See: *Man-Eaters and Jungle Killers.*

of their slain animals with this stuff. Almost always, success crowns this dastardly deed by poisoning the marauder when he returns for a second meal.

The results have been so disastrous that, particularly in Mysore state, tigers, panthers, hyenas, and even jackals, and to some extent vultures, have been practically wiped out by the misuse of this chemical—without taking into account the high mortality among human beings all over the country by suicide, murder and accidental poisoning. The old-fashioned and far slower acting, less deadly posions like arsenic, strychnine and zinc salts, which can only be purchased in minute quantities, are discoverable, but the government will give anyone pounds of deadly insecticide almost for the asking. It is deplorable that the authorities cannot, do not, or will not see the truth of this matter.

So we went to 'tiger-land', to a lovely cabin of bamboo and grass that we had built on a small plot of land I had bought many years earlier for the sum of 120 rupees (about seven pounds sterling). Two hundred yards in front of our hut flowed a river, its presence plainly indicated by the heavy growth of giant *muthee*, tamarind, *jumlum* and wild mango trees that lined both banks. Here and there were areas where dense clumps of bamboo had ousted all other forms of vegetation, bringing their towering, feathery fronds to overhang the cascades and pools of the stream, while dark and silent glades, covered with a carpet of rotting leaves, reached down to the water's edge.

The crocodile loves such places, for the deer like them too. The dense cover afforded by the bamboos, their shade, and the flooring of decaying leaves permit a silent, sheltered and comparatively safe approach for the sambar, nilgai and spotted deer when they come in the heat of the day, and also at night, to slake their thirst with the cool water that has cascaded down so recently from the cold of the mountains above the forest.

In their anxiety to escape the great carnivores that may be lurking behind any tree, any clump of bamboo, or any bush, the deer lose no time in drinking as fast as they can, with their noses and ears alert for the scent or sound of a tiger, and their eyes on the watch for a panther or for the cruel wild dogs. Often enough, in the anxiety of scanning the landscape, they overlook the ugly crocodile, who is invisible anyhow, his head and body below the surface of the stream and very close to the bank.

And so a sambar lowers its head to drink, and as it does so the crocodile rises from the water. Cruel jaws, with long, saw-like teeth, close upon the sambar's snout while almost in the same instant the reptile's flat, scaly tail swings out of the water and whips across with irresistible force, striking the sambar's legs or flank and throwing it off-blance into the pool.

Never loosening its grip on the sambar's face, the crocodile swims backwards into deep water, dragging its struggling victim with it. Once in its element, the crocodile throws itself into a spin of incredible speed in order to break its victim's neck or otherwise render it unconscious, and the next moment both crocodile and sambar vanish beneath the dark surface of the pool and only a series of large bubbles disturb the placid flow of water over the scene of the tragedy.

But we know nothing of the grim drama being enacted in the slime and ooze at the bottom of the jungle river. From the comfortable cane chairs on the veranda of our hut we listen to the loud cracking of the stems of giant bamboos as they are broken by a herd of elephants grazing on the opposite bank of the stream. Now and again comes the faint squeak of an elephant-calf and the dull thunder-like rumble from the digestive organs of an adult, or a contented cow-like mooing from a feeding female. All is peaceful and the faraway call of a peafowl alternates with the shrill, cat-like meowing cries that come from above us, made by the pair of brown vultures in their never-ending quest for scraps of food left by the great jungle cats.

Although there was apparent peace in the jungle there was some discord in our hut. Trouble arose between the caretaker, whom we employ to look after the place in our absence, and his wife, who brings us water twice a day in an old kerosene tin from the river. There was muttering and grumbling, and an occasional high-pitched female screech that put even the vultures to shame.

'Some trouble between Boora and his wife,' observed Donald laconically. 'Better see what it is about. She hasn't brought water for my bath yet, although I've told her twice already.'

So I got up and went into the kitchen, which is a smaller grass hut about twelve feet square, situated behind our dwelling-place. There sat Boora on the ground, idly poking a wood fire with a stick while his spouse sat opposite him, chewing betel-nut vigorously and spitting red saliva all over the place. An interested spectator was my *shikari* Thangavelu, originally from faraway Closepet, who had promoted himself into Don's services as a camp-cook, table-boy, dressing-boy, and every other sort of boy except a boy who honestly did any work.

'What's the matter with you two?' I asked aggressively, glaring at Boora and his wife alternately. Then, addressing the woman. 'Your bad language is disgusting.'

There was silence for a while, then Boora explained in the local dialect: 'Sir, I married this harridan three years ago. She has had three children from me but doesn't look after them. Neither does she feed me properly. She won't work because she's lazy, All day long she keeps chewing betel-nut and demands money to buy more. Altogether, she's too expensive a proposition.

'As it stands when I married her I paid ten rupees to her father for her. Now, old Javanna had offered me his youngest daughter for fifteen rupees. She's a comely wench and will look after me well. What's more, Javanna is willing to take over this bag-of-bones from me for five rupees, half the price I paid for her, so that the deal will only cost me ten. She can keep the three children she had from me—I certainly don't want'em!'

Further plans on the part of Boora were interrupted by the screeching voice of Devi, his wife.

'You lecherous old pig!' she cried. 'What do you want with a young girl like Lakshmi? She's only fifteen years old, although she's a bitch at that! You're already half-dead, and after a week with her I'll have the trouble of burying your exhausted bones! As for that old sod, javanna! He's so old he hasn't any teeth! Also, he's fond of young boys! Who's going to satisfy me? I'm young and vigorous still!'

A knotty problem, indeed! But there was one redemptive factor. Considering the rate of exchange at one shilling and four pence to a rupee, the cost-factor involved in this mutual exchange, in whatever way you might look at it, was not very high. Thangavelu summed up the situation concisely with a wide grin, and in the butler-English which he had picked up, chimed in:

'Sar I like this place. Plenty very much damn good place. Plenty shikar, plenty tiger, plenty deer got-it. Plenty women, too, plenty damn cheap-rate. Here five rupees, ten rupees get-it wife. Then too, can pay next month. When no want, can change-it. Another wife get-it. Only ten rupees! Damn woman won't go 'way after. Want-it more money. Can't get 'nuther wife less than 'nuther hundred rupees. Sar, this very damn good place.'

Thangavelu ended with a meaning grin.

'Thangavelu, tell that bloody woman to fetch my bathwater,' Donald roared from the veranda. Kunmarie, the local *shikari*, turned up just then with the information we had asked him to bring us. He had been scouring the jungle since dawn and reported that a tiger as well as a panther, had walked up the bed of a dry *nullah* about half a mile away. The panther seemed an old resident as Kunmarie said his tracks, both old and fresh, appeared many times. The tiger was evidently on a casual walk and could not be expected to return that way for some time.

So the prospects were that if we tied a bait with the object of taking a photograph later, it would probably be a panther and not a tiger that would kill it. We were after tiger only; we reiterated this fact to Kunmarie, asking him to go out again to try to find a place frequented by a tiger rather than a panther.

That afternoon he returned with news of success. Across the river, he said, was a well-frequented game trail on which were tiger-pugs, both old and fresh. Further, there was a convenient tree, safe from interference by elephants, from which we could easily take our photographs when the time came. The tiger was sure to pass the same way that night or the next.

We had procured four buffaloes as bait and decided to tie out two of them—the larger on the tiger-frequented gametrail across the river, and the smaller in the *nullah* four furlongs away, where the panther was almost certain to get it. Thangavelu went with Kunmarie to help tether the two animals, while Don and I went for an evening walk along the river bank.

This particular jungle was still a veritable paradise for game and we saw large herds of spotted deer, with a fair number of sambar and individual nilgai, browsing by the water-side. Around a curve in the river we came upon a bull-elephant having his evening drink. As we were not on a *shikar* trip we carried no firearms. For a moment or two the bull looked nasty; no doubt he resented our intrusion on his privacy. Then he thought better of it, wheeled and lumbered away into the thicket of overhanging trees. It was extraordinary how so large an animal could move so quietly.

The following morning Kunmarie went to the game-trail and Thangavelu to the *nullah,* to see what had happened to our baits during the night. In the jungle the unexpected frequently happens, and the reports they brought us were as surprising as they were heartening from the photographic point of view. A tiger, and not a panther, had come along the *nullah* where we had tied the smaller bait, expecting the panther to kill it. It had easily broken the tethering-rope and had taken the buffalo-calf a little distance away to a ditch. There it had eaten every scrap except the head and four hooves. Because they were sheltered by undergrowth the vultures had not discovered the remains.

Strangely enough a panther, and not the tiger we had expected, had come along the game-trail across the river. It in turn had killed the large buffalo-calf we had tied for the tiger, evidently with some difficulty, for Kunmarie reported marks of a struggle. But the panther had not been strong enough to sever the tethering-rope. So it had eaten a small portion of the buffalo-calf, leaving the rest by the side of the game-trail where we should be able to photograph it easily if we wished, from the big tree bordering the trail when it returned that night.

Don was in high spirits. He would photograph his tiger at last. Naturally he decided to sit over the scant remains, consisting of the head and legs, of the smaller calf we had tied out in the *nullah.* To make sure the tiger put in an appearance, he proposed tying our third bait near by, just in case the tiger thought the remains of the first one too insignificant to merit a second visit.

Incidentally, I might remark that this is a plan I have found most successful with both tiger and panther. After all, they are individuals just as we are; they differ among themselves just as we differ and they suffer from some at least of our faults. The commonest of these is greed. Some panthers and tigers hardly ever return to their kills a second time. Others return only after they have spent a very long time reconnoitering the locality and feel it safe to show themselves. It is in this process of surveyance that they frequently discover the presence of the hunter, perched in his tree-*machan* or wherever he may have concealed himself. To exploit this greed, I have found it good to tie another live bait within sight of the partially eaten one, and if possible to sit at a spot between them; or if that is not practical, to sit over the new bait in preference to the old, partly-eaten one.

What happens is this. The tiger or panther returns to the scene of its first kill but does not approach the carcase straight away. It is suspicious and circles the spot several times to discover the presence of the man its instinct warns is in hiding somewhere. During this manoeuvre it comes upon the new live bait. One might conjecture that this would make the feline more suspicious than ever. How does a live animal come to be so close to the place where he had left a dead and almost completely devoured victim? But you must remember that tigers and panthers cannot reason as human beings do. They are creatures of instinct, even if such instinct is often uncanny in its efficiency.

The immediate result is that the prowling tiger or panther kills the live animal. No doubt the prospect of fresh meat is always more enticing than the decomposing flesh that has been exposed to the sun and vultures throughout the day, and so the tiger or panther brings about its own undoing.

I had no camera suitable for night photography, and as we were not on a shooting excursion and carried no firearms there seemed no point in my sitting on the big tree across the river merely to hear a panther tucking into a good meal. So I decided to spend the first part of the night in sitting in the comfort of a cane chair on the veranda of our bamboo hut, listening to the sounds of the jungle; and the rest of it in bed.

Showers of rain had been sporadic in the area, and for this reason each of us had brought along a tarpaulin sheet to sling as a roof over the *machan* in case of necessity. This is a practice I do not recommend at all. Firstly, it makes the *machan* very conspicuous and calls for extra camouflaging. Secondly, when the rain comes the noise of the water on the roof is so great that your cannot hear a thing. Worse still, any creature on the ground below at fifty yards cannot help but hear the pandemonium overhead. It looks up, discovers the *machan* and knows you are there. But it certainly is no joke to sit up in a tree all night in pouring rain, even if you are waring a greatcoat or waterproof cape. The rain has a strange knack of getting inside anything.

Don decided to use the tarpaulin and I went along with Kunmarie and Thangavelu, together with another man named Bunda, to help him with his *machan*.

A soap-nut tree grew to one side of the *nullah* and on this Don decided to sit. It was within about thirty yards of the ditch in which lay the head and legs of our first bait and it overlooked the course of the *nullah* in both directions. There was a third advantage to this tree. The tiger, in stalking our bait the night before, had come down by way of a third *nullah*, which was more a shallow ditch, and the soap-nut tree grew just opposite the point where this ditch met the main *nullah*. So it was strategically in an excellent position and, according to all the rules of the game, with ordinary luck the tiger should make itself visible somewhere, and Don should get the chance of a good photograph.

Our three henchmen made an excellent job of the *machan*, and as the sky was clouding over Don decided to stretch the tarpaulin above the platform of the *machan*, across a stick cut and placed in position so as to afford a slope on both sides to allow any water to flow off. The tarpaulin itself was cunningly concealed with leaves and branches that entirely hid it from view. The four of us went away about 5 p.m. leaving Don with the camera all set for an adventurous night.

I will tell you first what I heard from our bamboo cabin, and then let Don tell his part of the tale.

Thangavelu served dinner early, and then I sat on the cane chair on the veranda, smoking my pipe and sipping rum and lime-juice. Darkness had only just fallen and the jungle was silent for the moment. The 'Aiow! Aiow! Aiow!' came the cry of spotted deer from across the river while a sambar stag on the near bank hoarsely took up the warning with his strident 'Dhank! Dhank! Oo-onk!' and a doe sambar, farther away, heard the signal of danger and in a higher tone not quite so hoarse, answered 'Wonk! Wonk! Wonk!'

A bribe of langur monkeys on a banyan tree, the top of which was just visible to me in the darkness to my right, had all gone to sleep long ago. All except the watchman who, with a true sense of responsibility, had remained wide awake. Later, when he began to feel drowsy, he would awaken his relief, who would keep watch till the time came to awaken the next big male, and so on, throughout the night and all day long too, for the big male langurs have an uncanny sense of disicipline and responsibility. They take upon themselves, each in turn, the duties of a watchman, perched at the very top of the highest tree, to look for possible danger and guard the females and young from an unexpected attack.

The langur watchman heard the sambar and the spotted deer and echoed the alarm to awaken the members of his tribe: 'Harr! Ha-harr! Harr! Ha-harri!' I could picture the mother-langurs clutching their young to their breasts while peering down from their perches on the banyan tree into the blackness of the night below to try to discover the killer and reckon from where it might be creeping upon them.

I could plot the progress of the tiger's approach by the cries of the spotted deer and the sambar. He crossed the river and frightened a barking deer in the act of drinking. 'Khrr! Khrr!' the little animal cried. Its cry is quite unlike any other noise associated with the deer species. It sounds more like the hoarse bark of a dog and accounts for the colloquial name by which this small creature, otherwise called the muntjac is known.

The tiger was now disdainful. It knew it had been discovered and scorned to conceal its movements any longer. 'Oo-oongh!' it roared, and then modified its utterance to a softer but deeper 'Aungh! Ughh; Ughh-aa!' There was not anger in the sound, nor was it very hungry.

As if by magic, at the sound of its roars, deep silence descended upon the forest. The deer and monkeys were stilled. Even the frogs by the riverside stopped their croaking. All living creatures, large and small, knew that the king of the jungle was on the prowl and they trembled in fear. Only a solitary wood-circket, ensconced in cool comfort behind the water-pot in what goes for the bathroom of our bamboo-cabin, disdained the challenge of the striped terror. Maybe it had not even heard. Maybe it could not be bothered with such big clumsy creatures as tigers. Probably its problem was more mundane.

Then the silence was shattered down by the river: 'Haa-ah! Haa-ah! Haa-ah!'

The panther had returned long ago and had no doubt been eating its fill of our larger bait. All this fuss had upset it, while the roars of its bigger, irascible and bullying cousin, the tiger, had made it jittery and irritable. It resented the proximity of that majestic terror, but did not know what to do about it. Angrily it repeated: 'Haa-ha! Haa-ah! Haa-ah!' while deciding whether to remain or slink away.

I knew that Don must have heard all these sounds too, and that he would be getting ready to take his picture of the tiger, which by this time should be near the remain of the buffalo calf it had killed the night before, and the live bait we had tied near by.

Silence fell over the forest again. The frogs resumed their croaking by the river and the night seemed to grow black and yet blacker. I looked up at the sky and wondered why I could see no stars. A moment later knew the answer as thunder rumbled across the range of hills behind our cabin. Repeated flashes followed, and the artillery of heaven was loosed upon us, each crash preceded by vivid forked lightning that snaked across the sky like rivers on a giant map.

Then the wind started. I could hear it howling in the distance as it raged down the hillside with a prolonged banshee wail rising ever louder and louder until it hit our own jungle. I could hear the trees tossing wildly as their branches clashed in agony, although it was far too dark to see a thing, and the bamboo supports of our cabin swayed, straining, creaking and groaning. I thought that the thatched roof would be blown away.

Then suddenly as quickly as it came, the wind passed. I could hear it receding into the distance across the forest tops as far as the distant horizon. But the lightning increased in intensity, and the crashes of thunder drew ever nearer and more intense. All at once a giant tree was struck. It was cleft asunder as a vivid flash lit the forest as bright as day, so close to our hut that the thunderclap was instantaneous. I thought of Don in his soap-nut tree and was worried. It was not a very big tree or a high one, however, and hardly likely to attract the lightning that had so many loftier trees to choose from.

The rain reached the cabin and for a moment even approaching down the hillside, long before it reached the cabin. Donald must be really glad, I thought, that he decided to put the tarpaulin roof above his *machan*.

The rain reached the cabin and for a moment even the thunder was drowned in the uproar of falling water. The grass roof above me hissed, and streams of water from a hundred leaks dripped, pattered and flowed in all directions upon our possessions. What had been, only a moment earlier, a cosy cabin became a wet and muddy hole with pools of water on the floor and no dry spot within sight. I sat on, inwardly cursing the labourers who had made such a poor job of the roof.

Thangavelu, awakened at last by the hubbub, in which perhaps he was dreaming of wives for sale by the dozen at five rupees a head, dashed in, gazing in dismay at all the wet things around him, and then scuttled about aimlessly, trying hopelessly to find shelter for them.

The deluge continued for an hour and then settled down to a steady drizzle.

'Quak-ker! Quak-ker! Quak-ker! Quak-ker!' The frogs had now changed their note. This was the mating call of a thousand throats from the river and surrounding puddles, to salute the advent of the monsoon. I rose and prepared for sleep. The only dry spot seemed to be under the bamboo bed rather than upon it.

At that moment I heard the unmistakable scream of an enraged elephant. It came from the direction of the *nullah* and Don's *machan*. Thangavelu, who was still pottering about aimlessly, heard it too. He stopped and we looked at each other anxiously. Then we both went out on to the soaking veranda in order to hear better.

The elephant screamed again. There was no mistaking the fact that the scream came from the *nullah*. Then I heard distant shouting, muted by the continuous pattern of the rain, but there was no doubt that it was a human voice, shouting words I could not make out. The voice came from the same direction as the elephant's scream. Who but Donald was out there in the *nullah*?

Then the truth dawned upon me suddenly. My son was in danger: the elephant was trying to pull him out of the *machan*, and he was trying to drive it away. And he was unarmed.

The irony of the situation struck me and I cursed myself for my overconfident carelessness. I should have known better; they boy was not to blame. We were defenceless. For we had brought no firearms with us, leaving them behind because we had come on a photographic excursion and did not want to be tempted to shoot!

Grabbing the larger of the two lanterns in one hand and, for want of anything better, a walking-stick made from sandalwood in the other, I dashed out and began to stumble through the drenched jungle as fast as I could to cover the half-mile to the *nullah*. I was hardly aware of the cold or the fact that I was bareheaded and without a coat as the rain soaked me to the skin.

I had run as best I could for quite a distance before I became aware of another lantern bobbing behind me. It was Thangavelu, carrying the other light. He loved Donald, and

I was grateful for his presence. No other servant would have dared to venture forth on that foul night, in pitch darkness and unarmed, to a place where a wild elephant was rampaging in fury.

Then we heard a tearing, rending sound, and a crash, and I knew the elephant had pushed over the tree on which Don had his *machan*. I tried to run faster and Thangavelu ran beside me. But I could not make the pace, so we resorted to shouting as we jog-trotted along, hoping to attract the elephant's attention and draw him away from Donald.

This is how Donald himself tells his part of this story: 'I don't know why my father, when he writes his books, brings me into them. For one thing, I hate writing and talking about myself. Actually, the entire incident appears to me now as "much ado about nothing".

'Dad had told how it all started and how I came to be seated on the soap-nut tree with Dudhwalla's flashlight camera to try to photograph the tiger that had killed and devoured our bait the previous night. There was so little left that I had decided to tie a live one near by to tempt the tiger when he prowled around, as tigers generally do, before approaching their kills.

'The *machan* was a comfortable one; the head and feet of the first calf lay in a ditch some thirty yards to my left, while below me was the *nullah* that Kunmarie, our *shikari*, said was a regular route for tigers and panthers on their way to the river. Entering it was a smaller watercourse which the tiger used the night before. A shade to my right, and in clear view, was our third bait—a live one—another buffalo-calf. The second bait was killed by a panther across the river the night before.

'Darkness had just fallen when the deer and langur monkeys sounded their alarm cries and I knew that a tiger or a panther was afoot—probably a tiger, to judge by the amount of noise the animals were making. Then the tiger roared fairly near, and soon afterwards I could hear a panther answering in the distance. Most likely it was the one that killed our second bait.

'I got ready to take my picture. All the same, I wished I had a rifle in my hands instead of a camera. The old man is always talking about taking photographs instead of shooting, and I guess he is right, but the temptation was there nevertheless. I felt strongly now and wished I had my .423 with me.

'The next sound I heard was a thud and the cry of the live bait. I knew it was a tiger and not a panther that was killing the calf, for a panther has to choke his victim, who naturally struggles. There was no sound of a struggle whatever, for the calf was already dead with a broken neck.

'I pointed the camera downwards and to my right, in the general direction of the live bait, and pressed the switch-button. There was a blinding flash and the tiger uttered a startled 'Gr-a-ahm!' This was followed by the faint crash of undergrowth. I knew that it had gone.

'There was nothing more for me to do and I stretched out to sleep, contented with the hope of a good photograph. The *machan* was a bit hard and I wished I was back in our bamboo cabin.

'I must have fallen asleep after that, for I woke with a start to find my *machan* swaying crazily as the tree bent and threshed in a mighty wind. The night was extraordinarily dark till a flash of lightning, followed almost at once by a crash of thunder, told me we were in for a storm, and a big one too. Branches and leaves were torn from the trees and they whipped past my face, while my tarpaulin roof was partly blown away. One end held, the corner that we had lashed to the tree-trunk, while the other threshed loudly in the wind, whipping against the branches and making a great noise.

'Then all at once the wind fell and the rain came. It was more like a waterfall than rain. I closed Dudhwalla's camera and flashlight apparatus and put them away in their case and hoped the water would not get through. I was like a sponge myself; so full of water that it seemed to be running through me. And the rain went on falling.

'Now something unusual occurred. The tiger came back. Probably the lightning had made it think himself a fool for running away in the first instance. What it had seen must have been only a flash of lightning, no more. So it came back and started tearing at the calf it had killed a short time before.

'I dared not attempt to take another picture. God knows what would happen to Dudhwalla's camera, I thought, if I opened it in the torrential rain. There was no point in trying to do anything; even the beam of my torch could not reach the tiger through the falling rain.

'Eventually the rain eased off a little and I could hear the tiger's gnawing more clearly. Then I heard a fresh sound: the squelch of giant footfalls approaching along the *nullah,* wading through the rushing water that I could hear gurgling down the watercourse below. An elephant!

'Probably is was too wet for it to eat and it just wanted to shelter, for he was breaking no branches. It squelched nearer and nearer.

'The tiger heard it too and did not like it. It let out a terrific "Wr-aah!" Ordinarily it would slink away, for tigers and elephants avoid one another as much a possible. But this tiger was an exception. It was eating.

'Moreover, it was angry. So he snarled again and again: "Wr-aah! Wr-aah! Wr-aah!"

'The squelching stopped abruptly. The elephant attempted to strike its trunk against the ground in the usual note of alarm and warning. But its trunk met mud and water instead of firm earth, and the resulting noise sounded more like somebody with a severe cold blowing his nose.

'This annoyed the tiger more and he growled louder than ever, and the elephant would have as likely as not gone away then and left the tiger to its feast, and me in peace, but for an unfortunate turn of events.

'There was a sudden gust of wind and the end of the tarpaulin waved like a flag, banging against the branches of the tree almost above the elephant's head. The tiger took off with a leap at hearing this new sound and crashed into the undergrowth at the elephant's side. This startled and angered the great beast; confused and alarmed, it did not know whether the tiger meant to attack it or if the strange object that was lashing about above its head spelled danger. It looked up and saw everything: the tarpaulin, the *machan*, and me!

'Jumbo let out a terrible scream and rushed straight at the soap-nut tree, its forehead banging against the trunk with a sickening thud. The heavy rain had saturated and loosened the earth, the tree-trunk went off the perpendicular and assumed a slant, and I knew well enough that with another push or two it would come crashing to the ground.

'Jumbo screamed again, backed a little and was obviously gathering itself for a further assault. Although it was very dark, I could faintly make out his shape, so close as to be almost within arm's reach, directly to my left. A faint streak of whiteness against that inky-black background indicated its tusks and confirmed that it was a bull. Moreover, I could smell him now. In spite of the rain that must have washed him well, his body gave out the rank, unmistakable odour of a wild tusker, especially strong when the animal is angry.

'In the next rush the soap-nut tree would fall to earth and take me with it. so I started shouting madly, at the top of my lungs, the first words, just any words, that came into my mind.

My voice had the desired effect—at least for the moment. The elephant delayed his charge and screamed again. The next second would decide my fate.

'My electric torch! Why had I not thought of it before? The light was sure to frighten him off. Hastily I grabbed it and shone it directly into the elephant's face.

'By all the rules of the game he should have beaten a hasty retreat. Instead, he screamed louder than ever, and a second later I felt as if a steamroller had hit me, when he dashed his forehead a second time into the trunk of the soap-nut tree. In slow motion, as if deliberately staged, the tree heeled over to the accompanying noise of rending roots. Then, gathering momentum, it crashed to earth, carrying me, *machan* and everything with it.

'When I felt myself falling I grabbed at the branch above my head so that, apart from the shock, I should receive no physical injury. I thought fast. The first idea that came to mind was to dash for it; but I was enmeshed in the branches of the blasted tree and could not find my torch. In falling I had let go of it in order to grab the branch. God knows where it had gone. It was pitch-dark and to escape from the entanglement of bamboos that formed the *machan* and which were now jumbled all around me, and from the branches of the tree itself, would take a considerable effort, and would lead the elephant to where I was.

'The elephant solved the problem by finding the end of the tarpaulin that had been threshing about in the breeze and seizing it with his trunk. One end was still tied to a branch, so he tore it in two and I could hear him tramping and stamping upon the other piece a few paces away.

'I cowered among the branches, but peeped out to see if I could discover how close he was. It was utterly black everywhere, but his movements betrayed that he was within fifteen feet. I could smell him strongly and hear him breathing as he slogged the end of the tarpaulin against the ground with his trunk, stamped upon it and tore it to shreds. The noise continued for a full minute or two when another noise reached me. I could hear men shouting.

'They appeared to be approaching, and soon I could make out dad's voice and another, which I recognized as Thangavelu's. The twinkle of lights in the distance showed that they were carrying lanterns or torches. Abruptly the bull stopped beating the tarpaulin. He was silent for a moment and then banged the end of his trunk against the ground in alarm and anger. I heard him turning around to face the approaching men.

'Dad and Thangavelu were coming in at the run now, shouting as they did so. I knew my father was unarmed and that it was going to be touch-and-go whether the enraged bull decided to charge them or beat a retreat himself. Perhaps if I started shouting it would help to confuse the dammed beast.

'Just then, stumbling and squelching down the water-filled *nullah* the two men came, holding their lanterns in front of them and shrieking like banshees. The old man was yelling "Don, are you all right?" but I dared not answer. The elephant was far too close and the sound of my voice would bring him down upon me.

'The flickering lights showed me the towering form of the creature as he faced them, his trunk curled inwards, the inevitable sign of an elephant on the verge of a charge. I would have to do something to divert his attention, so I let out a yell and kept on yelling.

'The elephant trumpeted shrilly. Dad and Thangavelu, who had now seen him, stopped running and held their lanterns aloft, to join in the general pandemonium, by yelling too. Dad was doing something so ridiculous that I almost laughed in spite of the danger we were all in at that moment. He was brandishing a stick.

'The screeching sounds we were all making must have sounded hideous. But, thank God, the bull thought so too and lost his nerve. He wheeled abruptly and thundered up the bank I lost no time in getting free of the tree and getting to Dad and Thangavelu.

'"Are you all right?" the old man asked.

'I could not help smiling. He appeared in worse shape than I was and his voice was hoarse from screaming.

'"Thanks. I'm fine." I assured him.

'"Thank God," he said, and then, "Let's get out of here."

'"That's a sentiment with which I fully agree. And fast," I added, rather unnecessarily.

'We stumbled away from the soap-nut tree as quickly as we could. Elephants are individuals after all, and this one could change his mind and return.'

The following morning we went back to recover Dudhwalla's camera and Don's torch. A sight awaited us.

Perhaps the camera had been thrown clear of the falling tree, or perhaps it had got caught up in the tarpaulin. Anyway, either deliberately or by accident, the elephant had stamped it flat. Gone was Dudhwalla's camera and Donald's precious flashlight photograph of the tiger eating its kill! But we found the torch unharmed.

Later that day we sat by the swollen banks of the river, watching the spotted deer and the langur monkeys feeding and playing upon the opposite bank. The wind of the previous night had knocked down the wild figs by the thousand from the great tree on the other side of the river. A herd of about thirty spotted deer were feasting upon them, while the family of langur monkeys that had found the figs earlier and had been tucking into them were now too full to eat any more.

They were frolicking and playing with one another and the spotted fawns like children. Now and again a half-grown langur would leap from the branch of a tree onto the back of a startled spotted doe, tweak her ears or pull her stumpy tail and then jump back again. The spotted stag was indignant at such activities and so were the older langurs, but the fawns frisked about, trying to play catch-as-catch-can with the younger monkeys. It was an unusual and pretty sight.

But as we were looking, death struck where all had been so peaceful. The herd of deer had moved away but the monkeys were still gambolling when a rusty brown streak leaped out of the jungle upon a half-grown langur that had strayed a short distance from the band.

For once the langur watchman had failed in his duty. Perhaps he had been too distracted in watching us to notice the lone, slinking wild dog that had successfully stalked the happy monkeys and now stood upon the opposite bank of the river with one of them dangling from his jaws.

Most of the monkeys scampered to the tree-top, screaming invectives, but the langur watchman and the big males leaped down in concerted attack, voicing the harsh langur war-cry: 'Hok! Hok! Hok! Hok!' They were too late. The young langur was already dead.

Don and I stood up and shouted in unison. My voice, already strained by my efforts of the night before, must have sounded ghastly, for the wild dog dropped the dead monkey in fright and ran a few yards away. There he stopped to gaze at us stonily. These creatures are exceptionally bold, far more so than the great cats of the jungle. They hardly fear man, although they do not attack him as a rule.

The river was swollen and too deep to wade across, but while still shouting to keep the wild dog at bay, we made it by clambering along the trunk and branches of an ancient tree that had fallen years ago and still spanned the stream. The silver-grey body of the black-faced little langur was warm when we picked it up, the great tail, nearly a yard in length, hanging limply from the carcase.

The monkey tribe was still on the tree-top, screaming invectives at the watching murderer, while the watchman and the other males bared their teeth at the wild dog and us alternately. Then they appeared to understand that we were not responsible for the little creature's death and fell silent as we picked up the lifeless body and placed it as high as Don could reach on the crotch of the tree where the monkeys were grouped. After that we returned to our side of the river.

The langurs came down now and surrounded the carcase of their companion. Some smelled it, others handled it. An old female, who might have been its mother, picked it up and kissed it. The large black eyes in those jet black faces seemed strangely shiny and moist. Do langurs weep?

We left 'tiger-land' that afternoon, disappointed but richer in experience for our little adventure with the elephant. The geese had come down from the Himalayas in larger numbers than usual this year, and Don had planned a geese-and-duck shooting expedition with some friends. So we had to return in time to meet them. I did not join the party.

Man-Eaters and Jungle Killers

Introduction

TIME AND CIVILISATION MARCH INEXORABLY ONWARD, BRINGING IN their wake industrialisation, higher standards of living, and greater amenities and comforts, but at the price, it seems, of an ever-diminishing appreciation of Nature. Her face has been scarred and furrowed by man-made projects and constructions. Every minute of the day hoary trees, the giants of the forest, some of them centuries old, crash to earth, felled by the hand of man, either for the sake of the timber they provide or to make room for the constant expansion of a mechanical culture: a condition in which only a few are happy and which is occasionally punctuated by the most barbaric atrocities.

With the crash of the forest giants, other things take their departure too: the wild animals, the birds and all the living creatures that once beautified our lands. They are all disappearing, and very rapidly too!

Such was the case long ago with the American prairies, once the home of countless bison and now completely cleared of its ancient tenants. Africa is rapidly following suit. Where are those myriad heads of game that once covered the face of that wonderful land? Some still remain; but long ago the bones of the vast majority lay bleaching in the hot African sun, scattered across those thousands of miles by the bullets of avaricious, unscrupulous and money-making hunters—men who sometimes shot the mighty elephant for commercial ends, literally by thousands.

India, too, has lost much, for the decrease in the variety and number of her wild life has been alarming. I know localities where until 1930 the moaning sough of a tiger or the guttural sawing of the panther were normal sounds in the night, followed always by the warning call of sambar and other members of the deer family. Now the night passes without a sound, except perhaps for a persistently chirping cricket. Where once the pug-marks of a tiger and other wild-animal trails would tell their morning story of the creatures that had passed that way during the night, the tiny tracks of a few rabbits might today indicate that they at least have not been exterminated.

I do not wish to enter into argument as to how and why a country loses so much with the disappearance of her wild life. Anyone who has never come to know and love the jungle, its solitude and all that its denizens signify, could never appreciate such sentiments, nor the sense of irreparable loss and sorrow felt by those who look for the once familiar forms that are no longer there, or listen vainly for those once familiar sounds that were music to their ears, only to be greeted by a devastating silence.

One cannot doubt that the time will come when even the few living creatures that today remain in their natural state will have vanished, and man may then, and only then, realise too late what a priceless asset he has wantonly allowed to be thrown away.

MAN-EATERS AND JUNGLE KILLERS

I write these stories not only in the hope that they may afford some degree of pleasure to the adventurous, but that they may also indicate what the conditions of living, in and near the great forests of India, were once like, and to show too that one of the greatest opportunities that any individual could desire, of showing his skill and perseverance in the fine sport of 'Shikar', is now in the process of vanishing forever.

One

The Marauder of Kempekarai

IF YOU TRY TO IMAGINE TWO PARALLEL RANGES OF LOFTY HILLS, averaging four thousand feet and more above the sea, with a valley between them about five miles across, covered with dense forest except for the craggy summits, you will have in your mind's eye the background of my story. It is set in the North Salem district of the Presidency of Madras in southern India.

The hills run from north to south, and the easterly range is the more lofty of the two, culminating at its southern point in the peak of Gutherayan, which is over 4,500 feet high. On its slopes stands a lovely little forest lodge, known as Kodekarai Bungalow, amidst some of the finest scenery in the world. Rolling hills and jutting cliffs are to be seen in every direction. The sun rises in shades of rose-pink above the billowing clouds of morning mist, to set eventually in the orange-bronze reflections behind the western range. Then the moon comes up in pallid splendour, tipping the hill-tops, and later the deep valleys, with her luminous wand. Through the night she rides the heavens, silent witness of many a jungle tragedy in the dark forests below. The scream of a dying sambar or the shrill shriek of a spotted stag have often gone forth in vain to that same full moon as they spilled their life-blood on the forest floor beneath the paws of a hungry tiger.

More than twenty years ago I had the honour of meeting the brother of King Amanuallah of Afghanistan, who was exiled from his native country and lived at Kodekarai Bungalow, which was his favourite abode. He told me that he loved the place, that its scenery reminded him of his beloved Afghanistan, except that the hills of Kodekarai were forest-clad while those of his country were bare. But both of them exemplified space and freedom.

Kempekarai is a small hamlet standing on the lower slopes of the western range. Around it lie a few fields and beyond the fields the forest of dense bamboo, intersected by a rocky stream that flows down the centre of the valley.

This valley, which I called 'Spider Valley' because of the immense spiders that spin their webs across the narrow footpath that runs beside the stream, broadens out toward the south into a larger tract known as the Morappur Valley where the rocky stream finally joins the Chinnar river at a spot called Sopathy, some ten miles from the Cauvery river.

I have described the area at some length so that the reader may, with a little imagination, share the stirring beauty: the dank smell of rotting vegetation, the twilight of a dense jungle, the distant half-roar, half-moan of a man-eating tiger searching for its prey, the eerie and deathly silence that follows those thrilling calls, and finally that faint rustle in the undergrowth, the indefinable creeping something that is the man-eater, watching as he becomes aware of your presence and pits the age-long hunting skill of his kind against the civilised intellect of man.

But let me begin my story.

Kempekarai was in a state of great fear, for a man-eating tiger had appeared, and three of its few inhabitants had already gone to fill his bill of fare.

The first victim, an old poojaree, had left Muttur, eleven miles away, to come to Kempekarai one month ago. He was never seen again. Elephants infest these areas, and very occasionally kill men, so when the poojaree failed to arrive at Kempekarai, a search-party set out towards Muttur. Perhaps the men who composed it expected to come upon the plate-like spoor of an elephant, and to find the squashed remains. But they found neither. About five miles from Kempekarai they did come upon the tracks of a male tiger, a little blood by the *path*-side, the old man's staff and his *loincloth*—and, nothing more.

Some ten days later, near sunset, a woman went down to the community well to fill her water-pot for the night. She never returned. At eight p.m. her husband and some of his friends, carrying lanterns and staves, visited the well to look for her. The brass water-pot, half-filled with water, lay on its side some twenty feet from the well, where it had been dropped by the woman on her return to the village. Of her there was no trace.

Next morning, a search-party was instituted, which duly came across the woman's saree, later a silver anklet, and finally her remains. Her head lay under a bush; her hands and feet were scattered about; of the remainder of her body, a goodly number of gnawed bones showed the tiger had indeed been hungry and had done full justice to a succulent repast.

A month dragged by. Kempekarai assumed the air of a fortress besieged. Nobody came in, and nobody went out. The immediate precincts, and in some cases interiors, of the few huts stank with human filth. Was there not a killer nearby, waiting for the first victim who was bold enough to even venture outside to answer the call of nature? The matter was particularly perilous at night; human beings, with their cattle and sometimes their dogs, were barricaded together within their cramped huts behind doors that were kept shut with logs of wood or rounded boulders from the stream. The huts became more filthy every day, under the force of the terrible circumstances in which the people were placed.

But the very best of precautions sometimes fall short of attaining their desired results. Mara, one of the sons-in-law of my old friend Byra, the poojaree, had spurned to live in such insanitary conditions. He had told his wife that, man-eating tiger or not, he for one would not soil the inside of his house. Nightly he had gone outside to answer the calls of nature, and nightly he had returned. Then one night he went out as usual for the same purpose, but this time he did not return. His wife, anxiously waiting inside, admits she heard a dull thud, a rasping gurgle, but nothing more.

After fifteen minutes she raised an alarm. Nobody would come to her rescue, for nobody dared. The inhabitants of the barricaded huts heard her shrieks for help. They knew that by this time Mara was beyond human assistance. He was dead, but they were alive! What was the use of going outside to join him among the dead! So they remained indoors, and listened to her screaming for the remainder of that long night.

Next morning, a half-hearted attempt was made to find what was left of Mara, and it would have been unsuccessful but that the tiger had boldly eaten his fill among the bushes within two hundred yards of the village. A little more was left of Mara than had been left of the woman who had gone to the well. Perhaps his flesh was tougher, or perhaps the tiger was less hungry. Who knows? His head and torso, at least, were still in one piece.

Because of the fate that had befallen his son-in-law, my old friend Byra, who happened to be at Kempekarai at that time, undertook the hazardous eighteen-mile journey to the village of Pennagram next day. He came by himself, as nobody would accompany him, and made the journey without sight or sound of the man-eater. At Pennagram he sought out his old acquaintance, Ranga, and the two of them came by bus to Bangalore. At 9 p.m. that night voices called me to the front door, and, going outside, I was surprised but delighted to see my old jungle companions once more.

The Salem district had meanwhile adopted 'prohibition' as a guiding policy towards physical, moral and, no doubt, spiritual uplift. But my two visitors, being simple, honest forest-folk, with no such high physical, moral or spiritual pretensions, enjoyed a shot of good spirits in the form of half a tumbler of neat brandy, each. Thus refreshed, they began at the beginning, or rather Byra did, and related the brief history of the coming and doings of the man-eater, as I have told it to you, closing with the flat statement that his son-in-law, Mara, must be avenged and that I was to do it.

In the face of that argument and his childlike confidence in me, I could find no very convincing reply. Three days later I was on the road to Pennagram, where I left the Studebaker. We bought supplies at the local market, and within a few hours the three of us were trudging those eighteen miles to the little hamlet of Kemperkarai, where the car could not go.

A couple of miles before our destination we found fresh pug-marks of a tiger on the footpath. No human traveller had passed along this track for many days, and the spoor was clear. I made careful measurements and noted that the pugs belonged to a male tiger of average size. This gave no indication whether the maker was an old animal, or of normal adult age, nor could any of us say at that time whether he was the man-eater, or just another passing tiger.

The few inhabitants of Kempekarai were unable to add much material information to that which had already been given to me by Byra. They thought the man-eater was an enormous animal, but, of course, all simple folk, when keyed up to a state of sheer terror bordering on panic, as had been the case with these poor people for the past few weeks, are given to attributing superhuman cunning and wholly impossible bodily strength and size to their oppressor.

The problem now was: how to proceed, and what to do? The answer was: wait for a kill, or present a live-bait. This particular tiger had not killed a single cow or other domestic animal belonging to the villagers. So far, at least, it had killed only human beings. The question was: would it kill an animal bait, or should that bait be human? To which the only answer was, that in the event of a human bait, it could be nobody but myself, an answer which I thoroughly disliked even to think about.

Byra, Ranga, and myself went into close conference, over successive mugs of tea, and eventually an answer began to take shape. I thought we should try animal baits, but they thought a human bait—myself, of course—would produce immediate results. I heartily wished they had reached a different conclusion.

In a three-man committee, any two of them form an overwhelming majority. The odd man must give in but I managed to force my point to the extent of agreeing that together with the human bait, there would be no harm in trying out a couple of young bullocks at selected spots as an additional attraction.

No buffaloes were available at Kempekarai, so I bought two bullocks, one of which we tied at the spot where we had found the pug-marks, and the other on the bed of the stream that meandered along the bottom of the valley. I sat on the stone parapet of the well, my back resting against one of the wooden uprights that supported the pulley-wheel, through which ran a rope for drawing water. I arranged for a metal pot to be tied to the end of this rope, which I kept beside me on the parapet. Fresh water is always nicer to drink than that from a water-bottle.

The jungle began some fifty yards from the well in all directions except one. Here somebody had planted a dozen or more papaya trees. With the occasional watering from the well that these trees received, an undergrowth, mainly of grass with a few shrubs here and there, had sprung up around the papaya tree. In daylight this undergrowth appeared negligible, but with twilight and approaching darkness, I began to feel it presented an admirable line of approach for the man-eater, which could easily crawl through it on its belly and come within almost springing distance of where I sat, without my being aware of its presence.

When this thought came to my mind, I changed my position to the other side of the well, using the opposite wooden upright as a back-rest, so that I now faced the papayas.

I had only decided to expose myself in view of the fact that we had fortunately come at a time just before full moon. Moonrise almost synchronised with sunset, but I had forgotten that the moon still had to top the range of hills to the east before it could cast its brilliance on that benighted well. This would only happen after 8 p.m. and I spent one of the worst ninety minutes of life awaiting—I cannot hope to express how eagerly and anxiously—the first rays of that longed-for moon.

The experience brought me back to the terrible hours I had spent before the huts of Gummalapur, awaiting that horrid panther, and to the day I had sat with my back to the teak tree, in the far distant Chamala forest range, hoping for a glimpse of a similar man-eater;* and I wondered what had made me so foolish as once again to place myself in such an awkward predicament. Then common sense told me that perhaps it was the only way.

The darkness was deathly still, and not even the familiar nightjar came anywhere near me. A few bats flitted down the well, to sip the limpid water in a series of flying-kisses, as they quenched their thirst after the hot day. I strained my eyes, not only towards the papaya trees, but also in all directions. Imagination created the form of the man-eater, slowly creeping, stealthily stalking me, from just outside my range of vision. I sat glued to the parapet, my .405 cocked, my thumb on the torch-switch.

The thoughts that spring to a man's mind at such times are often strange and unaccountable, but why should I burden you with them? The tiger first assumed the role of possible avenging fate. At other times it practically faded from conscious thought.

Shortly after eight o'clock the skyline above the eastern range grew more distinct; a pale glow diffused itself against the sky, dimming the stars, and then the moon appeared, lightening both the surroundings and my nervous condition. As the moon rose higher in the heavens, the scene became brighter, until I could see almost clearly between the stems of the papaya trees. Not a sound disturbed the silence of my vigil for practically the first half of the night.

Shortly after 11 p.m. a sambar stag voiced its strident call from the bed of the stream where I had tied one of my bullocks. I recognised the note of alarm and fear in its voice, as the call was repeated over and over again, to die away at

---

* See *Nine Man-Eaters and One Rogue*

last in the distance, when the stag ascended the rampart of the opposing range of hills to safety.

Again silence fell, and the night dragged out its last hours. It then struck me that I might perhaps be able to catch the tiger's acute hearing, if he was anywhere within a mile, by operating the pulley-wheel above the well, which, I had noticed earlier in the afternoon, creaked and squealed loudly as it revolved about its uncoiled axle. Perhaps he would hear and be attracted, thinking another prospective victim was drawing water from the well.

So I went around the well to where the water-pot rested on the ground. First of all I stood the firearm up against the wall, and then let the pot down till it touched the water, drawing it up and letting it down in slow succession thereafter. The pulley screeched loudly in the silence of the night, and I continued for nearly an hour, stopping every now and again to survey my surroundings intently, particularly the deep shadows cast by every bush. But nothing stirred, and in the breathless air not a leaf moved, nor did even a belated rat rustle the dried debris that carpeted the ground beneath the adjacent papayas. To all intents and purposes, I was the only living thing in that area, apart from the inmates of the huts, secure behind barricaded doors.

After 3 a.m. the moon began to sink behind the western range of hills, and the same conditions presented themselves as in the previous evening. It grew darker and darker, and soon I could see only a few yards around me, and that by the radiance of the stars that came to life, and twinkled overhead, with the disappearance of the setting moon.

There were only ninety minutes of darkness left, and I felt terribly sleepy. Still I had now to redouble my guard. Had I not been trying to attract the tiger for the past hour? As he had not passed that way all night, it was just possible he might do so now. Moreover, conditions for a surprise attack were all in his favour, as the papaya trees themselves now became undefined, except as a darker blur among the other shadows in my line of vision.

I realised that the man-eater had me completely at his mercy if he chose to attack. Should he roar as he charged, I could at least discharge my rifle at point-blank range. On the other hand, if he crept silently upon me, I would not be aware of his coming until actually struck down.

At the same time, all the rats and rabbits, and other small animals, which had been conspicuous by their absence all night, appeared to select this moment to rendezvous near the well. They scurried hither and thither, and rustled the dead leaves, sometimes noisily, sometimes barely audibly, while my excited imagination telegraphed the urgent message 'the man-eater is coming'.

Altogether I had a dreadful time. The false dawn came and went, and then at 5.45 a.m. the brightening of the skyline once more, above the eastern range, told me that daylight was at last at hand and that the tedious vigil was nearly over. It was well past seven before the sun peeped over the eastern hills, and I arose and dragged my wary, sleepy steps to the tent I had pitched at the southern end of the village.

Hot tea and a nap till ten-thirty. Then, accompanied by Ranga and Byra, I first visited the bait tethered in the streambed. It was alive and well. Closer inspection showed that a tiger had approached to within 15 feet of it and had passed on after a cursory inspection.

The sambar stag I had heard during the night had doubtless seen or scented this tiger and had voiced his loud alarm. The tiger's pug-marks were clearly identified as having been made by the same animal as had been those I had seen while coming along the *path* on the western range, where the ground was firmer and dimensions not exaggerated. Nevertheless, I had little doubt that this was the real man-eater, for a normal tiger will not readily leave a tempting, unguarded bait alive.

We then went to see the other bullock, where a surprise awaited us. It had been killed by a tiger, whose pug-marks were identical with those I had carefully measured the previous day, near the very same spot on the pathway.

The question now was this: were there two tigers in the vicinity, or had the second bullock been killed by the man-eater? If the latter was the case and there was only one tiger—and that the man-eater—why had he not killed the bullock which had been tied in the streambed instead of just looking at it and choosing to kill the other?

I formed the definite opinion that there were two tigers in the vicinity, and that it had been the man-eater which had ignored the bullock at the stream. Ranga agreed with me, but Byra would not commit himself to either opinion. He suggested that the man-eater might be the only tiger in the area, that it had not killed the first bullock, possibly because it was a white one. The second, being dark brown, had been above suspicion.

On the question of the colour of a live-bait I have a very open mind. In my own experience, colour makes little or no difference to a tiger, and he will kill your bait provided certain other conditions also exist. He must be hungry, for a tiger rarely, if ever, kills wantonly. Moreover, he must not suspect a trap of any kind. In these days when tiger-hunting is becoming intensified, tigers are learning their lessons quickly. Nature makes an effort to try to preserve a species which is rapidly becoming shot-out.

Thus a bait secured around the neck by a rope stands a very good chance of not being touched by a tiger. He cannot reason, but his instinct, or sense of self-preservation, tells him that it is unnatural of villagers to tie up their cattle for the night in a forest. A bait secured by a rope tied around the horns stands more chance of being killed, for it is possible for an animal to get entangled in the under-growth by its horns. A bait secured by its hind leg is also readily taken. The main point to be remembered is that both tigers and panthers attack the throats of their victims, and there should therefore be no visible obstruction to prevent this method of attack, or the attacker becomes suspicious.

Panthers are generally less careful than tigers in this respect, and take greater risks. Personally, I dislike tethering dogs as bait for a panther; I feel the practice is extremely cruel, for the dog is a very sagacious animal and knows well the purpose for which he is being tied. This being so, he must suffer terrible mental torture till his attacker arrives. When I was younger, and, I must confess, had fewer scruples, I tried to salve my conscience by protecting the dog's life. To achieve this I made a collar about four inches broad, using two pieces of leather, with numerous two-inch-long, sharpened nails in close array, protruding outwards, the heads of the nails coming between the two strips of leather. It would amuse me, in those bygone days, to watch the panther grab at the dog's throat, only to spring backwards in obvious dismay as the sharp nails pierced his mouth. Before he could solve the puzzle, of course, he was shot. But such elementary tricks cannot be played on a tiger.

Tying up a sickly live-bait is also fatal to success. The Badaga tribe, who inhabit the Nilgiri mountains, are very averse to selling healthy animals for bait, no matter what price is offered for them. They feel it is a sin to sacrifice the life of a good bullock. Invariably, they will offer only a sickly animal, whose days are numbered anyhow, for this purpose.

I well remember tying up a bullock in the last stages of foot-and-mouth disease. For three nights in succession, as tracks in the sand revealed, the tiger came to the spot, walked around the bait, even squatted before it, and then decided it was too diseased to kill. On the fourth night, my son sat up over the sick animal, but by eight o'clock its allotted span of life was running out. It collapsed and took the whole night to die. That night the tiger did not even appear.

Hunters of experience vary in their opinions regarding the colour of a live-bait, and I have met a few who avoid using white animals, either cattle or goats, because they claim that these are the least likely to be taken. A famous panther-hunter of days gone by, who had shot over a hundred panthers, was very averse to tying up a black goat, which, he claimed, made the panther extra wary in its approach.

I have digressed at some length on these points, as I feel many of you who read these stories will be interested to learn what might be called some aspects of the technique of tiger and panther shooting. In drawing-room circles we often hear of the extraordinary degree of 'good luck' that attends a certain *shikari* or big-game hunter. Actually, much of this 'good luck' is due to his previous experience of the innumerable factors that combine to make, or mar, a successful hunt.

Returning, to my story. There was obviously only one thing to do, and that was to fix a *machan* above the partly eaten brown bullock. Through experience both our baits had been tethered near suitable trees; so while I went back to the tent for a further nap, Ranga and Byra, both highly qualified in such matters, made a good job of slinging up the canvas camp-chair I had brought, neatly folded, with me. Next to a *charpoy*, or Indian rope-cot, a folding chair makes a good *machan*. It is not nearly so comfortable or roomy as the *charpoy*, but has an advantage in being easily taken to pieces and folded up.

Returning by 5 p.m., I took up my position, prepared for an all-night vigil.

The pathway, situated as it was on the western range above the village of Kempekarai, received the rays of the rising moon far earlier than did the village and the well, where I had spent the previous night. So it was that, soon after the sun sank below the western hill-tops, the moon peeped over the eastern range, and visibility was good all around me.

Nothing happened till shortly after eight, when I became aware that the tiger stood directly beneath me. How or from where it had come, I never knew. Certainly not along the *path* which was clearly visible in both directions as it stretched away into the forest. I knew the tiger was below me by the soft noise it made as it rubbed its body against the trunk of the tree in which I was sitting, and in doing so looked up and became aware of my presence!

Things then began to happen quickly. With a snarling growl, the tiger began at once to claw its way up the tree trunk. Fortunately, we had selected a tree with fairly straight trunk till the first crotch was reached at about fifteen feet above the ground—where I was sitting on the camp chair. I knew that this was the man-eater, for normally a tiger would have decamped at once on becoming aware that a human being sat above him.

Instinctively I drew up both legs as high as possible, while leaning over the chair sideways and to the left, to get in a shot. Unfortunately, I had leant in the wrong direction, for the tiger was trying to climb the tree on my right side. I quickly corrected myself, but now had to hold the rifle to my left shoulder.

It took you longer to read the preceding two paragraphs than events actually took that night. As I have said, I was sitting about fifteen feet above the ground. A normal tiger is about nine feet long from nose-tip to tail-tip. Subtracting the length of his tail and adding something in compensation for an outstretched forepaw, we may come by a working figure of almost 8 feet to cover the 'stretching range' of man-eater, or for that matter, of any tiger. Deducting these eight feet from the original height of fifteen feet, we get a difference of about seven feet, which was about the distance that the tiger succeeded in climbing the tree-trunk that night. In his eagerness to get hold of me he stretched out a forepaw, and as the sharp claws drove through the canvas of the camp-chair seat, and incidentally partially through my pants, the tiger lost his balance and fell backwards to earth, while instinctively, in my anxiety to protect my rear, I half-levered myself out of the chair. I was lucky not to drop my rifle and follow in the wake of the tiger.

Now it is a peculiar fact about man-eaters, both tigers and panthers, that they appear to be craven creatures, although they attack and devour human beings. Almost without exception, such attacks are made from behind, and when the victim is not aware of the presence of his attacker. Very rarely, indeed, has any man-eater been known to carry out frontal attack or rush a person who is aware of his presence and faces him.

So it was that night, for, as he fell backwards to earth, the man-eater realised his presence had been disclosed, and no sooner had he landed on the ground than, with a bound and a snarl, he disappeared in the surrounding lantana.

I cannot say to which of our good fortunes it was that he did so, for, although I had now become aware of his presence and was prepared for him, I might easily have overbalanced, or dropped the rifle, in trying to get a downward shot at that very awkward angle, directly below me. Be that as it may, he was gone in a flash, and as suddenly and as unexpectedly as he had come.

My presence having been discovered, there was now no point in remaining motionless or silent. Reviewing the damage done, I discovered three claw-marks through the canvas of the chair, each about five inches long, where the tiger's forepaw had swept. Of these, two had penetrated the seat of my pants — and myself inside them to a lesser extent. The flesh certainly smarted, to remind me of the fact.

Normally, the incident would evoke some mirth in the minds of mirthful people, but I would remind them that the claws of all carnivores are full of poisonous bacteria from the decomposed flesh at which they tear, and a man-eater is no exception to this rule, because the flesh happens to be human. The canvas of the chair, and the cloth of my pants, were not sufficiently thick to absorb all this poisonous material, so that there was some chance of my wound becoming infected.

I had brought with me a variety of first aids, including a good stock of procaine penicillin and my five c.c. hypodermic syringe. But all these were in my tent at Kempekarai, some two miles away. I had therefore to choose between returning immediately and taking medical precautions, or remaining till morning—which was at least ten hours ahead—by which time the poison might have spread in the wounds. In the one case I had to face the chance of an attack by the man-eater, which might be launched anywhere along the *path* for the distance of the two miles it extended up to Kempekarai. On the other hand, I had to face perhaps the more certain danger of sepsis, and a long period of incapacitation from pursuing the man-eater.

So I chose to risk the tiger, as the lesser of the two evils, and quickly letting my rifle down on the rope brought for the purpose, I quickly scrambled down myself, praying fervently that the man-eater would not choose that very moment for a second attack. Reaching the ground, I stood with my back to the tree-trunk, while I freed the rifle from the rope by which I had lowered it. All was as silent as the grave, and not a sound came from any part of the forest to give me any indication of the whereabouts of my recent attacker. For all intents and purposes he might be ten miles away, or behind the nearest bush! The brilliant moonlight bathed the jungle in its ethereal glow, making visible each leaf and grass-blade as they gracefully vibrated to the soft currents of the night-breezes that gently wafted the scent of night flowers along the glades of the forest, or blew in gusts between the aisles of its myriad trees.

After a few moments, I set forth along the path on the two-mile walk to Kempekarai. Now this path varies in width according to the nature of the soil, and the character of the vegetation, from fifteen feet at the maximum to hardly a yard. At certain spots it is fringed with long grass and at other places by lantana undergrowth. Several small streams have to be crossed, where bamboos grow in profusion, their tall swaying stems creaking to the gentle breeze, while the fronds, in obliterating the moonlight, cast ghostly, chequered patterns on the ground in front.

In such circumstances your heart thumps in your chest almost audibly and as if to leap from its cage; your nerves are frayed to breaking-point and every faint rustle heralds the man-eater's charge. The inclination is to hurry, if not break into a run. Your nerves signal you to look to one side or the other, for the tiger may be making an attack from behind or from either side!

All these emotions must be held under close restraint, for to give way to them in the least would mean panic, and panic will cause you to lose your presence of mind, with ultimate but certain destruction to follow.

The thing to make certain of is that the tiger is not in front, lying in ambush till you come abreast of him. To attack from the rear, he has to make at least some noise in the undergrowth in order to catch up with your normal stride as you walk forward.

It is wisest, therefore, to look in front, although your eyes must search every shadow before you come abreast of it, rather than keep turning the head from side to side. Keep your rifle cocked and held in the crook of your arm, for you will have to fire from your hip, and make certain of your shot. There will be no time to raise the rifle to your shoulder and aim, for the tiger is a killer, and it is not the habit of killers, either animal or human, to go about advertising their presence. For if they did, they would soon cease to be the killer—and become the 'killed' instead.

If your quarry is wounded, you may perhaps hear a snarl or growl, but most likely that unnervingly awful, earth-shaking *'woof'* as he charges. If he is not wounded, and a man-eater, you may expect to hear just nothing, for he will be upon you in the twinkling of an eye.

Hardly a quarter-of-a-mile before Kempekarai there is a low outcrop of boulders on both sides of the *path*. This is the most dangerous spot in the journey home, as the tiger could be behind any one of those boulders. However, seeing him head the other way when he made off, I felt he had not had enough time to retrace his steps. With this mental assurance, I negotiated the rocks, and soon came to Kempekarai and my tent.

Ranga and Byra were awake, as they always remained when I went out alone, in case I should require their sudden assistance. Telling them to make a fire and heat some water, I drank some coffee that had been kept ready, and got out my hypodermic, which I sterilized in the hot water. Thereafter, mixing two phials of eight-lakh units of procaine penicillin, I gave myself a shot with the syringe.

I got Ranga and Byra to wash the wounds with a strong solution of potassium permanganate dissolved in the rest of the hot water, followed by a dressing of sulphonomide ointment. The spot was one that could not be bandaged, or plastered, so I went to sleep hoping that no ill effects would develop with my wounds.

I was tired after my sleepless nights, and it was nearly nine before I awoke next morning. This is a very late hour for rising in any jungle, where one is usually up and out before sunrise. The wounds, I was glad to note, were not unduly painful.

Taking another four lakhs of penicillin, and after redressing the wounds, I breakfasted excellently on porridge, bacon and eggs, and an enormously large, ripe papaya fruit from the grove by the well-side, where I had spent the first night.

Then I set off to visit my bait on the streambed, which I found as alive and well as on the previous morning. Returning the two miles up the *path* to where I had sat the previous night, I found the tiger had not come back nor touched the bullock he had killed two nights before. His pug-marks, as he had approached the tree, identified him as the tiger whose prints I had seen first.

The forests of Salem, unlike those of the Nilgiris, Coimbatore and Chittoor districts, are mostly thorny in nature, lantana and the 'wait-a-bit' thorn predominating. Along the valleys and streambeds these give way to clumps of bamboo, massed in close array. In either case, the effect is the same, namely, to make roaming or stalking unprofitable, if not impossible.

A carnivore moves silently, and the secret of its success as a hunter lies in the animal instinctively watching where it places its front paw in order to make no sound. Next it places its rear paw in exactly the same spot, as the front paw moves forward again to take the next step. The human stalker must move silently, too. He must watch carefully where he places each step, for the smallest dry leaf will crackle when trodden upon; the smallest twig will snap. Those clutching 'wait-a-bit' thorns must be avoided, too, for a single thorn is strong enough to halt your progress if it catches in any part of your clothing, while it will rip your flesh in no uncertain manner if you are foolish enough to wear shorts.

All this will distract your attention from being on the lookout for the tiger, and if that tiger is a man-eater, who will not be deterred by thorns, you are at a distinct disadvantage.

The jungle at this spot was etremely thorny, so we returned to Kempekarai to hold a council of war with the 'greybeards' of the village. The facts, as far as we now knew them, showed that:

The man-eater was a male of average size.

He particularly frequented the *path* on the western range.

He did not particularly care for bullock meat.

We were still uncertain whether or not there was a second tiger in the vicinity.

The obvious conclusion reached after this discussion was much the same as that reached by Ranga, Byra and myself on the first day we had come to Kempekarai: either await the next human kill, or offer a human live-bait, preferably somewhere along the pathway to Kempekarai as it descends the western ridge. A couple of bullocks could also be tied out elsewhere in the jungle to tempt the man-eater, but more to find out if there was another tiger operating in the same area.

The scratches which the tiger had inflicted, being located where they were, made it impossible for me to sit still for more than fifteen minutes at a stretch. This fact precluded all chances of 'sitting-up', in the literal meaning of the word. True, if I was to act as a bait there would be no necessity for me to sit still. In fact, movement would be a necessary factor in helping to attract the tiger. On the other hand, the very act of sitting would not only be agonising, but would also retard the healing of the wounds, which I was naturally anxious to hasten.

The alternatives left were either to stand or lie down. The former course was naturally not advisable for a night-long vigil, so the only practical method under the circumstances was to lie down.

We did a lot of thinking that day and eventually came by what we all thought to be a very ingenious plan. How ingenious it actually turned out—or rather did not turn out to be—you will very soon come to know.

I have already explained that the footpath down the western range to Kempekarai was crossed at several places by streamlets, bordered by dense undergrowth and clumps of bamboo. The beds of these small rivulets were rocky and admirably suited the purpose I had in mind.

It so happened that the first of these small streams to be crossed on the way down to Kempekarai, from the tree on which I had sat the night before, was the broadest of the lot, and was, moreover, closely covered with rounded boulders of all sizes. My plan was to detach a cart-wheel from one of the only two bullock-carts in the village of Kempekarai, dig a pit in the stream-bed, get inside it, place the wheel above, and anchor it securely around the circumference with big boulders. Smaller boulders, and a camouflage of dry leaves, would help to conceal the cartwheel. I would also make a human dummy and seat it somewhere on the footpath, where it crossed the stream. The cartwheel would be raised off the ground at one end, facing the dummy, to allow me a range of fire in that direction.

This was my general plan. For the benefit of those who have not been to India, I would explain that the wheel of an Indian bullock-cart—I am referring to the large type of cart—averages five feet in diameter. The circumference is of wood, some six inches wide by three inches thick, shod with a hoop of iron to serve as a tyre. There are a dozen stout wooden spokes, all converging on a massive central wooden hub. The central hole in the wooden hub rotates around an iron axle, some one-and-a-half inches thick. The wheel is kept from falling off by a cotter-pin in the form of a flat iron nail, passing through the axle at its outer extremity. Similarly, the wheel is prevented from moving towards the frame of the cart by the axle itself, which is made suddenly thicker immediately beyond the bearing surface of the axle on the hub, which is perhaps a little over a foot in width. In what may be called deluxe models, a better bearing surface is provided by lining the hole in the wooden hub with a piece of iron or galvanised piping. 'High-grade lubrication', from the village viewpoint, is provided by applying old motor oil, perhaps once a fortnight, on the ends of the axle, after removing the cotter-pin and the wheel to do so. The oil is carried permanently on the cart in the shell of an old bullock-horn, suspended somewhere beneath the cart, and is applied to the axle at the end of any piece of stick that may happen to be lying handy, when 'servicing time' comes up.

It was too late to set the cartwheel that day, so we busied ourselves gathering old clothing from the villagers. Pants are unknown in such parts, so I contributed a pair of mine, into which we stuffed two 'legs', made of bamboo and wound around with straw. In case the pants might strike the tiger as being unfamiliar, we draped a *'dhoti'* (which is a cross between a sarong and a *loincloth*) over the pants. The body of the dummy consisted of straw rammed into an old gunny sack, over which we draped a couple of torn shirts, and a very ragged coat. The head of the dummy was a work of art; it was made from a large-sized coconut, complete with its coir fibre.

On dress occasions Indian women sometimes augment their natural hair with 'false hair', which they twist into a 'bun' or 'coonday' behind their heads, into which they stick flowers, particularly jasmine. Fortunately there was a 'belle' in Kemperkarai who was vain enough to be the owner of a coil of such hair. This we borrowed, combed out, and fixed around the coconut, to emulate the long hair of a villager. An untidily-tied, 'yokel-pattern' turban was then wound around the nut and a pair of 'chappals' or sandals were put on the dummy's feet.

Tigers, as I have said, have no sense of smell, so the dummy looked realistic enough to attract a man-eater, if only he did not watch it long enough to begin wondering at its uncanny stillness.

That night I applied fresh dressing to my wounds, and next morning helped myself to another shot of penicillin. I was thankful to note that so far no undue inflammation had occurred.

By 8 a.m. half-a-dozen willing helpers and myself had trundled the cartwheel to the crossing I had in mind. Here we busied ourselves excavating a hole nearly four feet across by about four feet deep. This was easily done, for we were digging in the soft sand of a streambed. Some grass was then cut and thrown into the hole to absorb, to some degree, the dampness of the sand which naturally increased with the digging of the hole.

Sitting inside, I found I could adopt only a semi-crouched position, which was going to be very uncomfortable indeed, the only recommendation it offered being that it saved me from a sitting position, which, as I have said already, would have been most uncomfortable in view of my recent wounds.

The dummy we placed with its back to a tamarind tree, some fifteen feet away, which stood on the western bank of the stream where it was crossed by the track to Kempekarai; it was so arranged that its legs stuck out on the track at an angle of forty-five degrees. Thus, it would at once be visible to the tiger from any point along the streambed or on either section of the track, if he happened to pass in any of those directions. Lastly, we collected some of the larger boulders, and, as I stood guard with my rifle, Ranga and Byra gathered brushwood and debris for camouflaging the wheel.

When eventually I got into the hole, the wheel was just a couple of inches above the top of my head. There was a space of six inches between the ground level and the wheel through which I could fire in the direction of the dummy; it was made by placing two stones of that size about three feet apart under the circumference, leaving the central portion open to the sky for the purpose of ventilation. Brushwood and debris were scattered and intertwined among the boulders; it would also give me warning if he came up from behind, when the debris would crackle as he brushed against it or trod on it.

For safety's sake, I had arranged that the men should return to Kempekarai in a body, and only come back next morning, again in a body. I would be imprisoned all night in the hole, as the weight of the cartwheel with the boulders above it was too great for me to lift unaided from inside.

It was 4.30 p.m. when I entered my voluntary prison. It had taken nearly another half-hour to position the boulders on the wheel and arrange the camouflage, so that it was almost five when I found myself alone. The heat inside the hole, despite the opening above, was stifling. I removed my coat and shirt, and would have removed the remainder of my clothes but for the fact that I did not want the sand to get into my wounds.

Peeping above the level of the ground, I could clearly distinguish the dummy and quite a wide extent of the background. A clump of 'henna' bushes grew halfway down the sloping bank behind the dummy. A slight movement in that direction caught my eye, which I found was due to the twitching, outstretched ear of a beautiful spotted stag that gazed in curiosity at the motionless dummy. The value of sitting still in a forest was then made apparent to me, for the stag gazed a full ten minutes at that still dummy. Then it appeared to lose interest in the curious object, came out on to the open track, which it eventually crossed, vanishing into the jungle on the other side. The distance between the dummy and the stag could not have been much more than twenty feet, and yet the latter was quite unalarmed. Had a human been seated in place of the dummy, he would surely have moved, even if it was an eyelid that flickered, and this would have sent the stag crashing away in alarm.

A pair of peafowl then came strutting along the track. The cock-bird stopped, fanned out his tail and rustled the quills in display to his admiring spouse. Female-like, she kept one eye on him and the other elsewhere! Anyway, she saw the dummy, took a short run, and sailed into the air. The cock, chagrined at her failure to appreciate his beauty, lowered his tail and saw the dummy too. A much heavier bird than the hen, he flapped wildly and desperately in an effort to take off, his wings beating loudly on the still evening air, before he finally managed to rise just clear of the surrounding bushes and follow his more wary partner to apparent safety.

'Kuck-kaya-kaya-khuck' crowed the grey junglecocks in all directions, as they came out along the streambed to peck a few morsels before darkness fell. 'Kukurruka-wack-kukurruka-wack' cackled the smaller spurfowl, belligerent little birds, as male fought male in little duels throughout the jungle for the favour of an accompanying hen. Drab and uninteresting as she looks, to gain her favour was for them the only interest in the world that evening.

Darkness fell, to the farewell call of the pair of peafowl, as they roosted for the night on some tall tree in the forest, perhaps a quarter-of-a-mile away. 'Mia-a-oo-Aaow' they cried, as the sun sank behind the western range.

Those of you who have been in an Indian forest will remember the almost miraculous switch-over that takes place at sunset, as the birds of the daylight hours cease their calls, and the birds of the night take up theirs. 'Chuck-chuk-chuk-chucko' cried the nightjars, as with widespread wings they sailed overhead in search of insect morsels, or settled on the ground, resembling stones against a background of sand.

It was pitch-dark where I sat and even the dummy was hidden under the shadows of the tamarind tree beneath which it was propped. I reckoned the moonlight would not reach that spot till after ten. At nine I heard the noisy snuffling and deep-throated gurgle of a sloth bear, as it wended its clumsy way down the stream in my direction. It almost fell over the outlying debris we had placed on the streambed to give me warning of the tiger's approach, and then saw the newly-heaped boulders placed upon the cartwheel! I could have read the thoughts that crossed the little brain beneath the shaggy black hair! 'Here's a chance to find some luscious fat grubs, or a beetle or two; perhaps a nest of white ants, or, most hopeful of all, a beehive built by the small yellow bees that can hardly sting a big bear like me.'

With those thoughts, the bear fell to work on the task of clearing away the boulders that so carefully anchored my cartwheel.

'Shoo!' I whispered in an undertone. 'Get away, you interfering...!'

The bear heard my voice, and stopped. 'Where did that come from?' he was thinking. A few minutes' silence followed, and then he started at the stones again. 'Out! Shoo!' I whispered. The bear stopped, climbed over the boulders, and looked down between the spokes at me.

'Aa-rr, Wr-rrr!' he growled. 'Get out, you idiot!' I growled. 'Wr-oof! Wr-oof! Wr-oof' he answered, as he scrambled, helter-skelter, over the boulders, stumbled over the debris, scampered up the bank and crashed away between the dried bamboos.

Hardly ten minutes had passed after the bear's noisy departure when I heard the most infinitesimal of noises, the soft tread of the padded foot of some heavy animal. It is almost impossible to imitate that noise in speech, and less so on paper. The nearest description I can give is the very muffled impact of a soft cushion when it is thrown on to a sofa.

The tiger had come and in his silent way was negotiating the fringe of the debris we had scattered on the streambed behind me. He was picking his way carefully across it.

Would he attack the dummy? Would he pass in front of me? These were the questions that raced through my mind as I awaited developments. My nerves were taut with anticipation.

The moon had already risen, but its beams had not yet reached the shadows cast by the heavy foliage of the tamarind tree. The dummy was not visible to me, but I knew that the tiger could clearly see it.

There was silence for a time—how long I could not say. Then came the clink of a stone as it rolled above my head. Nobody had anticipated an attack in that direction; but my recent visitor, the bear, had already shown that the unexpected could happen. Now the unexpected was being repeated by the presence of the tiger above me. What had caused it to ignore the dummy, and come straight to the spot where I lay, was a mystery. Very likely, the tiger had been watching the bear, had seen its strange behaviour, had noted its hurried departure and had come to investigate. Even more likely, the behaviour of the bear had caused the tiger to suspect human agency, which he had come over to find out himself. Or perhaps the wheel just happened to be situated on the shortest line of approach which the tiger was following to get at the dummy.

Whatever be the reason, the tiger was now barely two yards away, and above me.

As these thoughts raced through my mind, I heard the vague sound caused by the tiger's breathing. Then he stepped gracefully over one of the big boulders that held down the wheel, and peered down at me.

In the meantime I had not been idle. Screwing myself around, as best as I could, I now lay half on my back, gazing up at the tiger. The rifle I had drawn inwards and backwards till the butt came up against the side of the hole. I have already told you this hole was about four feet across, and about the same in depth. Hence it was impossible to get the rifle to point completely upwards. The most I could manage was an angle of a little more then sixty degrees with the bottom of the hole. Unfortunately, the tiger was not in the direction in which the muzzle was pointing, but was standing behind it, and directly above the spot where the butt of my rifle was stuck against the side of the hole.

Then events moved quickly. The tiger did not react quite as the bear had done. His features, dimly visible above me, contorted into a hideous snarl. A succession of deep-throated growls issued from his cavernous chest, and, lying down upon the cartwheel, he attempted to rake me with the claws of a foreleg, which he inserted between the spokes of the wheel.

I knew those talons would rip my face and head to ribbons if they only made contact, so, sinking as low into the hole as possible, I struggled desperately to turn the muzzle of the rifle towards the tiger.

All this took only seconds to happen. The tiger growled and came a little farther on to the wheel. The muzzle of my rifle contacted his shoulder and I pressed the trigger.

The explosion, within that confined space, was deafening. The tiger roared hideously as he catapulted backwards. During the next thirty seconds he bit the boulders, the wheel and even the sand, as he gave forth roar after roar of agony. Then I heard him fall amidst the debris, pick himself up, fall again, get up and finally crash into the bushes that bordered the little stream. He was still roaring, and continued to do so for quite fifteen minutes more as he staggered away into the jungle.

Finally silence, total and abysmal, fell over the forest. After the pandemonium that had just reigned, every creature, including the insects, decided it was wise to hide till with the passage of time they could forget their fright.

The hours passed. At one in the morning a stiff breeze began to blow over the hills, dark storm-clouds scudded across the sky, completely hiding the moon, and soon the distant sound of falling rain across the western range fell upon my listening ears. Not long afterwards, large raindrops penetrated between the spokes and splashed down upon me.

Then the deluge began, such as can only be experienced in tropical countries, and particularly forest regions with dense vegetation. I was soaked to the skin, and the water began to trickle down the sides of the hole. With that came the sudden realisation that the stream, which had been dry, would soon be flowing with the spate of rain-water that was running into it from all directions along a hundred tributaries. I would be drowned like a rat in a hole.

Jerked into frenzied action, I got on my hands and knees, placed my back to the wheel and pressed upwards with all my might. The wheel did not budge an inch! My helpers had done their work of protecting me from the tiger only too well! They had placed the heaviest boulders they could find around the circumference of the wheel and I was unable to move them unaided.

There was but one chance left, and that was to dig myself out through the six-inch-wide gap we had made for me to fire through. Desperately, with both hands I scooped the earth downwards into the hole, which was already half filled with water and sand; the damp sides were collapsing, making it very obvious that within the next few minutes, unless I got out quickly, cartwheel and boulders would all come down together on top of me.

When I judged there was sufficient room for my body to pass, I pushed the rifle between the spokes of the wheel and then rested it across them. Next I started squeezing myself through the opening I had just dug, wriggling in the sand and water like a stranded eel, till I finally struggled free onto the streambed.

The rain continued to fall in torrents. I had no idea how far the tiger had gone, or in which direction, so, picking up the rifle, I first carried the dummy off the streambed and placed it high up on the western bank. Then I started to recross the stream on the return journey to Kempekarai, and as I did so, I heard the dull roar of the spate of rain-water descending the streambed from the direction of the hills.

Within a few minutes it arrived, a wall of foaming water over three feet high, carrying all before it. Logs of wood, uprooted trees, dead bamboos and flotsam and jetsam of every description mingled with the crested, frothing waters. They reached the cartwheel and covered it; then the cartwheel and boulders were swept away downstream along with the torrent. In less than five minutes the stream had become a raging river, over four feet deep.

Thankfully appreciating the escape I had had, I began the return journey to Kempekarai. No other sound could possibly be heard above the splatter and swish of the rain. The darkness was intense, my torch throwing a circle of light before me. Moreover, the ground was extremely slippery to the soft rubber shoes that I was wearing. I had to cross three other streams, slightly smaller that the one where I sat, but all were raging torrents of water.

Half-way to Kempekarai, I saw the flicker of an approaching light. A little later, I met the party of men that were carrying it—Ranga, Byra and a few stalwarts from the village. They had realised the danger I was in when the waters rose and had risked encounter with the man-eater to come to my rescue.

Next morning the sun shone brightly on the saturated forest. We returned to the site of my adventure the night before. All streams were flowing briskly, although they were now no more than two feet deep. There was no trace of the cartwheel anywhere near the crossing. Evidently it had been borne downstream by the spate and probably smashed to bits. We combed both banks thereafter, without finding any signs of the tiger. The torrential rain had only too effectively obliterated any blood-trail or pug-marks.

Two hours later, a depressed and disappointed group, we returned to Kempekarai. There I remained for three more days, hoping to hear news of the tiger, only to be doomed to disappointment. Both Byra and Ranga felt it had died of its wounds, but I doubted this very much, as I knew I had not been able to aim sufficiently well to score more than a mere raking shot.

My period of leave, taken for the purpose of shooting this animal, had now elapsed, so I left Kempekarai on the morning of the fourth day, instructing Ranga to remain behind to assist Byra in reconnoitring. They were then to come to Pennagram, and thence to Dharmapuri, where there was a telegraph office from which they could send me a message. They were to await my reply there.

Ten days after returning to Bangalore, the hoped-for telegram arrived, stating that a pack-pony belonging to a Forest Guard of the Kodekarai Forest Lodge had been killed. Calculating from the telegram that the kill would be four days old by the time I reached it, I sent a reply, telling my henchmen to return to Kempekarai and wait there for any further events, which were to be reported by telegram in the same way.

Six more days passed, when I received a second telegram stating that a tiger had attacked the driver of a bullock-cart that was the last of a convoy travelling from the small hamlet of Morappur towards Sopathy on the Chinar River.

This, no doubt, was the man-eater again. Within an hour I was on my way by car to Dharmapuri, where I picked up my two henchmen. We continued to Pennagram, where we left the car and made a cross-country trip of about twelve miles to Morappur, passing the Chinar river and Sopathy on the way.

I had meanwhile learned that the cartman, who had been attacked by the tiger, had saved his life by jumping from the cart, in which he was travelling, on to the yoke and then between the two bulls that were hauling his cart. He had yelled vociferously and his yells were taken up by the other cartmen in the 'convoy'. The tiger had then made off.

I spoke to this cartman at Morappur. He said that the tiger had suddenly appeared behind his cart, which was the last in the line, and had attempted to leap into it from the rear, when he had dived between his bulls for protection. Asking him why the tiger had not succeeded in the comparatively easy task of getting into the cart, the man said it had jumped half-in, and he had not waited to see any more.

Meanwhile, a party of travellers who had followed us from Sopathy brought the news that they had come across fresh tiger pug-marks, made the previous night, leading down the Chinar River.

Hearing this, we hurried back to Sopathy, and it did not take us long to find the pug-marks. The water was running in the Chinar as a silvery stream, meandering from bank to bank, and in the soft, wet sand we clearly noticed that the tiger which had made the marks must have been limping badly. The weight of the body fell almost entirely on the left forefoot, the right being placed very lightly on the sand at each step.

I have said that, 'Spider Valley' met the Chinar river at this spot. A half-mile downstream, and in the direction in which the tiger had gone, was a small longish rock in midstream. It rose some four feet above the bed of the river and was about forty feet long by eight feet wide. I decided to sit on top of that rock that night, in the hope the tiger might make his way back up the Chinar and see me in my elevated position.

Borrowing Ranga's turban, old brown coat and *dhoti*, I donned all three, the two latter above my own clothing, and seated myself on the rock by 5.30 p.m. As Ranga and Byra were afraid to return to Morappur alone, they elected to spend the night on comfortable crotches, high up in the huge *muthee* trees that border the Chinar in this locality.

The nights were dark at this time, but from my position on the rock, and as the Chinar was about 100 yards wide at this spot, I relied upon the white sand to reflect the starlight and to reveal the form of the tiger from whatever direction it might come. Apart from being handicapped by its lameness, I knew the tiger would not charge its prey from a distance of fifty yards, but would try to stalk as close to me as possible before launching the final attack.

After testing my lighting equipment, I carefully loaded and cocked the .405, which I laid on the rock to my right, where it could not be seen by the tiger and create suspicion. I had also taken the precaution of bringing my .12 bore double-barrel Jeffries with me as a spare weapon. With L.G. slugs in the choke barrel, and lethal-ball in the right, I laid the Jeffries on the rock to my left. My flask of tea, some *chappaties* to satisfy my hunger towards morning, and my pipe completed my creature wants for the night. I sat on my great-coat, for the cushion it provided against that hard rock; I would wear it if the night should become too cold.

The usual animal and bird calls from the forest bade farewell to the day, while the denizens of the night welcomed their turn of activity with their less melodious, and more eerie, cries.

At seven-thirty it was dark; the reflecting whiteness of the sands of the Chinar surrounded my rock as if it were an island.

Just after nine there was a loud bustling and crashing and a tusker came down the bank, walked along the sands, passed the rock where I sat motionless, and continued beyond. There he met the current of breeze blowing down the river and caught scent of me. Banging the end of his trunk against the ground, and emitting a peculiar sound as if a sheet of zinc were being rapidly bent in half, he turned around, smelled more of me and hurried up the bank into the cover of the thick undergrowth that grew there. Such is the behaviour of an elephant when it is not a rogue.

At eleven I was still keeping my watch in all directions, as I had been doing since sunset. Then, half to the rear and my left, I sensed rather than saw a movement. Looking more intently, I could see nothing. No, wait! Was that not a blur against the faint greyish-white carpet of river sand? I looked away and then back again at the spot where I had just noticed the blur. It was not there!

'That's funny', I thought. 'Are my eyes playing tricks, or are they just becoming tired?'

Staring hard, I saw it again. Only it was much closer to me this time than when I had seen it first. Indeed, it was halfway between the further bank and the rock on which I sat.

I could not now risk looking in any other direction until I succeeded in defining this strange object. And as I looked it seemed to stretch, to float towards me, growing longer and shorter at intervals, but making no sound whatever.

Then in a flash I realized what it was. The tiger was crawling towards me on his belly, silently, in quick, short motions, till he judged he was within range to make his final, murderous assault.

Perspiration poured down my face and neck; I trembled with terror and excitement. But this would not do; so taking a deep breath and holding it, to allay the trembling, I offered a silent prayer to my Maker and drew the rifle on to my lap, raising it to my shoulder.

The tiger, now some twenty yards away, saw my movement and seemed to guess that his presence had been discovered. A thin black streak, his tail moved behind him. The blur became compact as he gathered himself for the charge. My torch-beam fell full on his snarling, flattened head. Then the rifle spoke, a split-second before he sprang.

With my bullet he rose and bounded forward. I owe my life to the fact that the torch did not go out, and I was able to fire a second shot. Then he had reached the rock.

Because of his earlier wound, or my recent shots—at that moment I could not tell which—he failed to climb up. My third bullet, fired at point-bank range through the crown of his skull, stopped the charge that had all but succeeded in reaching me, and he rolled back on to the sands of the Chinar, his career at an end.

Whistling on my way back to Sopathy, I gathered Ranga and Byra from the *muthee* trees on which they were sitting. Hearing my shots, and seeing my approach along the riverbed, they gathered I had killed the tiger.

Next morning we found him to be an average-sized, somewhat thin, male. My shot from beneath the cartwheel, fired seventeen days earlier, had done more damage than I had thought, for it had passed through his right shoulder, splintering the bone, and out again. But the wound was in good condition, and I have little doubt, would eventually have healed, although the tiger would have remained a cripple. My first shot of the night before had passed through his open mouth, and out through the neck, blowing a gaping hole. Still, he had come on. The second shot had gone high, entering behind the left shoulder, passing downwards through the lungs, and out again. And still he had come on. It was only my last shot, through the crown of his skull, that had shattered the brain that impelled his indomitable spirit.

What had made this tiger a man-eater? This is the riddle that every hunter tries to solve when he kills a man-eater, be it tiger or panther, not only for his own information, but for the education of the general public. And this beast proved to be no exception to the invariable rule that it is the human race itself that causes a tiger to become a man-eater. It had an old bullet wound in the same leg—the right —as had been injured by me in our first encounter, only lower down; embedded in the elbow joint was a flattened lead ball, fired from some musket or gun a year or more earlier.

This foreign body, embedded in that most important joint, had not only caused the tiger to suffer intense agony, but had greatly impeded his movements when it came to killing his legitimate food, wild game and cattle. It had weakened the use of the right leg, which plays an all-important part in gripping and pulling down his normal prey. Without a doubt, this was the sole factor that forced this tiger to turn to human beings as food, in order to keep himself from starving.

Two

Alam Bux and the Big Black Bear

THE STORY I AM NOW ABOUT TO RELATE CONCERNS A SLOTH BEAR. Quite a big, black and bad bear.

All bears, as I have had occasion to remark in other stories, are excitable, unreliable and bad-tempered animals. They have a reputation for attacking people without apparent reason, provided that person happens to pass too close, either while the bear is asleep or feeding, or just ambling along. So the natives give bears a wide berth; together with the elephant, they command the greatest respect of the jungle-dwelling folk.

This particular bear was exceptional among his kind for his unwarranted and exceptionally bad temper and aggressiveness. He would go out of his way to attack people, even when he saw them a long distance away.

The reason for his unusual conduct was difficult to explain. There were many stories about him, which were as varied as they were extraordinary. The most unpretentious was that he was quite mad. Other stories had it that he was a 'she' who had been robbed of her cubs and had sworn a vendetta against the human race. I think that the bear had been wounded or injured at some time by some human being. Perhaps the most fantastic of the stories was to the effect that this bear, almost a year previously, had kidnapped an Indian girl as a mate while she was grazing a flock of goats on the hill where he lived. The story went on to say that the whole village had turned out, *en masse*, to rescue the girl, which they had finally succeeded in doing, much to the bear's annoyance; he had then taken to attacking human beings in retaliation.

Whatever the reason be, this bear had quite a long list of victims to his credit; I was told that some twelve persons had been killed, and two dozen others injured.

Like all bears, he invariably attacked the face of the victim, which he commenced to tear apart with his tremendously long and powerful claws, in addition to biting viciously with deliberate intent to ensure the success of his handiwork. Quite half the injured had lost one or both eyes; some had lost their noses, while others had had their cheeks bitten through. Those who had been killed had died with their faces almost torn from their heads. Local rumours had it that the bear had also taken to eating his victims, the last three of whom had been partly devoured.

I had no opportunity to verify the truth of these rumours, but felt that they might be true to some extent, as the Indian sloth bear is a known devourer of carrion at times, although generally he is entirely vegetarian, restricting himself to roots, fruit, honey, white ants and similar delicacies. So fresh meat, even human meat, might not be unwelcome.

This bear originally lived in the Nagvara Hills, which lie to the east of the large town of Arsikere, some 105 miles northwest of Bangalore, and in Mysore State.

It was on these hills that he had perpetrated his earliest offences. Then, as he lost his fear of mankind and grew bolder, for no apparent reason he came down to the plains and commenced to harass people in their fields at dawn and dusk. He would come out from one or the other of the numerous small boulder-strewn hillocks that were dotted here and there, to forage for food.

I had been hearing occasional stories of this animal for about a year, but had not paid much attention to them, as I felt that, like nearly all the stories one hears in India of maulings and killings by wild animals, they were greatly exaggerated. Furthermore, as I think I have mentioned somewhere else, Bruin is quite an old friend of mine, against whom I have no antipathy. I was therefore most disinclined to go after him.

But there came an incident that made me do so. I have an old friend, an aged Muslim named Alam Bux, who is the guardian of a Mohammedan shrine situated on the main road which leads past Arsikere and on to Shimoga. This shrine is the burial place of a Mohammedan saint who lived some fifty years ago, and like hundreds of similar shrines scattered over the length and breadth of India, is preserved and held sacred by the Muslim community. Each shrine has its own guardian, or caretaker; invariably some old man who is quartered at the shrine itself to keep it clean and care for it. One of his particular duties is to light a lamp over the shrine, which is kept burning all night, to signify that the memory of the saint burns ever brightly in the bosoms of the faithful.

I first met Alam Bux on a dark night while motoring from Bangalore to Shimoga on my way to a tiger-hunt. The rear wheel of my Studebaker flew off, and the back brake-drum hit the road with a terrific jolt. I happened to be alone at the time and, stepping out of the car, viewed the situation with considerable disgust and annoyance. Fortunately for me, the incident had taken place almost opposite the shrine, and old Alam Bux, waking up at the noise made by the brake-drum striking and dragging along the road, came out to see what it was all about. Seeing my predicament, the old man volunteered to help me, which he did to a very considerable extent by bringing a lantern from his abode, gathering stones to serve as 'packing' while I raised the axle of the car, and last, but by no means least, by serving me with a bowl of hot tea. I thanked the old man, after he had replaced the truant wheel, and promised that I would look him up whenever I happened to pass his little hut again. This promise I had faithfully kept, and I never failed to bring the old man something, by way of supplies, on any occasion that I happened to pass.

Some four hundred yards beyond the shrine is a small knoll of heaped boulders, among which grew the usual lantana shrub. All around this knoll, and right up to the shrine and adjacent roadway, were fields in which the villagers grew groundnuts after the monsoon rains. Now, bears are very fond of groundnuts and our big black bear was no exception to this rule. The boulder-covered hillock offered a convenient lodging, and the groundnut fields were a great attraction. So he took up residence among the rocks.

He made his abode in a deep recess beneath an overhanging boulder. Hungry by sunset, he could be seen coming forth from his cave, and, as twilight deepened into nightfall, he would amble down the knoll and come out on to the groundnut fields. Here he would spend a busy night, eating, uprooting, and generally shuffling about over a wide area throughout the hours of the darkness. Early dawn would find him replete, with his belly full of roots and nuts, white ants, grubs and other miscellaneous fodder which he had come across during the hours of his foraging. Leisurely he would climb back to his abode, there to spend the hot hours of the day in deep and bearly slumber. I forgot to mention that a small tank, which is the Indian colloquial name for a natural lake, was conveniently situated on the other side of the hillock, so that our friend, this bad bear, wanted for nothing.

About this time the fig trees that bordered the main road which ran past the little shrine came into season, and their clusters of ripe red fruit filled the branches, spilling on to the ground beneath carpeting the earth in a soft, red, spongy mass. Hundreds of birds of all varieties fed on the figs during the day. At night, scores of flying fox, the large Indian fruitbat resembling in size and appearance the far-famed 'vampire' bat, would come in their numbers, flapping about with leathern wings, screeching, clawing and fighting among themselves as they gormandized the ripe fruit.

These numerous visitors, both by day and night, would knock down twice the number of figs they ate, which added to the profusion of fruit already lying scattered on the ground, blown down by the wind and often falling of their own weight. All this offered additional attraction to the bear, which now found a pleasing change to his menu. It was there in abundance, just waiting to be eaten.

So from the fields he would visit the fig trees, and thus his foraging brought him into the precincts of the shrine. That is how the trouble began.

Alam Bux had a son, a lad aged about twenty-two years, who, together with the guardian's aged wife and younger sister, lived at the shrine. One night the family had their meal at about nine, and were preparing to go to bed, when the boy for some reason went outside. It happened to be a dark night, and the bear also happened to be eating figs in the vicinity. Seeing the human figure suddenly appear, he felt that this was an unwarranted intrusion and immediately attacked the youth; more by accident than deliberately, the bear bit through the youth's throat and not the face, which was his usual first objective. The boy tried to scream, and had kicked and fought. The bear bit him again, this time through the nose and one eye, and clawed him severely across his chest, shoulders and back. Then it let him go and loped away into the darkness.

The boy staggered back to his parents streaming with blood. His jugular vein had been punctured, and although they had tried to staunch the bleeding with such rags as were available, they failed in their attempt to save his life, which ebbed away in the darkness, as cloth after cloth, and rag after rag, became soaked in his blood.

The false dawn witnessed the youth's passing while the old bear, replete with figs and groundnuts, climbed back to his cave among the boulders.

Alam Bux was a poor man and could not afford the money to send me a telegram, nor even his fare to Bangalore, either by train or by bus. But he sent me a postcard on which was scrawled the sad story; it was written in pencil, in shaky Urdu script. It was stained with the tears of his sorrow. The postcard arrived two days later, and I left for Asikere within three hours.

I had anticipated that the shooting of this bear would be an easy matter and that it would take an hour or two at the most. Therefore, I did not go prepared for a long trip. I carried just my torch, .405 Winchester rifle, and a single change of clothing. I reached Alam Bux shortly after five in the evening and it did not take him long to tell me his story.

There was no moonlight at this time. Nevertheless the plan to be followed seemed a simple one; namely, to wait till it grew quite dark and then set forth to search for the bear with the aid of my torch.

With this procedure in view, Alam Bux allowed me inside his abode by sunset, and closed the door to give the appearance that all was quiet. In the dingy little room we chatted in the flickering light of a small oil lamp, while he repeatedly lamented the death of his son. In fact, within a few minutes the whole family were weeping and wailing. I had, perforce, to listen to this continuously till eight, when I could stand it no longer and decided to go out in search of the bear.

Loading my rifle, and seeing that the torch was functioning properly, I stepped outside, Alam Bux closing and bolting his door behind me. The darkness was intense, and as I pressed the switch of the torch fixed near the muzzle of the rifle, its bright beams shone forth over the groundnut fields to my left, and the dense aisle of fig trees bordering the road to my right.

The bear was nowhere in sight and so I started to look for him, beginning with the fig trees. These trees grew on both sides of the road, so I judged the best thing to do would be to walk along the road itself, swinging my rifle from one side of the road to the other. I walked in this fashion away from Asikere for about a mile and a half, but saw no signs of the bear. I then walked back to the shrine and continued in the opposite direction for another mile and a half, but there were still no signs of the bear. So I came back to the shrine, and started to search the groundnut fields.

Bright glimmers of various pairs of eyes glared back at me, reflected by the torch beam. But they proved to be those of rabbits and three or four jackals. I circumvented the hillock and walked along the margin of the tank on the other side; where I came across a small sounder of wild pigs wallowing in the mud. But still no sign of the old bear was to be seen. I then walked closer to the foot of the knoll, and around it two or three times, shining my light upwards and in all directions. It was a tiring work, and the old bear did not put in his appearance. On the third occasion I almost stepped upon a very large Russell's viper that was coiled between two rocks in my direct *path*. Engaged as I was, looking for the reflecting gleam of the bear's eyes, I did not watch the ground before me. My foot was within a few inches of the viper when he inflated his body with a loud, rasping hiss, preparatory to striking. Instinctively I heeded his warning not to come any nearer and leapt backwards, at the same time shining the torch directly upon the snake, which lunged forth with jaws apart to bite the spot where, just a moment before, my legs had been. It was a narrow shave, and for the moment I felt like shooting the viper. But that would have caused a tremendous disturbance and might frighten away the bear, in addition to wasting a valuable cartridge. After all, the snake had been good enough to warn me, and so, in return, I threw a small stone at it, which caused it to slither away beneath the rocks.

By this time it was evident that the bear had either gone out earlier in the evening and wandered far away, or else he was not hungry and was still in his cave. I returned to Alam Bux's shack and decided to make another tour in a couple of hours.

This I did, and made two further tours after that, making four in all, but the bear was not to be seen, and the false dawn found me still vainly circling the hillock in search of the enemy.

With daylight, I told Alam Bux that I would return to Bangalore but he begged me to stay for the day and to climb the hill and search the cave for the bear. In the meantime his wife had prepared some hot *'chappaties'*—round flat cakes made from wheat flour—and a dish of steaming tea, both of which I consumed with relish. Then I fell asleep. At about noon Alam Bux woke me, to say that his wife had prepared special 'pillao rice' in my honour. Thanking him for this, I tucked into it too, and in a very short time polished off the lot. Mrs. Alam Bux appeared highly gratified that I so relished her cooking. The sun was now at its meridian and shone mercilessly on the rocks which blazed and shimmered in the noon-day heat. It would be a good time to look for the bear, I knew, assuming he was at home, as he would be fast asleep.

Alam Bux came with me up the hill and from a distance of fifty yards pointed out the shelving rock beneath which the bear had its cave. I clambered upwards on tiptoe, the rubber soles of my shoes making no sound on the rocks. But against this advantage I was soon to feel a greater disadvantage, as the heat from the sun-baked stone penetrated the rubber and began to burn the soles of my feet.

Coming up to the entrance of the cave, I squatted on my haunches and listened attentively.

Now a sleeping bear invariably snores, often as loud as does a human being. If the bear was fast asleep, as I hoped he would be, I counted upon hearing that tell-tale sound. But no sound greeted my ear, and after sitting thus for almost ten minutes, the sun began making itself felt through the back of my shirt. Some pebbles lay at hand and, picking up a few, I began to throw them into the cave.

Now such a procedure is calculated to make any sleeping bear very angry. But I could still hear nothing. So I went closer to the entrance and threw the stones right inside. Still nothing happened. I threw more stones, but again with negative results. The bear was not in his cave.

Descending the hill, I told Alam Bux the news and announced my intention to return to Bangalore, asking him to send me a telegram if the bear put in a further appearance. I gave him some money, both for the cost of the telegram and to tide him over immediate expenses. Then I left for Bangalore. A month elapsed, and I heard nothing more.

About twenty miles across country, and in a northwesterly direction from where the shrine is situated, the forest of Chikmagalur, in the Kadur district of Mysore, begins. About halfway between Chikmagalur and Kadur stands the small town of Sakrepatna, surrounded by the jungle.

The next news that came to me was that a bear had seriously mauled two woodcutters near Sakrepatna, one of whom had later died. The district Forest Officer (D.F.O) of Chikmagalur wrote to me, asking if I would come and shoot this bear.

I concluded that it was the same bear that had been the cause of the death of Alam Bux's son, but to look for one particular bear in the wide range of forest was something like searching for the proverbial needle in a haystack, and so I wrote back to the D.F.O. to try and get more exact information as to the whereabouts of the animal.

After ten days he replied that the bear was said to be living in a cave on a hillock some three miles from the town, near the footpath leading to a large lake known as the 'Ionkere' also that it had since mauled the Forest Guard, who had been walking along this *path* on his regular beat.

So I motored to Chikmagalur, picked up the D.F.O., and proceeded to the town of Sakrepatna, where there is a small rest house owned by the Mysore Forest department. Here I set up my headquarters for the next few days.

As luck would have it—or bad luck, if you call it that—the very next afternoon a man came running to the bungalow, to tell us that a cattle grazier—his brother in fact—had been grazing his cattle in the vicinity of the very hill where the bear was supposed to be living, when he had been attacked by the animal. He had screamed for help, and his cries had been mingled with the growls of the bear. His brother, who was lower down the hill and nearer the footpath, hearing the sounds had waited no longer, but had fled back to the bungalow to bring us the news.

Now bears are essentially nocturnal animals never moving about during daylight. At most, they may be met with at dusk or early dawn, but certainly not in the afternoon. Probably the unfortunate grazier had strayed too close to some spot where the bear had been sleeping, causing it to attack him at that unusual time. That could be the only reason for this strange attack.

It was nearing 4.30 p.m. when he brought us this news, and I set forth with my rifle and torch and three or four helpers to try to rescue the grazier who had been attacked. We soon found that the distance to the spot was much greater than we had been told by the unfortunate man's brother. I figured I had walked nearly six miles into the jungle before we came to the foot of a hill that was densely covered with scrub, including clumps of bamboo. It was then nearly six and, being winter, it was getting dark. The men I had brought along refused to come farther, and said that they would return to Sakrepatna, advising me to accompany them and suggesting that we should go back next morning to continue our search. The brother of the missing man volunteered to wait where we stood, but was too fearful to come farther into the jungle. The most he could do to help me in finding his missing relative was vaguely to indicate, with a wave of his arm, the general area where the attack had occurred.

I went forward in that direction, calling loudly the name of the man who had been mauled. There was no answer to my shouts, and I advanced deeper and deeper into the scrub. By this time it was almost dark, but I did not feel perturbed, as I had brought my torch and began to flash it about as I sought a way through the undergrowth.

Soon it became so dense that I could make no further progress, and was on the point of turning back, when I thought I heard a faint moan, away in the distance. The ground at this point sloped downwards into a sort of valley that lay between two ridges of the hill, and the moan seemed to come from somewhere in the recesses of this valley.

The missing man's name was Thimma, and, cupping both hands to my mouth, I shouted this name lustily, waiting every now and then to listen for a reply. Yes! There, undoubtedly, it was again! A moaning cry, feeble, but nevertheless audible. It definitely came to me from the valley.

Forcing my way through the thickets, I struggled down the decline, slipping on rocks and loose stones, catching myself every now and then on the thorns. After a couple of hundred yards of such progress, I called again. After some time I heard a moaning answer, somewhere to my right. I proceeded in this fashion, following the cry till I eventually found Thimma, lying at the foot of a tree in a puddle of his own blood. His face was a mass of raw flesh and broken bones, and the only way of distinguishing that he was breathing was by the bubbles of air that forced themselves through the clotting blood. In addition, the bear had raked him across the stomach with its claws, tearing open the outer flesh, so that a loop of intestine protruded. He was hardly conscious when I found him, and I soon realised that what I had taken to be a moaning reply to my calls were just the groans he kept making, every now and then, in his delirium.

The situation was critical, and after examination I saw that another night's exposure would cause him to die by morning. There was therefore no alternative but to carry him back to the spot where I had left his brother. Lifting him on to my shoulder was a tricky business, in the terrible state that he was in. To make matters worse, he was a heavily built man, equal to myself in weight. But I managed to lift him and, using my rifle butt as a prop, began to struggle upwards the way I had come.

I never wish to experience again so terrible a journey. I had almost gained the ridge down which I had lately come when the accident occurred. My left foot slipped and came down heavily between two boulders. There was a sharp, shooting, wrenching pain as I collapsed on the rock with Thimma on top of me, while the rifle clattered to the ground.

I had sprained my ankle, and was now myself unable to walk. From where we lay, I began to shout to the brother; but after nearly an hour I realised he either could not or would not hear me. There was no alternative but to spend the night with the dying man.

Desiring to make the torch batteries last the night, if that were possible, I refrained from using them more than was necessary. The early hours of morning became bitterly cold and Thimma's groans became more and more feeble, till eventually they turned into a gurgle. I realised he was dying. At about 5 a.m. he died, and there I sat beside him till daylight eventually came, shortly after six.

I then made a determined effort to drag myself to my feet, but found my leg would not support my weight. I tried to crawl, but the thorns formed an impenetrable barrier. They tore my hands, my face and my clothing to shreds. I soon gave it up and became reconciled to the fact that I would have to wait till a rescue party came to search for us.

It was well past noon before the Forest department people, accompanied by Thimma's brother and a dozen villagers, came anywhere near the scene. Eventually, guided by my shouts, they located us, and that evening I was back at

Sakrepatna forest bungalow, lying on the cot with an immensely swollen ankle. The D.F.O. turned up at about nine o'clock and drove me in my car to Chikmagalur, where I went to the local hospital for treatment. It was a week before I managed to hobble around. You may guess that by this time I was extremely angry with myself at the delay, and more so with the big, bad, black bear that had caused all the trouble. I was determined that I would get him at any cost, just as soon as I could walk.

In the meantime he had not been idle, but had mauled two more men who had been walking along the *path* to the lonkere Lake.

Four days later saw me back at Sakrepatna, just about able to walk, although not for long distances. Here I was told that the bear had taken to visiting some fields about a mile from the village, bordered by *boram* trees, the fruit of which was just then coming into season. At 5 p.m. I reached the trees in question and, selecting the largest, which had the most fruit, decided to spend the night at its foot, hoping that the bear showed up. I sat on the ground with my back to the trunk, my rifle across my knees.

Shortly after eleven I heard the grunting, grumbling sound of an approaching bear. He stopped frequently, no doubt to pick up some morsel, and as he came closer I heard the scratching sounds he made in digging for roots. He took nearly an hour to reach the *boram* tree, by which time I was amply prepared. Finally, he broke cover and ambled into the open, a black blob silhouetted in the faint glimmer of the stars.

I pressed the torch switch and the beams fell on him. He rose on his hind legs to regard me with surprise, and I planted my bullet in his chest between the arms of the white V-mark that showed clearly in the torchlight. And that was the end of that really bad bear.

MAN-EATERS AND JUNGLE KILLERS

Bears, as a rule, are excitable but generally harmless creatures. This particular bear carried the mark of Cain, in that he had become the wanton and deliberate murderer of several men, whom he had done to death in the most terrible fashion, without provocation.

Three

The Mamandur Man-Eater

THIS ANIMAL WAS A FEMALE, AND YOUNG AT THAT; SO THERE WAS NO apparent reason for her becoming a man-killer. But because she began her depredations shortly after the death of the man-eating tiger of the Chamala Valley—whose career I have told in the story entitled 'The Striped Terror of the Chamala Valley'*—and operated partly in the same locality, there were perhaps some grounds for the local gossip that set her down as the mate of that august killer. Another, and equally likely explanation, was that she was a grown-up cub, who had learned the evil practice of man-killing and man-eating from her evil sire.

Whatever her antecedents, this tigress made her first attempt at killing a human being when she attacked a herdsman, who attempted to succour a fine milch-cow, which she had

---

* See the author's earlier book, *Nine Man-Eaters and one Rogue*.

chosen to attack from amongst his herd of cattle, and whose neck she had just skilfully broken. The herdsman very bravely but foolishly attempted to frighten the tigress away from the fallen cow by shouting and brandishing his staff in the air. Mostly such tactics have the desired effect of frightening the tiger away, but in this case the effect was just the reverse. Instead of bounding away, the tigress bounded towards the herdsman, covering the short twenty yards that separated them at incredible speed. The herdsman turned tail and bolted, but the tigress dealt him a raking blow with her front paw that opened the flesh from shoulder to buttocks. The weight of the blow bore him to the ground; but in this, her first attack on a human being, the tigress apparently considered she had inflicted enough damage, for she turned back to the cow she had just killed.

With returning consciousness, the herdsman could hear the crunch of bones a mere forty yards away as the tigress fed on the cow. Fortunately, this man kept his head and did not attempt to get to his feet. In all probability any such movement would have provoked a second, and this time fatal, attack.

So he lay as he had fallen, on his face, but by stealthily moving his head very slowly and slightly, he was able to see the tigress as she fed.

He told me afterwards that he would never forget the next hour for the rest of his life. Apparently, the tigress stopped eating every now and then, raised her head and glanced in his direction. Once she got to her feet and even took a few steps towards him. The poor fellow almost screamed with terror, and nearly made the mistake of moving. Perhaps his very terror saved his life by making him incapable of movement. Fortunately, the tigress then changed her mind and returned to the cow.

It was more than an hour, the herdsman told me, before the tigress eventually decided she had eaten enough. She then leisurely sat on her haunches, licked her forepaws thoroughly and began to clean her face. With a final backward glance at his recumbent figure, she at last got to her feet, stretched herself contentedly and walked off into the jungle.

The herdsman lay still for another ten minutes, to make perfectly sure she had really gone. Then he got to his feet and dashed homewards as fast as he could run.

There is at least one other, equally remarkable, end to this story: the deep scratches the tigress had inflicted healed completely in spite of the absence of any proper medical treatment, apart from some crushed herbs, mixed with cow-dung, which the native doctor rubbed into the wounds. Perhaps the shawl he had been wearing, draped across his shoulders, had prevented the poisonous matter under the claws from entering the bloodstream.

This incident had occurred scarcely four miles from Mamandur railway station, where a rocky escarpment fell sharply for about three hundred feet into a forest glen, through which ran a little stream.

The next incident was also one of mauling, but this time the victim was not so lucky. Again it was a cowherd who was involved, an elderly man who died of his wounds. The events were much the same as in the earlier case. The tigress had dashed into a herd of cattle that was grazing a mile to the west of the railway line that cut through the forest, and had once more selected a milch-cow for her victim. As the frightened cattle stampeded past the elderly herdsman, he ran in the direction from which they had come to learn the cause of their alarm.

Soon he came upon the tigress, astride the dead cow. This time no attempt was made to frighten her off; the herdsman just stopped in his track in surprise. But evidently the tigress resented his appearance on the scene, for she attacked and mauled him severely. Then she walked back to the dead cow and dragged it away into the undergrowth.

It was three hours before help came to the old man. The cattle had stampeded across the railway line. The old man's brother, coming in search of him, saw that the cattle had moved and that their owner was nowhere to be seen. Standing on the railway embankment, he called loudly to his brother, but got no response. Then sensing that something was wrong, he hurried back to Mamandur village for help.

The search party, following the tracks of the stampeding cattle, came upon the mauled man. He was unconscious and almost dead from loss of blood. They carried him to the village and then to the station, intending to put him in the guard's van of a goods train that was due in half-an-hour, bound for the town of Renigunta, nine miles away, where there was a hospital. But the old herdsman died before the goods train reached Mamandur.

Only at her third killing did this tigress develop man-eating tendencies. She again attacked a herdsman, on this occasion at about nine in the morning. How it happened was related by a second herdsman, who was standing beside the first at the time of the attack. The tigress dashed out amongst the herd as usual and leapt upon a young bull. Somehow, she failed in her initial attempt to bring the bull down. On the other hand, the bull, with the tigress on his back, dashed madly to where the two herdsmen were standing. One of them—the man who lived to tell the tale—bolted. The other just did nothing, but appeared to be rooted to the spot with surprise.

The fleeing man looked back only once, in time to see the tigress leap from the bolting bull on to the terror-stricken herdsman. He saw no more, for the very good reason that he turned away and ran as fast and as far from the spot as he could.

When the rescue party turned up some hours later, armed with sticks and matchlocks, the body of the victim was not to be seen. So the party went back for reinforcements. Another three hours elapsed before the rescuers, now numbering nearly a hundred men, arrived at the scene of the attack. They followed a clear trail and found the corpse, lying on its face in the sandy bed of a narrow *nullah*. A part of the chest and buttocks had been eaten.

Three further human kills followed during the next couple of months. Of these, one was a herdsman, one a traveller on the Renigunta road, and the third a Lumbani, who had gone out to gather wild honey. Thereafter, all cattle-grazing stopped, as did also the collection of wild honey. No more travellers dared to come by road on foot. They came by train instead.

Mr. Littlewood, the district Forest Officer at the time, wrote to me, suggesting I might spend a few days at the beautiful Forest Bungalow at Mamandur and try to bag this tigress. With fifteen days' privilege leave to my credit, I caught the night mail-train from Bangalore; but it was 3.30 p.m. next day before I alighted from a slow passenger train at the little wayside station of Mamandur.

The forest bungalow lies a bare seven furlongs away on the top of a small hillock. The *path* to the bungalow traverses the small village of Mamandur, where I stopped for some time to make it widely known that I had come especially to shoot the tigress. My object was to get the news to spread from mouth to mouth, so that I would not only pick up all available known details about the animal, but, more particularly, would be acquainted with the news of any fresh kills that took place, either animal or human. I also negotiated the purchase of three buffalow heifers, which I paid for in cash, placing them in the charge of the local *shikari*, a man by the name of Arokiaswamy, whom I had engaged on earlier visits to Mamandur.

The bungalow had a wide and well-sheltered verandah. From its hillock fire-lines, or 'forest-lines' as they are sometimes called, radiated in five directions. Those south and south-westwards ran close to the village and railway embankment respectively. The other three struck far into the forest, and the eye could travel along them for many miles. The fire-line to the north stretched away towards the escarpment where the very first herdsman had been mauled by the tigress. Those to the east and southeast travelled in almost straight lines into the labyrinth of the jungle, like the spokes of some giant wheel. The country in both these directions was flat.

In years gone by, when game was far more plentiful, I had spent many a pleasant early morning or late evening, standing on the verandah or on the plinth of the bungalow with a pair of powerful binoculars, looking along those forest-lines. It was very common to see sambar, spotted deer and peafowl cross from one side to another. I had seen bear on three occasions, early in the morning, and a tiger crossing the northern fire-line at five in the evening. Also, although quite two miles away, I had witnessed a pack of eleven wild dogs 'ringing' an old bear. I had dashed after them on that occasion—to save the bear from the cruel fate that awaited it—arriving just as the eleven demons closed on the harried, exhausted, but brave, old beast. Three of the dogs lay dead before they realised they had to deal with a new foe. A fourth tumbled to the crack of my rifle as the pack began to run away, and a fifth joined the other four by the time the remnants of the pack were out of sight in the jungle.

I was using my old .405 Winchester rifle in those days, and had emptied my magazine. Only then did I realise I had to face a maddened bear, who had been infuriated by the dogs and the pain of the bites he had already received.

He was then about sixty yards away, and he charged straight at me, screaming, 'Woof! Woof!' I ran as fast as I could along the forest-line, and as I did so I opened the under-lever action of the .405, rammed home a cartridge in the breach, and closed the lever, which automatically cocked the rifle. Whipping around I faced the bear, which was scarcely fifteen yards away. In true bear style, when five yards away, he rose on his hind legs to deliver the final 'coup de grâce', which is popularly thought to be that most fearsome of caresses, 'a bear's hug', of which we have all heard so much.

Actually, the south Indian sloth bear does not 'hug' his adversary. He rises on his hind legs to tear at his victim's face with his formidable, three-inch long talons, or to bite him on the head with his powerful teeth. In rising to his hind legs, the bear exposed the broad white V-mark that all sloth bears carry on their chests. With the one cartridge I had in the rifle, I shot him in the base of the V. He fell forward and lay still, just two yards away!

Three of the wild dogs had been males, the other two were females. The forest department paid me a reward of ten rupees for each male and fifteen rupees for each bitch. As wild dogs are very destructive to deer, their shooting is encouraged. I was sorry to have had to kill old Bruin, but he brought it on himself.

All this had happened very, very long ago.

Another factor that made this bungalow very attractive was the sea breeze that blew in from the east shortly after two o' clock each afternoon. I think, as the crow flies, the Bay of Bengal is not less than seventy-five miles from this little bungalow; and I am no authority to argue about the distance at which a sea breeze ceases to be effective. I only know that, at almost two each afternoon it turns the verandah of that little bungalow into a delightfully cool spot on which to take a nap. If you don't believe me, visit Mamandur Forest Bungalow.

It was too late that evening to tie out more than one of the three buffaloes, which only arrived at 5.30 p.m. This buffalo I took for two miles along the northern fire-line, where I tied it at the foot of a large and leafy tamarind tree. It was past seven when I got back, so I kept the other two buffaloes in the garage and asked Arokiaswamy to sleep in the kitchen.

Early next morning we were astir. First we took the bait which we had tied two miles away the previous night, and which was still alive, right up to the foot of the escarpment where the very first attack had taken place. There we secured it to the roots of a tree in a beautiful glade of rank, green grass.

We came back to the bungalow and took the second heifer along the fire line stretching to the east, where I tied it at almost the very spot where my encounter with the wild dogs and the bear had taken place.

Returning for the second time to the bungalow, we took the third and last heifer across the railway line to the west, and tied it near the spot where the elderly herdsman had been killed.

It was past midday when I got back to the bungalow for the third time, and blazing hot too. Taking off my sweat-soaked shirt, I ate a belated cold lunch and awaited the advent of the sea breeze, which I knew would start at about two. Nor was I disappointed; for when it began, it turned that broiling-hot verandah to the likeness of the shores of some far-distant South Sea Island, where we read that 'the sea-breezes forever play'.

The next two days were uninteresting. I visited all three baits each day, but none of them had been touched. The evening of the fifth day brought a tragedy.

The semaphores along the railway lines of southern India are lit at night by kerosene oil lamps, except in the shunting yards of the larger railway junctions. As you are no doubt aware, every ordinary railway station has two sets of signals on each side of it; the near or 'home' signal, and a more distant, or 'outer' signal, as it is called. Normally, the kerosene oil lamps at these signals are cleaned, trimmed, refilled and lit by a pointsman or an other railway employee appointed for the purpose who does his job at about six each evening. But owing to the presence of the tigress at Mamandur, and the fact that the outer signals, both in the direction of Renigunta to the south and Setigunta to the northwest, were surrounded by forest, it had become the custom to light these lamps well before five, while the sun was still up.

That evening two pointsmen had set out on this task at 4 p.m., one walking towards Renigunta, and the other in the opposite direction. The second man never came back.

Shortly before six a body of seven men came rushing to the forest bungalow, sent by the stationmaster, to tell me what had happened. Hastily grabbing my rifle, torch and a few other necessities for a nightlong vigil, I sent the seven men back to the station, and Arokiaswamy along with them, as he absolutely refused to stay in the bungalow alone that night. Then I hurried up the forest-line that led to the west, which I knew met the railway track almost midway between the 'inner' and 'outer' signals.

When I reached the railway line, which here ran along an embankment ten feet high, I looked to my left and saw the 'inner' signal, with its red light twinkling.

'Stupid man', I thought. 'Instead of attending to the outer light first, while it was still early, and coming back to the inner on his way to the station, he wasted time on the inner light, and then went to the outer, when it was considerably later.'

Turning to the right, I walked along the embankment towards the 'outer' semaphore, which came into view when I turned a corner. As I walked, I looked along and about the tracks for signs of the attack that must have taken place while the pointsman was approaching the outer signal. I found nothing. Then I came to the foot of the 'outer', and looked up. The light was burning!

So the man had been attacked on his way back after he had attended to the 'outer' signal, and not before. Added to this was the fact that the light of the 'inner' signal was also burning. Perhaps he had not attended to that light first, as I had originally thought. Perhaps he had lit the outer, then the inner, and had been attacked somewhere between the inner signal and the station yard.

But was that likely in view of the fact that all the area from the station up to the 'inner' signal, and even a little beyond it, was open cultivated land? Would any tiger, even if it was a man-eater, walk about thus boldly on absolutely open land in broad, daylight? It was possible, but rather unlikely.

My watch showed 6.55 p.m., and it was rapidly growing dark as I began to retrace my steps towards the inner signal, keeping now a sharper lookout than ever. An early moon had risen, which was indeed fortunate, or it would have become quite dark by this time.

Almost at the spot where I had first come on to the embankment from the forest-line was a small culvert, crossing a narrow but deep *nullah*. Something white there caught my eye, fluttering between the sleepers of the railway track as it spanned this *nullah*. I stopped, and peered between the sleepers.

It was the white *dhoti* worn by the railwayman. Wedged under a boulder, twenty feet away and clear of the embankment, lay an elongated, dark shape, which I knew to be the body of the victim. Even in that uncertain light I could tell that the body had been partly devoured in the short time that had elapsed since the kill had taken place. The neck had been bitten through, and the head lay about a yard away. Because the tigress might perhaps be in the vicinity at that moment, or even watching me from the cover of the bushes, it would be unnecessarily dangerous to descend the embankment and make a closer examination of the body.

A hasty survey of the position made me decide to lie at right angles across the railway lines and exactly in the middle of the culvert. I would thus be safe from attack from the front or rear, as to do this the tigress would have to leap a clear fifteen from the bottom of the *nullah* on to the track. This left her the choice of attacking me along the track, either to my right or left. I should have told you that the span of the culvert was about twenty feet. Not much, but it would at least give me time to see the tigress.

Of course, there was the possibility that she would creep up at an angle to the embankment and attack me obliquely, either from the front, or worse still, from behind; and either to the left or right of me.

It was a chance that had to be taken.

I had already clamped my torch to the rifle walking from the bungalow. I placed my haversack beneath my chest, to soften contact with the rail. This section of track was broad gauge, which means that the lines were five feet six inches apart. By spreading my legs widely, I found my soles just touched the other rail and did not overlap it. The teak—weed 'sleeper', on which I lay, was perhaps eight inches wide: not over-comfortable to lie on and awfully hard!

The moon was shining brightly by this time and lit the scene clearly. The corpse and its severed head were clearly visible against the lighter colour of the rock and the finely-grained white sand of the *nullah* in which it lay. Everything was deathly silent.

The red light glimmered from the friendly inner signal; it seemed to remind me that help was close—but yet so distant.

The hours ticked by; a sambar stag belled from the jungle to the west. Perhaps that call heralded that the tigress was on the move! No, for it was answered by another stag, further away to the northeast, and then by another to the east. Periodically, the spotted deer also gave vent to their sharp cries of alarm, 'Aiow! Aiow! Aiow!'

But the cries did not come from any one direction; if they had done so, that would have indicated definitely that some carnivore was afoot in that area. They came from all sides, far and near, indicating that several carnivores were on the move. Also, being a brilliant moonlight night, it was possible that packs of wild dogs were on the hunt. These animals chase their prey by day and never on a dark night, but on brilliant moonlit nights, in certain jungles, they occasionally reverse their habit and hunt by moonlight.

At midnight silence reigned again. And then the hair at the back of my neck began to rise, for what I was witnessing was eerie indeed. The severed head had rolled on to its side!

All this time it had been staring heavenwards; now its lifeless eyes and face were turned to me. Yet no animal had touched it, for it lay in the open, clearly visible in the bright moonlight.

I felt myself tremble and grow cold. I licked my dry lips and stared at that terrible head.

Again it moved! It had tried to roll back to its former position; it had turned halfway and then, as if it lacked the strength to complete the move, it had rolled back again and was staring me in the face.

Now I may tell you I am a very practical person, not superstitious, nor afraid of the dark. I had spent many a night in a similar or even more dangerous position; I had sat over half-eaten human bodies before, and on earlier occasions I had imagined that I had seen them move. But never before in my life had I seen a severed human head actually turn around of its own accord, then try to turn back again and fail; finally, to roll back in obvious despair.

I almost cried out and for quite a while was seized with a powerful urge to get up and run towards the twinkling, friendly red light of the 'inner' signal. Then common sense reasserted itself. A dead head, human or otherwise, cannot move of its own accord. Something must have moved it!

I stared at the head intently, and the bright moonlight showed me the answer to my problem. Two black objects could be seen moving in the white sand. They were 'rhinoceros beetles': large insects, more than an inch-and-a-half long, with great spikes on their noses resembling the horn of a rhinoceros, from which resemblance they had got their name. Generally they are nocturnal, although one frequently sees them on forest roads, early in the morning, and again late at evening, busily rolling a ball of cow-dung, perhaps thrice their own size, to some unknown destination.

These two little creatures by their combined strength had succeeded in rolling this head over once, but the second time they had not quite succeeded. I had been so absorbed by what I saw that I had forgotten all about the tigress; she could easily have surprised me at that time.

It was now 1.40 and the rail beneath my chest began to tremble. Then I heard a distant rumbling sound which gradually grew louder and nearer. A sharp whistle rent the air and soon the brilliant headlight of an engine fell full upon me. It was the Night Mail from Madras to Bomaby.

Stiffly I got to my feet, lifted my haversack, walked to the end of the culvert, and then a couple of foot down the embankment. But I had entirely forgotten to take into account the vigilance of the driver of the train. He had clearly seen me in the bright headlight of the engine, although he had not noticed my rifle. As he was to tell me in a few minutes, he took me for a would-be suicide, deliberately lying on the track in order to be run over, whose courage had failed him at the last moment. I may mention, incidentally, that this method of committing suicide is rather popular in India.

Anyhow, with a grinding of brakes and violent hissing of steam, the train drew up just after the engine had passed me. The next thing I heard was the loud thudding of boots on the hard ground as figures ran towards me. It was the driver and his two firemen from the engine.

They charged up and grabbed me. Only then did they realise that I was obviously not what they had taken me to be. In the meantime, heads popped out of carriage windows, and a hundred voices began to question and conjecture. The guard came up from the rear with his bulls-eye lantern. So I had no alternative but to tell them what I was doing.

'Where is the man who has been eaten by the tiger?' asked the driver, a middle-aged Anglo-Indian. I pointed the corpse out to him. 'And you have been lying here in the open by yourself since evening?' he asked, incredulously.

When I replied in the affirmative, he added, very simply, 'You are quite mad,' and tapped his forehead significantly. His two firemen, and the Indian guard of the train, nodded heartily in agreement.

A few minutes later, the Mail puffed onwards, on its long journey to Bombay, and I was left alone once more. But I had little hope of the tigress putting in her appearance after so great a disturbance.

At 2.30 a.m. the rails began to rumble again. This time I lay flat on the embankment, hiding my rifle, before the engine's headlight betrayed my presence. As a result, the goods train passed me by without stopping. At 4 a.m. again the rails rumbled and trembled, and I hid once more. It was the return Mail, from Bombay to Madras, that thundered by at full speed, as mail trains do not halt at Mamandur.

The false dawn came and went. The distant call of awakening peafowl fell on the air, as they cried, 'Mia-a-oo-Aaow' across the forest valleys to be answered by the cheery 'Whe-e-e-Kuch-Kaya Kaya-Khuck'm' of that most lovely bird, the grey junglecock.

A pale shell-pink tinted the sky above the eastern hills that stood sharply outlined now in velvety black. Meanwhile, the moon, which had held sway all night and was now about to set, began losing some of her brilliance.

In the east the shell-pink turned marvellously to mauve, then to a deep rose, tinged at its edges by the palest of greens and the purest of blues. The rose became orange-purple then orange alone, then deep red, and finally flame, as the glowing tip of the sun peeped above the wave-like lines of hilltops to the east.

Radiating beams of sunlight, cast heavenwards by that rapidly growing orb, touched the racing, fleecy clouds in the sky with all the colours of the spectrum. Then, suddenly, just as a butterfly bursts forth from its chrysalis, the sun surmounted the hills, driving before her, in eddying swirls, the wisps of mist from the damp jungle below.

It was another day, and to welcome its birth a glad chorus of song burst from the birds of the forest all around me. Every bush and tree throbbed with life, fresh, clean and new. Those who have seen the marvel of an Indian jungle sunrise will never forget it.

The head still stared up at me, but it was still now; the two rhinoceros beetles that had worked so diligently throughout the night had long since abandoned the unequal task and gone to rest.

I made my way to the station, disappointed and slowly, to tell the stationmaster he could allow the relations of the dead men to remove the remains for cremation, and by eight I was asleep on the verandah of the bungalow. In the afternoon the sea-breeze lulled me to a deeper slumber.

At 4 p.m. I awoke, feeling refreshed and fit, and ate a quick lunch-cum-tea, while listening to Arokiaswamy's report that he, with four others, had visited all the baits and had found them alive. It certainly looked as if this tigress was not going to kill any of the heifers I had tied out.

Then came sunset and bright moonlight. I felt like taking a walk. If I kept to the centre of any one of those five radiating forest fire-lines, I felt I would be safe enough, provided I maintained a sharp watch while I walked. There was also the definite chance of attracting the tigress, should our trails cross during the night.

I dressed for the occasion. In my own kit I had only khaki clothes and a black shirt which was useful for night *machan* work. So I went with Arokiaswamy to his hut, where I slipped on a long white shirt, allowing the shirttails to flutter loosely outside my khaki pants. Arokiaswamy further completed the disguise by tying a white turban round my head.

I did not know what the tigress would take me for if we met; but I know I was a source of considerable amusement to the villagers, who were somewhat shocked to hear of my plan.

I debated for a moment which fire-line to walk up first and decided to follow the one leading in the easterly direction. It was 7.30 p.m. when I started to walk. I kept in the centre of the line, and as I moved I allowed my eyes to rove freely around and about the bushes and undergrowth on both sides. Occasionally I glanced backwards.

Although the moonlight was brilliant, the bushes cast long black shadows, and clumps of thorns and grass looked ghostly grey around me. I realised that, for all the moonlight, my eyes could never pick out a lurking carnivore in that unreal sheen, even if it showed itself, which it would not. I should have to rely on my sense of hearing—and that other, my sixth sense!

At ten-minute intervals I whistled a bar of some tune or other to advertise my presence to the tigress; but only for half-a-minute at a time, so as not to impede my own ears, that were attuned to catch the slightest sound.

Thus, many a subtle rustle did I hear in the grassy hillocks as I passed them. Invariably, the nocturnal bamboo-rat was the culprit, as he scampered for cover at my approach. Then an indefinable, prolonged, slithering rustle: that was a snake, probably a Russell's viper, coiling comfortably around and around himself in the grass, to be cosy and warm. Something heavy descended from the sky, neatly on the back of a hare as it scampered across the fire-line. The hare squealed, and the great horned owl, which had attacked it, pecked it sharply on the forehead. I approached the owl, which extended both its wings to the ground to hide the hare from me, much in the same way as does a hen with chickens. I approached closer and the owl glowered; I drew closer still and the owl flew away. I picked up the limp hare and rubbed its back briskly. With regaining consciousness, it began to kick vigorously. I let it go into the long grass.

There were no bison in these jungles, nor elephants, but in their stead bear were plentiful. Nor was it long before I came upon Bruin, engaged in his favourite pastime of sucking white ants out of their hills. A distant sound, midway between a buzzing and a humming, a queer noise rather like someone inflating a bagpipe, or the sound of angry swarming bees, first told me that a bear was afoot. It grew louder and louder and was punctuated by grunts, coughs, whimpers of impatience and growls of annoyance.

There, to one side of the line and to my right was a white-ant hill. There standing up against it, with its head inside a hole, was a shaggy, black shape. It was the bear, blowing, sucking, grumbling, swearing and complaining, as he met with little or no success. Rarely there would be a chuckle of sheer joy as something succulent went down.

He was deeply engrossed in his task as I padded silently on my way, and the sounds of his feast receded behind me, growing fainter and fainter. I walked for two hours along that line, then turned and retraced my steps. Bruin had gone home by the time I came to the ant hill again, and it was then only half its original height, due to his efforts. I saw nothing else till I reached the Forest Lodge.

Next, I turned up the northern fire-line and walked towards the escarpment. This line did not run straight like the one I had just abandoned. Rather, it twisted and turned considerably as I approached the escarpment. A stream intersected it at the third mile, in which a trickle of clear, cold water sparkled like silver in the moonlight.

Stooping down, I drank, conveying the water to my mouth in my left palm; my right hand held the rifle with its butt to the ground, while my eyes watched the jungle and my ears strained to catch the slightest sound. There was nothing visible, and the only sound was the gurgle of the water. I went on.

The bait I had tied was around the next corner. It was alive, and as I passed it looked at me with dumb reproach for the cruel fate to which I had exposed it. I had no answer, no excuse! That I was guilty there was no doubt. I turned my eyes away, but could not rid myself of the sense of guilt.

At last the base of the escarpment was reached. Here the fire-line stopped and became a narrow game-trail that plunged abruptly into the labyrinth of greenery. It was too dangerous to go any further under such conditions and I turned back.

All I passed on the return journey was a large cobra in the process of swallowing a bamboo-rat. Three-quarters of the rat were down the cobra's throat, only the hindquarters and tail protruding, when I came upon the scene in the middle of the fire-line. The snake saw me and raised its head two feet above the ground, simultaneously erecting the fine bones of its neck to form that most beautiful and at the same time most enthralling of sights to a newcomer to India; the well-known cobra's hood. The hind legs and tail of the rat still dangled incongruously from its mouth. The beady black eyes glittered malevolently in the phosphorescent light.

I rapidly stamped my feet and clapped my hands. The cobra became nervous and finally panicked. It vomited the rat, lowered itself to the ground with deflated hood, and slithered away into the bushes to one side of the fire-line.

Once more I was back at the bungalow. I had covered twenty miles, and it was 2.45 a.m.

Two fire-lines remained to be tried, but there would only be time to negotiate one, either the fire-line running to the south-east, up which I had not yet been since my arrival, or the line to the south-west, crossing the railway embankment, where I had sat the previous night over the dead body. For some unaccountable reason, I chose the latter.

I reached the railway track, crossed it, and had walked over a mile further towards the west, when suddenly the silence was shattered by the moaning call of a tigress. It appeared to come from a point no more than a couple of furlongs in front of me. Perhaps the beast was walking along the same fire-line; she may have been going away or perhaps coming towards me.

Doubling forward for the next 50 yards, I hid behind the trunk of a large wood-apple tree, cocked the rifle and raised it into position. Then I gave the deep-lunged moan of a male tiger.

Almost immediately it was answered, from much closer than I thought—perhaps a hundred yards away. I did not dare to call again, for fear that I should be recognised for the imposter I was.

Tiger-calling should not be indulged in at close quarters, for fear that the real tiger should discover a difference in the timbre of the call. Should he become suspicious, he may just fade away. One hundred yards is about the closest range at which such mimicry can be tried. Of course, man-eating propensities, and also curiosity, from which most animals suffer to some degree, might still cause the tiger to come forward, but there is always the risk that suspicion may drive him off. So I remained silent—and still.

Thirty seconds later, a tigress strode down the forest-line towards me, the moonlight playing upon the black stripes of her coat. She came abreast of me, then began to pass.

I shot her behind the ear. Only her tail twitched as she sank to the ground. She never knew what happened; she had no chance. It was an unsporting shot.

Anyhow, at Mamandur no human has been killed now for some years. The tigress, which was young, was in the best of condition and there was no reason why she should have become a man-eater. Perhaps, after all, the Chamala man-eater had taught her the bad habit.

Four

The Crossed-Tusker of Gerhetti

THIS IS THE STORY OF ANOTHER ELEPHANT THAT EARNED THE NAME of a 'rogue', and was proscribed by the government of Madras by notification through the Collector and the district Forest Officer of Salem.

The events I am going to relate took place quite a time ago. As usual with rogue elephants, no one knew just what caused this elephant to start molesting human beings. The forest guard then stationed at Gerhetti stated that, one night about a month before the rogue began his depredations, he had heard two bull elephants fighting in the forest. According to his story, the contest had raged off and on for over three hours, and had taken place in the vicinity of a water hole situated just about half a mile in front of the forest bungalow.

Next day he had found the jungle trampled down and great splashes of blood were everywhere in evidence of the punishment that had been inflicted. Judging by the account he gave me, and from the pandemonium that had raged, it must have been a mammoth struggle. Possibly the rogue, as we came to know him, had been the elephant that had got the worst of that fight and from this moment had begun to vent his spleen on all and sundry.

Another explanation might have been that the rogue, was just an ordinary bull elephant in a state of *'musth'* a periodical affliction that affects all elephants and lasts for about three months, during which time they become extraordinarily dangerous.

A third possibility was that this elephant had been wounded by one of the many poachers that are to be found in the forests of Salem district. These gentry sit up over water holes and salt licks to shoot deer that visit such spots during the hot and dry summer months. Generally, when a poacher sees anything more formidable than a harmless deer, he keeps very quiet or slinks away if he feels the going is good. Yet even amongst poachers we find a few that are 'trigger-happy'. They discharge their muskets at any animal that puts in an appearance, and it may have been that one of these adventurers had wounded the bull and started him on his career as a rogue.

It may even have been that a simple peasant, guarding his crops by night, had shot at him with his match-lock. Elephants are fond of destroying crops that grow close to the forest.

Whatever it was that had originally upset him, the rogue of Gerhetti started his career quite suddenly, and for the short time he held sway in the fastness of the jungle where he lived, he became a terror, bringing all traffic, both bullock-cart and pedestrian, to an end within an area of about four hundred square miles.

Gerhetti is the name given to a tiny hamlet comprising some five or six huts about two miles off the track leading from Anchetty to Pennagram in the Salem North Forest Division. The country here is very hilly, and thick bamboo jungle grows to a distance of about three miles from both banks of a rocky stream known as Talvadi Brook, which joins the Cauvery about fifteen miles southwest of the spot I am telling you about. This bamboo jungle nearly always harbours herds of elephant and quite often three or four independent elephants, which although not rogues, are very carefully avoided by the jungle folk.

Another stream, called Gollamothi, flows almost parallel with the Talvadi rivulet, about twelve miles north of it, and joins the Gundalam river, itself another tributary of the Cauvery. These three rivers, with the hills that surround them on all sides, and the thick bamboo jungle that abounds, makes an ideal habitation for any elephant, and it was here that the rogue started his career as a killer.

It began like this. With the midsummer heat, the Gollamothi stream had dried up, except for one or two isolated pools of water which had managed to survive, being formed between huge rocks that cropped up on the riverbed, and fed by subsoil percolation. One of these pools was known to hold fish of some size, perhaps six to eight inches in length, and one afternoon two men from the village of Anchetty, five miles away, decided they would go to this pool and net some fish in the restricted area that had resulted from rapid evaporation.

So they arrived at the pool and cast their nets. Soon they had made a considerable catch. They then put the fish into their baskets and lay down under a shady tree by the side of the water hole to enjoy a brief siesta.

It was about five when one of them awakened. The sun had just sunk behind the top of a hill that jutted out to the west of the pool, but it was still quite bright. As he sat up beside his sleeping companion, something caused the man to look behind him, where he saw the slate-grey bulk of an elephant descending the southern bank of the Gollamothi on its way to the pool.

The man reached out and vigorously shook his companion, to whom he whispered in Tamil *'Anai Varadhu'*, which means 'an elephant approaches'. Then he got up and ran to the northern bank and into the forest. His companion, suddenly aroused from sleep, did not quite grasp the significance of the warning, and as he sat looking around and wondering what had happened to his friend, the elephant was upon him.

The man who escaped told me he heard the screams of the friend he had left behind, mingled with the shrill trumpeting of the enraged elephant. Then there was silence. Naturally, he had not waited to hear more. Two days later, when the search party from Anchetty came to look for the remains, they found a pulpy mass of broken flesh and bones decaying in the hot sun. There was evidence that the elephant had first placed his foot upon the man and then had literally torn him apart with his trunk. He had carried one leg to a spot ten yards away, where he had beaten it against the gnarled trunk of a *jumblum* tree before finally throwing it away among the rocks.

That was the rogue's first victim. His second attempt was upon a herd-boy who was driving his herd at sunset to the cattle *patti* at Gundalam. This boy, being young and agile, had fled along the sands of the dry stream, hotly pursued by the vicious elephant. Finding he was losing ground, the boy had the sense to run up the steep side of the hill where the rocks were very slippery and small loose boulders abounded. This had enabled him to maintain his lead.

In his mad rush to escape, the boy cut his bare feet literally to ribbons on the protruding sharp stones, while his body was lacerated in a hundred places by the thorns and shrubs that sought to hold him back. But he had kept on running, and managed to escape the elephant by climbing on to a high rock that protruded about two hundred yards up the hillside.

He told me afterwards that when the bull reached the rock, he walked around it several times, trumpeting and attempting to reach his victim with his trunk. But the boy kept his head, and moved around with the elephant, keeping as far as possible from the tip of that dreaded trunk. He told me that the top of the rock was only about twenty-five square feet in area and that the snake-like tip of the killer's trunk had sometimes been within a foot of his ankles. Nevertheless he had managed to avoid it, and after an hour of this game the elephant suddenly lost interest in his victim and wandered away. Still the boy had been too frightened to come down and had spent the night on top of the rock, only getting down the next morning after the sun had risen high in the heavens, when he felt that the elephant was nowhere in the vicinity.

After this there had been a lull for a month, when the few folk who lived in the area began to feel that the elephant had perhaps departed to other regions, or alternatively, if it had been in *musth*, that *musth* season had elapsed and that its condition had returned to normal.

But they had been far too optimistic, for exactly five weeks after unsuccessfully chasing the herd-boy this elephant attacked two wayfarers as they were journeying through the forest to the village of Nattrapalyam, which lies about eight miles south of Anchetty. These men had been suddenly chased by the rogue and had begun to run along the forest path with the animal in hot pursuit about hundred yards behind them. One of these men was about thirty years old and the other some ten years older. Age soon began to tell on the older man causing him to lag behind, his breath coming, in sobbing gasps. He knew that a terrible death was behind him, and he tried his best to keep running. Unfortunately, he had quite lost his head, and made no attempt to circumvent the animal, as he might have done, by perhaps climbing a tree, or by getting behind a rock or even by throwing down a part of his clothing as he ran. This last action might have served to delay the attacker for a few minutes. For when chased by an elephant, it is advisable as a last recourse to shed some part of one's clothing; when the elephant reaches it and catches the strong human smell, he will invariably stop to tear it to ribbons. In the precious seconds thus gained, the victim has a chance of making good his escape.

But this unfortunate man simply ran on till he could run no more. The elephant overtook him as he lay sprawled on the *path*, his body heaving to the gasps of his tortured lungs. Soon their services on this earth were ended, for the elephant picked him up in his trunks and dashed repeatedly against a wayside boulder, beating him to pulp before finally tossing him aside into the jungle.

As a result of these incidents, petitions had been forwarded, through Forest authorities, to the Collector of Salem district to proscribe this animal 'rogue', which means that permission was granted for the elephant to be shot by any game-licence holder in the district. Normally, the elephant is strictly protected in India. Red tapism, as anywhere in the world, is a slow process, and this is particularly the case in India, so that three months or more elapsed before action was taken to issue the necessary order. A further month's delay occurred before all game-licence holders in the district were notified.

Meanwhile the 'rogue' was rather busy. He attacked a bullock-cart that was laden with sandalwood cut by the Forest department. The driver of this cart, and the forest guard who was accompanying the sandalwood, escaped by running into the forest, but the cart was smashed to pieces and one of the bulls slightly injured.

Not long afterwards, the rogue did rather an unusual thing. Cattle, let loose by graziers in the forest, generally scatter over a fairly wide area. One of these animals evidently strayed too near the rogue, which attacked and broke the beast's back.

A further short lull was followed by the news that he had killed a 'poojaree', one of a jungle tribe of this area, as he was returning with honey from the forest for the contractor who had bought the right from the Forest department to collect all the wild honey in this particular division.

Then the official notification reached me. As a rule, I take no pleasure in elephant-shooting, as I have a very soft corner for these big and noble animals. Secondly, I feel it is a comparatively tame animal itself; elephants invariably give away their position by the noise they make in the undergrowth when feeding. It is then a comparatively simple matter to get up-wind of the quarry and stalk to within a short distance of it. All that is required is a little experience in knowing where to place one's feet, to avoid stepping on dried leaves or twigs that crackle and so give away the stalker's position.

Another very important aspect of 'still hunting' is the ability to 'freeze', to become absolutely still in whatever position you may be at that moment, if the quarry looks your way. This may prove a little awkward at times, when in a half-crouched position, but to straighten up or squat down would be fatal, as the slightest movement involved in doing so will give the stalker away. The thing to do is to remain absolutely and completely 'dead', even for as much as ten minutes in the same half-crouching position. I can assure you that this can sometimes be extremely tiring.

By these methods I have often stalked elephants to within a few yards and watched them grazing peacefully, without their being in the least degree aware of my presence. But the slightest whiff of my scent, or the slightest crackle underfoot, would have sent them thundering away. An elephant has surprisingly poor sight, and if you are dressed in military khaki-green and you keep absolutely still, it will often look your way without ever becoming aware of your presence.

For these reasons, as I have said, I do not like shooting elephants. Also, many of the so-called rogues are not rogues at all. As I have mentioned before, poachers and cultivators are in the habit of firing at elephants and often wound them in the process, when they become embittered against the human race. Again, many of the incidents reported against the so-called rogues never occurred, for people interested in shooting an elephant sometimes concoct tales and urge the villagers to write exaggerated reports in order to induce the Collector to proscribe the rogue. Collectors as a rule go into such matters very carefully and thoroughly before issuing orders; but sometimes, with all these precautions, elephants are killed which are not rogues at all in the real sense.

So I did not pay much heed to the notification till it was followed, about three weeks later, by a letter from Ranga, my *shikari* who lived at the town of Pennagram. He wrote to report that the elephant had killed a poojaree woman four days previously at a spot called Anaibiddamaduvu, which lay about seven miles from Gerhetti. The literal interpretation of this name is 'the pool into which the elephant fell'. It is a natural pool, formed by steep rocks on the bed of Anaibiddahalla river, a sub-tributary of the Chinnar river, which itself is a tributary of the Cauvery, that largest of south Indian rivers. Moreover, this pool is deep and never dries up, and I am told that many years ago an elephant, while reaching for water with its trunk, fell in and could not get out again because of the steep and slippery rocks that ringed it. Elephants are good swimmers, and have herculean strength and endurance, but they also have great bulk; so this poor creature, after swimming round and round in the pool for three days continuously, slowly sank and drowned before quite a large crowd of people who had come all the eleven miles from Pennagram to witness the 'tamasha'.

After receiving Ranga's letter, and as some time had passed since I had last seen him, I got leave of absence for four days and motored down to Pennagram. I picked him up and covered the eighteen miles or more of terribly bad forest road that leads to the Gerhetti forest bungalow, passing Annaibidhamadhuvu on the way.

The forest guard at Gerhetti told me that the rogue was in the vicinity, as well as a herd of about ten elephants. All these animals were in the habit of drinking at the water hole in front of the bungalow, and as there were several animals in the herd of about the same size as the rogue, it would be difficult to know which was which. This precluded any possibility of following with any degree of certainty any particular set of tracks.

Further, the description of this animal in the notification was very vague; it merely stated that the measurement around the circumference of the forefoot had been 4'10", which made the elephant approximately 9'.8" tall, as twice the circumference of the forefoot is the approximate height. The colour was reported as black, but all elephants are black after they have washed, but they soon cover themselves with sand or earth. Sand in the forest is of different hues, varying from red to brown, grey, and almost black. So this was no distinguishing factor either. The only feature that appeared to identify the elephant was that the two tusks, which were reported to be over three feet long, met and crossed near their tips.

You will therefore understand that the last factor was the only one by which I would be able to identify this particular animal, for it was doubtful if he would give permission, to approach and measure his height! But to see if the tusks were crossed meant getting a frontal or head-on view of the elephant, as at an angle tusks may appear to cross without actually doing so. I certainly did not want to shoot the wrong animal, apart from the immense amount of trouble and official explanation that would follow.

This meant that I could select any set of tracks that came up to the measurement of the rogue and follow them till I came upon the animal that had made them, then manoeuvre for a frontal view of the animal to see whether he possessed the hallmark of crossed-tusks. If he did, he was my elephant. If he did not, I would have to start all over again by going back to the pool and following another set of tracks. It must be remembered that I had only four days at my disposal, and of these four days one had already passed in picking up Ranga, coming to Gerhetti and making the necessary inquiries.

At about ten that night I heard the sound of elephants feeding in the vicinity of the pool. This was undoubtedly the herd, and the rogue would not be with them. So I went to sleep again.

At dawn I started with Ranga and the forest guard on my plan of following up one of the sets of tracks. The margin of the water hole was fairly ploughed up by a mass of footprints of all sizes, where the herd had watered the night before. These included the tracks of some very young elephants, which could hardly have been over three feet tall.

Circumventing the pool, I found three sets of tracks which came near to the size of the rogue. Two of these three sets, I noticed, had been made on the same side of the pool as the herd had watered, while the remaining set had been made by an elephant which had approached the water from quite another direction. I therefore argued that this third animal might be the rogue, and we began to track him in single file. Ranga went in front, following the tracks; I followed, covering him with my double-barrelled 450/400 Jeffries; the Forest Guard came behind me, his duty being to guard against an attack from the rear in case it happened that the elephant had gone round in a semicircle, and was now grazing behind us.

For a short distance after leaving the water the ground was covered by long spear grass and clearly revealed the passage of the elephant the night before, being trampled flat in all directions. Then the spear grass gave way to the usual thorny growth of lantana and wait-a-bit thorn. Here also it was comparatively easy to see where our quarry had passed, but our own passage became more difficult by reason of the thorns that plucked and tore at our clothing.

Yet the tracks were clear and we made fairly good time for about a mile, when we reached the base of a small hill. The slopes of this hill were covered with heavy bamboo growth, and the elephant had passed through this, climbing the hill as he went. He had also stopped to feed on the tender shoots that spring from the end of the fronds of bamboo, as was clearly evident by the havoc he had created in the mass of broken bamboo stems we met along this trail. Here he had passed a considerable quantity of dung, and as we reached the top of the hill and went down the other side, it was evident that the elephant had fed until the early hours of that morning; for the dung was fresh and had not had time to cool.

From here onwards our passage became laboriously slow. The dense bamboo completely surrounded us and a careless step by any one of us resulted in a rustle or sharp crackle, depending on whether we trod upon the leaves or bamboo fronds.

I touched Ranga's elbow and motioned to him to stand still, the guard and myself doing the same. We listened for over ten minutes for the familiar sounds of a feeding elephant, or the deep rumble that issues from his cavernous stomach in the process of digestion. But the forest was comparatively silent except for the cheery calls of grey junglecocks everywhere around us, and the distant whoops of langur monkeys on the opposite hillside.

Evidently our quarry was resting, or had perhaps passed further down into the deep valley that lay before us. As the latter seemed more likely, we proceeded on tiptoe, slowly and carefully in his wake. We had all to keep our eyes down to make sure we did not trample on anything that would betray our presence. Another half mile brought us to the valley, where the undergrowth was extremely dense; wild plum, wood-apple, and mighty tamarind trees grew profusely everywhere, making visibility beyond fifteen to twenty yards impossible. Another two hundred yards brought us to the rocky bed of a small tributary of the Gollamothi river.

The elephant had here skirted the bed of the stream and crossed it at a sandy spot fifty yards further down. The opposite bank, up which he had then climbed, was fairly steep, so that we were now faced with the prospect of having the elephant above us, which is hardly the best way of meeting a 'rogue'.

We went forward very slowly indeed, and as silently as was humanly possible. Our quarry had stopped feeding, and was now on the move again. We soon saw that he appeared to be making for another valley that lay beyond the spur of the hill up which we were now climbing. Having reached this conclusion, we began to move faster, but had gone only another quarter-mile when we heard the rumbling sound made by the elephant's stomach in the process of digesting his heavy meal.

I sent Ranga and the forest guard up a stout tamarind tree and crept forward alone in the direction of the sound. The elephant was in a small depression, densely wooded by bamboo. Evidently he was resting, or perhaps lying down, as there were no sounds of his feeding. By this time the rumbling had also ceased.

Very carefully, almost inch by inch, I went down into the depression. Then stopping for a moment, I gathered a little soft earth in my hand and held it up before me, letting it drop in order to see from which direction any current of air might be blowing. The earth fell straight, indicating that there was hardly any breeze in the depression. This was a handicap, as there was a chance of the elephant smelling me in the still air.

So I went forward, still more carefully, if that were possible. The bamboos towered above me, and I peeped around each clump as I came abreast of it. A few more yards of this sort of progress and I saw what appeared to be a slate-grey boulder before me. It was the elephant, lying on the ground, and as my bad luck would have it, facing in the opposite direction.

I could now do one of two things: either make a detour and try to come upon the elephant from the front, where I might see his tusks and identify him as the rogue before shooting, or much simpler, rouse him from where I stood. He would undoubtedly turn around to face the disturbance, so that I could then identify him and shoot before he could know what was happening.

Deciding on this second and easier course, I slipped partly behind a clump of bamboo, then softly whistled. The elephant took no notice. Perhaps he was deeply asleep, or thought the sound had come from some forest bird. Then I clicked my tongue loudly. This had the desired effect, for the elephant scrambled to its feet and span around to face me.

He was a magnificent tusker, quite ten feet tall, and his ivory tusks gleamed magnificently in the early morning sunlight. But they were wide apart, not crossed in the least. I had spent my time tracking the wrong elephant.

The pachyderm looked at me in amazement for quite half a minute, his small eyes contemplating the creature who had disturbed his slumber. I could almost read the thoughts that were passing through his brain. His first reaction, after surprise, was annoyance and he moved forward a pace or two in a threatening attitude. I gave another sharp whistle, at the sound of which his courage ebbed away, and he turned tail and bolted into the forest, the crashing sound of his retreat dying away in the distance.

By the time I returned to the spot where I had left Ranga and the Forest Guard, they had already climbed down from the tamarind tree, guessing, by the sounds they had clearly heard, that I had found an animal which was not the rogue we were after. The three of us then trudged dejectedly back to the water hole, not only disappointed, but annoyed at the time we had wasted.

As previously related, there were two other tracks of approximately the same size. They had been made in the mud of the pool and nothing could be gained by measuring them with my tape to determine which came nearest to the notified dimensions of the rogue; soft mud exaggerated the track of any animal. Ranga followed one, and the guard and myself the other, with the understanding that we would return to the water hole in fifteen minutes for further consultation.

It was not long before I could see that the animal I was following had been one of the regular herd, for the broken undergrowth revealed the presence of the feeding cows and young that had accompanied him. He was obviously not the rogue, and in exactly fifteen minutes by my watch I turned and made my way back to the water hole. Ranga, having no watch, had not yet arrived, so I sat down to a quiet pipe and sip of hot tea from the flask carried by the Forest Guard. After about ten minutes, he came to report that the elephant had made a detour a quarter of a mile from the water hole, had moved around in a semicircle and passed through a strip of jungle that led to a hill in exactly the opposite direction, behind the bungalow.

This news seemed promising, so we were up and away. Nor was it long before we came to the spot whence Ranga had returned to report. It soon became evident that our new quarry was a traveller, for he had hardly stopped to feed, other than pluck an occasional small stem of succulent young leaves. That elephant led us on and on, over the hill behind the forest bungalow, over the next two hills, and then in almost a straight line to the Talvadi stream.

In all we covered well over four miles before reaching the bed of that stream, when we found that the elephant had turned southwest and was moving directly down the Talvadi river itself. I knew the Cauvery river lay within a distance of fifteen miles, and I began to feel our quarry had suddenly made up his mind to reach the big river. Once he did this, and particularly if he swam across to the opposite bank, it would be hopeless to follow him, as the terrain there is not only extremely dense, but leads on and on as unbroken forest and hill country to the Niligiri and Biligirirangan Mountains, over a hundred miles away.

So we passed on with all possible speed, casting discretion to the winds, but our elephant had had a lead of several hours, and judging by the long and determined strides he had taken, he had been bent upon travelling.

The soft sand of the riverbed was now scalding hot under the midday sun. It hampered my walking and trickled into my boots by means that only fine river or sea sand knows. Every now and again the streambed became rocky, and for long stretches the fine sand gave way to a succession of rounded, water-worn boulders. In such spots the elephant had pushed through the undergrowth of the banks to avoid the boulders, and we did the same, bent double to dodge the dangling lines of creepers, and pouring with perspiration from our exertions.

Fifteen miles of such walking brought us near the confluence of Talvadi and the Cauvery. A few hundred yards from the big river, the Talvadi stream is crossed by the rough track leading from Uttaimalai village to Biligundlu. The elephant had changed direction here and had followed the track towards Uttaimalai for another two miles, before turning southwards again towards a swamp that borders the big river. This swamp, known as Kartei Palam, which means Bison Hollow, was well known to me. Years before it had been a regular haunt for bison herds that swam across the Cauvery from the Coimbatore bank to the Salem side. At this time of the year the swamp was fairly dry except in places, but lush grass grew everywhere, while shady clumps of trees dotted the whole area.

We now met with signs that the elephant had begun feeding, and as we made our way towards the centre of the swamp mounds of fresh dung showed that the animal was not far away.

The ground also became boggy, and once more I sent Ranga and the guard back to minimise the squelching sounds that were bound to arise from three people walking in the mud. Progress was necessarily at a snail's pace, for I had not only to look out for the elephant, but study the ground carefully at each step, to avoid suddenly plunging waist-deep into the clinging black clay. Yet, several times I sank knee-deep, and to extricate myself I had to struggle and flounder about, making no end of noise, before I gained a firmer footing.

Several times I stopped to listen but heard nothing, and then, without warning, there came a violent 'swoosh' of the reedy grass, and the elephant stood some twenty paces away, all dripping and covered with the sticky muck in which he had been lying. It was a big bull, with gleaming white tusks, symmetrically curved. But they were not the crossed tusks of the rogue. Disappointment and disgust so overcame me that I fairly 'shoo-ed' that poor elephant away, and when I rejoined my followers, I was in no good mood, as they could clearly see.

It was now past 4 p.m., and we had some fifteen miles to retrace along the Talvadi Stream, plus another four to the Gerhetti bungalow. Alternatively, we could camp at Biligundlu and return next morning; but this would mean the loss of another half-day, out of the two days that were left to me. So I gave the order for the return march, much to the disgust of my companions, who reminded me that, as we had no light of any kind, the major portion of our journey would have to be performed in darkness, there being no moon. We might even meet the elephant! My reply, I am afraid, was terse, and consigned this elephant, and all other elephants, to a region they would find far too hot.

That return journey seemed one long succession of stumbling, slipping, slithering over rocks, or tripping over stumps, or being caught by creepers without sign or sound of the elephant. It was almost midnight before we limped into the Gerhetti bungalow, thoroughly exhausted and as fretful as children. We had been up with the dawn, walking incessantly, stalking through thorns, grass, river-sand and swamp, and had covered about forty miles. We were ravenously hungry and thirsty too.

Next morning I was cramped and footsore. The forest guard showed an ankle, which he had contrived to twist somewhere along the Talvadi stream, and begged to be excused from that day's operations. Only Ranga appeared fit, and ready for another hard day. Porridge, bacon and eggs, and strong coffee put new life into me, while a huge ball of 'ragi', which is a small foodgrain, boiled and made into a sphere almost the size of a tiny cannonball, washed down with coffee, would satisfy Ranga till nightfall.

We had all been too tired to hear any sounds during the night, but a visit to the waterhole now indicated the herd had returned while we had slept. There were also the fresh footmarks of two big bulls, one of which was probably the first elephant I had followed the previous day, while the other was the animal I had not followed at all. The third bull, as we well knew, we had left far away at Kartei Palam.

Nevertheless, nothing could be left to chance; so we followed the same plan as that of the previous day, tracking each of these two animals till we came up with them. By 9.30 a.m. we had come up to the first bull that we had decided to follow. He was slightly smaller than the two we had tracked the previous day, and he was not the rogue! No doubt this was the third animal of the trio whose footprints we had noted the previous day. Going back to the water hole, we set out on the remaining track, and came upon its maker at 2.30 p.m., quietly standing under a large and shady tamarind tree. Nor was he the rogue. I readily recognised him as the first animal I had tracked the previous day and had disturbed while lying among the bamboos.

Thus it was clear that the 'rogue' was not in the immediate vicinity. Three of the four days available to me had now gone, but I was still no further forward than on the day of my arrival.

At five we were back at the bungalow, brewing a large *degchie* of tea. Then at half-past five a party of bullock-carts arrived from Anchetty, eight miles away, to shelter for the night because of the presence of the rogue. The cartmen stated that at a spot about half-way from Anchetty, where the Gollamothi stream traversed the road, they had come upon the tracks of a large elephant which had crossed and recrossed the road at several points and was evidently hanging around not far from the ford itself.

Determined not to give up till the last moment, Ranga and I ate an early dinner and, bundling the still-tired Forest Guard into the car, motored to the ford of which the cartmen had spoken.

It was 7 p.m. when we arrived there and almost dark. The car lights revealed the tracks of the elephant where the cartmen had said. At the ford itself, with the aid of torches we made out the plate-like spoor of the elephant superimposed upon the narrow ruts made by the cartwheels of our friends. Elephants do not wander about in daytime in hot weather, and this clearly indicated that the pachyderm had been on the road that very evening, before our arrival. Perhaps he had even heard the sound of the car, or seen our lights, and had moved off just before we came on the scene.

We quickly lowered the hood of the Studebaker. I handed my 'sealed-beam' spotlight to Ranga, whom I placed in the 'dickie' seat behind, but kept the guard in the front seat. I myself sat on the folded hood, my feet on the driving seat, with my rifle and torch at the ready. Complete darkness soon enveloped us, overshadowed as we were by the towering *muthee* and *jumlum* trees that bordered the banks of the Gollamothi, together with bamboo clumps, whose stems creaked weirdly to the jungle air-currents that blew up and down the dry sandy bed of the river.

The prospects were poor. To begin with, we did not know whether the tracks we had seen belonged to the rogue. They might, indeed, have been made by any elephant. All we knew for certain was that they had not been made by any of the three big males around Gerhetti. Secondly, there was not the slightest reason for this elephant to return to the ford he had so recently passed, for he had the whole wide jungle in which to roam. Thirdly, we all knew that ten miles to an elephant is scarcely two hours' easy ambling, and that when he is really travelling he moves much faster. Fourthly, the wind was blowing in all directions, and would carry our scent to any elephant within a quarter-of-a-mile and, if he was not the rogue, drive him off. On the other hand, there was the slender hope that, if this was the rogue, our scent might attract him.

So we waited in the pitch-darkness till 8.30 p.m., and then the dull sound of a hollow log being turned over came to us form somewhere upstream. The elephant was on the move at last and, judging by the sound, was some four or five hundred yards away. Silence followed for another quarter-hour, when the sharp crack of a breaking branch, much closer, indicated that the elephant was feeding and moving towards the ford as he did so.

I knew he would take thirty minutes at least to finish eating the young leaves from the ends of the branch he had just broken, so that there would be plenty of time before he came near. The car, with us inside it, would be clearly visible to him as he came around the curve of the river, and there was every possibility, if he was not the rogue, that on seeing us he would just fade quietly away into the forest. But I had not taken the wind into consideration; just then it blew strongly from us towards the elephant.

Minuets of silence followed, and then we heard a slight rustling in the undergrowth from the bank of the river nearest to the car. It was a faint sound, apparently made by a small body in the bushes. Then the ominous crack of trodden bamboo came to us suddenly. Silence again, deep and enveloping. Even the breeze seemed to have died, to allow full opportunity for the next event.

This was the ear-splitting scream of a charging bull-elephant, mingled with the crashing of bamboos and undergrowth as they collapsed before the monster that rushed towards us.

Ranga never flinched! The beam of the spot-light cut through the enveloping gloom. My own torch-beam, mingling with that of the vastly more brilliant spotlight, showed an enormous tusker, his bulk pitch black, his trunk curled upwards and inwards, with two wicked white tusks that were crossed at the tip, thundering upon us!

At fifty yards range the bullet from my right barrel took him in the throat. He stopped with the impact, screaming with rage. No doubt this was more than he had bargained for! The explosion, the pain and the lights confused him, and he half-turned into the jungle. My second bullet, aimed hastily at the temple, struck him somewhere on the side of the head. He rushed into the jungle, stumbled on his forefeet, picked himself up again as I reloaded, and disappeared in the bamboos as my third shot struck him somewhere in the body. For quite fifteen minutes we could hear heavy crashes in the jungle as the elephant reeled, collapsed and then recovered, to continue his flight.

Starting the car, I reversed and returned to Gerhetti. I slept soundly that night, Ranga awakening me at dawn with a mugful of steaming, strong tea.

By 6.30 a.m., we were on the track of the stricken rogue. Great gouts of blood had issued from the throat-wound and had sprayed through his trunk over the surrounding bushes, which had been reddened by his passage. Soon we too were red with his blood as we pushed ourselves through the undergrowth in his wake.

He had lain, or fallen down, in several places, where the greensward had been dyed a deep red. He had leaned against several tree-trunks that were still sticky with his blood. Truly, if you do not finish the job of killing an elephant, you let yourself in for a gory trail. I really pitied this poor beast, murderous killer of men though he had been.

After two miles I found him, half-kneeling, half-lying against a tree-trunk. He was so weak from loss of blood that he could scarcely move, although he clearly saw me as I walked towards him. The only sign of life were his wicked little blood-shot eyes, that gleamed and moved as they watched my approach. Fifteen yards away I raised my rifle to deliver the coup de grace. As if to salute approaching death, that game and mighty beast shivered from head to foot as he drew up his mighty bulk to its full ten feet. The trunk curled upwards, the big ears flapped outward, and he staggered two paces forward in his last charge, when the heavy 450/400 bullet crashed into his temple and he collapsed, as if pole-axed, to earth.

Although a killer, the 'crossed-tusker of Gerhetti' was a brave fighter, and I honoured him as he lay before my still-smoking muzzle—mighty in life and even mightier in his death!

Five

The Sangam Panther

NEWS FILTERED THROUGH TO MY HOME IN BANGALORE THAT A leopard, or 'panther' as it is more commonly known in India, was killing people in the vicinity of a place called Sangam, a little over seventy miles south of the city.

Man-eating panthers are rare in southern India. To begin with, the jungles are not so extensive, or nearly so continuously mountainous as in the north, particularly along the foothills of the vast Himalayan range. The exception is the Western Ghats, which are almost wholly covered with forest for over four hundred miles, with an average breadth of ten to fifteen miles. But the other forest areas are of much smaller extent and are more or less surrounded by cultivation. This causes carnivores, and particularly panthers, to confine their attentions to the herds of cattle and goats, in which the country is abundantly rich, and to a lesser extent to village curs, locally known as *'piedogs'* which are, like the common monkey, the curse of the land. Prior to the advent to hydrophobia vaccine, large numbers of persons died yearly of infection from the bite of mad dogs, as these curs constantly contract rabies, especially in the hot weather. Monkeys are and always have been a major menace, doing untold damage to crops and fruit trees. The monkey has a strong religious significance to Indians, and great objection is raised against any attempt to harm it. Panthers—at least so far as the 'piedogs' and monkeys are concerned—therefore perform a great service to the land.

In the Western Ghats of which I have just spoken, the rainfall is very heavy, even exceeding hundred inches per year. They are covered with dense bamboo, long grass, and thick evergreen vegetation—the breeding grounds of clouds of mosquitoes, ticks, leeches, flies and other animal pests.

Panthers do not like much water—and they detest the pests, in any and all their many forms! So, in the only region where they could multiply unmolested they are hardly to be found! By a natural arrangement, therefore, panthers, which are found in all other jungles of southern India, generally have plenty to eat and somehow do not become addicted to the bad habit of man-eating. A notable exception to this was the panther of Gummalapur, a story I have related elsewhere*; in that case there were special circumstances that caused it to take to man-eating.

In Bangalore news often reached us of people being mauled by panthers and tigers, more often by the former. But nobody took particular notice of these rumours as on-the-spot investigation always told the same tale. Some villager, with his matchlock, or some inexperienced hunter would let fly at a panther, generally with slugs, and succeed only in hurting

---

* In *Nine Man-Eaters and One Rogue*, George Allen and Unwin, 1954.

it. Then, inexperienced in jungle-lore, he would attempt to follow it up, through lantana bushes or amongst rocks, and get mauled—sometimes severely—for his pains. In years gone by, over seventy-five per cent of such cases of mauling resulted in death from septicaemia. With the advent of the sulpha drugs, casualties dropped to below ten per cent.

So nobody took much notice when such news came in. Why should they? They had other work to do. Moreover, rumour is invariably much exaggerated in India! A slight scratch is magnified into a severed mauling, and a mauling into a killing. When an actual killing does occur, it is widely described in the Press as several killings.

Therefore, when I heard that a panther had killed a woman, and later killed and eaten a child at Sangam, I did not believe it. Then the panther killed a third and a fourth time. The Press got hold of the news and it was splashed across the front pages.

Several hunters from Bangalore, Mysore and Madras went after the animal, but for a month the panther did not kill. One of the hunters succeeded in shooting a panther; and this fact, coupled with the cessation of human kills, seemed to indicate that it was the man-eater that had been shot. The hunters returned to the towns.

Then the panther killed once more, but was prevented from eating its victim, a man who was sleeping in a shed-like room with a pack of four mongrel dogs, with which he used to hunt hare and sometimes deer.

A thorn fence protected the entrance to the shed. The roof comprised loose bits of zinc sheeting, and the wall consisted of wooden stakes driven into the ground in close formation, the gaps being stuffed with thorns. The panther came at night, and with its paws contrived to open a passage between the end stake of the doorway and the thorn fence across the entrance. The dogs panicked, barking and howling loudly and cowering to one side. But the man must have just woken.

The panther entered the shed. The dogs clustered together but did nothing, and the marauder, walking past them, grabbed the man by the throat. He died after uttering a single, piercing wail.

The people in the neighbouring hut had been disturbed by the noise made by the dogs' barking and growling in the shed. They wondered what was happening, but nobody would go outside to investigate. The panther then tried to drag the dead man out of the shed through the same gap by which it had entered. The gap was not big enough. So the panther itself passed through and tried to drag the man after it. But the body became entangled in the thorns and stuck fast. The panther then gave a mighty heave, which succeeded in unbalancing the fence, which fell with a crash on top of the animal. This must have frightened him considerably for he made off, leaving the corpse still entangled amongst the thorns.

The continued noise resulting from the efforts of the panther now alarmed the people in the next hut, who had been listening breathlessly all this time. They began to shout and woke other villagers. After quite a while, some of the brave men came forth carrying lanterns, armed with matchlocks, bludgeons and staves, to find the dead man, but no panther.

The alarm now spread afresh, and news was brought to me by the village *Patel*, or headman, who came to Bangalore expressly for the purpose. I was at that time able to take two days' casual leave, while Sunday made a third. So I agreed to go with him and attempt to shoot the panther within those three days.

The road to Sangam ran past the town of Kankanhalli, thirty-six miles from Bangalore, from where it began to descend sharply to the bed of the Cauvery river. The last ten miles of the track was really atrocious, and my Studebaker rocked and creaked and groaned in all its joints, in protest at such bad treatment. Hairpin bends at ridiculous gradients and sharp angles (where all milestones and furlong slabs were coloured black to prevent them from being uprooted by wild elephants, who have a great aversion to anything white), betokened my approach to journey's end, and soon I reached the little traveller's bungalow after a short but exceedingly tough journey.

The word 'Sangam' denotes a 'joining' or 'confluence', and was most appropriate, for it marked the junction of the Cauvery river with its tributary, the Arkravarthy, which flows in almost a straight line southwards from its source north of Bangalore.

The Cauvery here flows from west to east, Sangam being on its northern bank within Mysore state territory. The southern bank of the Cauvery comes within the jungles of North Coimbatore district (Kollegal Forest Division). Some thirteen miles east of Sangam, Mysore state territory ends and is flanked by Salem district, which thereafter holds the northern bank of the river with North Coimbatore district continuing along the southern bank. Both North Coimbatore and Salem districts belong to the Madras presidency.

Sangam is a beautifully wooded spot, offering in normal times first-rate masher fishing, with crocodile shooting among the sandbanks and rocks in any direction along the river. On the Mysore side of the forest there are spotted deer, sambar, barking-deer, wild pig, feathered game, and an occasional bear, panther or tiger. Elephants often cross over from the Coimbatore bank. Along the southern bank, in the Coimbatore jungles, all the above abound in greater number, in addition to several fine herds of bison. Elephant and bear are particularly numerous.

After parking the car under the huge *muthee* trees that flanked the river and grew beside the bungalow, I walked across to the small village where the dog-keeper had recently been killed and inspected the scene for myself, in addition to being given graphic accounts of what had happened by the neighbours, who had heard so much that day, but had done nothing to help the poor fellow. The *Patel*, who had returned with me joined in the voluble tale.

With much questioning and cross-questioning, it became apparent that this panther was going to be an exceedingly difficult animal to bag, as on the north banks of the river it had a very wide expanse of jungle to wander over, without taking into consideration the many square miles of forest on the southern or Coimbatore side. But the latter could reasonably be excluded, since panthers, unlike tigers, generally dislike swimming across big rivers, although they swim well when compelled to do so.

The first, and apparently only thing to do was to tie out baits. With the *Patel's* active help, I purchased five large bull-calves. The first of these we tethered about half-a-mile west of the bungalow and about the same distance from the river bank; the second, on a line roughly parallel with the river and a mile farther west; the third, a mile farther west than the second; the fourth, on the farther bank of the Arkravarthy tributary, about half-a-mile east of the bungalow and the same distance from the Cauvery; and the fifth, a mile east of the fourth bait. Thus the five baits were roughly in a straight line, flanking the river, about half-a-mile inland and with a distance of four miles between the farthest bait to the west and the farthest bait to the east.

It was sunset before I returned to the bungalow. A cold dinner appeased my appetite, eaten on the small bungalow verandah and washed down with two steaming mugs of tea.

After lighting my pipe, I sat with my back to the wall, listening to the subdued rush of the river as it sped along its rocky bed. It was a dark night and fairly cloudy. Such stars as could be seen peeping occasionally between clouds would be insufficient for night-watching, so I went inside and fell asleep.

Early next morning we checked the baits. They were all alive. I walked up the road down which I had come the previous day, climbing up the hairpin bends and ghat section. There were no panther tracks to bee seen. A herd of spotted deer and three sambar—singly and at different places—had crossed the road during the night, but no other animal had passed.

When returning to the bungalow, instead of coming back along the road, I cut down the hill through the jungle and came on to the dry bed of the Arkravarthy, where I turned southwards and walked in the sand, looking for possible pug-marks. There were none to be seen, but the same herd of spotted deer that had crossed the road had also traversed the sands. In due course, I passed my bait number four, and came to where the Arkravarthy joined the Cauvery.

A day and a half, out of the three days at my disposal, had now passed, and I had not even seen the panther's pug-marks. The situation seemed hopeless.

After lunch, I decided to walk in the easterly direction, downstream along the Cauvery for about three-and-a-half miles, to a gorge where the river narrowed to about twenty feet. At this spot it roared through a chasm, known as Meke-Dat. The meaning of that word, in Kanarese language, is 'the goat's leap'. Legend records that, years and years ago, a jungle-sheep pursued by wild dogs on the Coimbatore side and driven to the brink of the river, performed the prodigious feat of leaping those twenty feet to safety on the Mysore side.

Here, all other sounds are drowned by the roar of the turbulent waters, hurling themselves through the narrow opening, and a man can hardly hear himself even when he shouts his very loudest.

I sat on the edge of the rocks and watched the troubled, racing river. A hundred yards away, downstream where the surface had become placid again, an occasional fish broke water, leaping into the air, as if evincing sheer exuberance and joy of living. A fish-eagle circled in the ethereal blue of a clear sky. After a while, I rose and retraced my steps to the bungalow. I had still not found any panther tracks.

The night was clear. Although there was no moon, there were none of the previous night's clouds and the starlight was enough in the jungle to enable one to see for a few yards.

The watchman in charge of the bungalow owned a *'piedog'*—the name by which mongrels in India are known—and against my custom and only because time was so short, I asked him to lend it to me till midnight. He hummed and hawed at first, but when three rupees had changed hands he agreed.

While walking along the road that day, I had noticed a rock at its edge hardly a mile away. I took the dog, tied it at the foot of the rock and walked away down the road. When out of sight of the dog, I turned to my right and cut into the jungle, coming back to the rock on its 'off' side. Silently I clambered up, and lay flat on its top. The rock was still warm from the sun that had been shining on it all day.

Thinking it had been abandoned, the dog began barking, whining and howling by turns. Dogs are too intelligent, it is unfair to tie them out as bait. Unlike cattle and goats, they sense danger at once and, even if not attacked, go through hours of mental agony. I have known a dog which was tied out as bait for a panther—although it was not harmed—

become so nervous that it fell sick the following day and died within a week.

I watched from the top of the rock. Nearly an hour passed, and then suddenly a shadowy, grey shape came scampering down the road. It moved fast till about ten feet from the dog, then it stopped. Could it be the panther?

The stars shed just enough light to prevent the darkness from being total, but not more than that. I could just see the grey shape looking at the dog. The dog growled furiously as it turned round to face the intruder. It must be a panther, I thought, as I aligned my rifle in its direction preparatory to depressing the switch of my torch which was fastened along the barrel.

'Ha! Ha! Ha! Ha! Ha!' said the intruder, followed by a disparaging but loud 'Cheey! Shee-ay! Shee-ay!'

It was a hyaena, the common striped hyaena of southern India. The dog growled still more ferociously; then began to bark frenziedly..

Now began an amusing drama, such as watchers by night are sometimes privileged to witness in a jungle. The hyaena darted off the road into the undergrowth, where he began to say, 'Gudda! Guddar! Garrar! Gurr-rr-aa!' ending with his usual disparaging 'Cheey-ar! Shee-ar!'

The dog faced the noise and barked loudly. The hyaena reappeared on the road, beyond the dog but watching him, and crackled, 'Ha! Ha! ha! Guddar! Garrar! Shee-ay!'

Unlike his African cousins, the spotted and the brown hyaena, the former being the familiar 'laughing hyaena' we have all heard about, the Indian hyaena is generally a silent animal, hunting alone or at the most in pairs. Spotted hyaenas move in packs. As a rule, all hyaenas are cowardly animals, although they are extremely strong for their size and have enormously powerful jaws, which can easily bite right through a man's arm, bone and all.

Quite rarely, they display extraordinary courage, of which I once saw an example. I had been sitting over a panther kill. The owner turned up and began to eat. I had held my shot, as I wanted, if possible, to learn the sex of the animal before killing it. This was because I had been told a male and a female panther lived in the vicinity, and that the female was accompanied by two cubs about six months old. I wanted to make certain I did not shoot the mother.

While I hesitated, a hyaena had arrived on the scene, and his arrival, on that occasion, had been dramatic. He came as if from nowhere, and the first I knew of his arrival was when he had scampered boldly up to the panther, voicing the same medley of sounds I have just described. The panther, sprawled across its kill, had glared at the newcomer with blazing orbs, snarling and growling furiously. The hyaena had approached to within five feet, just beyond reach of the panther's paw-sweep, and had set up such a cacophony of hideous sound as to resemble a chorus of the demons of hell.

The panther had added to the noise by growling still louder, and every now and then striking at the hyaena with its claws. The latter just rocked backwards, out of reach of each blow, after which it would feint with a short rush forward, while gradually working around to the rear of the panther. At first the panther had turned around correspondingly, to keep the hyaena in view, growling even more loudly while making short jabs and slaps with its paws in the direction of the hyaena. But the hyaena, always out of reach, had haw-ed and sneered, gargled and gurgled with unabated zeal.

Frightened—or perhaps just disgusted—at the unseemly racket, the panther had finally risen from its kill and then walked slowly away with many a backward glance, amidst snarls, at the hyaena, who continued his weird din till the panther had vanished in the undergrowth. Then he had fallen upon the kill himself, with the greatest—and, no doubt, thoroughly deserved—enthusiasm.

But the hyaena which I continued to watch from the rock was undoubtedly a little scared of the mongrel dog. Frequently he would disappear to one or the other side of the road. Then would come a pitter-patter amongst the dried leaves as he doubled back and forth, this way and that, to reappear at all places while continuing to make his unseemly, weird and often comical sounds.

The lesson I learnt from these two experiences was that hyaenas try to frighten their opponents with their continuous, unseemly crackle. The first hyaena had frightened the panther off its own kill while this one was trying to frighten the dog, perhaps just to clear it off the road or into the undergrowth, where he could pounce upon it more easily.

But the dog was tied up, and so could not move away, which the hyaena could not understand. An hour of this sort of thing ceased to be amusing to me, and I realised the racket, especially the part played by the hyaena, was almost certain to drive away any panther in the vicinity, man-eater or otherwise. So, groping for a small piece of rock, I hurled it at the hyaena. My aim fell short of its mark, and the stone thudded on the hard surface of the road. The hyaena jumped nervously, and scampered into the bushes, while the dog stopped barking and began to whimper. I thought I had rid the scene of a most unwelcome visitor.

Perhaps a quarter of an hour had passed when I heard the furtive pitter-patter again, shortly followed by the hyaena's queer notes. The dog barked and growled. I threw another stone at the hyaena. He stopped; only to start again after ten minutes. Once more a stone; once more a silence, followed by a new beginning. Only after about the fifth stone did the hyaena feel that the spot had somehow become unhealthy, and with a final, 'Ah! Ah! Ah! Chee-ey! Shee-ay!' took himself off. It was past ten o'clock.

My watch showed five minutes to midnight when I heard the approach of human voices. A little later, I saw the twinkling lights of two lanterns, illuminating from that distance the walking feet of many men. The dog saw them and stopped its moaning.

When the party drew level with the dog, I counted eleven men, two of whom were carrying lanterns, and all of whom, except one, carried staves and lathis of some sort or another.

The one exception was armed with a matchlock. They had obviously come in search of me. I answered their call and came down from the rock.

The men then told me that, scarcely an hour earlier, the panther had made its way into one of the huts of the very village where the dog-keeper had been attacked by burrowing through the thatched wall, and had seized one of the five sleeping inmates, a woman about twenty-five years old. She had shrieked aloud as she found herself being dragged away, waking the other four persons in the room, who were her father, two brothers and mother.

Meanwhile, the panther was trying to drag her out through the opening in the thatch by which it had entered. The girl struggled violently. The panther dropped her and bit her viciously. One of the brothers struck a match to lighten the darkness of the hut's interior. Her father, with commendable bravery and presence of mind, hurled the only missile which came to his hand, at the panther. The missile happened to be a brass water-pot of some weight, and it struck the panther full on its side. Man-eaters, whether tigers or panthers, invariably have a streak of cowardice in their natures and this panther was no exception to the general rule. Leaving its victim, it had dashed out of the hut through the opening in the thatch.

The screams of the mauled woman and the general pandemonium had awakened the whole village. The menfolk came out with lanterns, armed as best as they could. The party of eleven had then come to the rest-house to find me, and the watchman from whom I had borrowed the dog had directed them to where I was sitting.

Telling one of the men to untie the rope and bring the dog in tow, we hastened back to the bungalow, and I brought out my first-aid kit from the back seat of the Studebaker. We then hurried on to the village, where an appalling sight awaited me. The poor girl had been bitten right through her right shoulder, and again in the abdomen, where the panther had seized her the second time when she had struggled to escape. One breast and her chest right down the side were in ribbons where the foul claws had buried themselves deep in her flesh, raking it open with their downward sweep. Her jacket and sari were torn to pieces, and she lay in a welter of blood, blissfully unconscious after her experience.

I saw at once that such meagre first-aid equipment as I had was totally inadequate to meet the situation, but we quickly washed the wounds with strong solution of potassium permanganate and roughly bandaged her chest and abdomen with strips torn from another sari. Her father, two brothers, and three willing men from the village then carried her on a rope-cot to the Studebaker. Placing her as comfortably as possible in the 'dickie', I took her three male relations aboard and set out for the town of Kankanhalli, which boasted the nearest village hospital. We reached there after three-thirty in the morning, when I awoke the doctor and handed over the injured woman. Her condition appeared to be very low, owing to the great deal of blood she had lost.

By four-thirty, I was in the bathroom of the traveller's bungalow at Kankanhalli, where I removed my blood-soaked clothing and took a cold bath. I had no change of clothing with me, having left them behind at Sangam in the confusion of the moment. So I borrowed a clean *dhoti* and a blanket from the bungalow-waiter.

Dawn was breaking when I knocked at the Post Office, awoke a most obliging postmaster from his sleep, paid the necessary late fee and despatched an urgent telegram to Bangalore requesting extension of leave for four more days.

When I returned to the bungalow I found the younger brother of the injured woman awaiting me in tears. He had come from the hospital to tell me his sister had just died. Shortly afterwards, the father came to ask me to take his daughter's body back in the car to Sangam for cremation by the banks of the river Cauvery, in which the ashes would eventually be scattered. It was a request I could not refuse. The bungalow servant told me he wanted his *dhoti* and blanket back. So I had to dress again in my blood-smeared clothes.

We drove back to the hospital, placed the still, limp body of the girl in the back seat, and set out on the return journey to Sangam, delayed by two hours at the Police Station, where we reported the occurrence.

After a bath in a quiet pool beside the river, free from crocodiles, a change into fresh clothing, a cold lunch and two big mugs of tea, I lay back in a rickety old armchair to review the situation. My loaded pipe, from which the comforting smoke arose in spirals to the roughly-tiled low roof, helped a great deal to soothe my ragged nerves after the events of the previous night and to prevent my eyes from closing with sleep.

What should I do with the remaining four days and five nights at my disposal, to rid these poor village-folk from another, and still another, and God only knew how many more repetitions of these terrible events. Facts appeared to indicate that: (1) the panther would not take animal baits, (2) it had a wide range of cover, and (3) it was predisposed to dragging people out of huts. Then, while I pondered, I fell asleep.

At 3 p.m. I awoke and a possible line of action appeared to have presented itself while I slept. It was this:

The small village of Sangam, with about a dozen huts, had been constructed in the usual fashion, on both sides of a central lane. I remembered that on the southern side of this lane, and not far from the river bank, small herds of cattle belonging to the villagers were corralled in a common enclosure, surrounded by a fence of bamboo, intersticed with cut lantana brambles. The only dogs left in the village, which had belonged to the man who had been killed, were enclosed in the shed-like room where he had been slain, which room happened to adjoin the larger cattle enclosure on its western side. The idea came to me that, if I posted myself at night in the midst of the cattle, not only would I be perfectly safe from unexpected attack, as the cattle would grow restive and give ample warning should the panther approach, but this very restlessness, and the fact that the dogs too would join in the alarm, would help me to learn of the panther's presence, should he enter the village. Meanwhile, I would keep my five live baits tied out on the off-chance that one of them might be taken instead.

With this plan in view, I dressed warmly for the night, wearing a khaki woollen 'balaclava' cap to keep off the dew. My usual night equipment included, this time a large flask of tea, some biscuits, and my pipe, as I knew that smoking, in this case, would do no harm.

Because of the panther's presence, the villagers were inside their huts, behind doors barricaded and reinforced with freshly-cut thorns, long before six o'clock. I took up my position in the middle of the cattle enclosure. About me was a space of about fifty yards in every direction, with nearly hundred nondescript cattle scattered around.

At fist the animals resented my presence and crowded to the corners away from me, leaving me isolated in the centre of the pen. I started trying to make friends with them. One kicked over my flask of tea and nearly broke it! Moreover, some of the bulls were rather truculent and made short jabs at me with their horns if I came too close. After an hour in each other's company, the situation eased a little, and I was able to make my way guardedly to the centre of the herd, about half of whom were now resting on the ground. I got down also.

As the hours dragged by, the silence was unbroken, except for an occasional snort from one of the animals, or the trampling of another as it altered its position. One cow became friendly and insisted in nuzzling her muzzle against my chest as a gesture of companionship. Eventually she flopped down contentedly on the ground beside me.

Then cattle-ticks began to bite me in many places and mercilessly. I scratched myself vigorously, although I knew that by doing so I would only increase the irritation. It grew colder, and soon I was glad to nuzzle myself, in my turn, up against the warm body of the cow who had chosen to open this strange friendship with me. Now and again, one of the herd would 'moo' contentedly, or snort, or kick, or flop down to the ground, or struggle to its feet.

The hours still dragged by, and the ticks continued to bite. At one o'clock a sambar belled on the small hill to the north of the village. It was a doe that had called, and she called again and again. Then her call was taken up by a kakar, whose hoarse bark resounded across the *nullahs* which furrowed the lower slopes of the hillock.

The sambar doe had stopped belling by this time, while the kakar climbed up, giving occasional vent to his guttural call. Whatever it was that had alarmed them had come down the hill.

Some twenty minutes later spotted deer began their warning cries, answering one another from the jungle that slopes from the base of the hill to the edge of the river. Either a tiger or a panther was afoot, and the next few minutes would tell whether the carnivore was just a normal animal or the marauder I was awaiting.

It was almost pitch-dark when the cattle grew restless. With one accord, those lying on the ground scrambled to their feet, and I did the same, keeping close beside the friendly cow. Some of the bulls snorted, and the herd were all turned towards the lane that divided the small village and passed by the thorn hedge that bordered the cattle stockade.

The animals became very restless and began to gather in a mass at the further end of the stockade, away from the hedge and lane. The four dogs in the neighbouring shed had been barking furiously; they now began to whimper. Whatever had frightened them was passing down that lane at that very moment.

I had got myself wedged in the midst of the cattle and had to watch carefully against being impaled on one of the many horns that were nervously tossing about me. I began to force myself through the herd to reach their front rank, hoping that I might be able to see something, but the darkness and the hedge revealed nothing.

I could hear the dogs howling and whimpering in the shed in which they were locked. My ears were attuned to catch the slightest sound, but the noise made by the cattle and the dogs gave me little chance. Some minutes later, I caught the faintest of scratching noises. Listening carefully I located it as coming from further down the lane. They became louder and more impatient. Then I realised that the panther was scratching at a door of one of the huts some distance away.

Breaking through the remainder of the cattle, I approached the fence on tiptoe, hoping to be able to peep over it and catch a glimpse of the panther when I switched on the torch at the end of my rifle. The inmates of the hut at which the panther was scratching chose that very moment to set up a bedlam of shrieks and shouts; the silence was broken by the most frightful din.

Thinking that the man-eater had succeeded in forcing his way into the hut, I threw discretion to the winds and rushed for the bamboo-and-thorn door that formed the entrance of the stockade. At dusk I had firmly wedged a huge Y-shaped log into place, and it took some precious moments to release its base from the big stones against which I had jammed it.

Dragging it aside and switching on the torch, I heaved the clumsy door back and stepped into the lane. Nothing was to be seen in any direction.

Keeping my back to the thorn fence to guard against attack from the rear, I shone the beam in all directions, but I still saw nothing. The panther had disappeared into thin air. Meanwhile, the shrieks and shouts continued unabated.

Then it occurred to me that perhaps the panther was inside the hut all this time, mauling and killing the inmates, and with this alarming thought in mind I began carefully to cover the intervening twenty yards.

When I came abreast of the entrance, I found it was shut fast. I called out to the inmates. At first, due to the noise they were making, they could not hear me. Then I called again, louder and many times. The the hubbub gradually subsided.

I shouted to the occupants to open the door. They would not do so. Then a tremendous voice from inside asked whether I was a man or a devil. I called back that it was I, and that the panther had gone. The voice replied that the inmates would open the door only when morning came. Meanwhile, my torch beam clearly showed the fresh claw-marks on the door of the hut, where the panther had just tried to effect an entrance.

I returned to the stockade, reclosed the door, replaced the Y-shaped log and the stones and went back to the spot where I had been lying against the cow when the alarm had begun.

To my horror, I found that the milling feet of the herd had smashed my thermos and it was now impossible to drink the hot tea for which I longed. My biscuits also had been devoured, and as I watched her ruefully, the friendly cow devoured the last of the paper in which they had been wrapped. Fortunately, I had kept my pipe and tobacco in my pocket, and with this I spent the rest of the night in comparative comfort, once again nestling against the side of the cow.

I returned to the bungalow at dawn, tired and disappointed. Worst of all, my body was a mass of tick-bites and itched abominably. Further, I knew only too well that each bite would fester during the coming ten days, and that I was in for a most uncomfortable time.

A cold bath and change, followed by hot tea, tinned bacon and bread and butter helped to ease my gloom, and by 7.30 a.m. I was asleep. I awoke for lunch at midday, and slept again till 3 p.m. Then I got up and began to work out another plan.

It would be impossible to sit with the cattle again, for if I was to get bitten once more by as many ticks as in the previous night, I might end with a dose of tick fever. Yet it was undeniable that both the cattle and the dogs had helped admirably in giving me the alarm when the panther had passed down the lane.

At last I had a fresh idea, that appeared to be the only compromise in the situation. The roof of the dog-shed consisted of scraps of zinc sheeting. I decided that I would lie on that roof, suitably camouflaged and overlooking the lane, so that I should be able to shoot the panther if it walked down the lane again. The cattle and the dogs would still help me by giving the alarm. I could protect my rear and both flanks by heaping stacks of cut thorns on to the roof. Any heavy body, like the panther, that leapt upon the zinc roof would necessarily give its presence away by the noise that would follow. Not only did this appear to be the only solution, but actually a good solution of the problem.

So I hurried towards the village, carrying my night-kit, biscuits, tea (poured into an empty beer bottle, borrowed from the bungalow watchman). After telling the villagers of my new plan, willing hands soon stacked piles of cut thorn branches on to the zinc roof of the goat-shed in the form of a square. Others brought dried straw, which they placed on the roof within the square of thorns for me to lie on.

At 6 p.m. I took up my position. There were two disadvantages that almost immediately began to show themselves: the first, that having to face the lane all the time, I would have to lie so that my legs would be slightly higher than my head, for the zinc roof sloped slightly downwards from back to front, to allow rain-water to flow off easily; the second, that I would have to remain lying on my stomach for most of the time, since my slightest movement sounded distinctly on the zinc roof. But the advantages were that I was safe from surprise attack from the rear; that I had a clear and unobstructed view of the lane and could hear distinctly, particularly if the cattle or the dogs became uneasy; lastly, that I was away from those awful ticks.

But that night was a peaceful one, without any indication whatever that the panther had come within two or three miles of the village. Back at the bungalow next morning I had another bath, and another daylong sleep. Each day I had had my live baits checked by a group of men, but none of these beasts had been harmed.

That night I took up position on the roof once more. It was past 2 a.m., and there had been no alarms from the surrounding jungle, and I felt very drowsy. Suddenly, as in a dream, I heard the cattle begin to stir restlessly. One of the dogs in the shed beneath me growled. Then all four of them began to bark or howl together.

Peering forward slowly, I began to scan the village lane in both directions. Starlight was not good at that moment, only enough to prevent the night from being obscure. The lane to the right and left appeared as a faint blur and of a slightly lighter shade than the surroundings. I could hear nothing and see nothing.

Then I caught the faintest of sounds. It appeared to be a hiss such as a cobra might make. Yes, there it was again! And it came from in front and directly below me. Was it the hiss of a snake or the faint noise a panther makes when he curls back the skin of his upper lip?

I peered downwards and at first could see nothing. Seconds later a faint elongated shape registered itself on my vision in that difficult light, a smudge of an infinitesimally lighter shade than the surrounding blur of the lane. I stared at it, and thought I saw it move. The hiss was repeated more distinctly this time. It appeared to come from this lighter smudge. The dogs inside the shed below me now started to whine and whimper. The cattle were very restless.

I realised that I could not point my rifle downwards from where I lay, I would have to move forward another foot perhaps, till my head and shoulders completely cleared the edge of zinc sheet on which I was lying. I began to do this, but despite my utmost care, the straw rustled and the zinc creaked faintly.

There came an ominous growl from that lightish smudge, and I knew that I was discovered and that within the next few seconds the panther would probably jump on the zinc roof and on to me.

Kicking myself forward the remaining six inches, I lowered the rifle over the side of the roof and depressed the torch-switch. Two gleaming orbs reflected the light from a spotted body, crouched for the spring. Only a single shot was required at that point-blank range and the spark of life slowly faded from those blazing orbs: from fiery white they became a dull orange, then a faint green, then an empty glimmer, and finally a purplish blue as the light was reflected back by the now lifeless retina.

It was an old female that I saw next morning, with canine teeth worn down almost to their stubs. Her coat was extremely pale; even her rosettes were ill-formed and dull. Her claws were blunt and worn. There appeared to be no other signs of deformity of any sort about her, or indication of an earlier wound. It seemed that only old age, and the prospect of gradual starvation through her physical incapacity to kill animals, had caused the Sangam panther to make war on the human race—a war which, however ghastly and fearsome while it lasts, invariably ends in the death of the feline. Modern firearms and the human intellect are heavy odds against the jungle instinct, cunning and pangs of hunger.

Six

The Ramapuram Tiger

THIS IS THE STORY OF A TIGER THAT FOR THREE MONTHS HELD SWAY over nearly half a district, an area some sixty miles long by another sixty or so broad. Although his reign was comparatively short, it was nevertheless hectic, for during this short time the Ramapuram tiger was literally here, there and everywhere within the 3,600 square miles of his domain. Like the Scarlet Pimpernel he was sought by all, yet found by none, till his end came in an unexpected manner.

The district of North Coimbatore is largely made up of hills and forest. Bounded on the south by the low-lying plains of Coimbatore proper, it rises abruptly to the Dimbum escarpment. On the southwest are the jungles of the Nilgiri or Blue Mountain range. On the west, the forests of Mysore. To the northwest is another high range of hills—the Biligirirangans. North, northeast and eastwards flows the Cauvery river, clothed on both its banks with heavy jungle, the northeastern and eastern portions abutting on the forests of the district of Salem.

There is only one town worthy of that name in the district of North Coimbatore: Kollegal, which lies at the northwestern corner, scarcely eight miles from the Cauvery. Four roads branch out of Kollegal. Those that run westwards and northwards into Mysore play no part in this story. The third leads southwards and is more or less straight and runs along the eastern base of the Biligirirangan hills. Seventeen miles along this road brings one to the large village of Lokkanhalli; thirteen miles beyond Lokkanhalli is Bailur, where the 'Bison Range' begins and reaches to Hasanpur at the forty-eighth milestone, and to Dimbum, at the top of the escarpment, fifty-two miles from Kollegal.

The fourth road leads in a southeasterly direction and cuts through the village of Ramapuram, about twenty-five miles from Kollegal, where it turns southwards and leads to Bargur, twenty-four miles further on, then to Tamarakarai, another five miles, and finally to the southeastern end of the Dimbum escarpment, where it drops sharply to the village of Andiyur on the plains. This road totals about eighty-one miles in length.

The Kollegal-Lokkanhalli-Bailur-Dimbum road carried sparse lorry traffic and a daily bus service; whereas the road to Ramapuram, Tamarakari and Andiyur was unfit for motor traffic, except jeeps or old-fashioned high-clearance American cars, over the last sixty miles of its length. The terrain is fearful, consisting of sharp rising and falling gradients strewn with boulders. It becomes a narrow track, cut deeply by the wheels of bullock-carts and hemmed in on both sides by dense forest. The sandy—and often rocky-beds of forest streams cross and recross this track at intervals. In the deeper valleys vast areas of the mighty bamboo prevail, the drooping stems touching the hood of the car as it labours and chugs along in low gear with its radiator invariably boiling. Occasionally a fallen bamboo stem, or the broken branch of a tree, lies across the track, torn down to appease the ravenous appetite of an elephant. The driver then halts, and with his axe, or 'chopper' as it is here called, cuts away the obstruction and drags it aside, then moves on until he meets another similar obstruction. Without the handy 'chopper', this track would be impassable.

Tigers normally dislike very dense vegetation, and keep to low scrub jungle, but it is preferred by elephants and bison. The tiger has various reasons for its preference, one being that almost impenetrable undergrowth prevents the tiger from carefully stalking his prey and hinders his terribly effective last-minute charge. Another reason is that the tiger's legitimate prey — deer of all kinds, wild pig and, of course, village cattle — do not enter very dense jungle, which is mainly inhabited by elephants and bison of which the tiger generally keeps clear. A third reason is that thick undergrowth harbours insect pests, such as leeches, many species of animal-ticks, and the horse or animal fly, as it is called in India; tigers have a great aversion to these pests.

The Ramapuram man-eater was reported to have come from the banks of the Cauvery river, from the region of a mountain known as Ponnachai Malai, over six thousand feet in altitude. A few minor coffee-estates, owned by Sholagas and other Indian planters, exist on the slopes of this mountain. It is said that the Ramapuram man-eater began his career as an ordinary cattle-lifter that made a habit of raiding these estates for what he could pick up in the way of domestic cattle belonging to the planters and the coolies. He is reported to have killed and eaten several cattle, till one planter, more enterprising than his fellows, went down to Coimbatore city and purchased a gin-trap of truly formidable appearance.

This trap was made of iron with two semicircular rows of teeth, which when opened and held apart, had a spread of almost two-and-a-half feet. The teeth were about two inches long. The jaws were kept apart by a hair-trigger arrangement, which, when released, allowed an exceptionally powerful spring to bring the jaws noisily together at lightning speed, so that the wicked teeth meshed with each other.

Soon afterwards, the tiger killed a milch-cow which it dragged into a ravine and concealed beneath a heap of dried leaves, without starting to feed. The kill was followed and discovered, and the trap was carefully set near the hindquarters of the cow, at which place the tiger would normally start operations when he returned for his meal. The same dried leaves that concealed the kill were used to hide the trap. The tiger returned, and to his bad luck and the future ill-fortune of others—got his head in the trap, which caught him firmly on both sides of the neck, just behind the ears.

The trap had been anchored to the ground with a stake. The tiger tore at the trap and succeeded in uprooting the stake, while the jaws held firm in his neck. He then rushed away into the jungle, dragging the heavy trap with him, till at a spot almost two miles distant the trap got itself firmly wedged between two big rocks. The tiger tried to drag itself free, but only succeeded in wedging the trap more firmly than before.

The tiger roared with pain, and struggled desperately. The roars were heard for half the night by the planter and his frightened coolies, two miles away at their plantation. Finally, the animal broke loose losing its left ear and eye in the process, with very severe injuries to the rest of the neck and face. It was heard in the area moaning with pain night and day for quite a week afterwards.

Then came a period of absolute silence. Everyone thought the tiger had died of its wounds. The planter and his hirelings kept a careful watch for vultures, who would doubtless spot the carcase and betray the whereabouts of the dead animal by swooping to earth for their meal. But the only vultures seen were those soaring in the high heavens, carefully scanning the earth below for the signs of death; but none swooped, for the very good reason that the tiger was not dead.

A fortnight passed; then one afternoon, along the *path* to one of the smaller coffee-estates, climbed Jeyken, a Sholaga, and his eighteen-year-old spouse. In accordance with the established Indian custom, Jeyken walked in front, with the woman about a yard behind him, carrying a sack of grain balanced on her head. They had crossed a dry streambed, and were just climbing its slight embankment, when, out of a clump of grass like sugarcane that grows only along river banks in these areas, a tiger pounced upon the girl, throwing her to the earth.

Turning, Jeyken saw his wife lying on the ground gazing at him with terror-stricken, pleading eyes. The tiger crouched upon her back, its two paws overlapping her shoulders, the wide-open mouth just above her head. It was a tiger with no left eye, and no left ear, while the wounds on its neck and face had not yet healed!

Jeyken was turned to stone. He could not move and he could not speak, but remained rooted to the spot in horror and amazement. The tiger snarled horribly, contorting its already lacerated features into a still more horrible mask. Then it grabbed the girl by her right shoulder and walked across the stream with its prey—the girl hung head downwards, her loose hair and left arm and legs dragging in the sand. A moment later, the tiger and the girl had disappeared in the jungle on the further side.

Evidently the poor woman had swooned, or may already have died of fright. That was the last Jeyken ever saw of his wife, nor had she uttered the slightest cry, even at the moment of attack.

A month later a herd-boy was killed by a tiger within two miles of Ramapuram. In this case the half-eaten remains were found in a bush. The third human kill occurred about three weeks later, almost at the twenty-first milestone on the Kollegal-Lokkanhalli-Bailur-Dimbum road. This time it was a road-coolie, a middle-aged woman, who was attacked in full view of her companions just before five in the evening. She had stopped work for a few minutes, and had gone some yards into the jungle, when a tiger pounced upon her as if from nowhere and carried her away. She had screamed frenziedly, and those who were in the vicinity had clearly seen the tiger. It had a scarred face and no left ear or eye!

It so happened that my game licence for the North Coimbatore area had at that time expired. This area is divided into two forest divisions: North Coimbatore proper and the Kollegal Division. For although Kollegal fell within North Coimbatore district for administrative purposes, the Forest Department had recently subdivided the district into two distinct Forest Divisions. My licence, which had expired, covered North Coimbatore proper and Dimbum; while Lokkanhalli, Bailure and Ramapuram fell within the Kollegal Division. I had intended renewing my old licence, and was about to send the required fee when I read in the papers about the latest outrage committed by this tiger. That decided me, and with ten days' privilege leave at my disposal, I left Bangalore early in the morning, reaching the Forest Department office at Kollegal, eighty-seven miles away, even before it had opened for the day. It did not take me long to get the required shooting licence, and all available information regarding the tiger.

The area where the man-eater had operated was comparatively new to me, so I decided, for a start, to camp in the small forest lodge at Ramapuram, twenty-five miles away, which I reached in an hour and a half, after negotiating an extremely bumpy road.

Obviously, the first thing to do was to try and win the confidence of the inhabitants of Ramapuram by telling them I had come to try to rid them of the tiger. The people did not know me and gave somewhat garbled accounts, indicating that the tiger might be anywhere between Ponnachai Malai, where it had struck down it first victim, and Bailur, a distance of about sixty miles as the crow flies.

Bailur, as I have told you, was a small village some thirty miles from Kollegal, on the Kollegal-Lokkanhalli-Dimbum road. Thus, I could either return to Kollegal by car and motor thence to Bailur, or I could leave the car at Ramapuram and cover the third side of the triangle by walking from Ramapuram to Bailur, a distance of nearly nineteen miles. I decided to follow the latter course, as it would give me the opportunity of passing through several Forest hamlets bordering the Reserved Forest, where I hoped to get some news of the tiger.

Accordingly, at dawn next morning I left the little Forest Lodge at Ramapuram and began my walk to Bailur. The path led in a generally southwesterly direction, alternatively through sparsely cultivated country and scrub jungle, which skirted the ranges of small hills lying a couple of miles southward, within the boundaries of the Reserved Forest proper.

I passed a few hamlets, but all the inhabitants were either indoors or squatting at the entrances of their huts. Their few cattle were kraaled outside or grazed at will on the scant herbage in the immediate vicinity of the huts, for the story of the man-eater had spread far and wide and the usual scare that attends such visitations had already set in.

I walked slowly making inquiries wherever possible. Almost all the Sholagas inhabiting these hamlets reported that they had heard a tiger roaring in the vicinity, either the previous night or within the past seventy-two hours. At one spot I was shown the clear pug-marks of a tiger as it had crossed a recently ploughed field, just a hundred yards from the owner's hut. I took detailed measurements of those pugs for future reference before moving on but it soon became evident that the people in this area were either so nervous that they were making completely false and exaggerated reports, or else that an unusual number of tigers were operating along the nineteen miles between Ramapuram and Bailur. For, according to the information obtained, a tiger appeared to have visited each hamlet within the last three or four days!

At about 5 p.m. I approached Bailur, a village of some twenty huts. Here I met members of the road gang who had witnessed the killing of the woman near the twenty-first milestone. They told me what I have already recorded and particularly stressed the tiger's deformities, which they had all clearly seen while they stood rooted to the spot with terror, while the tiger made off into the undergrowth with its still-screaming victim, the road-coolie woman.

The nearest Forest department Lodge was some three-and-a-half miles farther along the motor-road in the direction of Dimbum. The Reserve lay along both sides of the road. It was now 5.30 p.m., and I knew that night would fall in an hour, so I covered those last three-and-a-half miles at a brisk pace, reaching the little Forest Bungalow shortly before dark.

The sun had gone down behind the towering range of the Biligirirangan Hills, which lay some three miles west of the bungalow, and the twilight calls of roosting peacock and junglefowl welcomed me as I sank into an old broken armchair which I dragged on to the verandah. The distant challenge of a sambar stag, descending the western range, was music to my ears as it floated across the dense valley separating the bungalow from the foothills. The myriad tree-tops of this valley were like a dark carpet in the deepening twilight.

Scarcely half-an-hour had passed before total darkness prevailed, punctuated by the incessant flicker of a million fireflies. They floated everywhere, like tiny elfin spirits in the gloom, carrying their lanterns of pinpoint brilliance to every bush tree-top in the vicinity. At rare intervals their flashes would synchronise, and the tree or bush around which they clustered would throb and pulsate to one big and unanimous flash of light, made by thousands of these little creatures. The blackness of the jungle night would disperse before a phosphorescent and ethereal glow—but only for a moment—until that rare interval of synchronisation occurred again.

I made an early night of it, sleeping on the floor of the small central room of the lodge; but at about 2 a.m., the moaning call of a tiger woke me. I heard it call at intervals as it traversed the valley, until it died away in the distance.

Early morning found me back in Bailur village, where I enlisted the help of two local *shikaris* and purchased three young bulls for bait. One of these we tethered in the bed of the stream that traversed the valley west of the bungalow, where I had heard the tiger calling in the night. The second was tied in a small forest-glade a bare 100 yards from the roadside, midway between the village and the Forest Bungalow. To tie the third, we walked back to the twenty-first milestone, where the road-worker had been killed. Close to this spot the road was crossed by a forest stream, known as Oddam Betta Halla; its banks were clothed with bamboo, except for a small clearing made by the Forest department, in which seedlings of various forest plants were being experimentally grown. My helpers told me that a tiger often walked through this clearing, and I found this statement to be true, in that pug-marks both old and comparatively new were visible at three different place. I examined the most recent of these imprints, and compared them with the measurements of the pug-marks taken at the hamlet on the previous day. Both sets had been made by a male tiger, but those in the departmental plantation belonged to a much older and heavier animal.

We tied the third bait on open ground just where the Oddam Betta Halla stream flows past this plantation.

When all this had been done it was 5.30 p.m., and on our return to Bailur village I was approached by a sturdy, good-looking Sholaga, who introduced himself as Jeyken, the husband of the girl who had been the man-eater's first victim. He said that a party of travellers who had passed by the coffee estate on the slopes of Ponnachai Malai, where he worked, had informed him that a *Sahib* had come to Ramapuram to shoot the tiger. Filled with the idea of revenge for his wife's murder, he had obtained the planter's permission to go to Ramapuram to offer me his assistance. At Ramapuram he was told that I had gone to Bailur, whither he had immediately followed me, all by himself.

I thanked Jeyken for his offer, and the trouble he had taken to find me, and immediately recruited him as my personal helper. I liked his appearance and his calm determination to leave no stone unturned to bring the tiger to book. Jeyken smiled at my acceptance and thanked me in turn, but he staunchly refused to accept any payment; indeed, he made it abundantly clear that this was the condition of his offer.

I returned to the Forest Lodge, instructing Jeyken and the other two helpers to make an early start next morning and visit the bait near the twenty-first milestone. For myself, I would visit the other two baits. This I did next morning, first visiting the bull tethered on the streambed in the valley, then the bait that was tied midway between the Forest bungalow and Bailur village. Both were unharmed and no traces of pugs were to be seen in any sand that existed near the spots where they were tied. I then walked the remaining distance to Bailur village, where I awaited the return of my three scouts; within an hour they arrived, to tell me the third bait was alive.

Leaving Jeyken and one of the Sholagas at the village, I took the second man, who claimed to be well acquainted with the forest gamepaths in that area, and walked westwards till we entered the foothills of the Biligirirangans. As all this area was unfamiliar to me, I got him to walk in front, while I covered him from the rear with my rifle ready in my hands. Sholagas are born jungle folk, and my guide showed no signs of nervousness while we threaded our way thus, in single file, up one game-path and down another, across dark *nullahs*, often bending double to avoid overhanging fronds of bamboo or outcrops of wait-a-bit thorn. But no signs of a fresh tiger track did we see.

A large male panther had crossed at one spot, and at another spot a female, accompanied by her cub; but it was evident that the tiger we were looking for had not passed that way.

It was nearing 3 p.m. before we got back to the Forest Lodge and a late cold lunch. The Sholaga made a fire, on which I boiled some water to brew us several cups of tea. Then I drew water from the little well in the compound, to give myself the luxury of a cold bath.

At five I returned with the Sholaga to Bailur village, where I left him with instructions for Jeyken, himself and the third Sholaga to visit the bait on the twenty-first milestone early next morning. It was well past seven by the time I got back to the bungalow. I slept soundly that night, nor did the moaning call of any tiger disturb me. Early morning found me on my way to visit the other two baits. Both were unharmed.

Returning to the Forest Lodge, I ate a frugal meal and then walked towards Bailur, carefully watching the road for pug-marks. No tiger had passed that way and 9.15 a.m. found me awaiting my henchmen. They returned before ten, this time to report that the bait had been killed and removed by a tiger, which had contrived to bite through the tethering rope.

Fortunately I had come prepared for such an eventuality and had brought my torch and other night-shooting kit with me in a haversack. Back we went as fast as we could, and shortly after midday had reached the spot where the bull had been tied. The tiger's pug-marks, in approaching the bait, were apparent in the soft earth some twenty feet away, and an examination showed that the killer was a tigress and not a tiger. From there she had launched her final attack that had killed the bull, biting through the rope by which its leg had been tied.

We could not know how far the kill had been taken, so I told my companions to wait for me by the twenty-first milestone till 3 p.m., while I would follow the drag-mark. If the dead bull had been taken for some distance, I would try to build myself a hide-out to await the return of the tigress, and would make it an all-night affair. Under such circumstances, I would not be back by three and they were to return to Bailur. On the other hand, if the tigress had dropped the kill not far away, I would return to my companions and get them to put up a proper *machan*.

I found the tigress had half-dragged the kill for the first two hundred yards, by which time she had got clear of the bamboo jungle that grew on the lower land and in the vicinity of the stream. Then she had encountered some heavy lantana undergrowth, which had obviously been an obstruction to her passage, encumbered as she was with the dead bull. Here she had evidently slung it over her shoulder, as tigers sometimes do to carry their kills, and it then became extremely difficult to follow the trail.

A dragging hoof, or the horns of the bull, had here and there broken a twig, and these were the only visible signs of passage. The carpet of rotting vegetation, and fallen lantana leaves, effectively did away with any hope of finding pug-marks. Necessarily, the going was also very slow, nor did I like the situation at all, as almost my whole attention had to be given to following the trail, which prevented me from being fully on my guard against a sudden attack. Finally the lantana gave way to more open forest, sprinkled liberally with trees and a carpet of the dwarf date palm.

Twice I came across the spot where the tigress had laid down her burden and then picked it up again. It was now evident that she had some particular destination in view, most probably a lair where she had cubs to whom she was taking the meat.

Up and up led the trail; the terrain became more and more rocky, till finally, in a break among the tree-trunks, I saw a hillock, perhaps a quarter-of-a-mile beyond and about 200 feet above the spot where I stood. The trail led directly toward the hillock. By now I felt reasonably certain that the animal I was following was not the man-eater, because all the data gathered about the man-eater had classed it as a tiger and not a tigress, although the sex factor was not an established certainty. As it was a known fact, however, that the man-eater had lost its left eye and ear, if I could but catch a glimpse of the animal I was following, I would soon know whether it was the right one or not.

How to catch that glimpse was the problem. The obvious answer to it was to keep advancing till we met, but it was scarcely to my liking, as even if the tigress was not the man-eater, she certainly was unlikely to welcome any human being who knocked at the door of the lair where she had her cubs.

But I went forward. The trail was now easier to follow, as the tigress had brushed against boulders and rocks, where smears of blood betrayed the passage of the dead bull.

Half the distance was covered now; the other half would bring me to the summit. The boulders lay in heaps, and the trail I was following wound in and out between them, as the tigress picked her path to avoid any part of her burden becoming jammed between the rocks. It was ten minutes to three; the sun beat down mercilessly on the bare rocks, which in turn threw the heat back in my face as from the door of a furnace. My clothes were soaked with perspiration, which ran in rivers down my face, getting into my eyes, which burned and smarted, and into the corners of my mouth. I licked my lips and I remember that almost unconsciously, in the excitement of the moment, I noted the salty taste.

My rubber boots made no sound as I negotiated the heated rocks. One corner after another was turned, and at each turn I knew what lay beyond. Then I came upon a shelving rock which met the rising ground at an angle of perhaps three hundred forming a shallow recess rather than a real cave. Two large balls of russet brown, striped with black, white underneath, were tumbling over one another in a vigorous game of 'catch-as-catch-can'. They were two tiger cubs, and they were playing!

I stopped in my tracks; the only movement being an imperceptible cocking of the rifle, with the faintest of clicks. But it was enough! Although they were only cubs, generations of instinct were behind them. They stopped playing, disentangled themselves, and looked at me in alarm.

Even now, I can picture the scene: one cub with a look of innocent surprise, and the other with its features wrinkled to emit a hiss of consternation.

That hiss was the signal for all hell to break loose, for it awoke the tigress, who was sleeping. With a series of shattering roars she dashed out of the cavern, vaulted over the cubs and came straight at me.

The distance may have been twenty yards. I covered her between the eyes as she advanced. Then five yards away she stopped; she crouched with her belly to ground, eyes blazing and mouth wide, while her roars and snarls shook the very ground on which I stood. She was a perfect specimen but certainly not the man-eater!

Wonder of wonders, she had not charged home. Her courage had failed her at the last moment. She was telling me, in the simplest of languages: 'Get out quickly, and don't harm my cubs or I will kill you.'

I was glad to oblige. Step by step, I retreated backwards, while never removing my eyes from hers, never allowing the rifle sights to waver in the slightest, my forefinger still on the trigger.

And she remained where she was! It was as if she understood that I was going. I realised at that moment that she did not want to harm me; that she was only protecting her cubs. Perhaps she was afraid. I was afraid too! But I did not want to harm her, nor destroy that lovely happy little family.

So I continued to retreat backwards. The tigress continued to roar. Now I had turned the corner of the first rock that hid her from view. Only then did I dare to take a hasty glance backwards, to see where I was walking, although I still faced towards the tigress, who had now stopped roaring, but was still growling. I knew that, as long as she continued to make those sounds I was safe; I would know where she was.

Another big boulder was passed; then I turned and beat a hasty retreat before she had time to change her mind and come after me. She stopped growling, and I knew that the real danger had come. She might have gone back to her cubs, or she might be following. I made down the hill as rapidly as possible, glancing frequently behind me. Soon I came to the trees and the date palms, then the lantana belt, up which I had so laboriously followed the trail, and finally to the bamboos and the road.

It was 4.30 p.m. and as instructed, my companions had returned to Bailur. I had nine miles to cover, and only two hours before darkness fell. Nevertheless, I sat by the roadside for five minutes to enjoy a quick smoke. I felt I deserved it. I was thankful, too, that I had not been forced to shoot the tigress, for the sight of those two cubs was still fresh in my memory.

It was past six-thirty before I reached Bailur village. There my three companions awaited me, eager to hear my story. When I had told it, they agreed that it was unusual for a tigress to have failed to press home her charge.

Darkness had set in by the time I left the little village on the last lap of my journey to the forest bungalow. But as one of our baits was tied at a point about half-way between the village and the bungalow in a glade not far from the road, it occurred to me that I would pay it a visit. Why this idea came to me, I cannot tell particularly as I had already looked at it that morning on my way to Bailur. It was an impulse, and I have spent my life responding to impulses. I turned off along the little footpath that led away from the road towards the clearing where the bait was tied. It was quite dark, except for the diffused glow from the stars that shone brightly in a clear blue-black sky. The bushes around me assumed ghostly shapes, and the wind sighed fitfully among the branches of the 'rain-tree' that bordered the road. Now and again, a large teak-leaf fluttered to the ground with the softest of sounds, like some huge moth of the night settling down to rest.

I came up to the small wild-fig tree beneath which my bait was tied. The shadows were deeper there, and the bait was, moreover, a brown one. I could not see it till I came very close, when it lumbered to its feet, as if startled at my approach, even as I was startled by its sudden action. It was still unharmed. I walked around it to the other side, to inspect the rope that held it by the hind leg, in case it had become twisted.

And at that moment the man-eater charged.

It was fortunate for me that I had moved to the other side of the bull, which consequently came between me and the tiger. But I confess that I was taken totally by surprise.

There was tremendous '*Woof*' from the jungle from which I had just emerged. The bull swung round. I leaped behind it, with my back to the trunk of the fig tree almost tripping over the tethering rope. A huge grey shape vaulted on to the back of the bull, which collapsed beneath the sudden weight.

But the tiger had not seized the neck or throat. It had simply leaped upon the bull in order to reach me beyond it. Luckily, in falling the bull ruined the tiger's spring, which otherwise would have followed within a split second.

The tiger was extricating itself from the heaving body of the fallen bull when my bullet smashed between its eyes. Convulsively it twisted backwards, still lying across the bull, which now staggered to its feet with the tiger over its back, the head and forequarters sagging forwards.

Automatically, and without thinking, I fired my second shot at a spot which I judged to be behind the tiger's left shoulder. The bull collapsed! The tiger rolled off the bull and towards me, as my third shot took it in the throat.

The bull never moved. The tiger kicked convulsively. And then at last all was still.

The light from the torch on the rifle revealed that my first bullet had smashed the tiger's skull. My second had been too low. The heavy .405 missile had ploughed through the end of the tiger's chest and blown a tremendous hole in the bull's side. My third bullet, a quite unnecessary one, had passed through the tiger's throat, leaving a gaping hole. But I had killed the poor bull that had unwittingly saved my life.

My hands were trembling, my knees wobbled, and suddenly I felt very, very sick. The reaction, after the events of that evening, was sudden. I sat on the ground, with may back to the fig tree, and raised my hand to my forehead, which I was surprised to find icy cold to my touch.

How long I remained thus I do not know. Then I groped for my pipe, filled and lit it. The first few puffs steadied my badly-shaken nerves and I was soon able to get back to the road and retrace my steps to Bailur Village.

I found the inhabitants gathered in the streets, agog with excitement and anticipation. For the surrounding hills had carried the sound of my three shots, which had reverberated across the valleys and stony ridges. They had guessed I had been attacked on the way to the bungalow, but were wondering whether it had been by the man-eater, or some bear or elephant.

Seeing me emerge from the gloom, they rushed forward to welcome me, my three servants well to the fore. I sat down by the roadside and told them the story. Gasps of amazement and incredulity broke from their lips, to be followed by congratulations and a fervent expression of thanks for my safety.

A 'chattie' of fresh hot milk was set before me, and a bunch of bananas. As gifts go, it was not much, but it conveyed the heartfelt thanks of the villagers.

In another half-hour practically the whole village had assembled with lanterns and kerosene torches, a stout pole and coils of rope, to bring in the tiger. Back we went to the spot and over fifty people surveyed the strange scene, their eyes wide open with amazement. Jeyken was especially pathetic to watch. With his knife he started to stab the dead tiger—to my dismay, for he was doing further damage to a skin already well-nigh ruined by my bullets. Gently, but firmly, I drew him off; then he began to weep unrestrainedly, thinking of his dead wife.

The deep-hearted weeping of a strong and brave man is not pleasant to witness; it is infectious, and I felt a strange lump rising in my own throat—a lump which refused to subside for quite a time.

Not much remains to be told, except for a strange sequel. Next morning, when coming to the bungalow, Jeyken passed the spot where I had left the road the previous night. Fifty yards further on he decided to answer a call of nature and stepped behind a star-plum bush for the purpose. There he discovered for the first time that the tiger had been lying in wait for me the previous night; evidently it had been in the vicinity, and had either seen or heard me approaching along the road.

Jeyken told me what he had discovered, and I walked back with him to check it for myself. I found what he said was true. There clearly impressed on the soft sand, were tiger's pug-marks while the soft grass and rank weeds beneath the star-plum bush were still partly flattened by the weight of the tiger's body, although more than twelve hours had passed since he had lain there in ambush, awaiting my approach.

Yet some people tell me that there is no such thing as Providence, a guiding-spirit, intuition, or a sixth sense; call it what you will. I find it more difficult to understand the disbelievers than understand Providence itself!

Seven

The Great Panther of Mudiyanoor

MUDIYANOOR IS THE NAME OF A SMALL VILLAGE NESTLING NEAR THE southeastern end of a fertile valley that lies north of the Moyar river and the frowning crags of the Blue Mountains or Nilgiri range, and south of the foothills of the smaller mountain chain known as the Biligirirangans.

This little valley comes as near as possible on this troubled earth to the elusive 'happy valleys' of fiction, or of which we dream during our restless slumbers. Certain it is that rainfall is assured, even in a season of weak monsoons, due to the abutting mountain ranges at either end. The earth is very fertile, being particularly rich in leaf-mould and a fine red loam, for it was until recent years part of the primeval forest which is slowly, but ever steadily, being pushed back by the inroads of civilisation. The climate is temperate during the days and rather chilly at night, due to the cool breezes that blow down the mountain ridges.

Most of the people of Mudiyanoor are farmers, although a few are cattle-grazers, who maintain vast herds of animals which are driven during daylight into the surrounding forest for grazing. The milk from these animals is entirely used in the manufacture of 'ghee' which is simply melted butter, and is employed for cooking throughout India. Kerosene tins, filled with this stuff, are sent up the ghat, as the winding cart-track up the hillside is called, till it meets the main road from Mysore to Satyamangalam at the little hamlet of Dimbum. There the tins of ghee are loaded on to cart—and sometimes lorries—and taken away for sale. There are good markets for it in Mysore and Satyamangalam, and particularly in the more distant town of Gobichettipalayam.

So the population is happy and prosperous. Few strangers visit the valley, because the cart-track is practically unmotorable.

The herds occasionally suffer from a marauding tiger or panther: at other times the farmers awake to find sections of their fields trampled flat by elephants which have fed there during the night. Wild pigs and deer take a moderate toll of crops, but these are considered minor calamities and are accepted as the dictates of inevitable fate.

The 'great panther' earned that name because he was quite outstandingly large. He was suspected of having come from the fastnesses of the Blue Mountains, perhaps from Anaikutty or Segur, and across the Moyar river, or Mysore Ditch as it is more commonly called. He began his depredations on the village cattle, killing in true tiger style by breaking the neck, and was therefore mistaken for that animal for some time.

Then, with increasing boldness, this panther started to harry the herds of fine milch cows that were part of my friend Hughie Hailstone's estate. This estate, the Moyar Valley Ranch, is an outstanding farm which is natural, for its owner is an outstanding character. A brilliant engineer by profession, he has the quick brain of an inventor—quick at thinking and quick at assessing values—and from his cleverness have originated many devices and mechanical improvements. In addition, Hughie is a born *shikari*. He loves the forest and its animals, and he is never happier than when handling, or tinkering with, a firearm. From this rare combination of mechanical genius and a love of the wild, Moyar Valley Ranch was born; for with herculean effort and skill, tenacity of purpose and the will to surmount all obstacles, Hughie literally carved his ranch out of the heart of the virgin jungle.

Mighty forest trees had to be cut down and cleared. Hughie exploited this circumstance by converting them into charcoal, which he then sold by lorry-loads to the far distant towns. Bricks, cut-stones, cement, mortar, and all the other items used in building construction had to be brought from the same places. Carpenters were also imported, who, under Hughie's able directions, soon utilised the better forest-woods for building purposes. A modern building rose in no time. With a windmill battery-charger, the house had electric lighting, a refrigerator and many up-to-date conveniences. In addition, farm machinery was imported, so that in almost the twinkling of an eye Moyar Valley Ranch became a flourishing farmstead.

Hughie has many business interests and frequently travels abroad. Sometimes he returns in a few weeks, but at others he is absent for months, and the following story concerns one of his long absences. He had very kindly offered me the privilege of visiting his farm at any time, and has especially asked me to keep a watchful eye on his livestock. So one day, when we received a letter from Hugh's caretaker, a man named Varghese, that the big panther had killed Hugh's finest Alsatian, something had to be done.

At that time I was immersed in some heavy and urgent work and it was impossible to get away for the next fortnight. Varghese's letter, having travelled by village post, had already taken six days to reach us. But my son Donald volunteered to deal with the panther, and I gladly delegated this job to him. The Studebaker had broken an axle a month earlier and I was still awaiting a replacement from Bombay, so Donald rushed off to his friend's house to borrow a car.

From this point I feel I had better let Donald relate the rest of the story himself, as I took no further part in the affair, beyond giving him a piece of my mind when he returned from the expedition.

'When Dad told me to go to Mudiyanoor, the first problem was to find a car to travel by, as his Studebaker was laid up. So I thought of a friend who had been with me at school, named Rustam Dudhwala. Rustam is a nice fellow and owns three or four cars. So with a bit of sales talk I had no difficulty in getting him interested. It took me just four hours to get together the odds and ends necessary for the trip, and to borrow Dad's lucky tiger-charm, which was given to him years ago by a jungle man named Budhia. I know Dad does not talk about this charm, as he thinks people will make fun of him, but I also know that he appears to have much faith in it. The charm is actually wrapped in a small piece of bamboo, tied with a strand of hair from an elephant's tail. What is inside it I do no know. The whole thing can be worn around the neck, as the bamboo is tied to a piece of string, but Dad generally stuffs it into his pocket.

'Just before leaving I thought of taking another friend along with me, a fellow named Cedric Bone, who is a keen photographer and good sport, and can rough it out splendidly. Cedric was ready to come, and soon the three of us were on our way to Mudiyanoor. I carried my .423 Mauser, which is a far superior weapon to Dad's old-fashioned .405 Winchester. He knows this himself, but like all old-fashioned people prefers to stick to something that is out of date. I also brought my .3006 Springfield as a reserve rifle for shooting deer for the pot. My old man lectures me against killing deer and I pretend to listen to him. When he is around, of course, such killing is taboo; but when he is not there it is quite a different matter.

'The last seventeen miles of the track to Mudiyanoor is really bad, and it took us almost eight hours to get there. Varghese greeted me with a broad smile, although I felt he was a little disappointed because Dad had not come along. That is the trouble nowadays. Young people like me are often not appreciated and the older men seem to regard us as being somewhat irresponsible. They forget that they too were young once.

'Anyhow, Varghese told us that, apart from village cattle, the big panther had also killed a cow belonging to Mr. Hailstone three days ago. The immediate problem was therefore to buy some live bait in the form of half-grown bulls, and for this purpose Rustam came in very handy.

'Let me tell you something about this Rustam. He is twenty-two years old and a Parsee, which community are the descendants of early Persian settlers in India. He comes of a very rich family, who owns lakhs of rupees worth of property in Bombay, bringing in enough income in a single day to buy me several times over. Apart from this, Rustam's Dad is a shrewd businessman, who earns an income even larger than what comes in each month from the property. He is a very sporting chap and very fond of his son, but sometimes he gets unreasonably strict about letting Rustam go shooting. When that happens, Rustam and I generally contrive to invite my father to visit Mr. Dudhwala, for when these old men meet and talk things over for an hour or two, our hunting trip is assured.

'Well, to return to what I was telling you. Rustam bought four young bulls, which we tied out in different places near where the big panther had recently killed. The first of these we tied near the forest boundary line which runs beside Mr. Hailstone's estate. The second we tied about a quarter of a mile away, near a small lake surrounded by heavy bamboo jungle. The third we tied on the outskirts of Mudiyanoor village proper, and the last on the cart track itself, coming into Mudiyanoor. Dad always makes a practice of setting up his *machan* along with the baits; but as Varghese had offered the use of Mr. Hailstone's portable *machan*, I decided to set mine up only after a kill had occurred.

'We took care to secure our baits by tying the hind legs to stout stakes driven into the ground, for it is a mistake to pass a rope around the neck of a live bait. Sometimes panthers, and tigers especially, are reluctant to attack an animal with a rope around its neck. They kill by grabbing the neck, and they feel suspicious of a rope, which would get in their way.

'At the last moment Varghese informed us that a tiger had been calling in the vicinity of the bungalow for the past two days. So as an afterthought, instead of a rope I used Mr. Hailstone's chain for securing the bait tied on the forest line near his bungalow. This was because I felt that if the tiger killed this bull he might break the rope and carry it away. As there were no other chains, the other three baits had to remain roped.

'Rustam wanted to go shooting wild pig that night in the fields around Mudiyanoor village, but I stopped him, as a shot might disturb the panther. Next morning, all four of our baits were alive and we were disappointed. But shooting is a game of patience, as Dad has taught me, so I told Rustam to be quiet and not expect developments for another day or two. On the third night the big leopard killed the bull tied on the forest line near the bungalow. It so happened that the tiger also killed the second bait tied among the bamboos near the forest pool the same night.

'Now I was faced with a problem. "Damn the panther," I said to myself "I will get the tiger." But there were other circumstances to be considered: Rustam reminded me that my purpose there was to shoot the panther which had killed Mr. Hailstone's livestock. It was my business, therefore, to sit up for the panther. I knew that he was right and that Dad would say the same. Still, it seemed a bit thick to lose the opportunity of sitting up for the tiger, and I tried hard to persuade Rustam to take on the panther. But he has some of his father's business instincts, and clung to his previous arguments. So, realising I was cornered, I had to give in.

'Cedric elected to come and sit up with me, as he felt that there were more chances of seeing the big panther by being with me, than of seeing the tiger by going with Rustam. He thought Rustam would make too much noise and would drive away the tiger before it ever appeared at the kill.

'So I got to work and had Mr. Hailstone's portable *machan* hung in the tree that grew about thirty yards from the dead bull. Rustam, for his part, got the villagers to erect a *machan* in a tree that grew close to where the other bull had been killed by the tiger. I forgot to mention that, in tying all these four baits, I had taken the precaution of tying them close to trees, so that there would be no trouble later in erecting *machans*.

'Both parties left the bungalow at about 4 p.m. Rustam had a longer distance to cover, so he and Varghese, complete with sandwiches, water bottle, torches, warm mufflers, blankets and what not, started off at a brisk pace. Cedric and I strolled along to the forest line with our packet of food and a single water bottle. We felt blankets were unnecessary as the weather appeared to be warm.

'Sitting in any *machan* is a tiresome business, and I always find it difficult to remain still. My old man has told me many a time that sitting like a graven image is absolutely essential, but how he does it I don't know. I have sat with him often and his style is to fold his legs beneath him, settle himself very comfortably, smoke his pipe, drink a little tea from a flask, and then become a graven image for the rest of the night. But all sorts of things happen to me. I get pins and needles in my feet, my back feels stiff and begins to ache, and the mosquitoes worry me considerably: not only do they bite me, but they find their way into my ears and nose and the only method of getting rid of one is to wait till it settles down to feed, and then give it a smart slap. Dad tells me that this is not the thing to do when on a *machan;* but perhaps he forgets that my blood, being young, is probably more attractive to the mosquitoes than his. You will understand, I am sure, that old men take quite a delight in telling younger people what not to do.

'Anyhow, by the time it grew dark at seven o'clock, these mosquitoes were already very busy on both Cedric and myself. I had already told Cedric to abstain from slapping mosquitoes, which was probably why he nudged me, once or twice, when I did so myself. Time passed, and then, at about a quarter to eight, we saw a longish object, that looked grey in the darkness, appear as if from nowhere. I must explain that, although there was no moon, there was a diffused glow all around from the stars that always seem to twinkle much brighter in a forest. There was enough light, at least, to show up the bigger trees and this grey object, but not the dead bull, which happened to be black. Well, the grey apparition moved towards where the bull lay, and shortly after we heard the rattle of the chain, followed by the sound of eating, and the crunching of bones. Slowly, I raised my rifle to my shoulder, but as luck would have it, my torch, which was fixed to the rifle barrel, struck against the tree and made the slightest of noises. There was a loud growl from the direction of the kill and the same grey object began walking across the forest line towards my left. Soon it disappeared, and then, after about ten minutes, reappeared to my right, but almost beneath us. I heard the sound of licking, and it seemed that the panther was seated there on its haunches. This time I got the rifle levelled properly and pressed the switch of my torch. The bright beam lit the panther, sitting on the ground in a dog-like attitude, hardly twenty yards away, It looked up at me, and taking a quick sight, I pressed the trigger. My best friend, the .432, roared, and the panther fell over sideways. I thought it was done for, but then it suddenly picked itself up again and sprang into the forest below the tree where we were sitting.

'Cedric had been very excited while all this was happening, for no sooner did the panther disappear than he prepared to climb down. I restrained him, and he said, "Come, let's go after it". But I told him not to be a fool and that we had better wait till morning.

'We sat there for nearly another hour. The mosquitoes became so unbearable that we decided to get down and return to the bungalow. I descended first, and Cedric handed me the rifle. Then he followed with the water bottle. The last six feet he took at a jump, and as he hit the ground with a thud there was an awful roar from very near. I swung around, pointing my rifle, with the torch burning, in the direction of the sound, but we could see nothing. After waiting for some minutes, we went forward a few paces, but the lantana undergrowth was very dense here and it seemed unsafe to follow up in the darkness. We then went to the spot where the panther had been seated when I fired, and began to look around for blood.

'There were no traces to be seen by the light of the torch and the alarming idea occurred to me that perhaps I had made a complete miss. I discussed the matter in undertones with Cedric, but he was certain that my bullet had struck the panther. Still, I was doubtful and we eventually decided to go back to the *machan*, on the very slim chance that I might have missed and the panther might later return to its kill.

'The rest of the night was extremely uncomfortable, what with the mosquitoes and the intense cold that began to set in with the early hours of the morning. We stuck it out, however, and dawn found us a very dejected and disappointed pair. We climbed down from the tree and stretched out in the green grass below it for nearly an hour, in order to give the sun a chance to rise, and to relax our stiffened muscles. Then, shortly after seven, we began to look for blood tracks in earnest. In a little while I was heartened to find a few drops where the panther had entered the lantana, and then quite a considerable amount at a spot about forty yards inside the undergrowth. It was now quite evident that he had been badly hit and had lain down here; also that it was he who had growled so loudly the previous night, when Cedric had jumped down from the tree. In fact one realised that the panther had not driven home a charge at the time and caught us napping.

'Cedric photographed the spot. He is one of those camera-enthusiasts who take photos of practically anything and everything.

'I found that from this point a blood trail was visible for upwards of another hundred yards. Within this distance he had lain down once more, which confirmed the fact that he had been badly hit. Then the blood trail became less distinct, probaly because fat, or a piece of membrane, had covered the bullet hole and stopped the external bleeding.

'The undergrowth was fairly dense and we searched carefully everywhere, but there was no panther to be found. The forest line continued, and I walked along the edge of it, peering into the lantana in the hope of seeing the beast.

'I had gone perhaps another hundred yards, Cedric following with his camera at about twenty paces, keeping to the open of the forest line, when it suddenly happened. Evidently the panther had been lying concealed beneath a bush on the opposite side of the clearing and had escaped my notice. He waited till I had passed and then, with a characteristic coughing grunt, he charged me. Cedric was almost level with the place where the panther had been hiding, and how it had not seen him and charged him, instead of me, is a mystery and very lucky for Cedric. Probably the panther was too busy watching me and preparing to make his surprise attack. Anyhow, he charged, but hearing that coughing grunt, I sprang around in time to see him coming. Fortunately, my bullet of the night before had smashed his right foreleg, which dragged as he came on.

'Throwing my rifle to my left shoulder—from which I shoot—I pressed the trigger and sent the bullet crashing into his throat. He lurched forward on to his chest, still snarling vigorously, and this gave me time to put in a second shot.

'Only then did I notice that Cedric was close behind, and was fairly dancing with excitement. He had been in my direct line of fire, and I might have shot him instead of the panther. But this incredible enthusiast had actually taken a photo of the charge. How Cedric had the nerve to take it, when ninety-nine men out of a hundred, completely unarmed as he was, would have turned tail and fled, beats me. It only goes to show that an enthusiasm for photography enabled him to forget everything else. He tells me he just aimed the camera and depressed the shutter mechanically, without thinking what he was doing.

'When we returned to the bungalow to tell the good news, we found that Rustam and Varghese had already come back, having sat up till about 2 a.m. The mosquitoes had by this time got the better of them, and as the tiger had not put in an appearance, Rustam and his companion had decided to call it a day, and get back to the bungalow for a nap.

'We carried the panther in by nine o'clock and had skinned him in about an hour. It proved to be quite a large male, measuring 7'8" from nose to tail.

'After an early lunch, I suggested to Rustam that we should go and see about the bull over which he had sat. I must not forget to tell you that, in the meantime, Varghese had sent out men to see what had happened to the third and fourth animals. These men returned to inform us that both were still alive.

'When we reached Rustam's *machan*, we found that the tiger had returned to its kill, probably in the early hours of the morning after Rustam had got down. Perhaps it had been watching, and had come to know that he was up there. Later when the coast was clear, it had come back for a late meal. About three-quarters of the bull had been devoured.

'Rustam was extremely disappointed, but was determined to sit up again. Then I had an inspiration. Wisely, or unwisely, I sent Varghese with one of the men to fetch our fourth bait, which had been tied on the track approaching Mudiyanoor village. It took about two hours to bring this animal, and we tethered it about thirty paces from the remains of the old kill. My hope in doing this was that the tiger might be induced to attack it, in case he hesitated to return to the old kill, which had been dead for two days and was stinking horribly. Rustam opposed this plan, because he felt that the tiger would be frightened away by finding a live bull where he had left a dead one the day before. But I felt the chance was worth taking.

'At about 5.30 p.m., the three of us, Rustam, Cedric and myself, got into the *machan*, having already arranged fresh green leaves for concealment, those of the previous night having been withered by the heat. Rustam was to have the first shot, and I would follow up. Cedric had fitted a flash bulb and reflector to his beloved camera, in the hope of securing another exciting photograph.

'With the approach of dusk myriads of insects of all kinds came from the nearby pool to make our existence a torture. But we were young and extremely keen. Rustam had long been waiting for an opportunity to shoot a tiger.

'Eight o'clock came, then nine and ten, but a little later we heard the moaning call of the tiger, as it descended a hillside beyond the pool about a mile way. About forty-five minutes passed, when a kakar gave forth its hoarse call from the denseness of the bamboos to our left. It was clear the tiger was coming, and we were all keyed up with intense excitement.

'We waited. It was much darker here than it had been at my *machan* of the night before, because of the bamboos. I whispered to Rustam to wait till the tiger either attacked the live bull or came back to its old kill, when I would use my torch to help him aim. Fortunately, the live bull was a white one, and we could see it faintly, and hear it snorting and struggling, as it tried to free its leg from the tethering rope. It was clear that the creature must have had some inkling of the approaching danger and its ultimace fate.

'There was a silence for ten minutes. Then there was a deep "Woof" and the tiger sprang on to the live bull. Rustam was trembling like an aspen with suppressed excitement, but I gripped his shoulder firmly to keep him quiet. There followed a hoarse gurgle from the bull, and a sharp snapping sound as the vertebrae of its neck cracked and the carcase thudded to earth.

'I maintained my grip on Rustam's shoulder. Another period of silence followed for almost ten minutes, before the tiger began to bite the rear of the bull in its first operations to tear out and remove the entrails.

'Still we waited, and then we heard the scratching sound made by the tearing of membrane as the tiger started to pull out the bull's intestines. I judged that by now its attention would be fully occupied by its kill; so gently releasing my grip on Rustam's shoulder, I nudged him to prepare for the shot.

'He raised his rifle, as I did mine. After about ten seconds I pressed the button of my torch. As the beam shot forth, the tiger, which had been lying on its kill sideways to us, turned around and looked up. At the same moment Rustam switched on his torch too, and in the two beams the tiger was distinctly visible as he stared back. Seconds passed, and I began to wonder whether Rustam was going to fire. Then, just as I was about to press my trigger, the roar of the double-barrelled .405/400 rent the night.

'Rustam had fired both barrels simultaneously, and the kick from the heavy weapon must have been considerable; I felt him lurch violently backwards. Nevertheless, both bullets had sped true to their mark, smashing into the tiger's neck just above the shoulder. The animal shook violently and then sank forward, just as if it was going to sleep. The tail twitched a few times and then was still. Rustam had shot his first tiger.

'We waited for another half-hour, but there was no movement from the animal; so we got down from the *machan*, still keeping the torch focused on the tiger. But it never stirred. It was evident that the tiger was dead. Upon examination, Rustam was jubilant at finding he had killed a fine male, which measured 9'4" from nose to tail-tip.

'And so we returned to Bangalore, an extremely happy party. Rustam had got his tiger, and I had succeeded in killing the panther that had been harassing Mr. Hailstone's animals. But of the three of us I think Cedric Bone was the happiest at having taken a marvellously lucky photograph and a marvellously lucky escape from what would have been a severe mauling, if not a painful death, had the panther attacked him instead of me.

'I told Dad the story, and he congratulated both of us. But he never at that time realised the narrowness of Cedric's escape from the panther, as well as from my rifle bullet.

'Next day, when he saw the photograph, he started to say a lot of uncomplimentary things. At the time I felt he was rather harsh and quite unreasonable; but, as I think of it now, the old man was right.

'I had made two major mistakes. Firstly, I had not looked carefully enough in the undergrowth, and had passed the panther without seeing it. Secondly in my excitement I had fired with a human being directly in my line of fire, and about twenty paces away. They say fortune favours the beginner, and it certainly was so in this case.'

Eight

The Mauler of Rajnagara

AT THE MOMENT OF TELLING THIS STORY (NOVEMBER 1995), THE 'mauler' is still alive, having defeated every effort I made to 'bag' him. And not only my own efforts, but those of several other hunters over a period of rather more than two years.

The mauler is altogether an unusual tiger, in that his habits are very un-tigerish and his haunts are in areas where no tiger has been heard of for many years. His habits are untigerish in that the earlier records of his activities were entirely confined to mauling men by scratching them with his forefeet. There were thirty-three instances of such attacks by this tiger, his victims being mainly herdsmen. In not a single case did he either bite or kill his victim. In every case he severely scratched the man from the crown of his head, down his face and neck, and across his chest and back.

This conduct at first led me to think that the so-called tiger was really a 'panther' after all. But when at a later stage

I questioned several of his victims, every one of them affirmed that it was a tiger and not a panther that had attacked him.

I was also led to think that the animal had been wounded or otherwise injured in some part of its jaw, mouth, or face, so that he could not drive home his attack by biting his victim. This theory was entirely refuted by the herdsmen, who stated that during two years, the same tiger had killed and eaten over two hundred of their cattle. They had examined many of these kills after the event, and in no case was any evidence found that the tiger had been unable to use his teeth properly. He had not only killed his prey in regular tiger fashion by breaking its neck, but had eaten each animal in a very normal and thorough manner.

The next strange thing about this animal was that he had begun his depredations in a most un-tigerish stretch of the forest, consisting of low scrub and thorn: very rocky, undulating hillocks with occasional steep boulder-strewn rivulets between them, flanked by long grass and occasional clumps of bamboo. It was known that panthers frequently roamed this area, and had even been seen on the main road that ran through it; but a tiger was unknown to the existing generation.

This stretch of forest lies immediately to the south of the Dimbum escarpment in the district of North Coimbatore. A sharp drop of over 2,500 feet from Dimbum brings you to this region of arid scrub land, dotted with frequent palm trees, and consisting mostly of thorny bushes and lantana shrub. Other game is also scarce, being confined to a few peafowl and an occasional jungle sheep. The area is comparatively small, being about five miles from north to south, and about thirty miles from east to west, where it adjoins the Bhavani river, which eventually flows into the river Cauvery.

We are told that this tiger had originally come from the Nilgiri jungles, had wandered down to the Moyar river and then taken its abode in this region. Its fondness for this locality can otherwise be well understood, for it is an area scattered with small cattle-*patties,* and entirely devoted to grazing hundreds of cattle. Hence, what it lacks in natural wild game is more than balanced by the large number of domestic animals, which are much easier prey to any tiger.

The story goes that at the earlier stages the tiger killed normally, ate his kills normally, and decamped normally, when he was 'shooed' off his kills by enraged herdsmen. But, as the old proverb says, 'too much of anything is good for nothing'! Or, at least, this tiger seemed to think so. The herdsmen evidently made themselves too much of a nuisance to him, when too frequently they drove him off his kills.

The first attack, as is usually the case, was made on a herdsboy who had had the temerity to throw a stone at him, just as he was in the act of dragging away a fine fat cow he had killed. The stone is reported to have struck the tiger's flank; the tiger is reported to have dropped the cow and charged the boy, whom he severely scratched about the face and chest. Then he went back and carried off the cow, which he thereafter ate in peace.

On several later occasions herdsmen and boys tried to drive him off the beasts he had killed, or was in the act of carrying off, or was actually eating. In each case the tiger attacked and scratched the intruder.

Naturally, as such attacks multiplied, he was left more and more alone. He was evidently a very wise tiger and had arrived at the sensible conclusion that it paid him high dividends to scratch but not to kill the intruders; for they thereafter left him more and more to devour his kill untroubled.

And so time dragged on. Nearly two years had passed and the victims of his scratching rose to thirty-three. Of these eleven died of subsequent blood poisoning, arising from the putrid matter in the tiger's claws. But these deaths, of course, may not be regarded as intentionally caused by the tiger himself. They were only an indirect consequence of the attack.

And then, in July 1955, the first human being failed to return. It was known that he had been attacked by the tiger, for his screams for help had conveyed this information to another herdsman, who had been standing near. This individual, very naturally, had run away. In the earlier instances, the victims had generally managed to stagger back to the main road or to the cattle village, whichever happened to be nearer. But this victim did not return. Some two hours later a search party set out to look for him. They came to the spot where the attack had been made. This time they found the dead cow, but they did not find the herdsman. The party lacked the courage to follow up any further, and the herdsman was never seen again.

A half-dozen more attacks were made, in three of which the victims turned up as usual, badly scratched. But the remaining three did not. Nor were they ever seen again. So the official score, at the time my story really starts, amounted to four killings and thirty-six maulings; the mauling, in every case, only by scratching. Whether the tiger actually ate these four men it had presumably killed, or only dragged them off to some remote part of the jungle, where they had been later devoured by jackals, hyaenas and vultures, there was no means of knowing.

I had read, now and then in the papers, of this animal's doings but had no details until an official report reached me from the forest authorities. Also at about this time I had a few days' leave to my credit and thought it would be best spent in seeing if I could catch up with this tiger.

The forest map I possessed, together with the information received, indicated that the best place at which to make my headquarters would be the small village of Rajnagara, where there was a little forest 'choultry' that would give me and my belongings shelter. This place, via Dimbum, is exactly 147 miles from Bangalore, and the road being quite good, I reached it in my Studebaker in just over four hours time, at about four in the evening.

I had no idea that an exciting time was ahead of me, for I was only two miles from Rajnagara itself, and was driving along the road through the arid scrub area, when I saw three men in front of me, one of them being supported by the other two. As I drew abreast of them, I saw that the man in the middle was covered with blood. Stopping to enquire the reason, I was told that only a few minutes earlier he had been attacked and severely scratched by this strange tiger. Closer questioning elicited the fact that the tiger had attacked him after creeping up on him by stealth. The victim told me that, before he knew he was in any danger, he had heard a low growl; then the tiger appeared beside him, reared up on its hind feet and scratched him severely about his face and chest. He had fallen down with the tiger on top of him, and had shouted for help. The tiger then left him and charged the cattle, which were milling around. As he lay bleeding on the ground, he had seen the tiger kill a half-grown brown bullock, which it had then dragged away. As nobody had come to his assistance, he had struggled to his feet and stumbled towards the road, still shouting for help. His two companions had joined him a little later.

I regarded the opportunity as godsend, to be followed up at once, and asked him to tell his companions the exact locality where the attack had taken place. He did so, and I then asked for one of the men to accompany me to the spot, while the other went on to Rajnagara with the victim.

A heated altercation now took place between them, both pleading urgent business at the village. It was clearly apparent that neither wanted to expose himself to the risk of meeting the tiger. For this I could hardly blame them, as the animal had already established his ferocity, while I was a complete stranger to them. They had absolutely no guarantee that I would not run away when the tiger showed up, and leave my companion in its clutches.

By much pleading, coercion and even threats, I eventually induced one of the men, very reluctantly, to agree to come with me, while the other continued with the wounded man.

My companion and myself then left the road and walked into the jungle. All along the path we came on splashes of blood from the recently wounded man. In crossing a bare stretch of rock these were plentiful, causing me to realise that he had been more severely hurt than I had actually noticed during my hurried conversation. I began to think that I should have taken him in my car to Satyamangalam, where there was a hospital, rather than leave the poor fellow to get there as best he could. Against this admitted negligence on my part, however, was the fact that I had a unique opportunity to meet this tiger face to face and settle the score once and for all.

A little later we came to the spot where the tiger had attacked the man. The sand on the trail clearly told its own story. We began to look around for the place where the tiger had killed the brown bullock, and soon found it some thirty yards away. My companion now refused to go any further, nor did I want him to, as he was understandably in a state of abject fear and would be much more a liability than an asset. So I left him standing nervously and began to follow the dragmark clearly made by the tiger as he had hauled the brown bull downhill towards the ravine that lay between the hillock down which I was creeping, and another and much higher hillock a quarter of a mile away.

Unfortunately, I had not anticipated such early action, and was wearing ordinary leather shoes instead of the rubber-soled boots I favoured for stalking. Try as I would, these shoes made some noise on the hard ground and the rocky boulders that were scattered there. Nevertheless I proceeded as silently as I could, till I had almost reached the *nullah*. Then I stopped and gazed about me. The scrub just here was very thick, and grew thicker where the rivulet was actually winding. My eyes roved over the slopes of the opposite hillock, which were fairly open. No signs of the tiger or the bullock were visible, and it was obvious that he must have hidden it somewhere in the *nullah,* and most probably would be eating it at that very moment. Even if he was not actually eating it, he would certainly be lying somewhere in the vicinity.

My shoes put me at a distinct disadvantage, and would betray my further progress towards that *nullah*. If I removed them and attempted to advance in my stockinged feet, I was almost certain to step on a thorn, not to speak of the sharp stones that lay everywhere. At the same time, I realised the opportunity was too good to be lost, and should be pressed home somehow. It was a chance in a thousand, which I might never get again. The time was just 5 p.m., and there was an hour and a half before sunset.

While I stood debating the odds, the tiger made the first move. He had quite obviously heard me; probably he had seen me too. Anyhow he had, after the manner of a great general, decided to make a flank attack. Quite unsuspected by me, he had already crept up the very slope down which I was moving, but at a slightly different angle, which brought him above and behind the spot where I stood thinking. Then he had evidently crept on his belly towards me, and was hiding behind a large bush, scarcely ten feet away, all unknown to me. In this particular case, my sixth sense of impending peril quite failed to register. I had just decided to advance towards the *nullah*, when there was a shattering roar behind me, and the tiger sprang out; I spun around and fired at point-blank range, missing him completely.

Probably the noise of the explosion, perhaps the strangeness of meeting someone who was obviously not a herdsman, or maybe rather the loud scarlet-and-blue check bush-coat I happened to be wearing, scared him off. For with a series of loud *'Woofs'* he bounded into the thicket and towards the *nullah*. I followed as fast as I could, reaching the bed of the *nullah*, where I almost fell over the brown bull. Examination showed that the tiger had already begun his meal before he had heard or sensed my approach, and had come forward on his own to the attack.

There were no trees in the vicinity, so I sat under the thick bush till it began to grow dark, hoping against hope that the tiger might put in a second appearance. But this he did not do, and at 6.15 I cautiously retraced my steps the way I had come. Reaching the place where I left the herdsman who had accompanied me, I found him missing and concluded he had gone home. So I went on to the road where my Studebaker stood, and shortly after reached Rajnagara.

Here a considerable crowd had gathered, and from a forest guard who was among them I found that the wounded herdsman had already proceeded to Satyamangalam hospital, together with his wife and brother. The herdsman who had accompanied me, whom I had left standing at the spot where the tiger had made his attack, while I had followed up the drag-mark alone, had failed to return.

I knew that he had not been at the place where I had left him, also that the tiger had run away after I had missed it. Where had the herdsman gone? We all realised that he would not remain in the jungle, or on the road, in a vicinity haunted by this tiger. What had become of him? I pondered this question, while his wife and family, who were also among the crowd and had overheard my enquiries, began to weep and wail.

It was now quite dark, and to search for the missing man would be impossible, as no traces would be visible had the tiger taken him away. Nevertheless, calling the forest guard to accompany me, I drove back to the spot where I had earlier left the car. Here we halted for a while, and I instructed the guard to call the man by name. This produced no results. We drove a further mile along the road and then returned to the village. By now it was evident to me that my companion of the evening before had been taken by the tiger. Evidently, while I had spent an hour sitting in the *nullah*, watching for the tiger to return to the carcase of the brown bull, the tiger had done some hunting on his own, and had carried off the unfortunate herdsman.

We did not get much sleep that night, having to listen to the weeping and wailing of the man's family, who squatted at the door of the forest choultry and amidst tears, reminded me that I was responsible for his death. This though impinged itself on my conscience very forcibly, for had I not almost forced the poor man to accompany me he would have been alive at that moment.

Early dawn found me retracing my steps to the spot where I had left him. Reaching it, I began looking around for any signs of struggle or other marks of the tiger's attack. Absolutely nothing was visible on the hard ground.

In the course of my search I walked around in ever widening circles, but still could find nothing. What had become of him was a mystery. I knew he had not followed me while I had pursued the tiger the previous evening. It was more likely that, being afraid of standing alone, he had begun to walk back towards the road. Working on this theory, I now turned back and slowly retraced my steps, looking around for possible traces.

About three hundred yards from where I had left him I found the first evidence in the form of an odd leather sandal, and not far away its fellow. At this spot short dry grass covered the ground and so no footprints were visible. But the position of the sandals made it clear to me that he had kicked them off, obviously in order to run faster. Searching around as I walked, I then saw something white flapping in the breeze under a bush to my left. It was the man's *loincloth* in India known as a '*dhoti*'. On the grass, and sprinkled on the bushes, were tiny splashes of blood, while closer inspection showed where the tiger had dashed through the undergrowth and caught up with its victim. From here the tiger had dragged the man in a course almost parallel with the road, towards the same *nullah* in which I had been sitting all the while the evening before, but considerably further down from where he had hidden the brown bull.

I must have walked a quarter of a mile before eventually stepping on to the rocky bed of this rivulet. Nothing was to be seen and here was complete silence. I knew the tiger must have hidden the remains somewhere in the vicinity.

While watching quietly, a couple of magpies attracted my attention from a spot about one hundred yards downstream. They were perched on the top of a thorny *babul* tree, where they were jabbering excitedly, frequently looking downward. The signs of the jungle are very clear to those who can read them. The magpies had either found the body, or were looking at the tiger, who in turn was probably looking at me.

Keeping to the centre of the *nullah*, I began to tiptoe forward, the rubber boots I was wearing this time making no noise against the rocks. Halfway to the *babul* tree, the magpies saw me, ceased their jabbering and flew off.

I had marked the spot where they had been perched, and approached cautiously. Immediately below the *babul* tree, a small elongated black rock jutted from the bank on to the bed of the stream, and lying behind this rock were the half-eaten remains of poor Muniappa, the missing man. Soft sand at the spot also revealed the tiger's pug-marks, and a cursory examination of them showed that the animal was a male tiger of no great size or build.

Once again, there was no tree in the vicinity on which I could sit, except the aforementioned *babul,* which was unusable because of its thorny nature. Nor, as it happened, were there any large bushes or bamboo clumps under which I could shelter. In every way the spot was about the most unfavourable, if not impossible, one for 'sitting up' that I had ever encountered. Still, I would have to do something about it for by this time there was absolutely no doubt in my mind that I was, at least indirectly, possibly directly, the cause of poor Muniappa's death.

I knew the tiger was not likely to return to his meal until the afternoon at the earliest. If I left the body as it was, the vultures would see it within a couple of hours and pick it clean. So I removed the khaki coat I was wearing and spread it over the corpse, weighing it down here and there with small boulders that lay at hand. Then I went back to the car and returned to Rajnagara.

Here I was forced to give the bad news, which not only led to renewed wailing, but a demand from the bereaved wife that the body of her husband be brought back at once for cremation. It took us a full hour to persuade her to give me a chance, that evening, for a shot at the tiger by sitting over the body, a chance which would be entirely lost if she had her way. Eventually, she very grudgingly assented.

After breakfast, I called a 'Council of War', which consisted of the village *Patel*, the forest guard and myself. Explaining to them the position in which I had left the body, I told them that I would return to it at noon and sit beside the body to wait the tiger's return. They thought this was a foolish idea, and I heartily concurred. But as nobody could suggest a better one, there was no alternative but to carry it out, other than to bring the remains back to the village and thereby lose a possible shot at the tiger.

Shortly after midday found me seated a few yards from the cadaver, from which a distinctly unpleasant odour was now rising. In fact, millions of bluebottles had already settled on my coat, and as soon as I removed it they swarmed over the remains.

I was prepared for the unpleasant situation, having plugged small wads of cotton wool into my nostrils; but despite these measures that awful stench penetrated my defences, and in time I began to feel sick. The heat was terrible. The silence was absolute, except for the chirruping of the cicadas from the branches of the surrounding bushes.

Three o'clock passed, then four and then five. At five-thirty a peacock flapped down to the streambed. As I sat motionless he had not even noticed me, which goes to confirm how invaluable absolute stillness is when out in a forest. He walked up the bed and only when ten feet away did he become aware of the two strange objects before him. He rose into the air, hurriedly and heavily, with a tremendous beating of his wings to gain momentum before he was able to fly away.

As may be imagined, I was by this time in a state of great excitement, and even greater fear, and I was, besides, on the verge of retching from the awful stench that rose from the half-eaten man.

Then followed complete silence for fifteen minutes: a silence that was all-pervading, that envelops one, that is everywhere, even in the very air. There was not even the creak of the wood-cricket, nor the twitter of the tiniest bird, nor even the faintest rustle of a dry leaf falling to the ground. Only a total and absolute stillness. That is what silence feels like, when one sits waiting for a man-eater to appear.

Although I was sitting perfectly motionless, my eyes minutely searched the scrub before me and on either side. All my senses were fully and painfully alert. But no sight nor sound registered on them.

The cheery evening crow of a junglecock, a little further up the *nullah*, relieved the tension. Six o'clock came, and then six-fifteen. An early nightjar began his peculiar clucking call. I knew that the time had come for me to leave. In a short while it would be completely dark, and then to sit for the man-eater in the open would be suicide indeed.

Getting stiffly to my feet, I walked back to the car, where I had previously arranged for a party of men to meet me and bring back the remains of the unfortunate Muniappa. It was quite dark by the time I collected them. But I knew my torchlight and their numbers would render us immune from any attack by the tiger. We returned to the ravine, where we gathered up all that remained of the unlucky herdsman in an old blanket which the men had brought with them for the purpose. Then, while the little procession wended its way towards Rajnagara, I motored back along the road.

Early next day found me again prowling about near the little *nullah*. The tiger had not returned to the spot where the body had been, as I could see by the absence of tracks. I then decided to walk along the bed of this stream towards the place where the brown bull had been left two days previously. I did this very cautiously, as the stream bed narrowed in places to hardly more than six feet and at points was nothing more than a pile of boulders or was entirely overgrown with lantana shrub. The brown bull had been hidden more than half a mile from where the man had been eaten. It had been hidden well beneath an overhanging bush I knew was safe from vultures. But when I reached it, it was only to find that the tiger had returned during the night and demolished it completely. Perhaps he had lost interest in his human kill or may have seen me earlier in the evening, sitting beside it, and become suspicious. Anyhow, the fact was that no kill remained and I would have to try other means of meeting the tiger.

Up till noon that day, and again in the evening I roamed about over hillocks and through valleys, across other streams and along their beds. Many times I came across the tracks of the tiger, but never once did I see him, nor catch any sign of his presence in the vicinity.

I spent three days in this fashion, but with entirely negative results. I had taken only a week's leave and had scarcely four days left in which to shoot the tiger.

Next morning I adopted fresh tactics. Climbing to the top of a large hillock in the centre of the terrain, I called as loudly as possible, in tiger fashion. Every ten minutes or so I repeated the call, hoping to hear an answer. Two hours later I did the same thing on a neighbouring hill. No sound came in reply. In the evening I followed the same plan, and yet the tiger did not respond. It was clear by this time that he was not in the immediate vicinity.

On the fifth day the herdsmen went out again with their cattle. You, who read this, may consider it a very brave thing on their part, and doubtless it was. But you must also realise the cattle were dependent for their food entirely on grazing. No grazing meant no food, for no provision had been made in any of the cattle villages for a reserve of fodder.

That morning, I joined the herdsmen and wandered amongst their animals, doing the same thing in the evening.

But night fell without any sign of the tiger. The sixth morning found me very despondent, as I felt the animal I was after had moved away and would not give me a second chance to bag him. But there was nothing more I could do, beyond mixing with the various herds of cattle as they grazed in the area.

I covered a number of miles that morning and was about eight miles from the place where Muniappa had been killed when, at about noon a group of men came running through the shrub to tell me that another herdsman had been attacked three miles away.

I hurried with them to where the man was lying. I saw once more the familiar signs: severe scratches across face, chest and sides, but no bite whatever. This man had lost a good deal of blood and was too weak to walk, so I hurried back to my car, instructing the men to carry him to the road. From there I took him to Satyamangalam, where I left him in the local hospital in pretty bad shape. Then I dashed back to the spot on the road to which he had been carried, left the car and went back into the jungle. There was no difficulty in following the copious blood trail he had left behind him, and this led me to the site of the attack.

In this case I discovered that the tiger had not succeeded in killing any of the cattle, which had escaped by stampeding *en masse* to the road. So searching for the tiger seemed again a hopeless undertaking. I wandered around, and every now and again called in tiger fashion, hoping to attract him. There was no response, and so ended another day.

That night I thought of motoring up and down the road that led through the shrub for about five miles, using my spotlight in the hope of picking up the tiger's eyes, should he be passing anywhere within range. I began to put this plan into practice at about 10 p.m., driving slowly, allowing for a stop of fifteen minutes at the end of each trip. Six hours of this monotonous procedure found me desperately sleepy and with a very low petrol tank.

Thus dawned the seventh and last day of my leave. After the latest attack, the herdsmen had not turned out with their cattle, so for the last time I wandered alone through the scrub, hoping to meet the elusive tiger. Noon found me about six miles from my car, when I turned and began to retrace steps.

I was walking down hillock and just reached the small depression at the foot of it. Before me another hillock rose. No stream traversed this valley, which was dotted with a few stunted *babul* trees, growing amidst the usual lantana and other shrubs. Hardly fifty yards ahead, the tiger stalked out. We saw each other at the same moment, and then, with a short bound, he disappeared behind a lantana clump.

Raising the rifle to my shoulder I advanced slowly, expecting, and even hoping, for a charge that would bring him to my sights. At the same time I was mortally afraid, and my heart beat a loud tattoo.

The charge never came! A sixth sense appeared to have told him that here was no victim, but one who was deliberately out to destroy him. He must have slipped away before I drew level with the bush behind which he had disappeared, for he most certainly was not there. I walked around it and searched everywhere, but I never saw him again.

Thus ended my seventh and last day. The time had now come for me to return to Bangalore and duty.

Although this is the story of an unsuccessful hunt—indeed, a story of complete failure—I have told it so that the reader may realise that such adventures are not always crowned with success. Failure and disappointment are far more frequent. But the hard work, strenuous effort, the very thrill of the chase, the pitting of human brains against animal instinct—

all these factors are there, and to a considerable extent compensate the enthusiast for his failure. For although I was really sorry that I had to leave the herdsmen, at least for some time, to the continued ravages of this animal, I felt satisfied that I had done my best and I looked forward to returning, when I might meet with better luck.

I handed a cheque to Muniappa's widow and started on that five-mile stretch of road on the beginning of my return journey to Bangalore. As the thorn bushes flashed past the car, I bade a temporary farewell to that extremely cunning and quite extraordinary tiger, which had not only succeeded in outwitting me at every encounter, but had also successfully hidden the reason for his peculiar habit of only scratching and not biting his victims—except those he actually killed.